The copper-skinned wench stood on the vendue table.

Canfield climbed onto the platform and stepped up to the girl. He placed a hand on her shoulder and smiled to reassure her. Then he passed his hand around her throat, let it slide down to her breasts and he gripped one firmly and shook it. Then he passed his hands down the small of her back, across her buttocks and down her slim, shapely legs.

She was petrified with terror and Fitz's ire rose rapidly when Canfield's hand went up under the girl's dress for a fingering inspection.

Fitz called out, "I bid eight hundrud an' until you tops my bid, suh, you keep you goddamn hands off that gal!"

Later that night, Fitz's father agreed to pay the thousand and one dollars Fitz had bid for the girl. "Proud of you, son. You sho' let me know you're a man today. Bed 'er down, love 'er up, but don't treat 'er like she's human; don't fall in love with no wench."

Novels by Norman Daniels

Wyndward Fury
Wyndward Passion
Wyndward Peril
Wyndward Glory

Published by
WARNER BOOKS

ATTENTION: SCHOOLS AND CORPORATIONS

WARNER books are available at quantity discounts with bulk purchase for educational, business, or sales promotional use. For information, please write to: SPECIAL SALES DEPARTMENT, WARNER BOOKS, 75 ROCKEFELLER PLAZA, NEW YORK, N.Y. 10019

ARE THERE WARNER BOOKS
YOU WANT BUT CANNOT FIND IN YOUR LOCAL STORES?

You can get any WARNER BOOKS title in print. Simply send title and retail price, plus 50¢ per order and 20¢ per copy to cover mailing and handling costs for each book desired. New York State and California residents add applicable sales tax. Enclose check or money order only, no cash please, to: WARNER BOOKS, P.O. BOX 690, NEW YORK, N.Y. 10019

Wyndward Passion
Norman Daniels

WARNER BOOKS

A Warner Communications Company

WARNER BOOKS EDITION

WYNDWARD PASSION comprises:
LAW OF THE LASH Copyright © 1968 by Norman Daniels
and
MASTER OF WYNDWARD Copyright © 1969
by Norman Daniels

Copyright © 1978 by Norman Daniels
All rights reserved.

Cover art by Tom Hall

Warner Books, Inc., 75 Rockefeller Plaza, New York, N.Y. 10019

W A Warner Communications Company

Printed in the United States of America

First Printing: March, 1978

Reissued: December, 1981

10 9 8 7 6 5 4

Wyndward Passion

PART 1
Law of the Lash

Chapter One

THE CLIPPER *Wyndward* was six weeks out of its African trading port and making acceptable time toward Norfolk. Its plankings were holystoned to a bleached-out whiteness, the ship was scrupulously clean above decks. The food had been good up to now, but it was beginning to run out. Water, too, was low and getting both slimy and wormy. The little green wrigglers were easily seen and the water had to be filtered through layers of cloth before it was usable.

The *Wyndward's* skipper was Captain Jonathan Turner, a tall, lean man with considerable breadth of shoulder and rather long arms. He filled out his clothes with a muscular brawniness exceptional in so tall and slender-waisted a man. His uniform consisted of gray trousers, tightly-fitted, a long formal coat, gold-braided at the shoulders, a round black hat, similarly gilded, a white, ruffled shirt with a string tie.

He was 38 years of age, the product of Isaac Turner and Martha Archer Turner. Jonathan's father had been a plantation owner since the Revolution, and prior to his death in 1810, eleven years ago, he'd been considered successful. Of his wife, little was known. She'd arrived from England, accompanied by her uncle, and promptly married Isaac. In due time, she bore him a son and, having done her part to continue the Turner name, promptly died. The progeny was named Jonathan and he now stood on the deck of his own ship, his own son at his side.

Fitzjohn Turner, the eighteen-year-old, rapidly maturing son of Jonathan, had been so named after a considerable argument between his father and mother, even while she lay on her bed of pain thirty minutes after she'd delivered him in that gaunt, two-story, weather-beaten house close by the shores of Massachusetts.

"I am goddamned, Sarah," Jonathan had said then, in the vitality and strength of his youth, "if any son of mine will be called Fitzgerald, fo' a first name. Goddamn it, woman, he should be called Jonathan, like me. What's the matter with Jonathan? You used to say it mos' tenderly when he was co'tin'. Now you ups and says he's got to be named Fitzgerald, an' I tell you now, it ain't goin' to be. Mayhap up here in this No'thrun climate, a man kin git away with a name like Fitzgerald, but in Virginny, they'd sure as all hell think he was a fancy-named nigger!"

"He will be called Fitzgerald after my mother's family," Sarah said with insistency and tears, to which she felt she was entitled after the pain, the screaming and moaning she'd gone through to get the boy born.

Sarah was stubborn New England, Joanthan was set Virginian; neither of them completely yielded, but they did finally agree on a combination of both choices. Not good enough for Jonathan, but good enough to honor his own stubbornness. At least, he came out of the argument with something, which was unusual.

Now this boy was eighteen and, as if to refute the ancestor who had brought to him the name Fitzgerald, he bore not the faintest resemblance to his black-haired, stern-visaged mother. Fitzjohn was as tall as his father, filled out more, heavier and even better proportioned. He didn't have his long arms, for instance. He did have his light brown hair, almost golden in hue. And the blue-gray eyes, the square, aggressive-looking chin. Perhaps there was something of his mother in the mouth for it was soft, the lips not as thin as his father's.

He too wore a gold-braided uniform; while this was his first voyage, the log listed him as second mate, though he hadn't known a jib from a mizzenmast when he boarded the ship.

Captain Jonathan signaled the two sailors who stood by patiently. They promptly unscrewed the heavy wooden grating installed above the ladder leading down into the hold of the ship where the invaluable cargo was held.

"Reckon you got a s'prise comin', Fitz," his father opined. "You ain't never been in the slave hold yit and I'm tellin' you now, you-all'll 'member the stink fo' the rest of your life. So take a-holt of your guts. Five hundred nigger bucks sho' make a pow'ful stench, like to dry up your nostrils an' shrivel your balls."

"Whut," Fitz asked, "is a little stink, papa? You cain't see it."

Captain Jonathan roared and slapped his thigh before he whacked his stalwart son across the shoulders with a blow that staggered him forward a few steps.

"Cain't see the stink! Mebbe not, but you sho' kin feel it. Thicker'n treacle, 'tis, an' it clings 'bout the same."

The Captain descended the ladder, followed by Fitz. With each descending step the stench grew heavier and worse until it seemed to fill the lungs, and the eyes, the mouth and every pore in a man's body. It was a mixture of sweat and human excrement in which the slaves lay. They were packed as tightly as possible, all lying on their right sides, with their bellies pressed up against the man in front, their buttocks pushed against by the belly of the man behind. When they urinated, they did so against one another. When their bowels moved, they were lucky if they managed to get the excrement over the edge of the plank. When they vomited, which was six or seven times a day, it simply gushed out over those near them.

Each day, by gangs, they were led out on deck to be

hosed down, fed, given limes to eat, put to work stoning the decks. Then they were led below again and another gang sent up. The hold was cleaned and aired daily as well, but this was a ship that had transported slaves for so long, every plank, every peg, was impregnated with the smell.

There were two holds on the *Wyndward*. The after one held a hundred and fifty females; the other imprisoned five hundred bucks. There were two platforms, five to six feet deep. Both ran the length of the hold, one about four feet high, the other almost flush with the deck of the hold. At suitable intervals were heavy iron rings bolted to the beams. Through these ran long lengths of chain which, in turn, held the spancels and fetters keeping the slaves packed and docile because there was no escape.

Fitz watched sailors unlock the chains and pull them through the spancels and bolted rings until the slaves were free to slide off the platform and try to stand erect after twenty hours of being chained in place. About one third of them promptly vomited as the roll of the ship became more apparent to them now that they were on their feet.

Fitz mumbled something and turned to climb the ladder as fast as he could. He sped across the deck, leaned over the rail and puked until he doubted he had much stomach left. He doubled up with the pain of it, crossing his arms over his belly and bending over, hoping in that way to quell any further disturbance of gas and bile.

The sailors watched him with sympathy. None laughed or taunted him. He was the Captain's son and, as such, should be treated with the same respect as the Captain, especially this one.

The slaves, silently climbing out of the hold, made his stomach turn again, but he didn't have to endure any more of the stench. They were led far aft where two hoses drenched them with cold sea water. The sun on their naked, wet, black skin made them glisten. A cook in a soiled apron dragged over a huge kettle of something that steamed slightly. While the blacks held out their cupped and spanceled hands, he ladled into them some grayish, lumpy substance that bore a faint resemblance to gruel. They slurped the food eagerly, spilling some in the process. The hoses continued their work, keeping the decks clean of the slop. A wooden cask of the green, wriggler-filled water was brought and they dipped their hands into it to drink, heedless of the wrigglers, in their mad and frantic desire to slake their thirst. Then each was issued half a dried-up lime which they ate slowly and carefully, not wasting any of this. Not all slavers issued limes, but on Captain Jonathan's ship there had never been a case of scurvy and he didn't intend there'd be one on this, his final voyage. It was a simple matter of economics. Slaves were too valuable to be lost through a preventable disease.

This group was given stones and told to rub down the deck. They fell to eagerly, glad to stretch their aching, cramped muscles. Their cheeks bulged with the limes as they methodically rubbed the stones against an already smooth deck.

Fitz noticed how silent they were, how unsmiling. He didn't blame the poor devils, although it was hard for him to think of them as people. They certainly seemed more like dumb animals. He heard quick steps behind him and swiveled about in time to see his father rush to the rail and empty the contents of his stomach. There were a few supercilious smiles on the faces of some sailors, which faded instantly when they grew aware of Fitz's scrutiny.

He walked over to the rail to join his father. "Take a mighty strong man to stand up agin that stench," he said with the warm commiseration of a fellow sufferer.

"This is my last voyage an' goddamn glad of it, I am.

Don' think I could stand 'nother one. Stinkin' bastards ought've been left to eat each other in the jungle."

"But they's human, ain't they, papa?"

"Human? You 'gard them as human? Look at 'em, son. They's black as coal, they got big feet and big hands and they hung as heavy as your grandma's chandelier in the big house. They got wool fer hair an' they got teeth bigger'n piano keys. Shows they ain't been long way from eatin' their meat raw. You ever smell a human who stunk like that? They's animals, son. They's animals who can talk—when they git to learn our language, which they shore don't know now. An' you watch 'em too. They's treacherous as a cottonsnake. You don't keep eyes in the back of your haid, son, they up and slices you. They's good fo' two things—to work and to breed. Later, I got a surprise fo' you which you-all is goin' to like. Tol' you this was my last voyage, but what I got me planned is somethin'll make your jaw flop some. Been lookin' to this all my life, I have."

The slaves on deck were being herded below and moments after the last one vanished into the stinking maw of the hold the first of the second batch came up, blinking against the bright sun, smeared with excrement and vomit, shuffling with their eyes downcast, their wrists still spanceled, but with long chains so they had some freedom of movement. The two last ones were slower than the others and a sailor with a whip cut at one of them. The lash bit hard and deep, sending blood oozing out of the wound and brought a howl of anguish to the recipient's lips. The lash went back for another lick, but this slave suddenly, and without stopping his howling, made for the rail. At first, no one moved. It was impossible to determine what he intended to do, jump or puke, and everyone preferred to believe the latter, because why should this black man jump overside? Wasn't he better off here than being eaten alive by animals in the jungle, or perhaps feasted upon by some rival tribe with a taste for human flesh? Even such stupid creatures as these ought to know this voyage would ultimately benefit them.

But this black man evidently didn't believe it. He didn't slacken his speed and his intent was now clear. Captain Jonathan made a flying leap toward him, wrapped his long arms around his waist and tried to drag him down. He might have done so had not the second malcontent suddenly joined in the fracas by darting across the deck before he could be stopped.

He raised his two hands, with the chain between them, brought them down over the Captain's head. He yanked hard and the chain bit into Jonathan's throat, cutting off his wind completely.

Fitz leaped on the back of the Negro and punched at his neck. It was like striking the trunk of a tree. Two sailors moved up, but by now the rebel slave had lifted the Captain clear of the black man on the deck. This man slithered to his feet and dove over the rail before anyone could stop him. Fitz heard his scream as he plummeted toward the churning water alongside the ship. Suddenly, the scream ended.

Meanwhile, the attacker, now riding the Captain's back, was hit with a belaying pin that all but tore his head off. With a low moan he slid from Jonathan's back and fell to the deck, spilling out his blood over the freshly stoned planks. Fitz helped his father to his feet. Jonathan gasped for air, but even while he labored to fill his lungs he stepped up to the prone slave and kicked him several times, as hard as he could, aiming the last half dozen at his crotch, which drew a moan from him even in the depths of his unconsciousness.

"Stinkin' black bastahd," Jonathan howled. "I'll crunch off his balls afore I kill 'im. Go fetch ropes and the blacksnake. Drag him over to the grate and tie him to it. Shuck him down, all the way. Then git all them other bastahds on deck. All of them, heah? Wenches, too.

Time they was given a 'zample what it'll be like fo' them that don't obey, and them that mutiny."

"What you figgerin' on doin' to him, papa?" Fitz asked. He was nursing an aching row of knuckles that had come into contact with the splendidly strong black neck.

"Figgerin' on doin'? I figger on killin' him, that what I figgerin' on. But first he gets his fill o' the whup. I'll whup him 'till there ain't but a breath left in 'im and then I kills him. Goddamn it, you lazy good-fer-nothin' hands what calls youse'f sailors—git them niggers up here and be fast about it."

It took better than an hour to get the five hundred on deck, crammed into a deadly silent crowd against the after rail, with sailors stationed at intervals to prevent any more suicidal jumps. Then the hundred and fifty females were brought up. They were somewhat better off than the males for Captain Turner knew they were tenderer and more easily damaged—and a damaged slave wasn't worth the breath she breathed, so it was much more profitable to give them women more limes, even a few lemons, and supply them with sufficient food that they lost little or no weight. They were provided with a cheap, shapeless osnaburg dress of thin cotton fabric. Their heads were turbaned or bandanaed, their splayed feet gave them a fine purchase on the rocking deck, and they stood as silent as the males. They didn't know quite what to expect, but the sight of the black man tied to the wooden grate slanted against the port rail was a good hint of what was coming. Captain Turner accepted the blacksnake whip from the second mate. It was six feet long, with a black leather handle weighted to be used as a weapon if necessary. Jonathan flicked the whip along the deck until it lay straightened out, the tip of it almost touching the heels of the groaning, naked slave.

Jonathan called to the interpreter, a black man in a scarlet coat, striped pants, a red fez. "Now you tell 'em, in they's own goddamn language, that this here nigger is bein' whupped for two reasons. I'm cap'n of this here pigsty and hittin a cap'n on the high seas is mutiny. So I got to peel 'im down some. Then I peels him down some more on accoun' he's a slave, an' a slave that'll fight his master ain't fit to live. You tell that to 'em all, heah?"

"Yas, sah, Massa," the red-fezzed man nodded vigorously. "I'm a'tellin' 'em."

"You might also say he done he'p another slave git away an' the penalty fo' that is gittin' hisself chopped up, to git the meat took right offen his back 'til there's nuthin' lef' but bone. Tell 'em all that an' when you gits through, I'll snake this sunabitch 'til they ain't a howl left in 'im."

Not a black man looked up as Jonathan's speech was translated for their benefit by the black in the red fez. Jonathan motioned Fitz to stand aside. He flipped the lash experimentally, then drew it back and sent it streaking to the exposed flanks of the bound man. It cut deep, blood spurted, the now-conscious and terror-stricken man gave a yell of anguish. The whip cut him again and again, gradually crawling higher with each stroke until his back was a mass of raw, bleeding flesh, some of which clung to the tip of the snake as it was withdrawn.

The shrill cries of pain had lapsed to groans and then moans until there were only inhuman mewlings from the man whose body sagged in semiconsciousness. The whip lashed at him—thirty more strokes. There was no sound from him after that. A sailor approached him and pulled back an eyelid. Only the whites could be seen. He waved his hand in a signal the man was far gone.

"Cut the goddamn side of meat down, set 'im on his goddamn back," Jonathan ordered. He dropped the snake, drew a knife that was always sheathed at his hip. He bent over the man, secured a grip of his wool, pulled his head back and slit his throat with one pass of the knife. He wiped blood off his hand by passing it through the wool.

"Feed 'im to the fish," he ordered. "Iffen they's hungry

'nuff to eat somethin' like this. Now git the men below. The wenches too 'ceptin' fer the youngest and best of the lot."

The men were urged below with many a lash of shorter whips made eager by the bloodthirstiness of the sailors who had witnessed a man beaten to death. It seemed to whet their appetite for blood. Most of the women were driven below until only eight were mustered into a wavering line.

"March 'em below," Jonathan ordered, conscious of the fact that he couldn't very well manipulate these wenches to pick out the best one, with his crew looking on. It would make them horny and maybe mutinous, and he had no thought of turning any of these young girls over to them.

Fitz followed him below. The wenches were now lined up just outside Jonathan's cabin. Their eyes fell as Fitz and his father squeezed by them in the narrow width of the corridor as they entered the captain's cabin, a spacious one as clipper ship cabins go. There were two bunks, one which Fitz had refused to use, preferring to be with the officers and share their quarters so that there'd be no hint of favoritism. He'd insisted on this so strenuously that Jonathan had given him his strong-willed way.

There was a long table, on which were the maps, the instruments for charting their course. A shelf held several books, put there by Sarah, but never once taken down and looked at. Her every attempt to instill a little culture into the mind of her husband had been a miserable failure.

The portholes were covered with curtains, printed with red roses and pulled back by red sash cords—more of Sarah's ideas. There were two chairs, into one of which Jonathan sank wearily.

"Goddamn," he groaned, "usin' that snake sho' tires a man down. It bother you any to see that buck git his neck cut?"

"No, papa, it didn't bother me none."

"The wuppin' do anythin' to you?"

"How you mean, papa?"

"Goddamn it, don't it make you horny as hell?"

"Guess not, papa. Made me kinda sick to my gut, that's all."

Jonathan's eyes narrowed to slits. "You standin' there tellin' your pa that killin' a damn buck don't give you a hard on, an' on'y makes you sick to your stummick? You tellin' you pa you ain't got guts 'nuff to stand it? You answer me, goddamn you, afore I takes the snake to your mizza'ble hide."

"Papa, didn't say I'm agin it. Kinda liked to handle that whup some myse'f. Knows the buck he'ped that other'n jump and that cost us six . . . seven hundred dollahs. I on'y say it makes me some sick, tha'ss all."

Jonathan's eyes opened wider and he relaxed. "Tha'ss good, son. It make you sick all the time, I dunno what'n hell I'd done with you. Wasn't goin' to tell you 'till tomorrow but reckon I will now. Set down. It'll take some time."

Fitz jerked a thumb over his shoulder in the direction of the door. "Whut 'bout them wenches, papa?"

"You want one now? That whut you want, son?"

"No, papa, on'y they's standin' there. . . ."

"Now whut the hell's the diff'rence, son? I say they stands, they stands. I say they squats, they squats. I say they git on they'd backs an' spreads they legs, that's whut they do. Now set. Reckon I'm too damn horny right now to take on one of 'em. Got to settle down some or won't be worthwhile. You ready now, to hear whut I got to say?"

"Ready, papa, and mighty curious too."

"Told you this before, but I'm tellin' it again so you understands everythin'. My papa and mama had theyse'eves a big plantation, raisin' cotton an' corn, but the land played out. Mama died an' papa gave up. He sold the plantation 'fore it got run down. He died right after that. Reckon he didn't care no mo'. The money he got was a good sum. Let me buy the *Wyndward* an' pay cash. I was raised on a plantation and I wants to own one more'n anythin' else in this world. But a big one, an' so I carried slaves in my ship 'cause they was the bes' payin' cargo. Got rich doin' it. Rich 'nuff to buy me land, an' pay fo' a big house an' everythin' goes with it. Plenty left too."

"You fixin' to start the plantation right off?"

"This is my last voyage. Cain't stand no mo'. Stink'll stay in my bones 'til the day I die. Seems like it's way down deep inside me. Nuthin' I kin do about it an' I ain't cussin' it. Made plenty of trips to Afriky, brought me back anywhar from six to seven hundred head each time. Been frugal, puttin' away to this day, plannin' on it fo' years. Your ma's goin' to be pleased—I hope. Ain't tol' her yit. Savin' it fo' a surprise."

"Yes, yes, papa," Fitz said impatiently, "but tell me 'bout the plantation."

"Already got me two thousand acres seventy miles west of Norfolk. Not far from Richmond and plenty close to Lynchburg an' Petersburg. All prime land an' I'm aimin' to raise me three money crops. Tobacco, pureblooded horses and niggers. Ain't never seen a better combination of money crops. One fails, the others go right on makin' money. An' everythin' cash on the barrelhead. Lots of gentry goin' broke in Virginny on account of they gits theyse'ves in the hands o' them sheeny moneylenders and they goes busted. Loses ever'thin'. Money, clothes, niggers, horses, cattle . . . all gits mortgaged an' all gits foreclosed. Not me—I owe no man and I ain't aimin' to. Some ways I'm like your ma, son. She's close too. Closer'n the legs of a whore waitin' fo' her four bits."

Fitz whistled between his teeth in amazement. Not one hint of this had ever leaked out. He was astonished —and highly pleased—for he had little liking for the sea and these voyages. He was far more at home on land, wearing gentleman's clothes, ogling the gals and wishing he had the courage to take one for himself. Now his father would leave the sea, move into the life of a plantation owner dealing in the three richest crops in the South. The use of tobacco was increasing rapidly and a demand for good Virginia bright was high over most of the world. Slaves bought in Africa for paltry sums sold right off the clipper for four hundred each, in bit lots, with no questions asked and no examinations made. The culls could always be sold off. These slaves, fed, rested, cleaned and dressed, could be sold at the vendue table for six or seven hundred. An exceptional buck would bring nine hundred and a good wench whose breeding abilities had already been demonstrated could bring seven-fifty. But young as he was, Fitz looked as far ahead as his father and knew what would be in store for them if they were lucky. His father meant to breed slaves. That's where the profit was. No more long voyages, expensive ships, losses by death and sickness on the way. Weeks at sea . . . that would be over. All that was needed was to pair off a buck with a wench and wait for results.

"You thinkin' it's a good idee?" Jonathan asked his son, eager for his approval.

"Papa, it's a lot better'n sailin' this clipper. What you aimin' to do with her?"

"Paid no mind to that yit. Let her stay at anchor apiece, I reckon. In the mornin', we line up the bucks and take our pick. Wants fifty of the best. Then we 'xamine the wenches, and they's lots o' fun a-fingerin' 'em. Let you do as much as you like. Good trainin, an' any wench ketches your eye, you cover her. Don't mind none they pops out light-colored suckers. Don't mind atall. Got me a passle o' 'em runnin' 'round all over the world. Your ma's purely strait-laced, son, but her husband ain't, and I reckon her son takes after me. Ain't that right, son?"

"Reckon so, papa."

"You ever slep' with a wench?"

"Not even a white gal, papa. Goddamn, I on'y eighteen. Gimme time."

"At seventeen, I aweady knocked up five, six wenches. Afore I met your ma, 'course. That ain't sayin' I never slep' with any since, 'cause I did. Lots of 'em. White gals nice. Kinda sticky, but nice. They don't smell musky, but you gets kinda used to that, you screw enough wenches. Kinda like it after a while. Wenches got more juice in 'em too. They friskier 'n white gals. They ain't tryin' to be ladies. I'm tellin' you, no gal black, white, tan or blue, was ever a lady in the hay. Not with me they wasn't. But the wenches likes it better and aks like they like it better. Gittin' me all riz up talkin' bout it. Needs me a wench right now, son."

He jumped out of the chair, flung the door wide. The wenches were still there, one of them squatted on the floor. She lifted her eyes to glare at Jonathan.

"Git your black ass up out'n there," he ordered sharply.

She only looked at him dumbly and he kicked her in the side.

"Papa, she cain't unnerstan' English. She dunno whut in hell you sayin'."

"Fergits that," Jonathan admitted. He reached down, grasped the girl by the elbows and lifted her. She wasn't a big girl, not the kind who'd breed one sucker after another, limited only by the years of her childbearing days. She was too slight of build, too narrow-hipped, too flat-assed and too meagerly titted. But her eyes were angry ones and showed no fear of Jonathan. When she looked at Fitz, he turned his face away, unable to bear looking at her, knowing what his father meant to do and feeling some of the same urge himself in that inexperienced and youthful area between his legs.

Jonathan studied each girl, letting his fingers pass lightly over their bosoms. One he favored by lifting her loose dress over her head and thrusting an inquisitive hand between her legs. He dropped the dress and went back down the line to the girl who so openly defied him. He took a closer look at her.

She didn't have the large teeth, nor the thick lips, the sloping forehead of the others. Her features were finely chiseled. She had a small shapely nose without even a hint of a flareout at the nostrils. Her mouth was small and thin-lipped. Her cheekbones were high and her hair was straight, with a reddish tinge through its darkness, as if it had been lightly touched with a feather dipped in dye.

Her legs were fuller, not the spindly ones of most African girls. She had slender ankles and her thighs were slim and firm, as Jonathan discovered when he hoisted her dress up and ran his hands along her legs.

She gave a sharp, angry cry. He let go of the dress and looked at her without expression. "You don' understand whut I'm sayin', gal, but you sho' as hell needs to be settled down some. You don' know whut I'm sayin', you sho' unnerstands this."

He slapped her half a dozen times, rocking her back and forth until her knees sagged and she started falling to the floor. He seized her then, pulled her to him roughly.

"I din' want you 'fore now, I does now. You gotta be shown, gal, that you owned by your massa an' he kin do whut he likes an' you got nothin' to say about it. Now you comin' with me. If you fights me, I'll whup you." He drew back his hand to show her what he meant and she cringed away from him. He opened the door to his cabin, set his hand against the small of her back and shoved her violently across the floor until she fell onto the lower bunk.

Jonathan grinned happily at his son. "Gal's your'n, you wants her. She's likely not busted yit, but she sho' as hell will be when I gits finished. Howsomever, you my son, and I gives her to you first, you say you wants her."

"No, papa," he said.

"Gals skeer you, son? Now you go in there and you strip her down and then mount her. You do that an' you gittin' on to be a man."

"Cain't, papa. Too tired, I reckon. Maybe later."

"Well, I ought to make you do it, son, but that gal's a likely one. She'll fight me like a cat, she will, but when I gits through, she'll be purrin' away nice and gentle. Come wake me up 'bout four, five hours. An' you want any of these other'ns, just grab one by the tits. Say . . . the one on the end, she tittied up real good. Bet you'd make her a sucker first time. Tits like that, she's just awaitin' fer a pickaninny. But you's tired, ain't you? Some other time. Lots o' time fo' you. Lots o' wenches. We get that there plantation goin', be a wench ever' night in the year 'thout repeatin'. Fixes it so you kin bust 'em all. Afore we turns 'em over to the bucks, you do the bustin'. Gives a man lots of juice so when he gits himself a white gal, he shows her somethin' all right."

Jonathan stepped into the cabin and closed the door. Fitz, his lips in a tight line, signaled the wenches to file back on deck. One or two looked at him with considerable warmth and one even had the courage to touch him between the legs, where there was the beginning of a wetness.

Damn papa, he was thinking. He forgets—plumb forgets every time he starts that kind of talk that I been home with mama and she don't tolerate none of this wenching. In all Massachusetts there wasn't anybody as strait-laced as mama, and Fitz often wondered how it ever came about that Jonathan had managed to slip his tumescence between her legs.

Not that she was a solemn, prune-faced woman. Rather, Sarah Turner was a shapely, most attractive female just beginning to fill out to a more matronly form the last time Fitz had seen her. She wasn't above taking a glass of port —if it was the best—and she not only stayed with the ever changing fashions, but concocted some of her own. She was church-going—in fact, he thought she spent half her life in church, but that was her affair. He'd gone with her the first years of his boyhood without protest. Then he began to make excuses and finally he became an abandoned soul, as Sarah called him. He pulled away from the church—far away. As his father had done, Sarah complained, but she didn't try to force him to return.

She lived quietly and contentedly in the two-story frame house with its widow's walk overlooking the harbor. One servant was all she required, and she delighted in baking her breads, making her cookies and cakes. The house itself was immaculate. Her father had been a sea-going man and then an importer-exporter. That was how she met Jonathan. He'd come to consult with her father about a shipment and stayed for supper and then stayed the night. Before dawn, he tried the knob on her bedroom door, found it opened freely, and he stepped inside, wearing only his flannel drawers. A candle was lit, placed beside the bed and Sarah was sitting erect, motioning him to make no noise, but to slip into the bed quietly.

He'd stretched out beside her that night, he'd kissed her lips and her nipples and caressed her. He'd rolled on top of her, pushing his hardness against her belly. She clasped his middle with her legs, kissed him back, fondled him, but she definitely, completely and positively refused to allow him to penetrate her. That night he was the most frustrated man in the State of Massachusetts.

Fitz, of course, knew nothing about this and, while he loved his mother and respected her, he did think she was too austere and proper. He didn't know her as well as his father did.

She was, however, going to hide papa when he told her about the plantation in Virginia. But she shouldn't be too surprised to learn his plan; Jonathan had often talked about the happy days of his youth when his father ran a plantation. Furthermore, Jonathan was Southern-bred; all his relatives had been Southerners, his whole background was Southern.

He wasn't a highly educated man, but he was a smart and clever one. It was a known fact that he was the best trader in the business, and his ship never sailed with empty holds. He owned his clipper too, every inch of her. No bank held a mortgage, no builder worried when she put to sea, because Jonathan had paid cash for her.

Fitz heard the wench cry out once and he shivered and continued on his way. In the cabin, Jonathan pulled the girl to him and kissed her. Then he sniffed audibly and let her go. He pulled open a drawer, pulled out four limes and drew his knife, an act which made the girl shrink back in terror.

"Don't worry none, gal," he assured her, waving the knife and smiling. "Ain't goin' to cut you like I cut that buck. You're beter lookin' than him and he didn't have whut you got, gal. No siree, he didn't have nothin' like whut you got to pleasure me with."

He sliced the limes, reached for her, pulled her to her feet, snatched off her dress with one yank that pulled it free.. Then he proceeded to rub her with the cut end of the limes until every bit of her flesh was covered with the fragrant juice. He threw the lime shells out the porthole and reached for her again.

"Cain't stand musky smellin' wenches," he said, as if she could understand a word. "You ain't bad. Reckon you got washed good first, you wouldn't stink at all. Reckon them other wenches got you all muskied up."

He drew off his shoes, removed his shirt and stepped out of his trousers. He removed his drawers and stood there naked, his nudeness against hers. He kissed her gently, almost tenderly, but there was no mistaking his intentions. She didn't have to understand English to know what he was up to and she did her best to avoid him, but Jonathan was no inexperienced boy. He slapped her twice, let her cower down on the bunk until he gently straightened her out so that she lay on her back. Then he calmly mounted her. She gave a wild screech at the pain of her deflowering. That only made Jonathan grin. He liked them that way, and busting them was a master's privilege anyway. In fact, the girl ought to be grateful, for some big buck with an appendage as huge as most of them would have torn this little girl to pieces.

At the end of it, she had her arms around him and she snuggled up to him and responded well when he again asserted his authority. Then they both fell asleep.

An hour later, the girl awakened and quietly disengaged herself from Jonathan, who was snoring lustily. She gathered up her dress and pulled it over her head. Then she opened the door silently, started out and came to a stop with a smothered cry.

Fitz stood with his back against the bulkhead opposite the door. He nodded politely to her, pushed her aside slightly and looked in to make sure his father was safe. The girl began to cry softly, the tears staining her bright copper-colored cheeks. Fitz led her up on deck and sat with her, their backs against a hatch. It was evening now, the stars were out. The weather was warm, the sea calm. The wind in the rigging made faint sounds. Besides that, all they could hear were the steps of the men on watch.

"You poor chile," Fitz said. "You cold?"

She looked at him without comprehension. He drew off his jacket and placed it around her shoulders. She studied him very gravely and then said something which he didn't understand, but she laid her head gently against his shoulder.

"Bet you're mighty hungry," he said. "Come to think of it, so'm I. Now you wait here. Don't go 'way. Heah me now?"

She gave him a tremulous smile. He arose and she quickly grasped his ankles to keep him with her. He shook off the hold, bent down and patted her cheeks. His smile told her he'd be back and she was content.

He paid a fast visit to the galley where he poured a pitcher of what the cook called coffee and added a generous quantity of molasses to it. He prepared four fat sandwiches of cheese and thick bread. He pocketed three of the now very scarce oranges and he stowed a strip of dried, salted beef into another pocket. Then he hurried back to find her still there.

He sat down beside her. He unwrapped the sandwiches which he'd wrapped in a clean napkin. She took one and ate it hungrily, but daintily, he noticed. None of the slobbering he'd seen in the bucks, and most of the wenches. She drank some of the coffee, obviously enjoying its sweetness.

"I don' know whar you come from," he told her, "but you sho' got better manners 'n me. Yas, ma'm, sho' have." He peeled an orange for her and showed her how to eat it. The enjoyment she exhibited gladdened him more than anything he could remember. She wiped her mouth with the hem of her dress and leaned back. His arm had gone around her to steady her against the slow roll of the ship. Now she was enclosed by it and she settled there as content as a kitten.

"Wish we could talk some," he said. "I know whut my papa did to you an' I'm 'shamed for him. Yes, I am. 'Shamed he did that. I'd like to do it too, but I ain't horny 'nuff yit, I reckon. That'll come an' when it does, I hope you're 'round. Sho' find it pleasurable pleasurin' you. Ain't no nigger, you ain't. Leastwise, not a full-blooded one. Reckon your pappy was an Arab, anyway a mustee o' some kind. Reckon you don't have more'n a tenth nigger blood, but that's all it needs to make you a nigger. Papa 'splained it to me a hundred times. Don't make no sense to me sometimes, but I reckon he says it right. So I couldn't ever tell a gal like you that I loves her. Love got nuthin' to do with a white man pleasuring hisse'f with a nigger." He grinned amiably down at her. "Reckon you be a white gal, you got my eyes ripped out by now. But you're only a poor nigger gal who don't know what the hell I'm sayin'."

She tilted her head back, inviting him, and he bent over her and their lips met, despite the fact that with a nigger gal there could be no loving, his papa insisted. No white man could possibly love a nigger no matter how white her skin might be, nor how she responded to him. Fitz forgot all that. Her body rose up with the litheness of her youth and met the rigidity of his teenage strength, and their bodies fastened together tightly while he thrust his hand down the bodice of her loose dress and fondled her breasts until the nipples stood out firm and hard. He was exploring beneath the dress when he heard his father's voice. The girl did, too, and she shrank away in fear.

He thrust the leftover orange at her, added the strip of salted meat, retrieved his coat and shoved her in the direction of the hold for females. She slipped across the deck, making no more noise than a shadow. Once she looked over her shoulder and gave a little wave of her hand before she vanished. Fitz slipped into his jacket, pulled his cap down over his eyes, crossed his legs until the tumescence burned out, and pretended to be dozing. Jonathan sank down beside him.

"You sleep?" he asked.

"Reckon I ain't now, papa."

"The wench was good. Busted her . . . nobody else had her 'fore me. Likes 'em that way. Knows they ain't crawlin' with somebody else's diseases. You been eatin' oranges?"

"Had my fill of them, papa. Figger we make port tomorrow, no sense leavin' 'em. Sho' bought 'nuff of 'em from that boat-vender off Cuba."

"Sho' did. Want to talk awhile?"

"Reckon so, you got somethin' to talk about."

"Got 'nuff to keep us here 'til mornin', I reckon. First, we got to scheme us a way to git your ma down here, 'thout her knowin' too much whut we got in mind."

"Mama misses you," Fitz said. "Many a time she tol' me so. Even said she was set agin the way I talked—

like you, but when you away she say it sounds good."

"You like to talk like I do, son? Knows you kin talk the other way."

"Yes, father, indeed I can." There was a Boston accent to Fitz's immaculate speech. "Mama taught me well and I love her for it, but you're my father and I love you too. I want to be like you, and I can't very well be without thinking like you, dressing like you and talking like you. Therefore, Cap'n suh, I been gittin' my talk like your'n. 'Cause we livin' on a Virginny plantation, better had talk like this, or folks'll think me uppity."

"Appreciates that, son. Yes, suh. Makes me feel real good. Now we drop anchor early in the mawnin' of day after tomorrow. Man, we got us plenty work to do be done come day. We gits to pick the bucks we want to take to the plantation. The wenches too. We picks fifty of each, the rest we turn over to the auction or the buyers and traders. We take our coffle to the plantation. They all rested and soon's we make po't I'll fatten 'em up some. Put some lard on they's bellies an' they kin walk the fifty mile no trouble. Part way we go by barge. Make twenty mile an' better a day. Writ to your mama and sent the letter from Cuba by clipper to Boston. Tells her to pack up and git her ass down here—kinda more polite 'n that, but I tells her. Reckon she'll 'rrive three, four days after we git there. I'm prayin' my knees blue she'll like it. Don't reckon she knows 'xactly whut in hell I aim to do, but whut kin I do 'ceptin' go right on. Cain't drop the plantation now, cain I?"

"Nothin' else to do, papa. I'm growin' fast and I ain't 'zactly dumb. Mama sent me to school 'nuff. I kin he'p you. Knows a lot 'bout bookkeepin' and I don't mind usin' a snake to make the bucks work fo' they keep."

"Lots for you to learn, son. Learned it from my pappy, but I grew up when they wasn't much to teach. I knowed whut a buck an' a wench was doin' when they together, before I was old 'nuff to get horny myse'f. Son, whyn't you take one o' them wenches? Tain't no sin to pleasure yourself with a nigger gal. That's whut they's for. They ain't got no other reason on earth 'cept to breed and give us suckers."

"Reckon so, papa." He was thinking about the copper-skinned girl and grew a response to his thought to such an extent he had to casually cross his legs in order to keep Jonathan from knowing what was going on.

"Time your mama gits there, we have everythin' ready. Din't tell you this, but had me a new house built. New barns, stables . . . we goin' to raise us blood horses as good as blood niggers. Better, blood lines easier to follow with a horse. New furniture from Richmond there. Silver, best china, all the bed clothes we need. Had a man at Richmond's best store take keer o' everythin'. Got me twenty niggers workin' there now. Tobacco crop in, sheds ready for the curin'. Hogsheads stored. Goin' to be a handsome, right place, son. Some day be all your'n to do with whut you want. But now all mine and whut gits done is what I says gits done. Don't aim to be no whip slingin' overseer, boy, but you got to learn to toe the mark whut I says. Cain't be more'n one boss."

Fitz grinned at him. "Wait'll mama gits here, papa. Who you say gonna be boss?"

Jonathan scowled. "You figger on spi'lin' every evenin' of my life, son? Best we git to bed now. Like I said, want to pleasure yo'se'f, take any wench. Don't reckon you will tomorrow night. Last night out an' I got somethin' in mind would give a marble statue a hard-on. Ain't often a man kin git amusement don't cost him nothin', and make hisself a fortune at the same time. Don' ask questions. You see what I means soon 'nuf."

Fitz walked slowly around the deck before he went to his quarters. He couldn't hurry because if he walked in with that passion bulge in his tight trousers he would be mortified by the laughs and winks of the officers. It went away after a single trip around the deck and he was quieted down. Tomorrow would be the last day at sea. On the following morning they'd drop anchor at Norfolk. The *Wyndward* would be tied up somewhere, probably sold after a bit. Papa wouldn't sell her right off. Might be he wouldn't like plantation work anymore. Mayhap Sarah would put her foot down and send him back to sea. There was no more honorable a profession than master of your own ship, in her opinion. She had no idea of the cargo he carried. The only time she ever was on the *Wyndward* was when he put into the Massachusetts harbor, but that was always to pick up a cargo to be carried to Europe or Africa. She believed he brought back manufactured goods and foodstuffs from distant places. He'd always been careful to seal the slave hold hatches before she came aboard.

She was a Bible-reading woman who believed a black man was human. It would be impossible to convince her otherwise, but she was going to have to learn. No doubt she'd be kind to the slaves. Jonathan had no objection to that, provided she didn't interfere with punishment when it became necessary—like flogging that buck to death. The poor brute was dead before Jonathan slit his throat, but the other slaves didn't know that. This man was dead, he'd been killed before their eyes as punishment for a crime they now would remember for life as punishable by death. Those who tried to escape, or assisted another to escape would meet the same fate. It had quieted them down. There'd been rumblings in the slave holds as the endless voyage went on day after day, but no more. Now they knew better.

He didn't blame them too much. Being cramped up as they were, for six or seven weeks, was a form of torture only strong bucks could endure. Usually five or six died. This trip none had, which made him believe he'd picked well, only the absolute primes of the lot offered by the Arab slavers. He'd reasoned that if he selected six hundred and fifty of the best, then if he picked fifty bucks and fifty wenches from this lot, he'd have slaves anyone would envy. Healthy, strong, hard-working, hard-fornicating slaves, to become the nucleus of his farm. Before a year was out he planned to have six hundred slaves peacefully working his tobacco, procreating at the fastest possible rate, presenting him with scores of suckers a year. Each one was worth at least two hundred dollars with its first breath. After twelve more years each would be worth a thousand. The way slaves were growing in demand, it was even likely a good buck would fetch twice as much as that—and all he had to do was feed them, let them grow, work them in the fields, and work them with his horses. Whatever it cost to raise them was more than equaled by the amount of labor he got from them, and when they were sold, whatever he got was clear profit. His coffles would bring fifty thousand a year if he handled things right.

Virginia was rapidly becoming the breeding farm for the whole South. The niggers born and raised here commanded very good prices because they were of good stock, well trained, and willing to work. Very few ran away. Those who did were promptly tracked down, beaten until the flesh hung off them and then some were hanged. As a result, not many ran. They were easy to get along with if they were treated well, fed properly, not worked half to death, given their small pleasures and rewarded now and then with a castoff coat or dress. With a silver dollar for each sucker born and five dollars for twins.

His father had always declaimed the tendency of slave breeders to take the child away from its mother even before being fully weaned, and turned over to another woman with milk. Then the child was simply placed in a large cabin with all the other pickaninnies so that, in a few weeks time, even the child's mother would have had a difficult time picking it out. Jonathan's father had let the mothers raise their own children. Let them nurse them, teach them what little they needed to know. When it came time to separate them, which was not often necessary, for a mother and her children brought very good prices when sold together, the mother might carry on more than a woman whose child had been taken from her and with whom she'd had no contact in years. But the women got over it quickly. Had they been human, such a thing couldn't possibly happen. They'd have fought any and all who attempted to break up the family, but they were niggers and it didn't hurt them any. Besides, by the time the first child was grown, the mother had half a dozen more clinging to her skirts.

Reaching his quarters, Fitz went straight to his bunk. The other officers were tired too, wanting to get in as much rest as possible so when they reached port they'd be in shape to visit every whorehouse spread around Norfolk, or find their own particular girls who'd promised to wait. Nobody wanted to talk, for which Fitz was grateful.

He undressed, crawled into bed and lay there on his back, with fingers intertwined, pillowing the nape of his neck. He couldn't stop thinking of that wench, and thinking of her brought back the surging tremors of passion. If he didn't keep his hands at the back of his head, he was going to do something he'd be ashamed of. He fell asleep that way, but she was even in his dreams and in the morning his nightshirt was wet between the legs and he never did know if it was spontaneous, or if his hands had drifted down as he slept.

He was shaved, washed, dressed and on deck half an hour before his father appeared. The first order of the day was for the ship's carpenter to select a likely crew of his own and install on the main deck fifty iron rings to be bolted to the deck itself.

"Nev' you min' you hole the deck," Jonathan said. "Ain't plannin' to use this ship for a long time. Holes won't make no damn difference, but git every one of them goddamn rings in fast. You-all won't be sorry you done this, boys. Tonight I'm puttin' on a farewell show, Perfo'mance nobody but Cap'n Jonathan Turner could think up. Be quite an evenin', yes sir. Goin' to break out a whole bar'l of good rich old rum. Drink it all up. No sense havin' it go to rot with the ship. Nobody works hard today. Long's the ship sails on, don' care none if anythin' needs polishin'. Let it all go. Fitz, want you in my cabin now. You comin'?"

There was a pitcher of rum on the table, some of it spilled over the maps. Jonathan spilled more as he poured. Fitz realized his father had been drinking rather heavily already.

"Don' mind none," Jonathan brushed aside some of the soaked maps. "Knows my way to Norfolk with my eyes closed. Whut I got to tell you, son, is my plans. 'Fore we start workin' 'em, you got to understan' 'em. Got to do with the plantation. I'm callin' it Wyndward Plantation. Been cap'n o' this ship *Wyndward* a long time. Now I'll be cap'n this plantation, and it ain't goin' to rock under your feet or pitch an' toss in a wind. Solid as a rock this here plantation we got. Don't owe any money on it— not a goddamned penny. Soon's I git my coffle there and the bucks workin' they asses off, and the wenches screwin' they asses off, we go lookin' for blooded horses. Racin's not much so far, but it'll grow and them has the best hosses wins the best races and the mostes' bets. Now all folks got is buck fightin' and that's a hell of a waste of black muscle 'cause they lets them bucks fight 'til one of 'em's ruint complete, or daid. Wantin' you to see we git the hosses that'll win."

"Figured on tamin' them bucks and wenches," Fitz objected.

"Figured on the same, son, but I been thinkin' on that. You got too much o' your ma in you. Man can't be gentle with them bucks an' he can't be sentimental 'bout the wenches. . . ."

"Papa, I kin whale the ass off them bucks good as you."

"Mayhap you kin, but what 'bout the wenches?"

"Don' know whut you mean, papa."

"No call to lie, son. No call to be 'shamed of anythin' you do 'cause you feels it's right. Times it is, times it ain't, but man's got to do whut he thinks best. Now the wench I busted . . . sorta sneaked under your skin, didn't she? You fed her, an' you comforted her, an' you sat with her. You got yourse'f all hardened up 'counta her. Now I ain't sayin' you're wrong, son. Cain't help feelin' sorry fer some o' them wenches, way the bucks haul off and stab 'em with their big cocks, near kill some of 'em. But they's niggers. They cain't he'p it, but they's still niggers, and that's the way they got to live. You remembers one thing 'bout 'em and it comes easier to unnerstan' why we got to treat 'em like we does. They ain't human. That's all they is to it. They ain't human, and if you treats 'em like human, they goin' to kill you some day. You gives 'em orders and you whups 'em when they don't obey, or they git lazy. You beat the ass off 'em and they 'spect you fo' it. You mollycoddle 'em, like your ma would, an' they laugh behind your back and start thinkin' when they kills you."

"I ain't scared, pa. I kin handle 'em real good."

"Fitz . . . an' ain't that a hell of a name—anybody kin handle 'em. Judgin' a nigger ain't no great shucks. You fingers 'em, you asks questions, you gits 'em to run, you inspects they balls an' see they hung right good, and that's all they is to it. But a hoss don't answer questions, you don't finger a hoss, and they's all hung good. You got to git to know hossflesh an' un'erstan' it. You got to think like a hoss, you got to train 'em and they's harder to train 'an a nigger. I ain't smart 'nuff to do that —on'y smart 'nuff to handle niggers. Wants you to take charge of the stables. Mayhap, things go good an' you got time, you kin he'p with the 'baccy raisin'."

"Sho', papa."

"You ain't dis'pointed? You ain't jes' sayin' 'sho', papa' 'cause you my son and you showin' me respect?"

"Papa, I showin' you respect 'cause you sho' one of the smartes' men in the world. I means it. An' you knows well I loves hosses and I loves bein' 'round 'em. Mayhap I should ask, you doin' all this 'count of I'm your son?"

Jonathan roared and whacked him on the shoulder again. "Fitz . . . goddamn your ma for thinkin' up that one . . . you an' me, we's goin' to have the best, the biggest, an' the richest sonabitch plantation in all of Virginny. 'Fore we gits done, everybody in the country will know about us. Yes, sir, they'll smoke, chew and snuff our 'baccy. They'll admire our slaves and they'll bet on our hosses. On'y one thing we got worryin' us and it's got pretty far up my ass."

"Ma," Fitz sighed.

"She goin' to raise hell 'bout slaves, she going to say smokin' sinful an' growin' 'baccy sinful. She goin' to say racin' hosses sinful for gamblin's the devil's own wuk. How we goin' to 'commodate her, son?"

"We let's her think she gits her own way, papa. Whut she sees we lets her see, an' whut she ain't s'posed to see, she don't see. On'y one thing you better not let her find out. She catch you screwin' one o' them wenches, she goin' to cry her pore heart out fo' the wench an' bust the furniture 'gainst your haid."

"Well," Captain Jonathan Turner of the good ship *Wyndward,* sighed deeply. "Cain't do 'thout her, son. Misses her ev'y time I set out to sea. Cain't wait to git back an' she the same 'bout me. Guess you calls that love. Whutever it is, that's how it's got to be. Your ma's the right purtiest gal 'ever did see, an' she true, an' she 'spectful—her dander ain't up."

"Won't be so bad, papa. We spendin' much time in Norfolk?"

"Been figger'n that, son. Norfolk's where all the slavers make po't. Traders don' pay more'n they has to, but we have to push on ninety miles by river, mos' the way to Richmond; that's where we take over prime nigger flesh we intendin' to wuk the plantation. Figger we float all our best niggers there. Then we marches the coffle 'bout sixty miles to the plantation. These niggers make it easy an' we won't push 'em none. Wagons for the wenches. Picked the land myse'f long time ago. We be settin' an easy trip by water to Richmond, we got Lynchburg fo'ty five miles southwes' an Charlottesville fo'ty miles no'th. We right 'tween them towns and they goin' to grow fast. Reckon that's all fo' now. Got to look over the niggers. Want on'y the bes', so you mind me and watch the ways I picks 'em."

Again, the orders were given to fetch all bucks on deck, in the usual batches. This time they came up from the reeking hold with chained rings around their necks. The red-fezzed slave master was taking no further chances with any crazy bucks jumping overside. He lined them up, ordered them to shuck down and they dropped their pants indifferently, prepared for anything at the hands of these strange white masters. They'd seen one of their kind dive overside and nobody made the slightest attempt to save him, which meant they were all worthless in the eyes of the fair-skinned people on this ship. They'd seen another of their number lashed and then have his throat slit, further example of their worthlessness. So they were no longer lords of the jungles, or strutting bucks in their tribal villages, possessors of a lion's skin to prove their worth as warriors and brave men. Here there was nothing to be brave about. A man could fight a lion. Provided with a spear he could kill him or at the least, make a run for it. On this ship there was nowhere to go, no way to defend oneself, and there was always that cruel whip ready to slash a man to ribbons.

Jonathan, with Fitz at his side, stepped up to the first buck and looked him over carefully. He ran his hands down the slave's arm muscles, transferred this kind of attention to his thighs and calves, his back, looking for physical strength. He grasped the slave's penis, rolled back the skin, hefted his testicles and again nodded. He glanced at the man in the red fez, the representative of the Arab prince who had collected the slaves.

"When I signals, you git each buck to run clear 'cross the deck an' back. Wants to see how he handles hisself."

The buck raced across the deck and back at the command in his own language. He didn't know what it was all about, but he understood that a nod of the head of this man in all the gold braid was a signal of approval, and the more nods, the better the man he approved. So, as the inspections proceeded, each buck tried to outdo the other for his approval which might mean more food, a better place to be chained and a wench.

It was slow work and late afternoon before Jonathan had his fifty stalwart bucks lined up and the others headed back to the stinking hold. The females were brought up. Fitz looked eagerly for the copper-skinned girl. She was one of the last. She smiled slightly for his benefit and glared indignantly at Jonathan. He now had the women release their dresses to bare them to the waist. He felt of their neck muscles, their legs and thighs. He squeezed their breasts, bringing giggles from some, tears from others, and sharp, angry cries from the more daring. Jonathan paid them not the least attention. He had them open their mouths and he ran his finger over their teeth to make certain they were all sound.

"You looks for rotten teeth," he told Fitz. "Them that has too many, you throw back. You watches 'em run to make sure they got speed an' balance. You looks at they cocks. Mayhap you find they got clap. You weighs they balls. Heavier they is, better they produce suckers. You 'members which one's hung too heavy and you gives him a big wench. Like to kill a small one. You inspect wenches, same thing, 'ceptin' the best of 'em is real tittied up."

Fitz noticed that he passed up the copper-skinned girl

without an inspection, but he didn't send her to join the girls he picked either, and when the others filed down to the hold, the copper-skinned girl went with them, Fitz felt disappointed. He'd wanted her picked. He'd wanted her in the coffle and, finally, on the plantation. He thought right off she'd make a fine body servant for his mother, but Fitz was not about to ask his father to take her. Obviously, Jonathan was afraid the wench would one day learn how to speak English and perhaps let something slip about being deflowered by Jonathan. Knowing his mother as he did, Fitz hardly blamed his father for such a precaution, but he was sorely disappointed just the same.

Now Fitz saw the meaning of the iron rings bolted to the deck. Each buck was relieved of the chain around his neck, led to one of the metal rings and there an ankle cuff was closed around one foot. It was attached to a long chain so the slave had far more room to move about than he had enjoyed so far.

Once they were all secured, Jonathan ordered the cook to feed them well, and apparently the cook knew he meant it, for they were given gruel in bowls this time, fat chunks of pone and all the fatmeat they could eat. It was somewhat tainted, though it had been brought aboard at Havana, but the slaves' hunger for meat made toughness and ripeness unimportant.

Jonathan even ordered each to be given a full cup of rum. Some of them gagged on it and puked. Hoses cleaned up the mess. Most just plain enjoyed it and sat down, pulling their knees up to their chins and rocking back and forth and thinking perhaps this wasn't going to be bad after all.

Jonathan cupped his hands to his lips. "All hands, 'ceptin' the watch, are invited to the free show. You all git here sharp and fast. All lanterns lit. This will go on most of the night. You-all with the red hat—fetch them prime wenches over here."

WYNDWARD PASSION

The girls were lined up. Jonathan stepped before the first one, tapped her on the shoulder and pointed to the nearest chained buck. He motioned she was to go to him. He made an 'O' with his left thumb and forefinger, thrust his right forefinger through it and made the indecent motions signifying what was expected of them. With happy cries they raced for the buck assigned them and the bucks were ready.

The bucks were naked and their tumescence rose the instant they understood what they were being granted. Most of them gave cries of delight and greeted their temporary mates with outflung arms.

Within half an hour every wench was on her back and every buck was driving up and down energetically and happily. The noise and confusion was earsplitting and the laughter and filthy suggestions of the sailors added to the din.

"I bet five dollars on the buck, four from the left. Five dollars says he screws her four times 'fore midnight."

"He won't, you will, eh, Frank?" someone else yelled. "I take the bet. That buck ain't big enough for a four-rounder. He'll lose it at three."

Money was changing hands, the sailors moved closer to watch the couples their money was on. The slaves were oblivious to them. They'd been chained up in stinking holds for almost seven weeks and not one wasn't eager to get his or her fill of all the sex they could bring to bear.

Squeals, shouts, laughter, giggling, curses as a sailor lost his bet, yells as another won. Jonathan and Fitz stood above the writhing, pumping, jerking Negroes and the shouting sailors, watching it all with laughter of their own.

"You be tellin' this all your life," Jonathan roared. "Ain't never been anythin' like it in the world. An' we wins two ways, son. 'Fore this night's over, thirty of them wenches is gonna be knocked up. By the time we gits 'em to the plantation, we got thirty suckers started. An' ain't one of these bucks and wenches don't think this is how they be treated all their lives. Lots of food, rum and screwin?"

"Only thing I know," Fitz said, and the tears of laughter stained his cheeks, "this here's the fuckin'st ship on the ocean and that ain't no lie."

"An' the whorehouses in Norfolk goin' to do the best bizness they evah done." His father roared at the thought.

Chapter Two

NECKS AND WRISTS chained, linked in groups of ten, the four hundred and fifty rejected bucks, their nudeness covered by pants, were marched off the ship and paraded through the streets of Norfolk where traders and buyers flocked to watch them and try to remember those who looked the best fit. The wenches, without chains and outfitted in fresh osnaburg dresses, with bright new bandannas over their kinky heads, were likewise paraded for the benefit of the traders.

Norfolk was one of the main suppliers of slaves for the entire South. Many of the slave ships made port here. There were jails and barracoons to hold two thousand slaves if needed, and the buyers and traders flocked here at word of an incoming ship. The *Wyndward* was one of the best. Her cargo rarely failed to fulfill the needs of the most fastidious traders, for Captain Jonathan Turner was noted for his ability to pick only the best.

The slaves were marched into the barracoons, very long sheds with few windows, which were securely barred, and heavy doors. Inside were spaces for each slave, with iron rings fastened to the wall beams. It wasn't much different from the hold of the ship except that here a slave was encouraged to wash frequently, and to rest, although still chained. He was given hearty food, all he could eat, and oil to anoint his skin until it was burnished bright. At the rear were trenches where the bucks could squat and relieve themselves.

The wenches were locked up in somewhat better quarters, for it was well agreed upon that they reacted to kindness, rest, and plenty of food even better than the bucks; thus, on sale day they often looked healthier than they actually were. And they were content, not given to spitting at the buyers or shrinking away from the hands which prodded them, frequently more for the sex thrill than as part of a serious examination for defects or disease.

The pick of the lot, male and female, were shepherded down the street by Fitz to one of the better barracoons. The bucks were only lightly chained and this more as a token of their slavery than a protection against runaways because there wasn't a buck there who would have been tempted in any way to leave this coffle. Some were stumbling along weakly, as a result of the night of orgy, some had hangovers, but almost all possessed big grins as they looked about at the huge structures they soon came to know as houses and stores. They studied with much interest and respect the men in their white coats and striped pants and big plantation hats, their ruffled shirts and ties. At boots shining like their own skins. At white women who were by far the most beautiful and desirable they had ever seen. Not a buck but didn't begin to show his maleness at first look at these gorgeous creatures. Later, they would find it was better not even to raise their eyes when a Southern belle walked by, unless they were house servants.

The coffle paused before the heavy, wide doors of the

Armstrong and Perkins Slave Pens, while Jonathan approached to enter and dicker with the owners.

"Heerd tell you-all fetched up with the best bucks an' wenches evah to grace our pens," Mr. Armstrong declared. "Seen 'em marchin' this way, Cap'n suh. Mighty glad to put 'em up at two bits a day." He reared up to look out at the coffle. "But where at's the res' o' them niggers, Cap'n, suh? Reckoned you-all had least six-seven hundrud of 'em."

"Did," Jonathan said, "but I sent most of 'em to Fenwick's pens on account of they's cheaper and it don't matter none 'bout them. These here's the pick an' they ain't for sale. I'm takin' 'em by barge as near to Richmond as I kin get and then I walks 'em to my own plantation."

"Yo' own? Cap'n, suh, that mean you ain't bringin' us no mo' of these prime blacks?"

"Give me a few years," Jonathan said, "an' I'll bring you the best prime slaves in the world. Goin' to raise 'em from this stock waitin' outside. I suggest, suh, you git them in here so they kin rest up some. They's pretty much played out, but a few of 'em might git randy so chain 'em. Put up the wenches real good and see nobody gits near 'em. They's prime, suh, and I aim's to keep 'em that way."

"Whatevah you likes, Cap'n. But we goin' to miss you. Bein' a planter ain't like bein' a ship's cap'n. This here likely-lookin' boy you son? Looks mighty like you, suh."

"He's my son an' his name is Fitzjohn Turner and effen any of you gentlemen round here laugh at the name, I'll bust you good. Ain't my fault an' ain't his fault he got that name hung on him. I reckon you know whut I mean."

The trader shook hands with Fitz. "Name don't mean nothin' an' this boy's big 'nuff an' strong 'nuff to do his own bustin', Cap'n suh. An' no offense meant."

"March 'em in," Jonathan ordered Fitz. "He'p Mr. Armstrong with gettin' 'em bedded down. See the food's the best. I'm payin' extra, Mr. Armstrong, suh. See they gets the best."

"Whur you goin', papa?" Fitz asked.

"Whorin', son. Randy myse'f, an' I craves a white gal. By damn, been away from that clipper five-six hours now an' I kin still smell her. You smell her, boy?"

"Don't smell nuthin' now, papa."

"You finish up here. We be stayin' at the Union Hotel. Kin see it from here real good. Right over there. You gits randy, jus' ask Mist' Cooper at the hotel and he'll send you to a nice whorehouse. Me, I can't wait. Have yourse'f a time, son. Have yourse'f a real good time."

Jonathan walked off briskly, the late afternoon sun shining brightly on his gold braid. Fitz grinned at his retreating back. He was a fine father and a mighty good ship's captain, but a ship's captain was also a sailor who remained at sea for weeks and when he set foot ashore, the first thing he needed was a woman. The wench didn't count, but when Fitz thought about the copper-skinned girl he wanted her. His need was so bad that he considered going back to the barracoons where she was lodged and getting her out of there. Common sense told him that if his father had wanted the girl, she'd have become part of his coffle, but obviously he had passed her by for whatever purpose lay in his mind. Be it fear of his wife or some strange degree of shame because he'd deflowered her. The latter theory didn't hold water to Fitz's way of thinking.

He became engaged in dickering, in demanding the proper kind of food and in seeing that each of the selected slaves was as comfortable as could be in the barracoon.

He wandered around Norfolk for a time. He thought about entering a tavern for a drink, but decided he was too young, he really didn't want a drink. He walked toward the hotel, noting on the way that the offices of two slave buyers were in a building directly across the street. Signs in the windows stated that either would pay highest prices for prime slaves of both sexes and all ages.

Behind the building was the slave mart, a large, cleared area, fenced in, with a shed for the slaves and a vendue table for the auctioneer where the slaves could be properly exhibited.

Fitz regarded the table with a troubled look. It was no more than a simple platform of rough wood with a smaller table set on that for the auctioneer. But standing there, silently looking at the scene, Fitz could mentally picture that girl before a crowd of men who would bid for her. She wasn't the kind who'd be bought for field work or to bear suckers. She'd be meant for some white owner and if he was wrong for her, he'd wear her out in weeks, and then give her to the bucks.

Fitz turned away. Certainly this was how things had to be. Those people were blacks. They were slaves. They were to be given reasonable care, their health tended to, some sort of happiness provided for them, but somewhere in Fitz's Boston background and his New England forebears was a reluctance to accept this, although he knew he had to. Knew it was the proper thing. Without the slaves, the South couldn't possibly prosper. It had none of the great factories of the North, and the growing of cotton and tobacco, rice, wheat and sugar was an absolute necessity for the welfare of the country as a whole.

Fitz went to the hotel, an unprepossessing building two stories high, once painted white, the color now turned to a dirty gray. The lobby consisted of a small room with two rockers, a faded rug, worn through in places, a desk which hadn't been dusted in years, it seemed—though the street out front was dusty enough to make cleaning any polished surface an impossibility unless the dirt rag was applied every hour.

Jonathan had made their reservation and a bent old man silently handed Fitz a key. He walked up the stairs and unlocked the proper door.

Inside, he found all his father's possessions, some packed in chests, some in big jacks, others in carpetbags. His own clothing was also there, but he didn't bother to unpack. Late tomorrow, the slave boat would be ready for its slow trip up the river toward Richmond. He was too tired to dress up and see the town tonight. There wasn't anything to see anyhow.

He stood in the window looking out over the ramshackle city. It seemed to have come into being solely to process the slaves direct from Africa, or those brought in from points further north for resale. In the harbor, Fitz had seen the long slave boats which would convey the blacks south, most of them to New Orleans where the market was very high. Especially for freaks, or lightcolored wenches.

In a nervous state, uncertain of himself, and his desires, fighting back the urge to visit a whorehouse, Fitz had to call upon all the strength of cold, unyielding New England and there he found the capacity to withstand earthy temptations.

He undressed, though it was still early evening, and crawled into bed. He suspected it had been used before and the sheets unchanged, but he was too tired to care.

He lay back, glad that his first and last ocean voyage was over. Happy, too, that his father had decided not to go to sea again. He'd be glad to see his mother—at least, he thought so. What her reaction would be to living in the South, especially on a slave-breeding plantation, was problematical. There were few blacks where she had lived her life and those she did see had no appeal for her. Yet she was unable to reconcile herself to the fact that some of these dark-skinned people were worked to death without pay, bred like animals, housed like cattle, families rudely broken up in sales. The Lord moved in ways too strange sometimes. She was going to be aghast at some of the things that went on at the plantation.

He didn't awaken when his father stumbled in, doused

his face in the water basin, sloshed the water out the window, got out of half his clothes and gave up on the rest to crawl in bed and promptly begin snoring loudly and steadily.

Fitz stirred, rumbled in his sleep, pushed his father's carcass away, seized more than his share of the thin blanket and managed, somehow, to get enough rest.

In the morning he was up early. Jonathan lay on his back, mouth open, but he no longer had the stamina to snore. He was drained out completely. Fitz grinned and wondered how many women he'd favored.

The uniform he'd worn on ship didn't appeal to him this morning so Fitz unpacked some of his things and put on fresh undergarments, clean stockings, a ruffled shirt badly wrinkled from having been packed throughout the voyage. He slipped into tight, pearl gray trousers that strapped under the instep and square-toed shoes handmade in Boston. He tied a large light green cravat in place and donned a dark green frock coat. The wavy mirror indicated he was sartorially correct, though more for an evening out than a morning stroll. As if it made any difference in Norfolk.

He fastened a sheath knife to his middle because he wasn't certain what the town would be like. By night he had found it had been tawdry and rough, even though he hadn't ventured into any of the pleasure places.

The sunlight was warm; he began to sweat rather profusely and wished he'd dressed in more carefree clothes, but it was too late for that now. In front of the hotel and the slave trader's offices all manner of conveyances were being tied up. Wagons, barouches, rigs, carriages and a large number of saddled horses were in evidence. The noise came from the selling mart. This was what he wanted to see. Fitz walked through the gate and took his place well to the rear of the throng. He judged there were at least fifty men here, all impatiently waiting for the auctioneer to begin. The pen already held a dozen bucks, each frantically looking over the men, one of whom would be their master if only for a space of time long enough for them to be transported elsewhere.

The bucks were neatly dressed now, in clothes furnished by the slave traders. They wore white cotton shirts tucked into tight-fitting britches. Their feet were bare, they'd scrubbed themselves clean, and were already so well fed it showed on them.

Fitz had no difficulty distinguishing the businesslike buyers from the usual groups who came to ogle the wenches and find excuses for fingering them. They were mostly young, flamboyantly dressed, loud-spoken and hunting whatever thrills could be found in a city like Norfolk in 1821.

Fitz was attracted to a half dozen of these sports and he stood by while they argued the merits of a young, wiry fighter pitted against a huge, older buck. It was Fitz's first encounter with even a mention of nigger fighters except by his father, and then only casually.

"Effen he's spry 'nuff an' slipp'ry 'nuff," one man said, "he'll git away from the bigger man, that he will, and I'd put money on it."

"The man talks," another said. "The big man, Frank Tavers, he's talkin' an' he ain't sayin' nuthin' 'cause he ain't got nuthin' to say 'bout nigger fighters."

"What's yo' name?" Frank Tavers demanded. "Why you-all talkin' impo'tant?"

"Name's Winfield Kearney, suh. Kearney Plantation, suh. Knows my niggers, I do, an' don't take no big lump of a buck to whup every buck who's smaller'n him. I seed small men bite the balls off 'em big bucks. Kills 'em ever' time. Might as well. What's they got to live for—no balls?"

The others joined in the spirited and sometimes heated dialogue, but the voices of Winfield Kearney and Frank Tavers were the loudest and the most boastful.

"Yo' willin' to put up some money—an' I means cash?" Tavers demanded.

"Whut you jawin' 'bout now? Sho' I'll put up cash, but for whut?" Kearney asked.

"This here's a nigger auction, ain't it? We got plenty room here, don't we? So let's yo-all buy yo'se'f one big buck . . . big ox you like. I'll pick me a smaller one an' buy him. Then we put 'em agin one another. 'Sides payin' for my buck and givin' him to yo'all he loses, I put down a bet o' two thousand I'm right and yo're wrong. Now that's the way we plays it in Norfolk. No goddamn fancy plantation boy comin' here and tellin' me I'm wrong, lessen he can be willin' to prove it."

"By God," Kearney shouted, "suits me fine." He pushed his way through the crowd. "Mist' Coopah, suh, craves a moment of your valuable time."

"Hello, Kearney," the auctioneer greeted him. "Tho'ght your place crowded with niggers. Whut yo' doin' here at my auction, eh?"

"Craves to buy me a buck an' Mistah Tavers here craves to buy him a niggah. But kinda special they mus' be, suh. Wants a big buck, kinda bit older'n average. Mistah Tavers he's wantin' a young buck full o' juice an' not so big as mine."

"Glad to obleege you gents," Cooper said, "but whut you 'tendin' to do with these here bucks?"

"Got us a argyment 'bout who kin fight best. Gonna buy 'em here an' now, and fit 'em here an' now." He raised his voice. "Any yo' gen'men wish to make bets, small or big, I'm sho' Mistah Coopah'll be glad to handle 'em all. Now trot out them bucks, Mistah Coopah, suh. One big buck an' one small buck, and we'll see who's right."

"Whut them two crazy galoots aimin' to do?" Fitz asked a small, slim, gray-haired man who had moved to his side.

"Buy two bucks and fight 'em, that's whut they aimin'

to do, son. You come to town more often, you shorely will know this happens too much. Waste of niggers, I say. Sheer, damn waste of good strong backs an' muscle. Who do I have the honor of addressin', suh?"

Fitz used the plantation title for the first time and glorified in it. He wished his father could have been present to hear him. He bowed courteously. "I'm Fitzjohn Turner, suh, of Wyndward Plantation."

"Braxton Canfield heah, suh. Lives in town. Proud to make your acquaintance, Mr. Turner. Kinda young, ain't you to brag onto a whole plantation."

"I take it kindly you makin' no fun of me, suh. It's my papa who owns Wyndward."

"Cain't say I evah heerd o'it, young man."

"That's reasonable, suh, 'cause it ain't operatin' yet. My father was Cap'n an' owner of the clipper *Wyndward* which the plantation is named after."

The elder man smiled and offered his hand. "By God, Cap'n Turner's boy. Knew he had one, but figgered you lived up No'th somewhere. Many a fine niggah your papa brought me from Africa. Regards him as the bes' man in the business."

"Ain't in it no more, suh. We's settlin' down to raise us money crops."

"If anyone kin do it, you sho' got the pappy who kin. Well, looks like these two buckaroos goin' to git their crazy wish. Mistah Cooper's haulin' out one big buck an' one small buck. Sho' a waste of good niggah flesh. But younguns'll be younguns and them two the craziest of all."

The two Negroes stood on the vendue table, not knowing what it was all about. Fitz was happy to see that neither belonged to the group his father had just brought in. These were wise slaves. They had heard some of the argument over the compound fence. They knew what they were supposed to do. Neither hated the other, barely knew one another, but in a few minutes one was going to kill the other. Nothing less than that final burst of blood in which one man died would satisfy the crowd. Bets were being made already. Cooper had seen to it that word got abroad about the fight and the marketplace was already packed.

Kearney and Tavers bid five hundred dollars each for his man. No one made a counter offer for either, and while these were only slightly off being prime and might fetch more than five hundred each, Cooper wisely surrendered them because, with the auction coming up immediately after the fight, he'd have the largest audience in months.

"Cain't see much sense to it," Fitz confided in Mr. Canfield. "Jes' ain't smart to throw away a man that way even if he ain't human. Ain't nobody to stop this?"

"Nobody wants to, son. Ain't nuthin' we kin do but stand here an' enjoy it. Kinda like to watch 'em myse'f even if I ain't in favah of them. You a bettin' man?"

"Fo' fun . . . high as double eagle, suh. You lets me pick the big 'un."

They shook hands to seal the bargain. "Got me faith in the little one. Don't look so drug out," Canfield declared.

Kearney and his buck, Tavers and his, took up opposite sides of the squared-off space in which the slaves were expected to fight. Each master whispered to his man, offering rewards of corn liquor and a new suit if he won, or quick sentence to a road gang if he lost—and lived. Cooper, from the advantage of the vendue table, called out, "One—two—three—an' fight you black bastahds. Got us money ridin' so make it a good fight or we'll all slice you to little bittie pieces o' dark meat, we will."

The slaves calmly dropped their pants, stepped out of them, threw them aside. They circled one another, sizing each other up. The big man sneering at the smaller one's gall to even think of fighting, not giving any thought to the fact that the small Negro had no more to say about his being here and risking his life than the big one had.

The big one made a savage rush, the smaller man

nimbly stepped aside and the buck went crashing into the thickly packed crowd, scattering them. They beat at him with their fists, kicked him, until he had to cover up his face and go rushing back into the ring where he was met by the small buck who promptly delivered a murderous kick to the crotch. The big buck yowled and clapped his hands to the injured region. He began staggering about, still yowling, and the smaller man leaped on his back, spread his fingers wide and did his best to gouge out the big buck's eyes. The searching fingers warned the big buck of a danger far more imminent than the kick in the balls. He raised his hands, secured a grip on the small buck's hand, dragged it down and bit off the little finger, spitting out the amputated member disdainfully.

The small buck now did his howling while the blood ran down his body from the stump of the finger he was holding tightly against his chest to try and stave the blood flow.

The big one reached for the throat of his opponent and met a fist hammering straight at his broad, flat nose. It promptly disgorged as much blood as a stuck pig, and sent him reeling blindly about. The small buck was still in agony from the severed finger, but he was also enraged to a point of near madness. He flung himself at the taller and heavier man, brought one work-hardened bare heel down on the big buck's instep. Bone crunched under the force of the stamp and the big buck was unable to balance himself. He went crashing to the ground and the small buck leaped on him. He straddled the big man, who lay on his back, squirmed lower to gain a better aiming distance for those hardened heels, and proceeded to kick the big buck's face completely in. He broke his jaw with two kicks, he delivered another to the tip of his already bleeding nose, pushed it upwards, broke it surely, caused it to begin bleeding all over again. He was now astride a man, far larger than himself, but utterly helpless. The small buck squirmed forward, raised one foot and sent the heel crashing into the left eye socket. The eyeball bulged out after this kick. The next one must have blinded him. No one ever really knew because the big man lay there moaning, arms flailing and hitting nothing. The small man then arose slowly, walked up to the big buck's head, raised his foot and sent it crashing down against his victim's throat. He repeated this and each time bone bracked.

Blood was now pouring out of the big buck's throat, his mouth was wide open, gaping for air his broken windpipe couldn't deliver. Then he gave one convulsive heave, fell back and was still.

"Jesus Keerist," Canfield uttered fervently. "Evah see anythin' like that, Mistah Turner? Evah in your whole life seen anythin' like that, suh?"

"Wishin I hadn't now," Fitz said. "This here's your double eagle, suh, won fair an' square."

Canfield pocketed it, still far more interested in the fight. The small buck was parading about with his chest stuck out. He was the winner, he deserved the praise and he damned well wanted his promised drink of corn. Someone handed him a tin cup of it and he slobbered the liquor half into his mouth, half down across his chest. Then he toppled forward and fell with a crash.

"Whut in hell's the mattah with him?" Kearney asked. He went to the side of the buck and kicked him experimentally in the ribs. The buck didn't move. Kearney turned him over with his boot. The small buck was dead.

"Goddamn!" Kearney said. "I be goddamn. This musky sonabitch daid. The big 'un musta got in a good lick, I didn't even see. Be goddamn. An' all bets off. Nobody pays. Mista Coopah, I thank you to pay back the money dollah fo' dollah as you c'llected it, suh. Nobody won."

"Jes' a minute," Fitz moved up to Kearney. "Ain't right to call them bets off, suh. The little buck was on his feet when the big buck died. That makes him the winnah, suh, and ain't no doubt 'bout that."

" 'N how much you stand to win, boy?" Kearney asked.

"Mattah of fact, suh, I bet on the big buck and I consider I lost, suh. Man on his feet when the fight is ovah, and he wins."

Kearney put the flat of his hand against Fitz's chest and pushed. Fitz, forced back, tripped over the big buck and went sprawling. Kearney threw back his head and laughed heartily.

"Yo' a clumsy galoot, 'sides bein' a nosey one. This ain't none of your business, suh, so kindly keep out of it."

"Makin' it my business, suh." Fitz untangled himself from the dead man and straightened up.

Kearney waited for him, legs spread apart, balancing himself lightly and confidently. Fitz was just as confident. All during the long voyage he'd killed time by fighting with the best the crew could offer. Besides, the hard work had toughened him to a point where he could absorb a punch and go in for more. He'd been taught all the tricks of dirty fighting, he knew where to aim his fists so they'd do the most painful and crippling damage.

He didn't rush Kearney, but walked up to him and ran into a fist that caught him just to one side of his chin. Had it been centered and a little lower, the fight might have been over. As it was, Fitz went hurtling backward this time, but he didn't fall. He merely took off his jacket, folded it and was in the act of handing it to Mr. Canfield when Kearney chose that moment to come charging in.

Fitz dropped the jacket to the ground, swept off his hat, took a hard blow to the chest which drove all the air out of his lungs, but as Kearney stepped back to wind up another blow, Fitz smashed him full in the throat, much the same sort of blow that the small buck had inflicted on his victim with his heel.

Kearney gasped and air whistled down his half-paralyzed trachea. Fitz pumped two very fast punches low in the stomach, doubling Kearney up in a fresh wave of agony, but Kearney back-peddled so fast Fitz couldn't catch him, until Kearney had his wits and his strength back sufficiently to meet Fitz's onrushing attack with a slamming punch that hit Fitz high on the nose, making it gush blood and rendering him helplessly dizzy. Had Kearney taken advantage of that opportunity when Fitz was all but immobilized, he might have won the fight, but Kearney was too busy trying to adjust to the frighteningly painful area in his stomach and the swelling of his throat that was cutting off some wind.

Fitz, on the other hand, recovered nicely, but the pain had created in him a rage that made his face bestial and he grumbled in a low voice as he came dancing in. He then methodically proceeded to cut Kearney to pieces.

He tore an ear half off with one glancing blow, closed an eye with another, made Kearney spit blood and a tooth with a punch that landed squarely against his mouth. Fitz now turned to the man's already sore gut and slammed four hard punches to his stomach. Kearney doubled up. Fitz moved back to deliver an uppercut and end the fight, but it wasn't necessary. As Kearney bent forward, holding onto his stomach, he didn't stop. He simply fell on his head and his legs thrashed out with the agony of all that punishment.

"You had 'nuff, seems like," Fitz said in a stone-cold voice. "Reckon they ain't no call to kill you, suh. Ain't like the nigger fight."

He turned away from the stricken man and walked toward Canfield who had picked up Fitz's jacket. Canfield smiled as he held out the coat. Fitz turned around, slipped his arms into the sleeves. Someone shouted a warning. Fitz glanced automatically in the direction of the man he'd whipped, but Kearney was still on the ground, unable to do more than moan.

It was Tavers who now presented a more difficult problem, for Tavers held a derringer and he moved forward to get close enough so the small gun could do its maximum damage. Fitz, his arms half in, half out of the coat sleeves, was momentarily handicapped. All he could see was the muzzle of that little gun which he knew could kill him in the next two seconds.

There was a tug at the coat, it was stripped away from him. He reached behind him, grasped the handle of the knife he'd been wise enough to carry. He whipped it out. The derringer came up in line with his chest. Fitz threw the knife. It made one glittering arc and its point bit into Tavers's shoulder. The derringer went off. Someone in the crowd gave a yelp of pain, but Fitz paid scant attention to that. He rushed up to Tavers and wrenched the derringer out of his hand. He flung it as far away as he could and then he grasped the wounded man by the right shoulder, secured a grip on the knife and yanked it free to the accompaniment of a scream from Tavers.

Fitz moved back. "I'm warnin' you, suh, nex' time you pull a gun on me, I'll sho' kill you daid. You lucky I wasn't in no killin' mood when I flung that knife."

Tavers scowled at him. "A lucky throw, thass all."

Fitz walked to the vendue table on which rested the auctioneer's ledger and a large pencil. Fitz appropriated the pencil, walked to the fence and drew a circle about five inches in diameter. He returned the pencil, moved to the far end of the compound, grasped his knife lightly by its tip. His hand came up, the knife flashed and its point thudded into almost the very center of the circle.

A long sigh went up from the crowd. Tavers, considerably impressed, stepped forward and made a low bow to Fitz. "I'm beggin' yo're pardon, suh. No hard feelin's on my part, suh. If you-all excuse me, I bettah see the doctor."

"Bettah bring Kearney with you," someone shouted. "Needs a doctor more'n you."

A man stepped out of the crowd, nursing a bleeding arm. "Goddamn derringer winged me too. I'm comin' 'long. Reckon next time that young 'un comes to town, I'm stayin' home. Near onto killed three men this day, he did."

The wounded man stepped over the corpse of the big buck without a glance. He paused beside the smaller buck and kicked him, as if he couldn't believe he was dead.

Cooper's voice rang out over the excited crowd. "Git them daid niggers outa there. Got us an auction to start. Drag 'em out. I'll have my niggers bury 'em someplace later. Business first, gen'men. Now you-all ready, we gits down to the bizness of the day."

While the bodies were dragged out by the heels and the crowd settled down from its lively discussions of Fitz's prowess, Canfield helped Fitz on with his coat. Someone else handed him his hat, carefully brushed off.

"Remarkable, young man," Canfield said. "Made yourse'f some friends in Norfolk. Them two jackanapes been pesterin' folks here for months, swaggerin' 'round and talkin' how good they was with fists an' a gun. You made 'em eat dirt and nex' time they starts abraggin', they's goin' to be shut up real quick."

Fitz gently massaged his face. One side of it was swollen, his nose felt twice as big as normal and he ached considerably from some of the body blows that had landed. Despite that, he felt himself in excellent condition and it was the proudest day of his life. He wished his father had been present to see it.

"Reckon I better get cleaned up, Mr. Canfield," he said.

"Stay awhile," Canfield urged. "You ain't battle-scarred too much. You feelin' all right, I hope?"

"Feels fine. Reckon I will hang 'round. Nevah saw a slave sale, but I heered tell of 'em."

A husky-looking, eighteen-year-old boy stepped onto the vendue table. He was one of those brought by the *Wyndward* apparently, for he understood nothing of what went on. The auctioneer realized this and gave his orders by a sign language all his own. He flexed his arm muscles, indicating the slave was to do the same. The black obeyed willingly because he was proud of his biceps. He squatted, jumped up and down, turned around several times, all following the auctioneer's example. He might even have been enjoying it until the auctioneer indicated he was to shuck down—remove his shirt and his pants. The slave drew himself up in a haughty fashion.

The auctioneer sighed, put down the little hammer which was his insignia of trade and picked up a short whip. He lashed at the man, catching him across the chest. The slave slowly closed his eyes and realization penetrated his skull. He'd been told what to do. If he disobeyed, there would be punishment right up to the point of death. He'd seen the two dead fighting bucks in the compound. He didn't know why they'd been killed, but he supposed they must have rebelled. He peeled off his shirt and stepped out of his trousers.

The auctioneer nodded and smiled and laid down the whip. He even patted the boy on the shoulder in approval that he'd understood. The auctioneer signaled that the boy was now ready for inspection.

Three men clambered onto the stage to examine him. They felt his muscles, ran their hands down his legs, lifted his feet to examine the bottoms of them. They skinned his penis, weighed his testicles, all in a completely off-hand manner. They made him open his mouth and ran their fingers along his teeth, testing them for firmness and cavities. They made him bend over while they spread his cheeks and looked for hemorrhoids. Finally satisfied, they rejoined the ranks of the others and the auctioneer went into his patter.

"Now, gen'mun, evah see a likelier lookin' buck? Straight from Afriky. Got no bad habits like niggers a'ready trained. You kin do anythin' with him. Look at them muscles! An' he hung jus' right to pester all the wenches you want him to cover. I sweah he's sound. Good field han' make a good carpenter. Too big foh a houseboy, but make a mighty fine body servant, yo' got need o' one. Ready now fo' the biddin'. Do I heah five hundrud? Do I heah five-fifty? Fine, suh. Mighty good o' yo'. I have five-fifty an' I'm askin' six hundrud. Don't figger you folks 'spect me to give him to you-all. Heah, boy, show 'em how you kin run."

The slave looked at him numbly. The auctioneer had provided himself with a stick which he now threw into a cleared space beside the vendue table. By his gestures the slave understood that he was to fetch it. He climbed down off the table and sauntered toward the length of wood. The auctioneer waited patiently until he returned. Then he took it, threw it again and lashed at the slave with the short whip, making him understand by the language of pain that he was to look sharp and run for the stick.

The slave mounted the platform again, subdued, frightened to a point where his eyes rolled wildly.

"Got me five-fifty," the auctioneer began again. "Lookin' fo' six hundrud. Thank you, suh. Six hundrud it is, goin' to six-fifty. Do I heah six-fifty? Six-thirty? Givin' this man away, suh, but six-thirty welcome nobody goes no higher."

His eyes scanned the crowd, searching for the slightest move he could interpret as a bid. There seemed to be considerable reluctance to go any higher so he slowed down his speech and drawled the challenges to go higher, and the praises he heaped upon this black whose abilities were as unknown to him as they would have been to Fitz's mama back in Massachusetts.

Fitz listened, fascinated by this dealing in men, even though he could not regard the black as quite human. It was impossible to do so. However, somewhere in his makeup, Fitz was repelled by all of this. He kept reminding himself it was necessary. Without it the South could not flourish and would die quickly under the driving competition from the North. Without slaves, Wyndward Plantation would cease to exist, even before it was really begun. Still, fascinating or not, there was something wrong about it. Fitz thrust this idea as far back into his mind as possible. It wasn't difficult to do. He regarded himself as a true Southerner and this was a part of Southern life.

"Bettah speak up," the auctioneer was saying. "You-all'll lose him, yo' don' bid. I got six-thirty . . . six-thirty . . . My compliments, Judge. Six-seventy-five. You're a fine judge of stren'th an' vital'ty. That's why I called you judge, suh. I got six-seventy-five . . . Once. Twice . . . Three times an' sold to the gen'man fo' six hundrud an' seventy-five dollahs."

For an hour, the auction went on. The slaves were all prime and bringing good prices. Often a batch of ten were sold at one time and at a discount to a trader who would send them to the New Orleans markets. Fitz shifted his feet, growing tired of it all and about to take his leave when the auctioneer decided it was time to arouse the interest of the crowd again. He had the copper-skinned wench from the *Wyndward* brought to the vendue table.

He smiled and winked lewdly at the crowd. "Now, if they's any gen'mun desirin' to make a close 'spection of this here gal, yo' welcome to come onto the table."

Fitz held his breath. If anyone began to paw that girl, he was going to start another fight. Some men moved up, intent on this sort of an examination. They had no intention of buying, but the girl was there and was in no position to resist their lascivious pawings. Fitz opened his mouth to sing out a challenge, not a bid. To his complete confusion, Canfield, at his side, called out the opening bid.

"Seven hundrud dollahs with no 'spection," he shouted. "Provided, suh, no man lays a hand on that gal."

"You biddin' fo' her?" Fitz asked.

"Wasn't makin' noise, suh. Wants her. Looks fresh. Virgin to me. Wants her fo' my own bed."

"Ain't you married, suh?"

"What's that got to do with it?" Canfield demanded. "I got a wife who gives me white children. No pleasure in that. Only real pleasure a man gits is from one o' these here wenches an' I likes 'em light-colored. Got ten-fifteen light suckers in my slave cabins. Made two mustees, I did. Real white they is. Reckon I kin get me more outa this gal."

The auctioneer raised his gavel. "I got seven hundrud," he shouted. "Mist' Canfield bid seven hundrud. Do I heah eight? Lookin' for eight . . . ."

"Eight hundrud," Fitz sang out loudly.

Canfield gave him a puzzled look. "Yo' means that, suh?"

"Like you said, I ain't talkin' to make noise."

"Makes a difference now," Canfield said. He moved forward. Fitz didn't know what he was about to do so he remained where he was. Canfield climbed onto the platform and stepped up to the girl.

Like the first buck, and most of those put up, she didn't know what it was all about, though she certainly suspected by this time. Canfield placed a hand on her shoulder and smiled to reassure her. Then he passed his hand around her throat, let it slide down to her breasts and he gripped one firmly and shook it. He turned her around and passed his hands down the small of her back, across her buttocks and down her slim, shapely legs.

She was petrified with terror now, not able to exhibit the fiery temper Fitz knew she possessed. His own ire was rising rapidly and reached its highest point when Canfield's hand went up under the girl's dress for a fingering inspection.

Fitz called out, "I bid eight hundrud an' until you tops my bid, suh, you keep you goddamn hands off that gal."

"One thousand," Canfield shouted, his own dander

rising. Fitz forced his way through the crowd, scattering those reluctant to move with vicious shoves. He made the platform in one jump. For a second, his eyes locked with those of the scared girl and he saw the appeal in them. He stepped up to Canfield and spoke in a gentle voice.

"Knows that gal, suh. Wants to make her part of my papa's coffle. You bid a thousand dollahs 'cause you on'y wants to take her home and make a whore outen her. You an old man. You cain't have much juice lef' in you balls. Me, I got plenty. I'm goin' to outbid you once more, suh. If you bids agin me, I'll bust you so there ain't no wench ever made kin bring it up, ever again. I'm right sorry to do this. I been takin' you as my fren', suh, but nobody gits this here wench 'ceptin' me."

"Bid," Canfield said bitterly.

"One thousand an' one dollahs," Fitz roared and doubled his fist, daring Canfield to speak. Canfield merely bowed, stepped off the stage.

Fitz drew a breath of relief. No one else bid. The amount was already far too high for a wench, even if she was young and a handsome piece.

"Ain't got that kind of cash on me," he addressed the auctioneer, "but I git it from my papa right away. Wantin' to take the gal with me now. You trust me, suh?"

"I'd trust Jonathan Turner's son with the whole goddamn fuggin' coffle I got me to sell. Yo' takes her along, son, and happy evenin's with her."

Fitz turned beet red and the crowd roared. All except Canfield who stood by in gloomy silence. Fitz grinned abashedly at the crowd, seized the girl's hand and pulled her down off the vendue table, through the crowd and out onto the street.

There he stopped long enough to touch her cheek fondly and smile at her. She would have flung herself into his arms, but he pushed her away and motioned that she was not to walk with him, but follow behind. She meekly obeyed, trotting like a cat at his heels.

The startled hotel clerk opened his mouth to protest the bringing of a wench into his place of business, but a look at Fitz's battered face warned him not to. Fitz pulled the girl up the stairs, down the corridor and into the room where his father lay propped up in bed with a ledger in his hands and a pencil over his ear. He stared at the pair of them. His swollen-faced son, his excited and breathless son—and a very pretty wench who faced him hand-in-hand like two people about to confess to an elopement.

"What in hell's this?" he demanded as he swung his legs off the bed. "Where'd you git that gal, son? Why you hangin' on to her like she was runnin'? Whut happened to your face?"

"Saw two bucks fight," Fitz began, determined not to leave out anything. "Like to kill theyse'ves, which they sho' did. Nevah saw anythin' like it——"

"Your face! The wench!" Jonathan reminded him to get at the meat of the situation.

"The big buck was killed first off by the little buck and then the little one fell daid. I spoke up and said the little buck was on his feet at the end of the fight and he won. There were some who said I was wrong so I had me a fight. Had me a derringer pulled, and I flung my knife an' wounded the goddamn dude. Then this here wench was put up an' a friend of mine by name of Canfield——"

"Brax Canfield? That who you mean, son?"

"Yes, papa, that his name. Well—he bid for this wench an' told me all he wanted her for was to bed down with."

"An' whut's the matter with that?" Jonathan demanded. "She's a likely piece. Yes sir, sho' is."

Jonathan hadn't even recognized the girl yet, though

she knew him beyond any doubt, for she shrank back the instant she saw him.

"Mistah Canfield, he's an old man, suh. Ain't right he gits a nice young gal like this," Fitz explained.

Jonathan began to nod slowly. "Mistah Canfield done bid and you done topped him. That right?"

"He bid a thousand, papa," Fitz said reluctantly. If there had been any possibility whatsoever of his getting that sum, he would never have confessed to Jonathan.

"A thousand? Fo' this wench? An' you topped im?"

"By one dollah," Fitz said sheepishly.

"One stinkin' dollah an' he didn't come back?"

"Told him he did I'd fix him so he'd never git another wench, for she'd be no use to him."

Jonathan stared at both of them in considerable awe. "You know Mistah Canfield, he's an impo'tant man hereabouts. He's a rich man too, an' he don't cotton much to wet-eared boys who take his wench away. Whut you do this for, son? Tell me why?"

"Tol' you, papa. This wench too goddamn good for old man like him."

"You aimin' to use her fo' your own wench?"

"Wasn't aimin' to do nuthin' with her 'cept put her to work."

"Hell of a thing. One thousand and one dolahs for a wench. It don't make sense, son."

"Papa," Fitz said desperately. In his frantic search for an excuse, he'd discovered the only one which would impress his father. "Papa, you know mama's comin' soon. She gits here she needs a wench fo' a personal maid. Ain't that right? An' mama ain't the kind to take to jes' any wench. She want a clean, smart one an' a pretty one. You evah seen a prettier one, papa?"

Jonathan got off the bed and approached the girl. "By damn," he said, "she come on our clipper?"

"Yes, suh, she did."

"I be damned," Jonathan exploded, "ain't she the gal

I busted? Sho' she is. Son, why'nt you bust her? Why'nt you take her? You admires her this much, it don't make no sense you don't take her."

Fitz inhaled slowly. "Papa, I am aimin' to do that soon's I git time. Wants her for mama's body servant and wants her for my wench. You got to pay the money, papa. I got some comin' to me. You add 'nuff to make it up, I work my ass off 'til I pays you back."

Jonathan sat down again. "Son, you been in these here town less'n a day and you see two bucks kill one 'nother, you gits into a fight, you beats up one man, knifes 'nother one. You insults an old friend of mine, rich man, pow'ful man. You buys you a wench fo' twice what she'd bring on the vendue table."

"Yes, papa, that's whut happened all right. Cain't he'p it."

"I'll pay fo' the wench. Don't owe me nothin'. Present from me 'cause you sho' let me know you're a man today. Proud of you, son. You wants me to clear out so you kin pleasure this here wench?"

"No, papa. I'm aimin' to save the pesterin' 'til we gits to the plantation."

"We got us a trip, son. You don't pleasure her soon, be goddamn, I will." He waved his arms dramatically and grinned at the storm growing on Fitz's face. "You right, son. She all yours. Won't lay a hand on her, I promise. But you lingers too long an' she's sho' goin' to spread her laigs for some buck."

"She does," Fitz declared, "an' there'll be a dead buck, I'm tellin' you, papa."

"No more'n right," Jonathan agreed. "Now you git down to the kitchen and fetch us some grub. I'm too hungry to wait for some slothful nigger to bring it. Anythin' they got and lots of it. Rustle up a nigger to tote it and git back soon's you kin. We got work to do an' tomorrow we start for Richmond."

At the door Fitz paused. "Papa . . . she's mine. You 'members that?"

"Course I cain't touch her you say so. She your'n, Fitz. I wants a wench I gits one, but reckon I'll sorta spend tonight at the whorehouse. Got me a nice fat one there, dreens me proper, she does, and reckon I better git myse'f dreened 'fore your mama comes. Git 'long now."

Fitz raced down to the kitchen, arranged for three trays to be sent up by relays of slaves. He hurried back to the room, not trusting his father too much, but Jonathan was back in bed and the wench sat cross-legged in a corner solemnly regarding him and looking as if she was prepared to leap to her feet and scoot for the door if he came toward her.

The tables arrived, two of them, and the contents of the trays were set on them. There were platters of pink ham, eggs cooked to perfection, hot, light biscuits, honey, a big ball of pale yellow butter and a large enameled pot of coffee.

Jonathan regarded all the food, the three place settings. "You ain't aimin' to have the wench eat with us, son? You ain't lost you mind complete?"

"No, suh," Fitz explained hastily. "Knows you was mighty hungry and so am I. Ordered 'nuff for three and they figured we was three humans so they sent all that stuff."

"Slaves eat whut we leave on our plates, you 'member that, son. That's all they eats 'ceptin' whut reg'lar vittles . . . slave vittles . . . we give 'em. That clear?"

"Sho', papa. I know that without proddin'. But way I figgered, we want mama to love this here wench an' she won't if all she gits is a skinny gal."

Jonathan clapped hands to his balding head. "Fitz, boy, this here gal white, I says you better marry her quick. Son, don't fall in love with no wench. Bed 'em down, love 'em up, do whut you wants with her, but don't treat her like she human. 'Cause she ain't. All she's good for is to pleasure you and tend to whatever your mama wants. Nothin' more than that, or you got more trouble'n you kin handle. I'm warnin' you."

"I knows that, papa. Only wants to fatten her up some."

Jonathan seized one of the plates and heaped it with some of everything. He walked to the corner where the girl sat. She tried to push herself through the wall until he proffered the plate. She took it and smiled tentatively.

Jonathan smiled despite himself. "You pleasured me right good, gal. I 'members that. Now you pleasures me son an' you got nothin' to worry you black hide about. But you step outa line and I sweah I lambaste you like you nothin' but a no-account nigger."

She nodded happily and began to eat the food with her fingers. She was obviously very hungry. Neither Jonathan or Fitz knew that she'd been offered special food in the slave jail in return for her favors to one of the guards, and she'd spurned him and therefore she'd been allowed to go hungry.

Jonathan sat down at the table and began to eat. "Got yourse'f a real nice wench there, son. Treats her right an' she treats you good too. She got a name?"

"No, papa, she cain't even speak a word yet."

"Got to have a name. Take us three, four days sailin' up the river to Richmond and I aimin' to name all them bucks and wenches so we kin make a record of them. Then we knows which buck's hung right and which wench pops us the mos' suckers. We is in the business of raisin' slaves and we keep books like we keeps 'em on our 'baccy crop an' our hosses—when we gits 'em."

"Whut you want we should name her, papa?"

"Been thinkin' 'bout that. Been sailin' the world mos' my life. Don't want to leave it entire, so I'm thinkin' I name our wenches after ships I've known. Ships are female anyways and it's no more'n right we gives the wenches female names."

"Sho' is a bright idea, papa. Whut the bucks named after?"

"Ports of call. That's it. Wenches for ships, bucks for ports. Lessee now . . . she bein' the first one . . . an' we better begin with the first ship. . . . Whut was the first?"

"I don't know, papa."

"You been to school—you studied in them No'thern schools. Whut was the first ship to reach America? Knew it once, but sorta disremember . . ."

"The Nina, Pinta and the Santa Maria, papa. Them was the ships Columbus sailed."

Jonathan grinned broadly. "Then we calls the wench Nina. First wench for Wyndward, first ship whut landed here."

He had finished his meal. The girl had eaten her plate clean. Jonathan arose, scraped what was left on his plate to hers and then added the leavings from Fitz's. At first she seemed puzzled and by her expression, not complimented. Fitz then carried the platter with an entire slice of ham still on it, along with three eggs and some biscuits and honey. He took the plate of leftover food and gave her the platter instead. He also provided her with a knife and fork which she examined critically and laid aside. She'd never seen such instruments before.

She ate with her fingers, daintily and slowly. Every move she made was ladylike. Fitz watched her, fascinated, while Jonathan chuckled, let his belly rumble and relaxed.

"Don' recommend you fo' overseer," he grinned. "You too goddamn kin'. She nothin' but a nigger wench, but you're makin' a pet out of her."

"That's it," Fitz declared. "That's whut I want. Nina as a pet."

He knelt before the girl and pointed his finger at her.

"You Nina," he said. "Nina... Nina... Nina...."

She wiped her mouth and smiled. "Nina," she said clearly on the first attempt and Fitz let out a howl of pleasure. "Papa, she's sho' smart." He pointed at her again. "You, Nina." He pointed at himself. "Me—Fitz. You git that, gal? Me—Fitz."

Her first attempt sounded like "Fizz," but she finally managed it. She pointed at herself and said, "Nina." She pointed to Fitz and said, "Fitz." Then she took his hand and kissed the back of it while Fitz squirmed.

He got up and faced his grinning father. "Papa, I declare soon's I git rested up, I goin' to pester this here wench 'til she dreens me out. Cain't wait."

"Neither kin I," Jonathan said. "Pays you fifty dollahs you lets me watch."

"You go to hell," Fitz said in his embarrassment.

That night Jonathan repaired to the whorehouse and spent all the time until dawn with his fat prostitute. Fitz went to bed early, undressing in front of Nina with some trepidation that she'd notice his manhood straight out. He threw a blanket on the floor for her, crawled into bed and snuffed the candle.

He lay there, all but panting for her. Asking himself what the hell was wrong. The girl belonged to him. He could do as he liked with her and here he lay like a dummy, afraid to take her.

He felt the covers move and she slipped into bed beside him. She pushed herself against him and she was as nude as he. Fitz closed his eyes and then sat up and uttered a loud, mighty oath. He drew back one leg, lodged his foot against her and kicked her out of bed. She literally was hurled half across the room. He lay back, cursing her, cursing his New England upbringing, cursing a cold mother whose sex chill he seemed to have inherited. He heard the girl squirm back to the blanket at the foot of the bed and presently her sobs tore at his already frayed nerves. When he could stand them no longer, he slipped out of bed, trotted to the foot of it, fumbled for her in the darkness, picked her up and carried her to the bed. He crept in beside her and drew her to him. He could feel the wetness of her tears and he gently dried them with the edge of the sheet.

She was making small cooing noises that somehow delighted him. Once she said, "Fitz," which delighted him even more. He kissed her, very softly and then the passion mounted in him until it was uncontrollable and he rolled over on top of her and penetrated her as if this wasn't the first time in his life he'd had intercourse. Her slim legs clasped him like hungry arms, pulled him down hard upon her. He felt her still budding breasts harden against his ribs.

"Whutever happens," he told her later in a low voice, "you is always mine. No buck'll ever lay his black han's on you. Papa says sell you an' I kills him if they's nothin' else to do."

She clung to him. There was about her only a womanly smell. She'd been bathed since coming from the ship and she didn't possess any of the musky odor of a black.

Fitz spoke again, this time forgetting his Southern background. "I know you don't understand a damn thing I'm saying, Nina, but some day you will. I know there's not much of a future for you, but whatever there is, you'll get the best of it. Someday I'll marry a white girl. I'll likely be very much in love with her, but you are my first love. To you I promise to be as true as a white man can be to his slave. If I marry, I'll still want you. If my wife finds out and objects, she can leave me. You and I are as one—forever. And damn this law of man that says we are different."

"Fitz," she said softly and snuggled while his passion began to rise again.

"I don't know who you really are or even where you came from, but you're not a nigger to me, Nina. You never will be. If Mr. Canfield had insisted on taking you today, I'd have killed him."

"Fitz," she said, and her hands moved down along his belly to clasp him firmly. She drew him over atop her and buried her face against his throat while they gave to one another the only form of love permitted between a white and a black.

Chapter Three

BARGES REGULARLY TRAVELED the river to and from the nearest landing point eleven miles south of Richmond, and they were used for freight and slaves. There were no holds in which the slaves could be chained, but the decks were equipped with rings to which the blacks could be tethered. The weather was mild at this time of year and for Jonathan's coffle an ideal way to travel. In the winter the wenches half froze to death.

Snug in a cabin, Jonathan and Fitz spent the time making their plans. One entire afternoon was used to name the slaves and the wenches who were now listed as Nina, Pinta, Santa Maria, Philadelphia, Monmouth, Bedford, Resolute, Washington, Republic. One enormous female had proudly accepted the name of Neptune.

The bucks sported names like Tripoli, Newport, Naha Quiberon, Fayal, Liverpool, Melbourne, Pago-Pago, Havana and London.

Each was given a separate page in a new ledger. On these pages would be listed whom they mated with, their progeny, mentions of illnesses. With new slaves, bought for cash, the purchase price was also listed as well as the names of their old masters and whatever talents the slave possessed.

Jonathan was concerned lest the letter he'd written to Smithson Livery in Richmond had not been received and the conveyance he'd ordered would not be at the barge landing, but by this time he was inclined to fret over any little thing. There'd been no snags so far and he wasn't used to an operation as huge as this without something to slow him down.

Fitz did his share of book work, added his opinions to their plans. It was a pleasant, slow voyage north from Norfolk. Someone gave a buck a drum on which he rapped the heels of his hands while the other bucks sang the songs they'd been taught at their own campfires.

Nina had become Fitz's personal servant and waited on him hand and foot. She was standing quietly by each morning to help him on with his clothes. Since the last night in Norfolk, he hadn't bedded down with her and he'd said nothing to Jonathan about the experience.

Nina still had a tendency to shy away from Jonathan until she grew accustomed to his gentle pats on her behind, or the occasional light touch of his hand against her breasts. Now that she was an established member of the team, Jonathan seemed to like her.

On the third day they reached the landing and there Jonathan's fears vanished, for there were six large wagons, a comfortable stagecoach and a mound of supplies waiting.

Because the barge, at this season, was unable to proceed all the way to Richmond, Jonathan planned to bypass the city and head straight for Wyndward, which met with Fitz's approval. There was no village here, only a way station, so they encountered few delays. The women were put aboard the wagons, crowded in with supplies. The men were spanceled, chained together in groups of ten. They followed in the dusty wake of the last wagon.

None minded, for they were again stiff and sore from the journey from Norfolk and were glad to stretch their legs. They had sixty miles to go, however, and before they reached Wyndward, they'd be slowed down and tired.

Nina, enjoying her special status, was allowed to climb onto the seat alongsides the stage driver, and there she perched, a diminutive figure, proud as a peacock and interested in everything she saw. Even the black driver, who at first resented her, began to appreciate the fact that she was no ordinary nigger. He took great care not to slap her knees or nudge her breasts. He knew it portended trouble for any buck who did, for he'd seen the look of fleeting tenderness on Fitz's face as he regarded her.

They proceeded slowly in deference to the marching bucks. Jonathan saw no point in exhausting them. Once they arrived at Wyndward there'd be much work to be done at once, and a coffle of tired niggers would be of no use to him. Besides, he was enjoying the last leg of the long journey because he now basked in the developing anticipation of his own first look at Wyndward.

All the work had been done—from his approved plans, of course—but so far he hadn't seen a stick of any structure. The only thing he remembered were the rolling pastures, the tilled land already growing tobacco. He recalled the oaks and poplars, the meadow flowers and the rich earth which gave promise of fine crops. His father had sworn by this region and his father had been a wise and successful man.

The first night they stopped at a way station where the horses could be baited and rested and the slaves penned up in a barracoon. There was another shed for the females, a cook house so they could prepare their own meals and a small house for the use of the whites. An aged crone and an old black were in charge and the house was as filthy as the barns.

Nina, still favored, angrily began cleaning the bedroom and then she rudely pushed aside the sputtering crone to not only clean the kitchen, but prepare food as best she could with what was at hand.

"Gal's turnin' out real fine," Jonathan told Fitz. "Kinda takin' over, and maybe we best give her a lick or two. . . ."

"The hell we will," Fitz declared, as his father laughed.

"Didn't mean it, son. You picked her and she's your'n, until your ma gets here, and then you better not let her catch you fiddlin' 'round with no light-colored gal. Cain't say I blames you. More I see her, more I likes her—an' don't git your dander up. I don't mean to pleasure myse'f with her. Kinda think I'm slippin'. That fat whore crawled in bed with me and I been a diff'rent man ever since. She just dreened me 'til there wan't one speck of juice lef' and all I been doin' is eatin' heavy to get it back. Your ma gets here I sho' better have juice 'nuff to say howdy, or she'll know I been pleasurin' myse'f with the wenches. Your ma, son, ain't no ordinary woman. No sir, not by a jugful she ain't. Don't know you gettin' outa hand lately. Lookin' for fights, knifin' a man, insultin' an old friend of mine, takin' up with this here wench. Maybe best I give you a lick or two with the whup so's you be proper respectful when your ma gits here."

Fitz grinned at him. "Think you kin do it, papa?"

"Might have me a time, but I could do it, son. On'y foolin' though. Boy turns into a man he gits in trouble an' he starts screwin' everythin' that comes along. Jus' natchural like. No harm done."

Each night Nina slept on the floor at the foot of the bed. She was comfortable enough with blankets to soften the hardness of the bare boards, and more to cover her well. She ate from her own somewhat cracked plate, scraping the leavings of the men onto it, but adding all she wished from the untouched food still in the kitchen. She was learning that a slave submits, but she was doing it in a way that suited her.

She was careful to maintain no contact with the other women and boldly flaunted her sex at the bucks, not one but knew what would happen if they laid a hand on her or even made a suggestion.

She was learning a few words and knew how to jump when Jonathan called for a glass of rum. She washed their personal clothing. More menial work she turned over to the women. She selected one young buck and gave him the job of polishing boots and shining the stagecoach, much to the amusement of the driver who knew it would be dusty after four turns of the wheel.

The second night they stayed in a small town hotel, little better than the wayside stop, but everyone was too tired to care. Even Nina, with her everlasting curiosity, was content to go to bed at the first fading of daylight.

The third night the caravan turned off the road, passed between the opened, wooden gates and under the archway that had the name Coldwell Plantation burned into it.

"These here be our neighbors," Jonathan said. "Name of Chauncey Coldwell. Kinda fancy. English way back, I reckon, but Virginians all the way through. Known Chaunce for years. Played together when we was kids. Laid our first wench together an' we weren't no more'n twelve, thirteen. Figgered we was men after that day, 'til we caught all the fancies on the plantation laughin' at us, an' we got so mad we wanted to whup the lot of 'em, but then our folks started laughin' too and pretty soon we figgered we had a little more growin' up to do."

"Reckon I'd ruther keep goin', night or not, papa. We's six-seven hours away from Wyndward and I'm cravin' to see it."

"Seems like you ain't usin' your haid, son. March them bucks ten more miles 'thout rest an' food, they'd like to die on us, they would. Don't ever fo'get—slaves are money. Fifty bucks wuth seven hundrud fifty dollahs each and yo' got yourse'f a heap of money, son. More'n we want to lose. Do we turn in at Colonel Chauncey Coldwell's place an' you stop your grumblin' 'bout it? I your papa an' I say we stay. You aimin' to argufy the point?"

"Not me, papa. On'y one argue with you is mama."

"By damn, Fitz, you kin think of more ways to make my life mizzable than anybody I knows. Now hush up 'bout your mama. She'll be here soon 'nuff. Tonight Colonel Coldwell gives us food an' hospitality. Never yit known him to forgit to pervide a fresh wench for his fav'rite callers and I be one of his real fav'rites. He offers you a wench, you take her, mind? An' you fix her good so she kin tell her massa in the mawnin' you a heavy-hung young buck an' she ain't been pleasured so complete in all her charmin' little life."

"But papa. . . ."

"No aryments. You insult the Colonel an' I tans your hide like you was nothin' better'n a nigger. You takes that gal an' you rapes her good."

"Yes, papa," Fitz said. "Reckon I randy 'nuff for it. I'll sho' make her squeal some."

The procession wound its way toward the huge two-story house, white-pillared with a three-sided porch set with cane chairs on every side. Two dogs came yapping loudly down to meet the caravan. They were followed by a plump little man with a white mustache and a grandee goatee. He was coatless and his pants were held up by wide galluses over a white shirt. His wild mane was tossed by the breeze which carried away his shouts of welcome. Behind him strayed a motley collection of house slaves.

"Cap'n Jonathan," he roared when he was close enough to be heard. He had a stentorian voice for such a small man. "Goddamn if it ain't Cap'n Jonathan hisse'f."

Jonathan jumped out of the stage and enveloped his host in a great hug of friendship. Fitz, slower in climbing down, glanced up at Nina and smiled. She nodded, but her face remained composed. She didn't know how to act in the presence of this fat little man who she gathered was an individual of some importance.

"An' this is your son." Colonel Coldwell made a rush at Fitz who was so taken aback that he retreated a step or two in dismay, but there was no evading the Colonel's brand of greeting. He tried to sweep Fitz off his feet, but the boy wouldn't budge and Colonel Coldwell thought that amazing.

"He's full-grown," he chortled. "Big's a moose too. Figgered not many men hung as heavy as you, Cap'n, but reckon this here boy hung lower, I sho' does. Now you got yourse'f a funny name. . . ."

"Fitzjohn," Fitz admitted. "Reckon it's kinda funny at that. I'm mighty happy to meet you, Colonel. Papa been talkin' 'bout you for three days entire now. Have to admire your plantation too. In all my life, never saw anythin' like it, suh."

"Come in, come in," the Colonel invited. "How many in your coffle?"

"Fifty bucks, fifty females," Jonathan said.

"Have my boys put 'em up in two o' my barns. Better leave 'em spanceled. Don't look like they's heavy irons, an' we got chains long 'nuff to let 'em bed down real fine." He raised his voice to one of those shouting yells that seemed so uncharacteristic of this little man. "Pomroy . . . you, Matthew . . . where at your black ass, Prince? Git yourse'ves down here quick, heah?"

Three slaves rushed up. They were middle-aged, going to fat, but still sleek, and they moved with considerable alacrity.

"You, Pomroy," the Colonel ordered, "run tell Minnie we got company an' set the table for two more. Matthew . . . Prince . . . you bed the coffle down and bait 'em. See the hosses rubbed down an' cooled. Watered an' baited too."

"An stay away from them wenches," Jonathan warned, "or I'll have your massa tan your asses good. I'm breedin' them wenches an' I wants 'em special bred, not by any damn nigger happens near 'nuff to smell 'em. Now, Colonel, we don't crave to discommode you. We's tired, but ain't no call we cain't put up in the barn too."

"My old friend in the barn?" the Colonel roared. "You come right in, suh, and you, Fitz . . . what in hell your name is. Cain't stand them No'thrun names. Don't mean to be disrespectful, son, but I feels that way an' they's nothin I kin do about it."

Fitz indicated Nina who had climbed down from the box. "If you got no objection, suh, I'd like to bed down this here wench in the house. She's light an' she's kinda purty an' it ain't safe to leave her near them bucks."

The Colonel jabbed Fitz in the ribs. "Warms a bed real good too, don't she, son? Wouldn't mind havin' her my own se'f." He noted Fitz's look of anxiety and dug him in the ribs again. "Don't crave her so much I kin take her away from you, suh. Likes your judgment of good female flesh, suh. Yo' git her knocked up an' she'll give you some mighty bright suckers. Sho' will, an' wish I could breed some by her too."

"You don't mind," Fitz said, "I'm dusty and I stink some. Mayhap I kin go to my room, suh, to get myse'f clean?"

"Go right ahead, boy. The house is your'n and don't doubt it. You the son of my best boyhood friend. Ain't nothin' I got you cain't have."

"Thank you, suh." Fitz bowed and motioned that Nina was to follow him. They entered the house while Jonathan and the Colonel strolled about inspecting the immediate portion of the plantation.

Fitz found the door opened for him by a white-haired, bent slave in a black suit, white shirt and flowing tie. His eyes rested suspiciously on Nina and he seemed about to make some sort of remark, but decided against it. They walked into a massive reception hall, two stories high with great chandeliers suspended from the ceiling, elaborate sconces for a hundred candles decorating the walls. The staircase was winding, making a graceful turn halfway up its length.

Fitz ducked into the ballroom just off the hallway and was awed by its grandeur, complete with thick, burgundy-colored rugs, hangings of the same hue, more chandeliers, stiff, awkward-looking furniture in bright red, and a fireplace capable of taking tree trunks. He hoped Wyndward didn't look like this.

Nina walked up the wide staircase beside him and he let his hand drift down to her rhythmic-moving buttocks. She gave him a ready, warm smile, one filled with promise and gratitude.

At the top of the stairs they were in a long hall overlooking the entrance. The bedrooms were to the left and Fitz suddenly realized he hadn't asked which one he would be using. He was on the verge of calling down to the butler at the front door, but there was no need. A heavyset woman in a cream-colored frock swept grandly out of one room. Her hair, a brassy blond color was done up in as many curls as could be coaxed out of it. She used an ample amount of rice powder so that her face was almost pure white. The effect was ludicrous, but Fitz's features remained composed. She blocked the corridor and looked at Fitz with distinct disdain.

"Who you, suh?"

Fitz bowed. "I am Fitzjohn Turner, son of Cap'n Jonathan Turner, your servant, ma'am."

"Humph," she scoffed. "Your pa will git my husband drunk tonight. He shorely will. Never did see a sailor who drew a sober breath."

The smell of corn whiskey emanated from her with every word she spoke, but Fitz was far too much the gentleman to comment on that.

"Reckon they might at that, ma'am," he conceded.

"They good friends an' been a long time they met."

Mrs. Coldwell pointed a finger at Nina. "Whut that wench doin' in my house, suh?"

"She he'pin' me to unpack, ma'am. We's stayin' the night, with your kind permission."

"I got nothin' to say 'bout who stays, but I got somethin' to say 'bout randy boys like you bringin' a wench into my bed. Git her outa here. They be no fornicatin' 'tween white and black in my house."

"But ma'am . . ." Fitz tried to protest reasonably.

"Whut's the matter with that slut? She cain't understan' what a mistress say?"

"Ma'am, we brought her from Afriky on'y three-four days ago. She don't speak much and she don't understand."

"Then she a stupid gal an' all she good for is breedin'. Now you git!" She prodded her thick finger into Nina's chest and the startled girl fled down the stairs and out the door, expectantly held open by the butler.

"Mind now," Mrs. Coldwell warned the stunned Fitz, "you don't take no wench to your bed, suh. It's agin nature for a white to bed down with a gal who ain't human. It stinks up my bed an' I burns the sheets they lays on 'cause I sho' wouldn't want to sleep on one by mistake. You come down to supper in ten minutes, heah?"

"Yes, ma'am," Fitz said. "Be obleeged you tell me whut room to take, ma'am."

"Room? Down the hall—take any of 'em, but no niggers sleepin' in my house."

Fitz selected a room at random, murmured a few mild oaths at the obstinacy of the Colonel's wife and then he stripped down and washed off the dust and grime from the day's travel. He dressed in fresh clothes, taken from the carpetbags brought up by two house servants.

Sartorially correct, he walked down the staircase in

his tight-fitting gray pants, ruffled shirt and cutaway pale violet coat. Jonathan stared.

"Whut in hell you made up for?" he demanded. "Never knowed you had fancy clo's like that."

"No reason to bring 'em out," Fitz said. "But in this here house, we be guests and I dresses fo' the occasion. I might remind you, papa, that there is a lady present."

He bowed elaborately to the Colonel's wife, and she rendered him a rather awkward and possibly somewhat tipsy curtsy. It was evident that both the Colonel and Jonathan had been drinking, probably in copious quantities to get as much inside them as possible before the Colonel's wife appeared.

Jonathan slapped his thigh and roared with laughter. "Goddamn," he chortled, "effen you don' look like a half-fucked he-whore. Mighty good thing you didn't wear them duds aboard my ship or sho' as hell you'd been raped by the whole goddamn crew. Lavender coat . . . looky them pants! They's so tight in the crotch his balls show."

"Umm . . . umm," the Colonel commented, "mighty well too, suh. Mighty well."

His wife tossed her head dramatically. "Such language in my own house. I declare, Captain Turner, ever' time you comes here to visit, you set Chauncey back years an' years of my teachin'. Ain't you men got anythin' mo' impo'tant to talk 'bout than . . . than . . . women an' wenches an' . . . an' them things you just said and no lady will say."

"Ma'am," Jonathan swept a low bow, "you makes me feel to home like no place else I ever go." But he addressed Mrs. Coldwell's back as she headed for the dining room. In an aside to the Colonel, he whispered, "Effen them two . . . your wife an' mine, ever git together, they's sure goin' to play hell with everythin' we hold dear."

The Colonel nodded sagely and beckoned the old

butler. "Samson, when you-all serves the coffee, you puts in it half corn, y'heah? Don't say nothin' 'bout it, jest put it in. That's for me and my friends."

"I understands, suh," the old man bowed. "Got three glasses waiting down the hall, suh. Yo' kin grab 'em 'foah goin' in."

"Now there," Jonathan said, "is the kin' of a butler I wants. You wouldn't sell him to me, Chaunce?"

"Never. Won him in a card game in New Orleans when I wasn't much more'n a young buck myse'f, Jonathan. Samson's my right arm, even if I gits mad 'nuff to whup him sometimes. Never done it, never will, and damn his black hide, he knows it real well."

They got in line to file past the little table in the hall where a silver tray and three copious drafts of pure white corn waited them. Each tossed down the drink, replaced the glass with hardly a ripple in their continuous forward movement to the dining room door.

Just before Fitz turned into the dining room, he caught a glimpse of Nina halfway up the staircase. She'd found some other way to get in. He grinned. It wasn't going to be a bad night after all.

The meal was superb. There was roast chicken and stuffing, potatoes white and yellow, greens, carrots, conserves, light as air biscuits, red gravy, and pink succulent baked ham.

Near the end of the meal, eaten in comparative silence, broken mostly by the ultra-polite compliments both older men paid to Mrs. Coldwell, Fitz began searching his pockets.

"Fo'got you seegars, papa. Better go git 'em. 'Scuse me, ma'am, with your kind permission."

Jonathan patted an inner pocket which was full of cigars. He began to take one out automatically, but pushed it back before Mrs. Coldwell saw him. Fitz was up to something, but Jonathan couldn't figure it out.

Fitz meanwhile had rushed down the hallway behind

the staircase and continued on to the kitchen at the rear of the house. In its steamy interior, he found an emaciated, middle-aged cook still fussing at the stove. Two teenage houseboys stood by to do whatever she would command. She eyed Jonathan politely but suspiciously as well.

"Wants you to fix me a tray with some of everythin' on it," he said.

"You-all din' git 'nuff at table, suh?" she demanded.

"Got plenty, and mighty good cookin' too, but this here fo' a fren' of mine."

"The wench?"

"That's who. Ain't havin' her eat nigger food they give to the coffle."

"Sho' nuff? You is goin' to slip this past old . . . past Mist'iss Coldwell's nose?"

"Sho' nuff," Fitz replied. "An' quit askin' questions. Ain't proper."

The cook found a tray, loaded a plate with enough food for four, added extra butter, filled a small pot with coffee, dumped in a large quantity of molasses and poured in plenty of thick cream.

"Thank you," Fitz said.

"That wench sho' been pleasurin' you real good, suh."

"You sho' is right," Fitz assured her. " 'Spect would be kinda nice pleasurin' you, too. Might git 'round to it, 'ceptin' we ain't stayin' long."

"Git," she pushed him gently. "Yo's talkin' to a ol' lady, but I does say it sounds good. Git now, 'fore things git cold."

Fitz knew how unorthodox this was. Not only smuggling food to a wench, but actually serving her. Yet he wanted to do it. Something within told him that there was no harm in it and custom be damned.

He kicked open the door to his room, which Nina had discovered by searching for his things. She was seated on the floor at the foot of the bed, patiently waiting for him. He placed the tray on the floor before her and motioned that she was to eat.

She smiled, took his hand and kissed it again. He yanked it away roughly. "Don' want you to do that no mo'," he said angrily. "Ain't no call for that. Now eat. I got to go downstairs again."

She seemed to know what he was talking about and though her eyes followed him all the way to the door, she was already quietly eating.

Fitz burst back into the room, thrust his hands through the contents of one carpetbag and found the cigars. He seized a handful and fled.

If anyone wondered why it had taken so long to simply fetch cigars, no mention was made of it. Jonathan accepted them with a word of gratitude and a sorely puzzled look. He gave one to the Colonel and they promptly lit up. Mrs. Coldwell sat between them and after a few moments she was all but obscured by the thick, heavy smoke. She waved her hand to drive the smoke away from her, but it was useless. When she realized she had received all the attention she was going to get, she excused herself.

Fitz listened to plantation talk for half an hour and then he yawned and excused himself. He went upstairs, dragging his feet from sheer exhaustion. He was so tired he didn't even look forward to sharing his bed with Nina and he felt considerably relieved when he opened the door and found her gone. So was the tray.

He took off his clothes, tumbled into bed, snuffed the solitary candle and pulled the covers up as he dropped off into a deep sleep. He had no idea how long he'd been asleep, but he was awakened by the sound of raucous voices from downstairs. Apparently, Jonathan and the Colonel were reliving some of their boyhood experiences, now fortified with plenty of corn.

Then he heard the door click, felt a slight draft as the door opened. Someone stepped into the room, closed the door again and moved toward the bed. There was a rustle of thin cotton as the osnaburg dress was hauled over the head. The blankets moved and a warm body slid under them and moved up against him.

The rest had done him a great deal of good, for his tumescence seemed to bob into being and he reached for the girl.

"Nina," he whispered, "I been hopin'. . . ." He paused, shoved his face closer to the lithe body and sniffed. Then he hurled back the covers, jammed one leg beneath the supine girl and used it as a lever to unceremoniously dump her out of bed.

"You ain't Nina," he accused her. "You smells like a regular nigger. Want no truck with a stinkin' nigger . . ."

"Whaffo' yo' do that, suh?" a plaintive voice came from the floor. "I on'y come to pleasure yo', massa. I likes pesterin' but I sho' doan like gittin' kicked outa bed, I doan."

"Where's Nina?" he demanded.

"Sleepin' in the kitchen."

"You git," he said. "Tell the Colonel I got my own wench."

"Colonel din' send me, massa, suh."

Fitz sat up, swung his legs off the bed and sat there regarding her in the faint light from the open window. "You jes' came lookin' to be pestered?"

"No, massa, suh. Nina sent me. She say ain't no good time to favo' yo', suh. Wrong time of month, she say. Thass why I come, suh. To pleasure yo' 'stead of Nina."

"Nina sent you," Fitz marveled. "Well, get your ass up off the floor, an' crawl into bed, y'heah? Reckon I kin hold my nose long 'nuff for you to pleasure me some. Come on, gal, while I'm in the mood."

Downstairs, Jonathan and the Colonel were holding a serious, if somewhat drunken conversation. As old friends, they confided in one another, held little back.

"Been some worried 'bout that son of mine," Jonathan said. "Been livin' with his ma up there in Massachusetts. Now I ain't sayin' she done wrong, but she sent him to No'thrun schools."

"Shore don't speak like no No'thruner," the Colonel commented.

"He speaks No'thrun like he teach school hisse'f, but when he 'round me, he talks like me. Knows it pleasures me, he does. His mama, she don' believe in slaves. She a smart woman, lots of ways, but she sho' ignorant 'bout slaves."

"Mebbe she's comin' down to manumit 'em all," the Colonel shuddered. "My wife ain't like that. She hates niggers, and on'y likes 'em when they's bein' whupped. Orders too many of 'em whupped. Got an idee she finds much amusement listenin' to 'em howl and watchin' the blood run down they backs. I took the snake away from her. She like to spoil ev'vy nigger I own."

"She use a blacksnake?" Jonathan asked incredulously.

"I'd put my foot down real hard. Don't want my niggers all scarred so they don't bring top price when I gits to sell or trade 'em. Uses a strip of cowhide, Jonathan. Good thick wide piece. It slaps them black asses and makes 'em jump, but it don't do no cuttin'. 'Sides, makes so much noise, the niggers think they gettin' killed. Reckon I got me an extra one."

He raised his head and bawled out a command for one of the kitchen boys to come fast. The boy appeared, breathless from his burst of speed begun in the kitchen as the Colonel's voice penetrated his dozing.

"Yassuh, massa, suh."

"Billy, yo' git down the whupping shed and fetch me up one of them cowhide ass warmers, an' be quick about it."

The boy stood there, open-mouthed, and beginning to tremble. "Massa, suh, I ain't done nothin'. Swears I ain't done nothin'. Please doan whup me, massa, suh. Ain't done nothin'. Swears it."

"Who said anythin' 'bout whuppin' you? But you sho'll get it, you don't bring back that ass warmer quick, y' heah?"

The boy sped away. The Colonel lit another of Jonathan's fine cigars, purchased in Havana. There was half a trunkful of them on the wagons.

"Hosses," he said. "You aimin' to raise 'em?"

"Race 'em too, I kin find a track. I cain't, I'll make one."

"Ain't yo' takin' on too much, Jonathan? Breedin' niggers, raisin' 'baccy and now racin' hosses. You goin' to be one busy man, suh."

"Been busy all my life. Couldn't loaf I wanted to, Colonel. This don't work out way I aims it to, I kin always go back to my ship. Lef' her tied up at Norfolk so all I has to do is go there, git aboard and I'm in business again."

"Do consid'able hoss breedin' over in Kaintucky. Might do you some good you-all go there an' see. They got pure Arabian stock I knows of. Other'n too, I reckon. Richmond a good gamblin' town. Mostly nigger fightin' or they tantalize a bear with a dog and watch 'em go to it. Some cock fightin', and gamin' as good as in New Orleans."

"Look into it, I shore will. Worryin' some 'bout Sarah. She agin slavery, bein' she raised in the No'th. Whut she goin' to say she finds out I got a couple hundred niggers workin' on the plantation?" He clapped a hand to his brow. "She goin' find out too, and whut she goin' to say she hears I been sailin' 'em from Afriky? She goin' to have my hide, Chaunce. She goin' to flay me alive. Mos' righteous female, Sarah is. Church-goin' an' there sho' ain't no church hereabouts. An' she got to boss the house slaves. How she boss 'em she don' believe in 'em? Colonel, I got me a problem worser'n my son. Ain't scared whut'll happen to him, he big 'nuff to keer for himse'f. But I sho' scared whut'll happen to me, Sarah gits here. Things all wrong, Colonel. Shoulda made women milder an' meeker. Not like niggers, mind you, but kinda like they keeps they mouths shut and listens to whut we tells 'em."

"Cain't get my mouth open my wife's 'round. Your Sarah don' like slaves. My wife don' like nothin'."

They were suddenly aware of the houseboy standing behind them, holding the cowhide strap in both hands and presenting it in their direction like a plague-ridden blanket fresh off a dead man.

"'Bout time," the Colonel said. "Now git!"

The slave disappeared promptly and thoroughly. The Colonel held out the eighteen inch wide length of hide. It was supple, heavy and when Jonathan slapped the back of a stuffed chair with it, the whole room seemed to shake.

"Don' bust no skin." The Colonel praised his instrument of torture. "Never dreened blood yet from even a scratch. Makes kinda big welts, but they don't count none. Sho' makes them black bastahds howl though. Heah 'em fo' a mile sometimes. An' 'nother practical thing 'bout this here whup, stays soft an' don' need no oilin'. Hang it up for five-six months and it's ready to go when you takes it down. Don't believe in usin' a snake myself. Cuts too deep and raises scars that'll make any buyer turn away, figgerin' a slave whupped that many times an' that hard got to be rebellious and sassy. Take it with my compliments, suh."

"Thanky." Jonathan flexed the strap a few times. "Likes it tremendous. Kinda minds me of the strap your pa used on us that day his two house wenches started bulgin' at the same time an' he'd never set them out to breed, but we'd bred 'em. Whaled the hell outa our asses that night. I kin still feel the sting, I think back."

"They sho' was good pesterin'," the Colonel acknowledged. "Nevah did tell yo' one sucker come out white 'nuff to be a mustee, other'n was black . . . like no human blood in it atall. But the mustee was kinda dull. Nevah did amount to very much an' died 'bout when he was ten. Been tryin' to figger out what one was your'n and what one was mine. Knew what wench berthed each one, but I disremembered complete which one I had that night. You 'member, Jonathan?"

"I 'members she was black an' soft an' hotter'n pepper. She come near makin' me a ruint man. But which was which, cain't 'member that. Likely 'cause it's of no impo'tance nohow. We was randy though. They wasn't the on'y ones, not by a jugful they wasn't."

"You still any good?" the Colonel asked bluntly. "Me, I had a nice wench back maybe six, eight months ago. She was more'n willin'. Wanted a light sucker. She tried everythin' she knew and I tried whut I could think of and I didn't get it up no bigger'n a jelly bean. Mortified? I was never so 'shamed in my whole life. That wench laughed at me that night, I'da strangled her. I'm tellin' you I would, but she didn't laugh. She jes' kep' tryin' and gettin' nowhars. Reckon I's all played out."

"You see Fitz's wench? She was ridin' the high seat on the stage."

"Likely lookin' gal. Told your son so."

"Night 'fore we dropped anchor I busted her. An' she knew goddamn well I did. Hollered like hell. Guess I got juice in me yet. Don't know how long I'll keep it, Sarah comin'."

They both sighed deeply in mutual sympathy. They had another large portion of corn brought by the butler and then they went upstairs. In Jonathan's bed was a wench, nude and big. Big enough to take on the biggest buck. She was waiting, eager and impatient. She removed his boots and wiped the dust from them. Jonathan knew they'd be shining by morning. She took off his socks, shirt and tie, hung them neatly along with his jacket.

She stripped down his underwear, all the while jiggling her bare breasts for his entertainment. Jonathan had been firmly and frequently instructed by Sarah not to miss a night kneeling at his bedside. He hadn't done so since the last time he saw her, but Jonathan regarded the black giantess who stood waiting to pleasure him, and decided this might be the night for a little prayer. He knelt.

Further along the corridor, Colonel Coldwell climbed into bed where his wife lay snoring. He sighed too, but he found no cause for prayer.

Fitz arose at dawn. The wench had slipped out of bed during the night and disappeared. It occurred to him that if he met her face to face in the next five minutes he wouldn't be able to recognize her. He dressed hastily, in clothing rough and serviceable for the final leg of the journey to Wyndward Plantation. He was excited and wanting to get started, but he knew his father and the Colonel had held their reminiscing into the late hours and had staggered to their beds, so they'd not be up for a spell of time.

He hurried down, hoping the Colonel's wife was also still asleep. He would have had no fear of being discovered by her, had he looked into her room. She was sleeping stuporously, lying on her back and arching upwards with each bellowing snore, as if she were trying to recapture it.

Fitz found Nina in the kitchen having her breakfast off a tin plate. She was eating fatback and pone. He wrenched the plate from her hand and threw it, food and all, out the door. Then he took down a china plate and thrust it at the angular cook. She asked no questions, but filled the plate with white-folk food. Bacon, ham, eggs done to a perfect state and basted with bacon grease. Biscuits, strawberry jam and a tin cup of coffee.

"You able to talk to this wench?" he asked the cook.

"Yassuh, massa, suh. She come from same part of

Africa I does. She likes yo', massa, suh, and I kin see yo' likes her. That ain't good, suh. Ain't right nohow."

"She my wench," Fitz declared stubbornly. "No buck gits her, an' she gits treated right. My papa he give her to me."

"Talked lots last night, suh. Hopes the gal she sent pleasured you good."

"She was fine. Tell me whut else Nina said."

"Figgered yo'd like to know, suh. Reckon she's octaroon, but I ain't sho' 'cause the blood she got 'sides black ain't 'zactly white. Comes from kinda close to the border where the Ayrabs used to live, suh. They was bad folks, raidin' our villages and rapin' anythin' they could lay down. Nina's ma was in one o' them raids and give to a man, a Moore or Ayrab, don't rightly know which. Nina got borned and she 'members her pa. Wore big turban with stones—shiny ones—in it, and he wore rings with mo' shiny stones. He was sho' a busy man 'cause he had fifteen-twenny wives. An' I don' mean wenches, massa, suh. Wives . . . they got married to him legal."

"Reckoned she was some kinda princess," Fitz nodded approval and smiled for Nina's benefit. "She smart gal."

"She been schooled some, she say. Massa, suh, she no breedin' wench. She quality folk. She near good as yo'. . ."

The cook clapped a hand over her mouth, knowing she'd said too much. A sound lashing was in order for a less serious slip than that, but this man only agreed with her and evidently had no thoughts of the whip.

"Hungry I am," he said instead of scolding her. "Cain't tell when my papa come down. Got plenty to do 'fore he's ready so I eats now."

Out of sheer gratitude, the cook sent Nina to serve him and she did so in a dainty and bothersome manner. Fitz didn't like his passion aroused so early in the morning. If she was aware of it, she serenely disregarded it and stood close behind him as he ate, trying to anticipate what he wished and reaching for its first. Once she placed a hand on his head lightly and then gave a nervous look about and lowered her hand to her side again. Fitz didn't comment, gave no indication he was aware that she had touched him, but he liked the gesture.

Breakfast over, Fitz went out toward the barns where the bucks were already chained, lying on the grass in the morning sun, getting all the rest they could for the last segment of the long journey. They were still too travel-weary to talk, but they'd been well-fed and were reasonably rested. Some distance away, the wenches were busy washing clothes and themselves. A dozen of them cavorted in the shallow stream. They'd been given tins of soap and they screeched, lathered themselves, ducked, screeched some more. They were all skinned down and Fitz damned the eagerness that always kept rising in him. At least, he thought, he was healthy and certainly not as badly off as the bucks, chained in groups, who were compelled to watch the wenches sauntering about naked and not being able to do anything about it except yearn.

Fitz supervised the hitching up of the wagons, ordering the Colonel's slaves about as if they were his own, which was standard procedure, unless the owner of the slaves gave express orders to the contrary. He inspected the horses to be certain they'd been well rubbed down and properly baited and watered. He tossed four bits to the chief groom and received a dozen low bows and expressions of gratitude. He wondered why he did these things. Goddamn nigger worked for his keep, nothing else. And here he squandered four bits just to see the black bastard bow and scrape. Was that the reason, he asked himself. Had to be. Satisfied with the answer, he dismissed the troublesome thought from his mind.

The stage was ready, the wagons loaded. The wenches hoisted themselves into their wagons, showing plenty of black thigh as they did so, deliberately teasing the bucks, knowing very well that as quickly as they were settled at the plantation, each would be given a buck to cover her and start the breeding process in those not yet pregnant. Most of them, even now, had their men picked out and they would somehow contrive to bed down with him. The experience on the deck of the *Wyndward* had taught them which men had much juice, and were properly hung.

Fitz returned to the house. Jonathan, breakfasted and ready for the road, was bowing over the hand of the Colonel's wife.

"Ma'am, been an honor to partake of your table. In my life, I never tasted better. Your husband the only friend I got 'round here an' I been complimentin' him reg'lar on how lucky he is to have found a wife like you, ma'am."

The Colonel was even more enthusiastic, notwithstanding his bleary eyes and somewhat shaky hands. "My dear, Jonathan will come through again in about three weeks. He's going back to Norfolk to fetch his own dear wife, and he wishes to stop here, so that you two ladies may become the same kind of friends, Jonathan and I be. Everlastingly faithful and true, ma'am."

She simpered at Jonathan, delighted with the news. "I'm sho' I'll like her. You say she goes to church regular an' she agin' sinnin'?"

"That she be," Jonathan confessed, wishing the fool Colonel hadn't mentioned the return journey to pick up Sarah. It had been in Jonathan's mind to prevent these two women from meeting for as long as possible—like ten, fifteen years.

Mrs. Coldwell accepted Fitz's hand and she curtsied, or hinted at it, her sudden smile gone. She wasn't forgetting how he tried to smuggle a wench into one of her beds. She could well do without these young men, though she had thought that Fitz had a most interesting hump in those tight pants he'd worn. If only she'd been younger and not gone to fat. . . .

Nina was on the high seat with the stage driver. The Colonel's slaves were gathered around to bid the others goodbye. It was, Fitz thought, much like a ship leaving port where everyone left behind waved energetically to rid themselves of the frustrations from not being able to go along.

Jonathan yelled an order, the caravan began to move. The bucks picked themselves up from the grass where they'd been lying for the last half an hour. The wheels of the stage and the wagons threw up much dust and the hard feet of the slaves kicked up even more, until the tail end of the procession could be followed for a considerable distance because sometimes the dust rose above the tops of the trees.

Chapter Four

THE DIRT ROAD led directly past Wyndward Plantation. The mansion itself stood half a mile off the road, atop a plateau, and was reached by a drive paved with fieldstone. On both sides of it was a bowling green, stretching almost as far as the eye could see. At the rear were the separate buildings used as kitchen, bakery, dairy, curing sheds, storehouses, cold spring and the rather elaborate outhouse divided into two sections with a door for each. It looked like a miniature cottage with overhangs, a random roof, two chimneys to accommodate the round pot-bellied stoves in each segment. A stone walk, beneath a narrow arcade, made visits to the outhouse protected in all manner of weather, though the womenfolk would rarely make the trip without an open parasol over their heads.

The mansion itself was square, uncompromisingly plain as befitted the house of a captain of a clipper ship. Four double chimneys rose above the slanted roof and accommodated eight fireplaces, one for each room in the house, and each fireplace large enough for a tree trunk. One thing Jonathan remembered about his boyhood, the winters were cold.

Set well back were the stables and stalls for the thoroughbreds not yet obtained. An oval track, a mile in circumference, had already been laid out with stakes and string, waiting for the strong backs of the bucks now being unchained by Lithian Carter, the white overseer who'd merely shaken hands briefly with Jonathan and Fitz and gone directly about his business of getting the slaves settled.

Jonathan and Fitz had not yet gone in. They stood at the north end of the veranda which went around three sides of the house and Jonathan pointed out what he wished Fitz to know.

"Got me twelve hundrud acres here. Seven hundrud in woodland and permanent pasture. Five hundrud in one hundrud acre sections where we'll raise 'baccy mostly. Hired Lithian to buy me enough slaves with trade skills, to git the place started. Contractors from Richmond did the rest and I sure reckon they did it well. Son, mos' my life I been closin' my eyes and makin' a picture jus' like this. Used to see it so goddamn clear, I writ it all down and drew plans. Take us a year or two and we gits this place runnin' nice. 'Baccy growin' its haid off to make us a good crop, slaves screwin' they haids off makin' suckers to increase our wealth. Hosses learnin' how to race, an' breedin' jus' like them niggers."

"Lithian done a good job," Fitz said. "You keepin' him on, papa?"

"Fire him soon's I git back with your ma. He's a good overseer in gittin' the work done, but he works the slaves too hard, and he's always pesterin' wenches and lashin' niggers for nothin'. No man I wants around me—but don't tell him yit. You do, an' he drags his ass slow, killin' time and drawin' his pay. Time comes I'll throw his rump off here. That sound like I ain't grateful for what he done here—I am—but he been paid well. Stay outta his way, son. He's a mean bastahd to tangle with."

"Looks mean," Fitz commented. "I take orders from him, papa?"

Jonathan stabbed him with a stiff forefinger emphasizing each word. "You my son. This plantation as much yours as 'tis mine. You give orders just like me and they gets obeyed just like mine do."

"Yes, papa, an' I'm mighty grateful. . . . I . . . be right back. Seems like Lithian got his goddamn eyes on Nina a'ready. I'll bust him effen he lays a hand on her."

Jonathan watched his big, strong son stride angrily toward the wagons and the stage. Nina was being handed down some luggage by the stage driver and Lithian moved up to her. He pushed her gently aside and reached for a carpetbag. In setting it down, he pretended to accidentally brush his head against Nina's breasts, straining against the thin material of her dress. He looked at her with a knowing grin.

Fitz had paid scant attention to him before, but now he studied the man as he might some specimen of vermin. Lithian, years later, would have made the perfect caricature of a slave driver with a bullwhip coiled at his feet. He was thin enough to be called skinny. His face had a sallow, unhealthy look to it and his eyes were cold and deadly in the stares he cast at the slaves, bending them to his will without a word said. He wore white trousers and a white linen coat that hung so loosely on him it looked like a hand-me-down. A stubble of gray-brown beard lent nothing favorable to his appearance.

He wasn't aware that Fitz stood not more than twenty yards away. Lithian was much too intent on this light-skinned wench, in the ripeness and fullness of her young womanhood.

Nina, instinctively aware of the type of man he was, moved aside after that first encounter, but Lithian never gave up easily. In his twisted mind, he wanted this wench. If she refused him, he would merely bed her down in one of the cabins, set a buck to watch her and when the day's work was done, he'd visit the cabin and pleasure himself, even if she wasn't pleased. Her kind were easily cowed by a series of hard slaps that would knock them down. Then a few lusty kicks followed by the main business of the evening. Getting her on the bed, tearing off her clothes and divesting himself of his. He was mentally licking his chops at the anticipation of enjoying this girl.

"Mista Cahtah, suh," a soft voice said behind him, just as Lithian passed the palm of his hand over Nina's buttocks which were stiffened in terror.

Lithian turned around angrily, not enjoying having his little session with this wench interrupted. But he was properly respectful to this tall young man from up North somewhere, and who likely knew nothing about the handling of slaves.

"Mistah Turner, suh," he bowed. "Yo' servant, suh."

"Keep your goddamn hands off'n that wench, heah me? Off any wench in this here coffle. We's breedin' right, an' we don't aim to breed 'em with no redneck like you. Now that's settled, you get these bucks an' wenches set in they cabins and you treat 'em like the valuable propitty they are. Nina, you come along."

He walked away, paying no heed to the darkening of Lithian's face. Nina walked past him with her head in the air and a picture of studied insolence. She trailed behind Fitz, at the proper distance for a slave. Jonathan waited for him on the porch.

"Seems like you riled Lithian some."

"Don't like him, papa. Good overseer he is, but I don't like him."

"Takes it you pesterin' this heah wench maybe too much, son. She on'y another nigger. No way to argue that, is they?"

"Papa, I likes her and I kin tell she likes me. I want mama to have her and like she is now, not like she'd be after a bastard like Lithian got done with her. 'Sides, I been pesterin' her and might be she's carryin' my child inside her an' I don' want no sunabitch like Lithian fussin' 'round."

Jonathan nodded. "Reckoned you been pesterin' her. Known you likes her that much, sho' wouldn't have busted her aboard ship. She coulda been yours. 'Members offerin' her to you. Din't make no difference to me which wench I busted. We had a hundrud an' fifty of 'em to pick from."

"Reckon I hadn't grown up enough then, papa, but I'm growed now."

"Likely," Jonathan nodded with grim satisfaction. "Pesterin' this here wench, buyin' her 'ithout my say-so, insultin' an impo'tant man in Norfolk, getting into a fight with one gentleman and knifin' another. Oh, you growed all right. I'm pleased we didn't stop in Richmond. Norfolk musta shook some afore you left and no sense Richmond shakin' too."

"I gits to keep Nina. Gits to have her when mama comes. An' she sleeps in mama's room from now until mama gits here and after, mama wants her."

"Sho' ain't goin' to need no overseer, time you take charge. But Lithian stays 'til I git back with mama. Now come on inside. Kinda achin' to see whut them folks in Richmond done for my money."

Jonathan pushed open the door and they walked into

a reception hall much larger than the one at Colonel Coldwell's mansion, though it wasn't two stories high. There were, however, larger chandeliers and more sconces to light up things well indeed. The hallway was carpeted in a rich gold-colored rug and this followed on up the winding staircase, graceful as the arching of the *Wyndward* in a mild sea. Fitz had never seen stairs carpeted before.

They entered the ballroom which also served as the drawing room. Here again was an opulence which Jonathan had bargained for and received. The furniture was along massive lines, all of it upholstered except for a row of gilded cane-back chairs to be used when the room was converted into a ballroom. There was a very large oval rug, varied in color, woven tightly and expertly. Around it, mahogany flooring had been polished to a brilliancy which made everything stand out in bright reflection.

The fireplace was framed by a mantel of white marble, with two enormous andirons holding up massive logs ready to be lighted. The side windows were mullioned, hung with pale green draperies over filmy curtains. The draperies were edged with gold fringe and tied back with thick, golden-threaded cords, heavily tasseled.

Nina skipped about, touching this, adjusting that, finding herself enchanted with a huge seashell that served as a decoration, and by the oil lamps with their bright glass shades.

"She sho' likes everythin'," Jonathan said happily. "Whut 'bout you, son?"

"Papa, it's the biggest and the most beautiful house I ever seen in my life. They ain't nothin' to compare it with. Mama's goin' to bawl minute she walks in."

Jonathan said, "Son, that wench of yours kinda musky?"

"Nina? Hell, papa, she never stinked I knows of."

"Well, I smellin' somethin'. . . ."

Fitz called to Nina and she turned to face him, her happy smiles fading as he strode in her direction. He seized her hand, lifted her arm and applied his nose to her armpit. He looked around.

"She don't stink, papa. You c'mere and sniff. Don't stink nohow."

"Nev' mind, son. Take your word for it. Reckon whut I smellin' is the *Wyndward*. Reckon I sailed her so long and carried so many niggers, the smell of 'em got into my nose and can't get rid of it."

"Cain't carry no stink 'round like that, papa. You just think you smell musky niggers."

"That it," Jonathan agreed. "Pay no mind."

They examined the dining room, rather bare for the sake of practicality, Fitz thought, but the long table and the twenty heavy chairs indicated that Jonathan possessed hopes of building some sort of a social life. Fitz knew very well how difficult that would be. Most visitors to these plantation houses were aunts, uncles, nieces, nephews and all the cousins down to the fifth or sixth. Jonathan had no one; therefore, Fitz had no one, and his mother would arrive as a complete stranger. Things would have to work out, especially for his mother. She'd never be content seeing no other member of her sex except niggers. They certainly counted for nothing. Not that his mother would think that way, but she certainly wouldn't socialize with them.

There was a bedroom on the first floor, spacious and nicely furnished. There was also a room fitted like an office, with a long table, a large desk with a high-backed leather chair behind it. Walls of mostly empty bookshelves, a brightly polished spittoon done in what looked like gold plate.

"Plenty of book work runnin' a plantation," Jonathan explained. " 'Spect you gonna handle most of it. We'll see. Come upstairs."

Nina, in her eagerness, slipped past them and bounded

up the stairs showing an interesting length of copper-colored legs. Jonathan made noises in his throat.

"She got to be learned, Fitz. Sho' she you wench an' I see she a real nice gal, but she be a bad 'zample to the other wenches. Cain't have 'em runnin' 'round like they owned Wyndward, not us'n."

"She'll learn," Fitz told him. "She kin speak a little English now. Picks it up real quick."

They examined the four upstairs bedrooms. The master was elaborately furnished and for some reason brought back memories to Fitz, though he couldn't explain to himself what the memories were of.

"Remind you of anythin'?" Jonathan asked.

Then it came to him. "Papa . . . you done had the room fixed like back home in Massachusetts, Mama goin' to love this. Love you fo' doin' it too. How'd you do this so good?"

"Last time I was home I drew pitchurs of ever'thin', put down colors an' sizes an' I gave it to the people in Richmond and tol' 'em if they had to send to Massachusetts for these things, I'd stand the expense."

"Papa," Fitz asked with naked curiosity, "you a rich man? I'm askin' for no reason, 'cept if I see somethin' the place needs, kin I buy it?"

Jonathan walked slowly to one of the windows overlooking the sloping green in front of the house. Sunlight beat at his face, showing every weather-beaten crease, every wrinkle. He was in his prime, but he looked tired and older. Fitz hadn't noticed it before.

"Don't know 'zactly how rich," Jonathan said, "but they's a bank in Richmond knows how much half of it is and another bank up in Boston knows how much the other half is. On'y know it'd take me a hell of a long time to spend it, so they's anythin' you want, you buy it."

"Ever'thin's nice as kin be," Fitz said. "Mama sho' goin' be surprised."

Jonathan gave him a wise look. "She sho' goin' to be

'sprized you pesterin' Nina. She gits here, you be mighty keerful whar you lays her."

"I be keerful. Mama say so, you tell her Nina sleeps in her room. Knows mama, I do. I wants Nina sleepin' off the kitchen. Soon's I git time—an' before mama comes—I goin' to build a little room off'n the kitchen an' that's whar she'll sleep. Mama won't have no nigger sleepin' in her room."

Jonathan took his arm. "Son, you and me better have us a talk. 'Bout 'baccy an' hosses an' crops an' niggers, an' one special nigger."

"You think it best, that's whut we do, papa. Reckon Nina better fetch her sack and bring it up here. 'Til mama comes, wants her sleepin' in my room."

"Suit yourse'f, son. She you wench."

Fitz managed to make Nina understand that she was to bring her meager possessions here and install herself in his room, stay there until he returned. She happily bustled out of the room and ran down the stairs, letting her hand rest lightly against the burnished bannister, as if the feel of the smooth wood was new to her and she enjoyed it.

Downstairs they found a young buck, not more than sixteen, waiting for them. He was attired in knee-length white cotton hose, through which his black skin showed, shoes, for his feet were enormous, short pants buckled just below the knee, a white cotton shirt and a white coat. Against the whiteness of the clothes nearest his face, he looked blue-black. He was nervous, bug-eyed scared, but he was doing his best to stand ready for the orders of his new master.

"Who you?" Jonathan demanded.

"I Lucifer, massa, suh. I yo' houseboy and I yo' body servant, massa, suh."

"Who says so?" Jonathan asked, not unkindly.

"Massa Cahtah, suh. He says Lucifer, yo' get yo' big ass ovah to the house an' yo' put on them clothes I bought an' yo' serve Massa Jonathan. Yo' run yo' ass he says jump. Yo' listens all day and night so's he calls, yo' come runnin'."

"Know how to mix rum an' water, Lucifer?"

"Knows to mix cawn an' watah, massa, suh."

"Good." Jonathan walked to the pile of luggage, delved into one of the carpetbags and came up with a bottle of Barbados rum. "This heah like cawn. You mixes a little water, not much. You gits the water from the springhouse so it's cold. Then yo' finds us and brings it. Now git, yo' black sonabitch, an' you sloth, I wakes you up with a kick in the ass. Mind now?"

He backed away hurriedly, as if the kick was already coming. "Yassuh, massa, suh. I fetches it real quick."

"Wait a minute," Jonathan said. "Your name ain't Lucifer no mo'. Now your name Calcutta. Kin you say that? Calcutta."

"Yassuh, massa, suh. I'se Ca'cutta I is. Thanks you, suh. Likes mah new name."

He scampered away. Jonathan led Fitz into the room furnished as an office. They sat down in the leather chairs, in solid comfort. Jonathan chewed the end of a cheroot and applied flame. He puffed slowly, regarding the cigar thoughtfully.

"We aimin' to grow better t'bacca 'n this. Now son, we got us a heap of work. We got a hundrud slaves don't know they ass from the Liberty Bell 'bout how things is done. Yours firs' job is to make 'em unnerstan'. Learn 'em an' do it real fast. I plannin' on stayin' here one week 'fore I set out fo' Richmond to meet you mama. While I gone, you be in charge. Now you been studyin' 'bout 'baccy raisin'. Lithian, he already got seedlin's growin' in cold frames. Soon's they git the right size, you waits 'til it rains an' the fields are wet. Field got to be plowed an' ready. Got good iron plows waitin' in the barn and real good farm hosses. You hitch four to a plow. You gits more done that way an' you don't wear out you hosses."

"Then I puts every nigger to work transplantin' the seedlings an' work 'em until it's all done without no stoppin'."

"Books showed you somethin' after all," Jonathan granted. "Raisin' 'baccy a tricky business. I was raised on a plantation an' I knows t'bacca, but I got much to learn too. Then you plants the field in wheat and the other in corn. Ev'y slave cabin git half a acre goes with it. You gives them wenches, seeds fo' corn, beets, carrots, yams, potatoes . . . everythin' else you kin think of. They know whut to do with 'em. Don't have to speak English to plant a seed. Ask any buck." Jonathan roared at his own joke. " 'Fore long we buy more slaves—three, fo' hundrud. The bucks who ain't got wenches, they lives in the curin' sheds 'til the crop is in or they git wenches."

"You sho' got eve'thing figgered out, papa."

"Got five bathin' tubs ordered from Richmond, one fo' each bedroom. They ain't no way to connect 'em yet, but we sho' got the manpower to tote the hot water and empty the tubs."

"Be better'n swimmin' down the pond or tryin' to get clean in a wash basin," Fitz agreed. "I tho't you sent that Calcutta fo' rum. Musta figgered his name Calcutta tha's whar he ought to go to fetch the rum."

Calcutta may have heard the comment, for he appeared instantly, but not too steadily. He held a silver tray on which were two glasses so amber colored that there was certainly not much spring water added to the liquor. The glasses slid down, almost fell off the tray and he saved them barely in time. He was grinning foolishly as he passed one glass to Jonathan and the other to Fitz.

Jonathan said, "You been drinkin' my rum, Calcutta?"

Pop eyes rolled whitely. "Naw, sah, massa, suh. I din' touch none. No suh, massa, suh. I knows betta . . ."

"You stink of it," Jonathan said. "You evah tasted rum befo'?"

"Naw, suh, massa. Naw, suh, never did."

"Yo' like it, Calcutta?"

"Sho' do, suh. Sho' do."

Jonathan said, "Now you set that there tray down, go into the hall and open the green carpet bag. Yo' know what color green is?"

"Oh, yas suh, I knows."

"In that bag you'll find a strip of cowhide. A wide one. Fetch it here."

Calcutta's silly grin died away, the eyes rolled again. "Yas, suh, massa. Whaffo I tote strip o' cowhide, suh?"

"Since when do you niggers ask questions? Now you git and fetch that strap 'cause I'm goin' to make your ass redder'n it's black. You don't fetch it real quick, I'll use a snake on you."

Calcutta streaked out of the room. He knew what the blacksnake whip was like; he'd seen it rip a man's back wide open. The cowhide he knew nothing about. Even so, he preferred it, sight unseen, to the whistling, crackling snake. He found the strap and groaned as he pulled it free of the carpet bag. This thing, he realized, could create real pain. But there was nothing he could do but carry it across both hands, into Jonathan's office. He could still taste the sweetness of the rum and he felt dizzy from it, for he'd consumed half a tumbler under the impression it was too sweet to be very powerful. He could taste it strongly. It was no wonder Jonathan smelled it on his breath.

Calcutta emitted a long, long sigh and walked into the office with the strap. Jonathan took it from him. He motioned toward the end of the desk.

"Shuck your pants," he ordered, "an' bend over there. Git a move on, you black imp o' Satan."

Uttering small cries, Calcutta dropped his pants and hobbled over to the desk.

"Shut your cryin'," Jonathan ordered casually. "You ain't been swatted by this thing yit." He flexed the wide strap, slapped it against the back of a chair and the sound of it made Calcutta cringe.

"Stick you' ass in the air mo'," Jonathan said. "Git it up!" He glanced at Fitz. "Been wantin' to try this out. Kinda achin' for a chance. The Colonel give it to me an' say it don't cut the hide none. On'y raises it up like a blister."

He stepped back, measured the distance to the black behind arched upward. He swung the strap, but very lightly to gauge it. Calcutta emitted a wild howl of anguish. Jonathan drew the strap back again and delivered a full strength blow. It made a sound like the splatting of a cloudburst on a tin roof. Calcutta screeched.

"Wheee!" Jonathan gloated. "Seems like they 'vent new things ever' day." He stepped closer to the boy and bent down to examine the results of the blow. "No skin busted, not one drop of blood."

"Please, massa, suh," Calcutta wailed. "No mo', please. That sting like whole hive of bees pecking at my ass, it do."

"All right," Jonathan said. "Hi'st your pants and go fetch two more drinks. An' if you so much as licks the cork, you git ten whops with these here cowskin."

Calcutta hastily pulled up his pants and hobbled away. He seemed to sting from head to foot. He dashed down the corridor to the kitchen where he quickly poured two more drinks, added the traces of water, rolled his eyes to the sky at the temptation of the sweet, wonderful smell and finally took a swig of the young master's. Somehow, Calcutta guessed that the young massa wouldn't make a fuss, but he must be careful not to open his mouth close to the older man. Calcutta didn't want another taste of that strap as long as he lived.

He held the tray steadily this time as he served the old massa.

" 'Bout time you got heah," Jonathan said, on the theory that no matter how prompt a slave might be, he must always think he could have moved faster.

"Mmmmm," Calcutta said.

"Whut you say?"

"Mmmmmmm . . ."

"Ain't you forgettin' somethin', you black bastard?"

Calcutta bent his head down as far as it would go, not in a token of humility, but to keep his breath from soaring up and out.

"Mmmmm, massa, suh," he managed.

"Better. Mind your manners, heah? Now serve my son his glass."

"Mmmmm . . ." Calcutta murmured and moved to obey with considerable speed. Fitz accepted the glass.

"You tongue-tied?" he asked.

"Mmmmm . . . naw, suh, I ain't tongue-tied, massa, suh."

As he spoke his head came up and the powerful odor of rum reached Fitz. He didn't say anything more. Calcutta, believing he'd gotten away with it at last, turned around. Fitz kicked him soundly in the behind, half lifting him off the floor.

"Git back to the kitchen," he ordered. "You been dippin' in that rum some more."

"Naw suh, massa. I ain't . . . I sweah I ain't . . ."

"Black boy's goin' straight to hell with all his lyin'," Fitz said. "We ought to use the strap on him again, but I too tired and I knows you are too."

"Reckon so," Jonathan agreed. "Now you git—but not far. I calls you, an' you don't come in two seconds, you gits ten licks with the cowhide."

"I come soon's yo' calls, massa, suh. I sweah I do. Yas, suh, I sho' do."

For another hour Fitz and Jonathan talked about the plantation. It was Nina who came to announce that supper was ready to be served. Apparently she was going to assist, with or without orders, in the serving. She took up a position behind Fitz's chair and displayed a gay smile. One of the kitchen maids came in with a platter of stewed chicken and dumplings, all covered with red-eye gravy and giving off vapors that set the salivary glands drooling. She held the tray for Jonathan, who carelessly shoveled a third of it onto his plate. She moved to serve Fitz and Nina sprang to life, spooning the choicest pieces to his plate, poking the dumplings to find the tenderest. She disappeared into the kitchen and came back with the biscuits, steaming hot. She placed them and the dish containing the round lump of pale yellow butter before Fitz.

Jonathan watched all this with considerable amusement. "Tell you, son, you git that wench to unnerstan' you soon's you kin, so I kin tell her who the hell is the Big Master 'round here."

"She don't mean no harm, pa," Fitz said in a worried voice.

"Reckon not." He held out his hand for a biscuit. Nina tilted the plate so that several of the smaller ones were within his easier reach and even Fitz burst out laughing.

"Son," Jonathan said, "you trains 'em mighty good. Kinda like this wench myse'f jest like she is."

"Told you, papa, she not a common nigger."

"Kin see that. We puts her in charge of the whole goddamn house, she learns to talk. Mama kin gt 'nother wench. Got me an idee Nina'll run a tight ship, eh, son?"

Fitz wished he could relay his father's praise to her, but it was impossible. Soon as it became necessary to light the candles, Jonathan called it a day. Fitz, too, was tired. He went to his room to find Nina there waiting. She had learned a great deal in a very short time. His clean clothes for the morning were already laid out. Those he removed were gathered into a ball and he suspected they would be washed and ironed before daybreak. He washed up and then he sign-languaged to a startled wench that he was very weary. by staggering toward the bed, closing his eyes on the way. She held the sheets back for him, he tumbled in. She bent over him, tucking the sheets in place. He wanted to reach up and grasp her breasts, with their hard nipples all but dusting his face, but he couldn't make it. He was asleep in one minute and it was Nina who snuffed the candle and then sat on the floor at the foot of the bed until Fitz's rhythmic breathing assured her he really was fast asleep. She gathered up his soiled clothes, his boots, and quietly left the room. She was glad he didn't want her to pleasure him tonight. She had many things which must be done.

In the morning, Fitz found his yesterday's clothes laid out, and also an outfit which he himself would have chosen for his work around the plantation. Nina was enterprising enough to have learned what he'd likely wear.

She waited for him in the dining room. Jonathan was already at the table wolfing two thick slices of ham, four eggs, several strips of bacon and slices of savory hot bread.

"Seein' you ain't here 'til now," Jonathan grinned, "your wench been takin' mighty fine keer o' me, son. You looks fresh an' horny. You sleep with the wench las' night?"

"Papa, I so goddamn tired I just flop in baid an' 'member nothin' else 'til I woke up this mornin'. Nina crawled in bed with me, she did the rapin'."

"Good thing. Got you a job to do," Jonathan said. "Wants you to git that racetrack begun. Leave it to you how you do it. Take all the bucks you want."

"Sho', papa, that's a job I relish real well. Quicker we git that track done, quicker we fetch our hosses. Reckon I'm goin' to like trainin' an' racin' 'em."

They set out together, with Jonathan taking a course

in the direction of the untilled tobacco fields where slaves, horses and plows were waiting his orders. The overseer was there too. His greeting gave no evidence he bore Jonathan any grudge because of Nina and he got the blacks working fast and hard within minutes.

Fitz surveyed the outlined track, determined what should be done, and then called together twenty bucks. Most were those direct from Africa, but there was a sprinkling of those Carter had acquired, who could interpret and instruct the others.

One of these was a tall, sleek buck, very black, not quite as broken as the others, for when Fitz gave him orders, he looked Fitz in the face. Other slaves would lower their eyes and mumble assent. This one spoke out.

"Yas, massa, suh," he said. "Reckon tha's the bes' way. We digs up the grass firs' an' then we plows an' rakes the dirt 'til it soft. Yo' says so, massa, we can fix the lawn real fine with the sod."

"That's a good idea. What's your name, boy?"

The big black grinned from ear to ear, again defying the established relationship between master and slave. "Was Emmanuel, suh, but yo' papa say I now Hong Kong. Whaffo, this here name, massa, suh?"

"That's the name of a big city near China. Big, strong city. Thass why papa give you that name, 'cause you big and strong too. Likes Emmanuel myse'f, but papa says Hong Kong, you Hong Kong. Now you git these here black buzzards workin', while I figger out how we tamp down the dirt."

Hong Kong turned around and shouted his orders. The men fell to with a surprising will. They'd expected far harder toil than this, though they were soon sweating and their sleek bodies glistened with moisture before the morning was half over.

Hong Kong approached Fitz diffidently enough, taking off his frayed, battered excuse for a hat. He knew his place, but he also knew he could provide help for this rather strange young master who didn't seem to quite treat him as an animal.

"Massa, suh, this heah goin' to be a racetrack, ain't it?"

Fitz regarded him sternly. "Who gave you leave to address me? I wants you I calls and then you come hoppin'!"

"Massa, suh, I work for massa over in Kaintucky an' I he'p him make a racetrack. I knows how to tamp down the earth, suh."

Fitz said, "Hong Kong, if you know how to do that, and you do it, I'm goin' to give you a silver dollah. Fact—two dollahs. Now how you aimin' to do it?"

The slave gave a prompt and credible plan. First, the track would be lightly plowed to loosen the earth well, then carefully raked so that not the smallest stone remained. Meanwhile, one of the huge hogsheads in which tobacco was sent to market, would be sealed with pitch so it would hold water without a bad leak. After drying, a shaft would be poked through its center, a horse hitched to it, a hole created through which water could be poured into the hogshead. Then the hole would be plugged and the now very heavy barrel rolled over the loose earth. True, it would leak where the shaft went through, but again, there was more than ample manpower to keep bringing buckets of water.

By midafternoon the plowing was done, the hogshead was ready, a fresh horse hitched and the cumbersome thing rolled onto the track. There it flattened the earth well. Hong Kong, now sure of himself and in full charge, had water sprinkled on the track just before the hogshead rolled over that area so the surface was slowly turning solid and smooth. It would take a week to finish the task, but there was no question of its success.

Fitz was able to saunter over to the tobacco fields where Jonathan was yelling at the blacks who couldn't manage a four-horse team hitched to a plow. He had to get behind the plow himself and crack the whip to direct the horses. Fitz clambered onto a fence and sat there in idle watching.

Jonathan, dripping with sweat, turned the plow over to a buck who seemed to understand what was wanted. Jonathan stumbled his way across the plowed portion of the field, removed his hat and drew a forearm over his brow.

"You feelin' a mite run-down, son?"

"I feel fine, papa."

"What in hell you sittin' there? Told you to git the track ready."

"Is, mos', papa. Trundlin' it smooth. Take three, four days to do that right, but it'll be done."

Jonathan grabbed his hand, hauled him down off the fence and walked him to the edge of the track where he stood in honest, open admiration.

"What's in that hogshaid . . . see it now—water leakin'. Whar'd yo' git that idea?"

Fitz pointed him out. "Big buck you named Hong Kong."

"I declare. How'd he know about it?"

"Made 'nother one over in Kaintucky for his last master. Real smart nigger, papa. I put him in charge o' the track."

"That was right an' proper."

"Told him I'd give him two silver dollahs, the track comes out good. Reckon I'll make that five."

Jonathan shook his head. "One thing, son, you got to learn. If you spoils these niggers, they ain't wo'th a bundle o' coon shit. They git lax and lazy an' begin expectin' things no slave ever gits. You wants to manumitt him, thass the on'y way, but then he gits off'n this plantation. Cain't have no free niggers mixin' with the slaves. An' you got to know how much you lost in lettin' him go. That buck's wu'th twelve hundrud and fifty dollahs now. Come next year he'll be wu'th fifteen hundrud. You thinkin' of throwin' away money like that?"

"Two silver dollahs," Fitz said. "Promised. Aim to keep my promises."

"You handle them niggers right—like slaves ought to be treated—they happy. They got more'n they ever had in Afriky an' they don't worry 'bout gettin' theyse'ves served as the main course fo' dinner, or runnin' from them hungry wild animals over there. They git to work hard, here, but they git all they kin eat, they git clothes, they gits a toothache, we pulls it. They get sick and we send fo' the veternary. They don't work on Sundays nohow, we gives 'em wenches, all they kin handle. Now who'd want more'n that, son? 'Specially when they ain't human."

When the work was done four days later, Fitz gave Hong Kong his two silver dollars and, surreptitiously, he added a lavender-colored formal coat he no longer liked, and a pair of shiny boots which would have to have the toes cut away so Hong Kong could slide his big feet into them.

Two days later, Fitz had the stagecoach, which his father had bought at the river stop near Richmond, made ready for the journey to Norfolk. Fitz had worried considerably about being able to handle the plantation and all the people who worked it, but by the time Jonathan stood by while his carpetbags were flung onto the boot, Fitz no longer had any fears.

"Mind now," Jonathan warned him, "I don' want you spoilin' the niggers. Got ev'rythin' workin' fine. Wench for just 'bout every buck who got juice in him. Want it to stay that way. Work the ass off'n 'em and listen to Lithian Carter's advice."

"Yes, papa. I know whut to do now."

"Wants the house clean as a deck after stonin'. Wants the house niggers shined up real nice and see they minds they manners. Be gone 'bout ten days, I reckon. Aimin' to spend a day or two at Colonel Coldwell's plantation. On'y right I should pleasure your ma that way. Your ma goin' to be lonesome she ain't got 'nother woman to jaw with, an' on'y a day's ride to the Coldwell place. Ev'ry woman likes neighbors."

Jonathan boarded the stage as Nina arrived to wave goodbye. She stood very close to Fitz and he automatically let his arm drift around her supple, young waist. Jonathan, looking back, didn't like that. Fitz was getting too soft around the slaves, especially Nina. Maybe the best thing he could do when he returned was turn her over to a buck. No sense that she wasn't earning her way by starting a sucker. It seemed strange to Jonathan that she wasn't pregnant already, after all those nights Fitz had spent pestering her. Maybe, he thought with horror, Fitz was one of these big, handsome young men without juice. The idea of not eventually having grandchildren alarmed Jonathan more than the anticipated arrival of Sarah.

As the stage disappeared in its cloud of tan dust, Nina raised an arm and pointed in a sweeping gesture at the plantation.

"Good," she said with a smile. "Ve . . . ry good."

Fitz grinned. "You're learnin' fast, Nina. Wants you to know as many words . . ." he paused. "You don' know whut I'm sayin' yit, but you will."

She giggled happily and went racing back to the kitchen, running like a doe, with her shapeless osnaburg plastered against her ripe young figure by the breeze she created with her speed. Fitz knew only too well that the day was coming when she'd creep into the arms of some buck and try to find her own brand of happiness there. It was only right and proper she should do this. What did the future hold for a slave with too much affection for her master. But then, he ruminated, what future did a slave have no matter what.

He walked toward the newly finished racetrack. It was a fine job. No white contractor could have done it better, but the rules said a slave must not be given too many compliments, and work well done didn't mean he was entitled to rest.

Fitz went to the tobacco fields to inspect the seedlings, which looked firm and healthy despite the fact they'd been in the ground only a few days. All the acres were planted in Virginia bright, a tobacco much in demand in England.

Lithian Carter, a short quirt under his arm, stalked the field, issuing his orders, now and then caressing the back of a slow-moving slave with just enough quirt to make him jump. He showed no favoritism toward the wenches either; in fact, it seemed to Fitz that he liked stroking them with the quirt and cussing them out in the vilest language he knew. Fitz found his dislike for Lithian increasing, and he was going to insist the man be dismissed as soon as Jonathan returned and the whirl of excitement over the arrival of mama settled down.

Fitz, now that the track was finished, had spent more time on reading about thoroughbreds, their raising and training. In some old newspapers, sent for prior to his arrival at Wyndward, Fitz read advertisements for racing horses. Most of the farms in Kentucky, but that presented no problem other than a tedious journey. However, once the plantation was running smoothly, either he or Jonathan could feel safe to leave.

Fitz made many notes as to what to look for in a horse. His father knew all about them and had already given him important information.

It was lonely now sitting at the big table, being served by two wenches and by Nina who always remained directly behind his chair. She'd learned a few more words and was showing an intelligence quite surprising in a wench. Fitz drilled her when he had time, but it was the cook who did most of it.

After the meal, Fitz usually returned to the office for more work and Nina helped clear the table. She followed the maids and sat down at the kitchen table to help herself to the ham, bacon and fried potatoes which had been served. The cook, who'd served another family for twenty years and then been put on the vendue table, was a woman made enormous by her constant nibbling and her craving for her own cooking.

Her name had been Belle before she'd been purchased by Lithian and installed at Wyndward. In accordance with his policy of naming all females after ships he had known, Jonathan had changed it to Elegant, because the ship of that name had been a wide, slow, massive monster, and Belle had reminded him of her at once. She could speak Nina's language and she was busily engaged in teaching her enough English to get by.

The maids washed dishes rapidly but thoroughly. Elegant inspected a dish at random and if she found one not absolutely clean, she would bat the offending maid with the back of her hand, hard enough to send her reeling.

Tonight she was calm and comfortable in the massive chair she'd caused to be built especially for her comfort. In Nina's language, she spoke very well.

"Child, this is a strange land. I was brought here more than twenty years ago and it took me five to get used to these people. I was sold to a master who ravished me the first night I was in his house. That was in Richmond—a great city not too far away. In those days I was not fat as I am now, not ugly."

Nina said, "You are not now ugly."

"I know I am," she contradicted sharply, "and I don't care. I began eating anything I could get into my stomach because I knew if I became fat enough, none of the white masters would look twice at me. I was set to work in the kitchen where I learned to cook. I made many mistakes and for each I was whipped. Not hard, but only to warn me I must be more careful. There are times when I think that was right. I might have become slothful."

"It is so strange," Nina confessed. "There are many things I do not like here, but there are others . . ."

"My child, I know you mean the young master."

"Is it right that I love him and sleep with him?"

"If you do not, child, you will never know what love is. It is possible that you will be turned over to one of the bucks for breeding. I pray that day never comes, for you are too sensitive to be treated that way. Yet, I sometimes feel the young master cares for you too much to see that happen."

"But what will become of me, aunt?" Nina used the expression as one of endearment. "I cannot live without him and his love for me."

"Do not be too sure it is love," the cook warned gently. "He is very young and he is full of the urges of young passion, which is right. But that may be all it is—passion."

"I do not think so," Nina declared confidently.

"Nina, some day he will have to marry and it cannot be you. It will be to a white girl whom you may have to serve, and that would break your heart. It would be better to console yourself with a buck and accept your lot."

"Aunt, cannot he love two women?"

"My child, it is possible. It has been done many times and perhaps in this case . . . who knows? Things are not so bad here. I see the old master as stern, but I believe he is also fair. He is of the South, as they call it here. In the North are people who do not believe in slaves. Some of us have escaped to there, but it is better we remain where we are. A few who ran have been hung. Always rewards are offered and when the slave is returned, he is beaten very hard."

"The young master is not like that."

"Yes, that is so. I think he is more of the North than the South, but I await with much worry the arrival of his mother who is the old master's wife. I keep my ears open and I hear enough to know she is a very stern woman, but one who worships the God they have here and it has become plain to me that she does not believe in slavery."

"Then that is where he gets his kindness," Nina said. "Aunt, will you make me work very hard that I may soon know the language. And tell me how best I may serve the young master."

"I will help you, child. Already you are doing well and I am sure he appreciates it."

Nina rinsed and washed her plate, not a cracked one, or a tin plate as the maids were required to eat from, but a good piece of china suitable for her former status before being stolen and sent here. She was in the midst of this when she and the cook heard the voice of Lithian cursing and raving down by the slave cabins.

"We got troubles," the cook said in English. "Been 'spectin' that redneck bastahd gettin' his juice up."

"What is he doing? Why is he so angry, aunt?"

"He has probably taken the girl from some buck who is brave enough to try to save her from being raped. It is best you do not go down there now."

In the office, Fitz heard the voices and then a shout of pain. He left the house and hurried toward the scene of trouble, at a dead run. Outside one of the newly built cabins, he found a wench crouched on the ground, naked and crying. Hong Kong, the slave Fitz had so recently rewarded, was standing firm and tall before Lithian, who was in a blind, drunken rage. Lithian had slashed him a dozen times with a short whip and he was circling the buck to get in more licks while he bellowed his vile language loudly enough to have aroused the entire plantation. Lithian had shucked his pants and was naked from the lower edge of his dirty undershirt.

Fitz reached for the whip as it was drawn back, and he jerked it out of Lithian's hand. The overseer whirled about, facing Fitz, and his anger overcame his usual wheedling self in the presence of those who hired him.

"Yo' gimme back that whup," he shouted. "I aims to beat this here niggah 'til they ain't no skin lef' on him."

"What happened? What the hell's going on here?"

"Whut happened? I tol' that goddamn buck to git somewhar else while I raped that wench. Found I had to draw my derringer. . . ."

"No call to pull a gun on that man," Fitz said, trying to hold his temper down.

"Who yo' to say so? Whut in hell yo' think yo' are, comin' down heah from the No'th and givin' us orders? I'm goin' to whup this bastahd 'til he near daid. Yo' heah that?"

Fitz handed him back the whip. "You do that, Mistah Cahtah, an' then you turns about an' uses it on me, 'cause I goin' to knock your fool haid off."

Lithian, half mad from drink and by the fact that his tumescence was still strong and crying to be slaked, yanked the whip from Fitz and lashed at the slave. Fitz grabbed him by the shoulder, whirled him about. Lithian made a serious mistake. He raised the whip. Fitz hit him low in the stomach so hard the tumescence vanished in a second and Lithian doubled up in pain, but he was trained to rough fighting and, without raising his head, he charged at Fitz and almost bowled him over.

Fitz grappled with him, flung him angrily aside and let him come in again. This time Fitz met him halfway with a fist that had demolished far better men than Lithian. He proceeded to cut the overseer to a wheedling, whining, pitiful excuse for a man. He closed one eye, broke his nose, shattered four or five teeth and cut his knuckles in the doing. He hammered blow after blow to Lithian's midriff, knowing that was his softest spot. Lithian finally slid to the ground, gasping for breath. Fitz grasped him by the hair, hauled him halfway up for the required leverage and then he brought his knee up hard. Bone broke with an audible cracking sound and Lithian stopped his groaning.

Fitz wiped his bloody knuckles on Lithian's pants which he picked up from the ground. He spoke to the wench. "Git inside an' go to bed," he ordered. He raised his hand toward a pair of bucks watching it all, fascinated, making no pretense of their delight.

"You two, haul this man to his cabin and throw him on his bed. Take his goddamn pants. You, Hong Kong, c'mere."

The big slave obediently approached. This time he hung his head. "Massa, suh, I knows I did wrong, but couldn't he'p it. I likes this wench and old massa tol' me she mine an' nobody gits to her. Then Mr. Cahtah, he come in all drunk an' evil an' he say 'git outa that bed, niggah, so's I kin rape that wench o' your'n.' Old massa say she mine. I tell 'im and he so liquored up an' bothered, he caint heah me. He likes to kill that po' wench, way he jump her. So I hauls him off'n her. Like old massa say, she my wench."

"You kin bet your black hide that was the wrong thing. You laid hands on a white man an' you knows whut's got to happen."

"I gets whupped."

"There ain't no black touched a white 'thout he gits whupped."

"Wuth it." Hong Kong took courage again. "Sho' wuth it to see yo' bust him up. Sho' wuth it, massa, suh."

"In the mornin'," Fitz said.

"I be in the whuppin' shed, massa, suh. Don't mine none yo' do the whuppin'."

"I don't whup nobody," Fitz said. "He do that—Mistah Cahtah. He does the whuppin'."

"Think he able?" Hong Kong asked in a freshly worried voice.

"Cain't do it tomorrow, he do it nex' day. Reckon he gits strength back in the mornin'. After this, you be mo' keerful, Hong Kong."

"Massa, he goin' to kill me sho'."

"You deserve it," Fitz said. He'd already made up his mind as to the number of lashes, but it was better to let the buck worry rather than tell him now.

"Yas, suh, massa, suh. Reckons I does. Don't mind the whuppin' so much, 'ceptin' it be done by him."

"You watch youse'f," Fitz warned, "or I might do some whuppin' myse'f when Cahtah gits through. Now git youse'f to bed. Rest of you-all, git back to whut you was doin'—makin' suckers."

They all filed back into their various cabins, the bachelors heading for one of the big sheds where they were bedded down. Fitz walked over to the two-room cabin especially built for the overseer. He found Lithian sitting up in bed, trying to maneuver a bottle through his aching lips and his broken jaw.

"Tomorrow," Fitz said, "you pack your things an' git. Don't want you 'round here anymore."

Lithian managed to speak, although every word was painful. "Gits . . . to whup . . . that niggah. Law says . . . I whup him . . . yo' cain't go . . . agin the law. . . ."

"You whups him," Fitz said. "No more'n right, he lay a hand on your precious white hide. Ten o'clock in the whuppin' shed. You cut him once 'fore I gits there, I'll pull you up and slice you to pieces."

He walked out. Lithian hurled the empty bottle at the wall, went to the door and tried to call out to a slave he'd bought for Jonathan as a carpenter. But Lithian couldn't speak loudly, couldn't open his jaw, so he trudged painfully down between the rows of cabins until he came to the right one. He used his foot to kick in the door.

The carpenter and his woman, both well on, sat up in sudden fright. They peered at Lithian, barely able to recognize him.

"Yo' hi'st yo' ass outen that baid now," Lithian managed. "Wants you in the carpentry shop. Yo' ain't there in fi' minutes, I whale yo' ass off."

He left the cabin and made his way to the shed designated as a carpentry shop. He lit candles, placed them on the workbench and sought a piece of wood the right size for his purposes. He found one about four feet long, meant for a light beam or support. He raised it above his head, hefted it and found it met with his requirements. The carpenter, still half asleep and buttoning his cotton shirt, came hurrying in. Lithian handed him the length of wood.

"Wants you to trim this down so it be fat on one end, thin on the other. Like a club I kin hol' tight. Like a club y' kin bash a man's haid in. I be here 'fore ten an' you ain't got it ready, yo' be the firs' one I use it on."

He walked out, returned to his cabin and got himself another bottle of corn from his trunk. He drained half of it, lay down and consoled himself with dreams of what he'd do to that insolent buck in the morning. And what he would one day do to Fitzjohn Turner, whom he hated even more than the buck.

He ached all over and he kept spitting blood. He grasped one shaky tooth and pulled it to the accompaniment of a wail of anguish and a torrent of angry curses.

His jaw was fractured, he knew, but that could be taken care of. His pride was wrecked even more than the jaw bones. He'd been beaten by a boy half his age in the presence of many of the slaves on the plantation. The news would travel fast, spread all over this region in a matter of days. Plantation owners who might have hired him would shy away. He'd have to move on some distance where the word didn't reach, and he hated Fitz for being responsible for this. It was incomprehensible to Lithian why Fitz had interfered. All he'd done was take a wench away from a nigger. What difference did it make if he raped her? Whose business was it anyway? He didn't doubt but that a dozen light-skinned children ran around the immediate area, all of them resembling him in one way or another. It was an overseer's privilege to take any wench he desired, except those reserved for their owner. This husky young man from the North had changed all that and Lithian resented it to a point of being willing to murder. He was consoled only by what he intended to do to the buck. At least he could take out his rage on him.

Hong Kong entered the whipping barn at ten minutes of ten to find Lithian already there, the snake under his arm, its length trailing sinuously behind him. Lithian had brought in two bucks and they awaited his orders. Propped in a corner was the club fashioned during the night. It was a formidable looking weapon.

Lithian had also tied up his flopping jaw so that he had more difficulty than ever in speaking. "Shuck yo'se'f down," he ordered Hong Kong thickly. He indicated the other two. "Git the hoist ready."

Hong Kong removed his shirt, lowered his trousers and stepped out of them. He was bent over, extracting one leg from the garment when Lithian struck him on the head with the weighted butt of the whip. Hong Kong simply fell forward without a sound.

"Tie his goddamn ankles," Lithian ordered. "One ankle at a time. I wants him hauled up so his laigs are wide and his knockers showin' real good."

"Yo' gonna cut his balls off, massa?" one of the bucks asked in fear and awe.

"Don't know 'zactly whut I does, till I ready to do it. Now hi'st him up."

Lithian hurried to the door to look out in the direction of the house. Despite Fitz's orders, he intended to inflict as much punishment as possible before he arrived and then finish it with the bloody, bestial plan that had kept him awake all night in the anticipation of these moments.

The bucks were slow. They knew if the young master arrived in time, it wouldn't go too badly with Hong Kong. If this sadistic white overseer went to work before Fitz arrived, there was no telling how far his rage would take him.

Lithian was no fool. He knew why they stalled. He lashed out with the snake and cut through the cotton shirt of one buck, drawing blood until the back of the shirt was soaked with it. The bucks fell to with more energy, though they could have moved faster.

They had to hoist him up by one leg because they couldn't attach two ropes to one pulley, but after he was upside down so that his fingertips just cleared the floor of the barn, they roped and pulled the other leg as far as they could get it and tied that rope to another post.

Hong Kong hung there, conscious again, his eyes rolling in terror. He was praying that the young master would come at once. Even now, Lithian was experimenting with the snake. Twenty lashes and Hong Kong knew he'd either be dead or ruined for life, the way Lithian would swing it. He knew his legs had been pulled apart and he guessed Lithian intended to somehow manipulate the whip so that his testicles would be cut up. Hong Kong began to moan in anticipation of the agony.

"Now yo' gits it, you black bastahd," Lithian said. "Firs' I goin' to cut yo' back up 'til the bones show. Then I goin' to chop off yo' balls and ever'thin' else yo' got down there, af'ore I cuts yo' back some more. Yo' gittin' fifty lashes. They be slow so yo' don't pass out. No sense hittin' a nigger he don't feel it. When they hauls yo' down, yo' goin' to be chopped up so yo' fitten to feed to the hogs. An' tonight I pleasures myself with yo' wench and nobody to tell me different. Heah comes the firs' one. Jes' a little taste whut yo' goin' to git."

The whip snaked out, wound itself around the buck's back and drew blood welling up from the deep slash. Hong Kong moaned and then shrieked. Not so much in the agony he felt, but as a voice of alarm for the young master.

Fitz was inside the barn before Lithian used the snake again. He yanked it out of the man's hand.

"Done tol' you, no whuppin' till I gits here. You deaf, Lithian? You wants I should bust your jaw agin?"

"Hates him I cain't wait," Lithian excused himself "He's gittin' fifty lashes."

"He gits five an' not with that whup. How you got him strung up? You crazy, Lithian? You miss with that whup an' you shorely cuts his balls off. That buck's wuth fifteen hundrud he's wuth a dollah. You lose you mind complete?"

"I whup him. I skin him alive," Lithian snarled.

"Five licks you give him. Got me a new kind of whup comin' from the house an' that's the one you goin' to use. Don't cut none, but sho' stings."

Fitz walked over to the swinging buck and bent down to study his pain-wracked face. "You got no call to complain," he said. "Raisin' your hand to Mistah Cahtah the wust thing a slave kin do, 'cept kill a man. You gits five good ones, 'cause you too valuable a buck to hurt much, but you evah raise your hand agin, you gits strung up by the neck, not the heels."

Nina was bringing the wide strip of cowhide. She stepped into the barn and gasped at the sight of Hong Kong's broad back dripping blood and the way he had been hoisted up. Fitz took the cowhide from her and handed it to Lithian.

The overseer examined the hide and sneered. "This

here wuth nothin'. Ain't goin' to use it. Law says this here buck gits whupped reg'lar, not some fancy No'thrun way. Yo' kindly stands back, Mistah Turner, suh, an' I gits at it."

Fitz yanked the strap from his hand, pushed him back and approached Hong Kong. The wide paddle-like affair swished through the air and smacked the buck squarely across the buttocks. Fitz was avoiding the cut area. He swung again. Hong Kong pressed his lips hard. This was painful. He didn't know how he could bear it in silence, but he knew this form of whipping would not harm him permanently and he only had four more strokes to go. He was wrong. Fitz counted the lash of the whip as one, and only administered four.

Then he hurled the cowhide aside as if it were tainted and walked toward the door. He had no warning except the way Nina suddenly flinched and her eyes widened in terror. Fitz, not knowing what to expect, looked over his shoulder. Lithian, with the new club held aloft, was already bringing it down to smash it against the suspended buck's groin. The weapon crashed. Hong Kong emitted one soft sigh and went limp. Blood spurted up from severed veins. The black body went slack.

"You sonabitch," Fitz roared.

Lithian raised the club. "I goin' to brain yo'. I goin' to bash in yo' haid. I goin' to. . . ."

He swung the club. Fitz dodged it, threw himself to one side, streaked past Lithian and picked up the blacksnake. Lithian stared at him in panic. He had the club, but to use it he had to get in close and the whip could cut him to pieces before that was possible. Yet he had to take the risk and he charged.

The whip opened his face so badly, his mouth was extended two inches further on each side and the parted lips revealed the yellow teeth, what was left of them, covered with blood. The whip whistled again. It cracked against Lithian's chest, ripped through his shirt and penetrated the skinny rib cage clear to the bone. The whip whistled five more times until Lithian was swaying drunkenly. He finally managed to lift the club and hurl it. Fitz only had to sidestep a foot or so and let the club hurtle by.

Then he cut the man around his buttocks, severed the flesh of his legs, raised the whip and with one final snap, wound it around his throat. The scream from Lithian was cut off sharply.

Fitz freed the lash, threw it aside. Lithian was lying on his face in a pool of his own blood. He wasn't dead, but by his moans he didn't seem far from it.

Fitz reached the side of the unconscious buck still hanging from that pulley. "Cut him down," he roared at the two stunned slaves. They quickly obeyed. Nina was already beside the injured man. Fitz knelt at her side. He ran his hand gently along the buck's inner thighs, feeling for the severed artery. By some miracle the blood had clotted and the flow stopped. He placed an ear against the broad black chest. There was a heartbeat. It was a source of amazement to Fitz how much these men could take.

He signaled the slaves. "You-all fetch a litter. You cain't find one, make one, and git it here fast. Go!"

They fled. Fitz nodded approval when Nina carried over a pail of water and a rag with which she proceeded to wash the slashed back and remove the clotted blood from between the legs. Her ministrations were gentle and careful, and she showed no reluctance to get her hands smeared with blood.

It required twenty minutes before the bucks returned with a door, torn off its hinges, to act as a litter. It was better than nothing. Fitz helped raise the silent form. He ordered him carried to his cabin. He gave Nina a gentle shove as a signal to follow the litter. She nodded and hurried alongside the unconscious buck, lifting his arms, which swung freely over the side of the door, and crossed them over his chest.

Fitz walked over to where Lithian lay. He turned him over contemptuously with his foot. "Git up," he said. "On your feet, you mizzable nothin'. On your feet, heah me?"

Lithian struggled to a kneeling position. His wits were clearing somewhat, although the hatred befogged him far too much. On his knees this way, he was able to reach under his blood-soaked coat for the derringer he always kept there. He drew it while Fitz was turning away. The small gun exploded. Fitz felt the roaring pain as the pellet sliced through his arm. He whirled and kicked Lithian under his bound-up chin. Bone grated and Lithian fell back. Fitz took the gun away from his inert hand, dropped it into his back pocket and then, holding onto his wounded arm, he ran toward the house.

Nina, attracted by the sound of the shot, had stepped out of Hong Kong's cabin. She saw the blood on Fitz's arm and she screamed and ran after him. He strode on, oblivious to her, angry at himself, mad enough to return and kill Lithian, and thoroughly dismayed at the results of his guardianship of the plantation for the first time. The overseer didn't matter. He was going to be fired anyway, but a healthy buck had been certainly turned into a eunuch, if he lived at all. It was all Fitz's fault. He should have been attending to business better than he had. His father wasn't going to like the outcome of this.

Nina passed him and held the door open while she screamed for the cook to come and help. They finally got Fitz seated in the kitchen where Nina promptly cut away his shirt sleeve. She murmured small sounds of anguish over his pain and she had the gentlest fingers imaginable when she prodded for any sign of the bullet. It seemed to have gone clear through, but there was still danger of infection.

She rushed out to return in a few moments with some leaves caked with fresh, wet mud. This she applied to his arm, despite his protests. The cook had torn cloths into strips for bandages. The arm did feel better once it was bound up.

"You-all think the nigger daid, suh?" the cook asked.

"I don't know," Fitz replied shortly. "Where's that no-'count boy . . . what the hell's his name . . . ?"

"Calcutta," the cook roared. "Gitten the iron outa you pants an' come yere. Quick, now!"

Calcutta appeared, hastily buttoning his white coat. Fitz eyed him sharply. "Fetch me some rum and a little water. On'y a little now, an' jump."

The boy raced away, snatching up a tray and darting out the backdoor to fetch cold water from the springhouse. Fitz went into the office and sat down. A great way to begin the day. Shortly, Calcutta arrived with the tall glass on the silver tray. Fitz ordered him to bend over and exhale. There was no smell of rum emanating from him. Fitz drank a third of the drink in one gulp. Nina sidled into the room and moved to a corner at the rear where he couldn't see her and yet she was there ready to serve him at his first gesture.

He opened a metal box and took out two double eagles. He beckoned to Nina. "See if you unnerstan' this. Fo' Mistah Cahtah. The sonabitch I whupped. Give these to him."

She nodded brightly and tucked the coins tightly into the palm of her hand, but then she hesitated, fearing to go near the man. Fitz sensed the reason for her hesitancy.

"Hell, Nina, you don't have to fear him none. They ain' 'nuff lef' o' that skinny bastard to feed the hens. Go 'long now."

She nodded, reassured more by his manner than his words. She scampered across the rear yard and reached Lithian's cabin. He was sprawled out across his bed, face congealed with blood, his jaw hanging lopsided. Nina held out her hand, opened the fingers and let the two double eagles fall onto his chest. He muttered something and tried to brush them away. Nina turned and left him.

She walked slowly back to the mansion, considering solemnly the fact that in this strange world inhabited and ruled by men with white skins, there were certainly two distinct types of men—the cruel and the kind. She didn't even understand Fitz fully. She wanted to, but there were times when he seemed to be two different personalities, one a Southerner going strictly by the rules, the other a kindly man, undecided himself what he really was.

The only thing she knew was that he was never deliberately cruel to those unable to defend themselves.

Chapter Five

WITHOUT LITHIAN to supervise, Fitz was kept extremely busy. Three days before Jonathan was due to return, it began to rain. Fitz had gone down on his knees to earn that. The tobacco seedlings had grown avidly through their protective covering of dead leaves and small twigs and were in need of transplanting, but it couldn't be done unless the earth was moist. Now the gentle rain of summer pattered the ground and provided the water that was necessary. He called together every buck and wench available and sent them into the three tobacco fields to do the transplanting.

His wound had been minor, healed quickly and now only a little stiffness troubled him. He stopped by the cabin of the injured slave to see how he was coming along. He was still weak and in much pain but he refused the proffered services of the veterinary. Fitz suspected it was because he wanted no man to gaze upon what was left of his manhood. Fitz was wise enough not to ask about it, only his general health. Nina and Elegant had babied him, along with his own wench who seemed to be absolutely devoted to him, but Fitz wondered for how long. Once she was convinced that he could no longer pleasure her or procreate, her interest was very apt to die off. Not many slaves were castrated, but those who had been, according to the stories Fitz heard told about the subject, their wenches had quietly gone away and left them to their boring days of bachelorhood.

By the time Jonathan was due, Hong Kong was up and around though leaning heavily on a cane like an old man. Whatever happened to Lithian, Fitz had no idea. When he'd gone to seek him out and drive him off the plantation, he had already packed up and left.

A slave, mounted on a swift horse, which was highly unusual, galloped up to the mansion in midafternoon. He was shouting as he dismounted.

"Massa Turner he comin', Massa Turner an' Mist'iss Turner, they comin', they comin' home . . ."

Fitz strode out to meet the man. "How you know they comin'?" he demanded.

" 'Cause Massa Colonel Coldwell, he sen' me, suh. He sen' me to tell yo' they was comin'."

Fitz was appreciative of the Colonel's warning. Perhaps he thought the house might be full of naked wenches. Fitz said, "When they git here?"

"I git here 'bout hour 'fore they do. Ride hard, massa, suh. They comin'."

Nina had responded to the excitement as she always did. Fitz was now able to give her orders and they needed no translation. It was amazing how this copper-skinned girl had picked up English.

"Take him to the kitchen and stuff him good," he ordered. "Then have Elegant fix him a ham an' pone or whatever, so he don't go hungry on his way back to Coldwell Hall."

"Yes, massa, suh." She bobbed her head and grasped the rider by the arm to pilot him at top speed to the kitchen. Moments later, Fitz heard her shouting sharp orders to all the maids and house boys. In one hour, the house would be absolutely spotless and shiny.

Fitz called for Calcutta and had him bring a glass of rum and water. He drank this while he nervously paced the verandah, waiting for the arrival of the stage.

When it did finally appear at the bottom of the driveway, it turned in slowly, not with the dash Fitz had expected. Then he saw why. Trailing behind it were more laden wagons, three filled with wenches. After that, trailed a coffle of bucks—at least a hundred, for which Fitz was most grateful. The plantation needed them all and more.

Nina suddenly popped out of the door armed with a rag and a whisk broom. She quickly brushed him down, knelt and ran the rag over his dusty boots until they shone, then she hastily retreated with a thousand more things to be done, casting one nervous glance over her shoulder at the oncoming stage.

Fitz hadn't seen his mother in almost two years, but he knew she wouldn't have changed much. He remembered her black hair had begun to show touches of gray. In would perhaps be more in evidence now. He was certain her black eyes would still have that snapping look and her mouth would be tightly compressed, as if in constant disapproval of everything about her.

The stage drew up before the door and stopped. Jonathan flung the stage door open and jumped to the ground. He was somewhat more resplendent than Fitz had ever seen him. He wore a bowler-shaped hat, morning coat with M-notched lapels; breeches which buttoned below the knee at the sides, white silk stockings and shoes tied with a bow. Though the garments were travel-stained, they were still impressive. Fitz couldn't believe his eyes.

Jonathan gave a loud whoop of welcome and grabbed Fitz. Then he took a moment to feast his eyes on the mansion and the plantation and his chest swelled with pride. Fitz moved to the stage to help his mother down. Her eyes regarded him serenely and she turned her cheek for his kiss. She was dressed, as Fitz knew she would be, conservatively but elegantly. Her bonnet of cerulean blue satin, topped with ostrich feathers, was of the same color as her shoes and reticule. Her gray dress was the latest fashion, with tight high bodice, revealing the outline of her ample breasts. Her double skirt was flounced and headed by rouleaux of satin. She looked fresh and serene, despite the eternity it must have taken to get from Boston to Norfolk by boat, and then the long stage ride, enveloped in dust and heat. His eyes beamed with pride at sight of her.

"He's grown, Jonathan," Sarah said, surveying her son. "You didn't tell me. He's a foot taller if he's an inch."

To Fitz, it was wonderful to hear Boston English. He impulsively hugged her, then with an arm around her, faced her in the direction of the mansion.

"Mama, if that ain't the mos' wonderful house you evah laid eyes on. . . ."

"What kind of English are you speaking?" she asked him sharply.

"Mama, you're in the South now. This is Virginia. Ever'body speaks like this. You're the one who has the accent down here."

"I daresay, but to me, the language of the South sounds downright primitive. As for the house, I'll give you my opinion after I've seen it."

"Papa fixed it up just for you. Bigger'n anythin' we ever had and ten times finer."

His mother gave an impatient toss of her head. "Please speak so I can understand you."

"All right, mama," Fitz acquiesced, glad to humor her, hoping it would soften her mood. "Look beyond the house. As far as you can see and further is our plantation. It's one of the biggest in Virginia now and in a year or two, it'll be the biggest."

"The biggest is not important," she said, "unless those who possess it deserve it. I am now prepared to enter the house. I won't like it, and I doubt very much I shall remain long, but I have a certain duty to my husband and to my son, so I consented to come. It has been a frightful journey and made horrible by the presence of those poor Negroes your father chained up and compelled to walk all the way from close by Richmond. I declare, such inhumanity I've never before witnessed."

Jonathan, behind her back, made a hopeless gesture. Fitz gave his father a reassuring nod and led his mother into the house. Jonathan took the opportunity to speed down to where the coffle had been given permission to lie on the grass. They were a likely-looking lot. Cost him seventy-five thousand dollars, but worth it. This was the first time he'd had a chance to really inspect them. Drat the woman, who had insisted they be allowed to rest every hour, and be given more food and water than they needed. As a result, their march had been slow despite the threat of the whip. A man can't march fast or far except on a lean belly, but Sarah would never in her life understand that.

Jonathan saw the completed track and tested the surface by stamping it with his heel. He only did that once. The shock of the contact sent pain shooting up his calf. He strode over to the tobacco fields and saw that they'd been successfully transplanted and doing well. The corn was coming along and the wheat was showing with a promise of a fine crop.

He slowed down at the springhouse and searched about for a bottle. He found one of corn whiskey and, tilting it, he drank copiously. He put the bottle away and inserted a cheroot between his teeth so he could chomp on it and hide the odor of the corn.

In the mansion, Fitz showed his mother the drawing room. If she was impressed, she didn't show it. The dining room met with her approval because of its starkness. The office interested her not at all, nor did the first floor bedroom. When they entered the kitchen, Elegant bowed very low and welcomed her.

"Mist'iss, ma'am, mighty glad to have yo' heah. Yo' tells me whut to cook and I does it, jus' the way yo' wants it, mist'iss, ma'am."

"Well," Sarah said somewhat mollified by Elegant's attitude, and noting her ample proportions, "you seem to thrive on it. What's your name?"

"Elegant, mist'iss, ma'am. Thass whut Massa Turner he name me. Likes it, I do."

"It's a silly name, but it suits you. Now, what are you cooking at this moment?"

"Roastin' a ham, mist'iss, got some chicken stewin', slab o' bacon to fry. Got biscuits ready . . ."

"What's this red stuff?" Sarah demanded, eyeing the boiling pot with some doubt.

"Red-eye gravy, ma'am. Admires it yo' try some."

Sarah was persuaded to accept a hastily wiped spoon and taste a speck of the gravy. Then she took more and nodded. "That's very good, Elegant. Very good indeed. And I suppose these two girls are the housemaids?" She looked doubtfully at the pair.

"Mist'iss, they be sluts. Housemaids upstairs gettin' yo' room slicked up. Got us a houseboy . . ." she opened her mouth wide and bellowed for Calcutta. He came rushing in, out of breath and pop-eyed at the sight of the grand white lady.

"This here Calcutta," Elegant explained. "He no-'count, shorely ain't, but he runs fast yo' tan his hide. I yells at him, he gits his black ass humpin', I kin tell yo'."

Sarah gasped and turned away hurriedly while Fitz smothered his grin. Elegant went serenely about her business, unknowing her earthy reference to Calcutta would never meet with Boston standards of language servants were expected to use when speaking to their mistress.

Nina was standing at the foot of the stairs, wearing a new maid's uniform of black with a trim white lace apron and a little white cap. She curtsied politely.

"Mama," Fitz said, "this here Nina."

"Well," Sarah said, "I'm glad at least one darky has an ordinary name."

"Jes' happen that way, mama," he said. "The next two gals in line papa named Pinta and Santa Maria."

"Your father sometimes has a strange idea of humor. To settle upon these poor defenseless people such names as that! What about this girl, Fitzjohn? She's very pretty."

"Mama, she's a slave like the rest of them, but she's very special. Her papa is an Arab prince and her mother is a princess of some sort in Africa. Very important people. Her family background is probably about as good as ours, if we look back real close." Fitz reverted to his Boston style of speech because he was so anxious for his mother to like Nina.

"Impossible," Sarah said, "but I like the girl. What is she capable of doing?"

"She can either run the house, which she does very well, or be your personal servant. It's up to you."

"We shall see. For the time being, she can be both. I wish to go to my room now to freshen up. Whatever happened to your father? I had the most difficult time keeping track of him in Norfolk. He was away much of the time buying these slaves. I insisted he purchase some new clothes. I wish to get cleaned up." She tapped Nina with one extended finger. "Come along, girl."

Nina followed her up the stairs and then led her to the bedroom which Jonathan had so faithfully copied from her own back in Massachusetts. Sarah stepped in and gasped. Then she unaccountably began to cry and Nina's consternation was such that she slipped out of the room and called down the stairs for help.

"Let her be," Fitz said. "Ain't often she cries. Do her good. Reckon it was the room. She knows now papa loves her."

Nina nodded silently, not quite understanding, but she had presence of mind enough to go to the kitchen and have Elegant make up a pot of coffee, which she carried upstairs and served to Sarah.

"Thank you, Nina," she said. "You're very bright, but then, how could you be otherwise, coming as you do from royalty."

Nina smiled and nodded and said, "Thank yo', mist'iss, ma'am."

"You sound like all the other nig . . . the other blacks. I shall endeavor to teach you to speak like a civilized person. You may pour me more coffee."

Fitz took advantage of his mother's resting from her journey, to hurry out to greet his father again. "Got the tobacco plants all set," he said. Corn been hoed, wheat showin' real fine."

"Good," Jonathan said. "What happened to Lithian?"

"You knows 'bout that?" Fitz asked sadly.

"He came by Coldwell Hall some days ago, lookin' like he been in a fight with a bear. You cut him up like that, son?"

"Yes, papa, it was me. Lithian, he got hisself drunk an' horny one night an' he busted in the cabin of Hong Kong . . ."

"Who the hell he?"

"The buck who built the racetrack."

"Valuable buck. Lithian knew that."

"Lithian hauled Hong Kong's ass outa bed, took off his pants and raped Hong Kong's wench."

"Then the sonabitch got whut he deserved."

"That ain't all, papa. Hong Kong hit him. But Hong Kong was fas' asleep. It was dark, I reckon he din' know Lithian was black or white."

"No mattah, Hong Kong gets lashed for that."

"Already done it, papa."

"Well, that's good. You promise them bucks the whup and hold off, and they git thinkin' you don't mean it, or they git scared too long and don't git no work done."

"Lithian strung him up by the heels with his laigs spread apart far as they'd go. He whupped him once with a snake, busted right through his back. I pushed him away, and used the cowhide strap. Worked real fine, but when I turn my back, Lithian picked up a club he'd had the ca'penter make an' he struck down agin' on Hong Kong's balls. Sure busted him up like to die. Walkin' round now . . . but he sho' ruint. Lithian shot me too . . . nothin' much. Jes' a stiff arm for a couple of days. I busted him best I could and not kill him."

Jonathan said, "Next time I meet him, I'll kill him on the spot. You did everythin' real fine, son. Proud of you. How's you mama takin' it—and, fo' God's sake, don't tell her 'bout you bein' shot."

"Not likely. She fuss too much. Mama likes the house fine, but she cry her heart out she see the bedroom just like her own back No'th."

Jonathan grinned. "She sobbin' too much you jest go up there an' tell her you been screwin' that fancy wench and you'll see how quick her cryin' stops. A wonderful woman. Pain in my ass, but a wonderful woman."

"You went cattin' 'round Norfolk?"

"Now how'd you know that?"

"Mama said you was very busy."

"Figgered it fo' youse'f, did you? Well, maybe I catted some. They's a fat one . . . had her when we came through. Dreens a man proper, she does. Reckon I better wash up an' get ready for . . . supper, is it?"

"Reckon that's whut'll be. Want me to see the coffle gets bedded down?"

"You do that. Prime stock, I got. Cost a fortune, but slaves is runnin' into big money these days. By the time we got our crop of suckers grown, they be worth three times as much. Whut you aimin' to do with Hong Kong?"

"Got to keep him, papa. Won't bring more'n three, four hundrud on the vendue table. Nobody wants a buck with no balls. He's a good worker an' smart too. Best we keep him."

"Put his wench to one of the new bucks," Jonathan ordered callously. "No sense wastin' her time with a man who ain't got balls."

"Sho, papa, soon's I git to it."

Fitz didn't plan to get to it for quite some time.

Sarah, seated in state at the foot of the long dining table, seemed to enjoy being served by two maids and helped by Nina. The food was even better than she'd anticipated during her brief tour of the kitchen. Her conversation was mainly about Boston, but when she realized there wasn't much interest forthcoming from either her husband or her son, she switched to Nina.

"I shall make her my personal maid, after all. She's very clean and intelligent. I can tell you those we brought here from Norfolk were not too sweet smelling."

"They was musky," Jonathan admitted. "All niggers musky, Sarah. Cain't he'p it, cain't do much 'bout it 'cept wash. But that don't mean it makes 'em stink any better, 'cause they cain't he'p it."

"Nina has no odor," Sarah insisted. "I don't believe she's an African anyway. There certainly must be a difference between a black African right out of the jungles and this girl whose father was a prince or emir, or something, and her mother a princess."

Jonathan shot his son a swift glance of appreciation. "She shorely ain't," he agreed. "Plenty human blood in her, there is."

"Human blood?" Sarah asked in surprise and anguish. "Don't you consider that these others . . . these slaves . . . have human blood?"

"They got one drop nigger blood they ain't human, Sarah. Eve'body 'grees to that. Doctors an' lawyers, an' 'specially plantation owners."

"Jonathan, that's the most atrocious thing I ever heard you say."

"They gits sick," he said, giving her the most reasonable backing for his argument he knew, "you call a white man's doctor, he don' know how to treat 'em. We got to call the veterinary 'cause he knows they animals and not human, so he knows how to treat 'em. Works that way ever' time." He wanted to get off the subject quickly. "Tomorrow mornin', Sarah, we take the coffle we jest brought in. We line 'em all up and match the bucks to the wenches. Figure maybe you like to see how we match 'em up."

"It sounds ridiculous to me, though I admit I don't quite know what you mean, Jonathan. However, I'll be glad to watch. I do declare, these are the best melon pickles I ever tasted. When and where do the servants eat?"

"Whar?" Jonathan looked up in surprise. "Kitchen, back porch, any goddamn place but near us."

"Are they given the same food we eat?"

"Sho' they are."

"Jonathan, don't lie to me. I didn't see any extra food being cooked in the kitchen."

"But Sarah, whut in hell you talkin' 'bout? They gits whut we leaves. They scrapes our plates—don't eat off'n 'em. You ketch a nigger eatin' off'n our plates, you send him to the whuppin' shed right quick and then you bust that dish to pieces."

"Savages," Sarah said bitterly.

Jonathan thought she meant the slaves. "That's jes' 'bout right, Sarah."

She concluded her meal abruptly when Calcutta slothed his way into the dining room with the bottle of rum and a pitcher of cold spring water. As she departed rather indignantly, summoning Nina to follow her, Jonathan pushed back his chair and delivered a well-placed kick to Calcutta's slow moving rump. He let out a screech of surprise and pain and scooted for the kitchen.

"I goin' to set him out in the fields, he don't wake up some," Jonathan told Fitz. "Mighty glad your mama likes it here. She didn't, would be a hell of a thing."

"Way she talked didn't seem to me she liked it, papa."

"Thass jes' her way. Findin' fault like breathin' to her. Soon's she gits used to the niggers, she'll change her mind. Figgered she'd bust up more'n she did."

"Well, kinda surprised me too."

" 'Member this, son, ain't no better woman than Sarah. Might be she don't show it, an' maybe I don't neither, but we in love. We always been in love. She don' spread her laigs easy, but that don't make no diff'rence long's I got me a wench to pleasure." He mixed his drink, sipped it. "Goddamn water ain't cold 'nuff." He shouted, "Calcutta, c'mere yo' black bastahd, an' fetch some cold water. You slips agin, you git whupped. Means it."

"Yassuh, massa, suh. I git mo'. I gits it real cold. Yassuh, but don' whup me, massa. I on'y po' nigger don' know much. Don' whup me."

"I said next time," Jonathan reminded him. "Up to you there is a nex' time. Git!"

Jonathan and Fitz, armed with cold drinks, went out to sit on the porch, but after awhile, the mosquitoes got too thick and they were forced inside again. Jonathan yawned. "Gittin' too goddamn old for them long journeys.

We needin' hosses to start our stables, you goin' to go git 'em. Tell you whut to look for and how not to git cheated. Ain't no worse man for skinnin' a buyer'n them hoss dealers. Ruther deal with a slave trader any day. I goin' to bed. Been many a month since I slep' with Sarah. Cain't leave her up there apantin' for me. Goodnight, son."

Jonathan climbed the stairs wearily. It was true, he did feel older, but perhaps he lacked his usual spryness because of the fact that he knew very well what reaction his bedding down with Sarah would be. He found her chattering to Nina, who listened without too much comprehension.

"Jonathan," she said, "I'm going to teach this girl to read and write as well as I. She's very smart. I like her."

"Sarah," he said, knowing she wouldn't understand, "we don't teach niggers anythin' like school learnin'. Makes 'em kinda rebellious sometimes, they git to know too much. Better leave 'em dumb like they is. Cain't pound much sense in 'em anyway. Can't learn, lessen you stand over 'em all the time and even then they gits slothful."

"Nina is different, Jonathan. I am taking her in full charge."

Sarah had her hair down over her shoulders. There were a few added gray streaks in it, but she still looked youthful and tempting to Jonathan who hadn't known her embraces in more than two years. Her thin dressing gown barely concealed the curve of her creamy-skinned breasts and he noted that the nipples stood out hard and clear which was sometimes an indication that she too had her mind on carnal enjoyment. Though not always. In fact, not even often.

Jonathan removed his coat, sat on the edge of the bed and took off his shoes. Nina, in an attempt to help each, was rushing about in what seemed to be an aimless manner but actually was a most precise one.

Jonathan hauled off his stockings and rubbed his feet. He looked up at Sarah's back. "Got us'n four bathin' tubs comin'. Be here in a month or two. Cost twenty-seven-fifty each. Ain't nothin' like 'em in the whole goddamn state."

"I'm grateful for the bathing tubs," Sarah said, "but must you curse everything, Jonathan?"

She turned about to emphasize her words and gave a scream. Jonathan, who had removed his shirt and pants and stood there in his underwear, stared at her in complete wonder as to what the scream was about.

She enlightened him. "Jonathan, do you realize we have an innocent girl in this room? Are you insane, disrobing in front of her? Have you no sense of decency?"

Jonathan glanced at Nina, who was showing no interest in his thin body encased in the underwear, which covered him anyway. But looking at her, he began to feel his penis harden. Should Sarah see that, everything would bust loose. He moved quickly to the adjoining bathroom where he washed up and muttered a few indelicate phrases about the habits and the motives of women, especially those from Boston.

Sarah sent Nina away before Jonathan came back into the room, his tumescence conquered. He crawled into bed and propper himself up.

"Been a long time I slep' with you, Sarah. Kinda been lookin' forward to it. Don't blame you none not wantin' to in the hotels and the inns. Folks all about. . . ."

She carried the single candle to the bedside table, slid under the covers he held for her. She turned her back on him to snuff out the candle and then she lay down in the same position. He pushed his maleness, rampant again, up to her. She snorted something about being too tired. Jonathan sighed, turned over on his back and then sat up with a jerk as Sarah screamed once more. She was the goddamnest screamingest woman he'd ever known.

"Whut's up?" he asked.

"There is someone else in this room, Jonathan. I felt a draft as the door opened and closed and I heard the latch—"

" 'Course they is, Sarah. That'll be Nina. She sleeps on the flo' at the foot of the bed. That's whar all wenches and slaves sleep."

"In our room, on the floor? What kind of madness is this?" She sat up. "Nina, is that you?"

"It's me, mist'iss, ma'am."

"Jonathan, is there a room she may use? I will not have her sleeping on the floor, nor will I have her in this room which I share with you."

Jonathan wondered what she was bashful about and what her conception of sharing a bedroom was, but he called to Nina. "Yo' fetch them blankets you got down to the room side my office. You knows whut I means, Nina?"

"Yes, massa, suh. I knows."

"Then git," he said, and wished he could git with her. He lay back, wondering if he should make another attempt to pester Sarah, now that she was wide awake. He twisted over, reached a hand and curled his fingers around her breast. He squeezed it tentatively. She gave forth with a loud snort that startled him until he realized she was already asleep and snoring.

He lay on his back while his maleness woke up completely. Jonathan quietly lifted the covers, took a great amount of time easing himself out of bed without awakening his wife. He didn't dare put on his clothes. It was a warm night anyway, so he sneaked from the room, padded in bare feet down the stairs and paused at the bottom of them considering a little side visit to Nina, but decided against it. He'd have Fitz and Sarah joining forces to punish him if he raped Nina.

So he went out into the night and got to thinking about the coffle of new wenches he'd brought back today.

There was one—a little on the black side with a trace of brown so he suspected she had some human blood. She also had a neat little figure and she wasn't more than sixteen, all of which removed his objections to a black skin.

He knew where Fitz had housed them for the night, awaiting the morning when they'd be assigned to their bucks and then removed to their new cabins. He opened the barn door and cursed the way it creaked. Inside, the wenches and women were sprawled out, sleeping away the effects of the long journey. He stepped over a dozen of them. Two or three opened their eyes, saw their white master and didn't move. They knew what he was after and most of them hoped to be favored by him. He came upon the one he had in mind. She hadn't awakened. He gave her a sharp kick in the ribs and she sat up, brushing away the sleep.

Jonathan reached down, grasped her hand and yanked her to her feet. He paused beside the shielded candle burning near the door, and inspected her casually, running his hands up and down her legs, baring her breasts and then sniffing of her. Lately it seemed everything had that nigger smell. It lived with him, haunted him.

He dragged her out of the barn and down to the plantation pond, ten feet deep in one spot. She shivered slightly as the night air penetrated her thin dress, despite the fact that the breeze was warm. Jonathan led her to the deep end of the pond and pushed her into the water where she gave a shriek, paddled about and then with a whoop she peeled off her wet dress, splashed water all over her, crawled out and was ready to be raped.

Jonathan, between slapping mosquitoes, considered taking her then and there because his swollen maleness demanded it, but that would be too undignified. He led her to the nearest shed. It was crowded with bucks. He headed for a barn. There, too, part of the coffle was sleeping in packed formation. Still another shed was too crammed with tools. His impatience was getting the better of him and so were the mosquitoes. His thin underwear was little protection.

He didn't dare take her in the house; every damn shed and barn he looked into was either crowded or not suitable. He assumed a dog trot, dragging her along. He came to the cottage-like building with its two doors and considered whether it would be proper to take her in the men's or the women's outhouse. He decided it didn't matter one damn and if he didn't take her pretty quick, there'd be no juice left to take her with. He kicked the door shut and reached for her. It was going to be a bit inconvenient, but it didn't matter. At least he wouldn't have an audience.

Next morning, Jonathan looked with great pride at the coffle now grouped before the porch of the big house. Other slaves were working in the fields, among them twenty-seven pregnant women, the result of the orgy on the deck of the *Wyndward*. Soon now, there'd be many more. The planting of the seed was always promptly reported, for the pregnant women were soon given much lighter work. When their bellies reached noticeable proportions, they were sent to the birthing houses where they had little to do except eat and feed the fetus growing inside them.

Fitz was on the lawn, getting the new slaves into position. Sarah was seated on the porch, and, despite the heat, she was wearing a high-necked, dark blue satin dress. Her hair was concealed by a mob cap of rich lace trimmed with flowers and she manipulated a fan impatiently, her stern features showing open disapproval of the scene before her.

Nina stood directly behind her, impassively watching the slaves being readied for matching. Jonathan had tried to reason with Sarah to let Nina fan her, asserting that's what niggers were for, but Sarah would have none of it. Her one concession to being waited on was to allow the girl to bring a footstool for her to rest her feet on.

Jonathan had his ledgers before him. On each page was the name of the slave and his pedigree, or what was known of it. The day of purchase, the price, the original, and the various masters who'd owned that particular slave were also entered. If a buck's back bore a welt or two from the lash, that was duly noted. If he looked much like a buck whose sexual appetite would be insatiable, and he'd produce many suckers, that too was noted—and underlined.

Jonathan was ready now to give the bucks new names, all of them from ports or cities around the world. The wenches would adopt the names of ships, though Jonathan was beginning to run out of them and was beginning to consider such names as Santa Maria Two. The most important listing, however, was the name of the wench whom a certain buck would cover. Jonathan was breeding slaves. He knew little and cared less about the various African tribes from whom the blacks were kidnapped. It was his theory that no matter which tribe, it was the individual who was more important. Therefore, a big buck, heavily hung, and a sturdy wench, would produce strong and fast-growing suckers. Smaller bucks and frailer wenches would produce in their kind and these suckers would be no less valuable because the smaller slaves were trained for work in the house where strength wasn't so vital.

"We-all's ready now?" Jonathan shouted. "I'm callin' buck name of Julius, wench name of Matilda."

The tall, glossy-looking buck came forward eagerly and he grinned widely in appreciation of the heavyset wench who came out of the ranks to join him.

Jonathan's pencil made marks on the page. "Julius, your name now be Rangoon. Matilda, you now Enterprise. Make this heah plantation lots of big bucks and pretty wenches and a silver dollah for every wench, two silvah dollahs for every buck. Five if they twins. You gits your pick of any new cabin. Blankets, pots an' pans ready fo' you—jes' ask Master Fitz. You craves to cover her now, Rangoon, you craves to be covered, now, Enterprise . . . go do it."

Sarah suddenly came to her feet. "Wait," she cried out. She tapped Jonathan with her fan. "Is it true that you have just mated a man and a woman with the intention of having them breed children?"

"No sense in 'em breedin' cats an' dogs, Sarah. Whut else a man and a woman breed?"

"But they are not married."

Jonathan said, "Whut?" in a voice spilling over with surprise, wonder and outrage.

"I asked you if they are now married, or if they will be married."

"Sarah, fo' Chris' sake, we don't marry niggers. They changes all the time. Maybe this here buck hung heavy, but ain't got much juice in him. Maybe the wench got somethin' wrong and she cain't git pregnant. Then we switches 'em 'til we got a pair who'll produce."

"That is inhuman," Sarah said, her black eyes snapping angrily.

"Sarah, how the hell else do we git niggers? We runnin' this heah plantation to breed niggers. They get trained here, and then we sells 'em. Whut you thinkin' a nigger farm does?"

"It was my understanding that you were to grow tobacco—which I do not approve, I can assure you. And you were to breed horses. That I approve of if you do not use them for the purpose of gambling."

"We aimin' to have three money crops," Jonathan explained, for what he thought was the fiftieth time. "We breeds niggers to sell 'em. But it takes niggers to make niggers, so them doin' the producin' they got to have somethin' to do 'sides screwin' the wenches. We got to keep the wenches busy too. So we raise t'bacca, usin' the nigger labor. We goin' to have thoroughbreds pastured pretty soon too. We breeds them an' git's mo' horses. Breedin' hosses and breedin' slaves all the same."

"Jonathan, are you so unintelligent or unfeeling that you believe there is no difference between animals and humans?"

Jonathan scratched his head in bafflement. "Sarah, I know they's a difference. But we talkin' 'bout hosses and niggers."

"Exactly."

"Then what we argyfyin' 'bout? They's all animals."

Sarah shook her head in dismay. "We will never agree on that, Jonathan, but I am going to insist upon one thing. When you pair these people, you will marry them. Otherwise, you are running on a huge scale just . . . well, you know very well what I mean."

"You meanin' whorehouse?"

"I do not care to use that word."

"You wants we should marry up ev'y buck with a wench? Sarah, first place there ain't a preacher fifty miles in any direction. If we bring one in further'n that, he'll want four bits a couple, sides which he won't do it anyway. That'll run to a lot of money, even if he'd do it."

"Jonathan," she said, in her most practical manner, "you are still a ship's captain. No matter that you are not aboard a ship, this is your property and you are master of it. In my opinion, you can marry these people and I insist you do so or I swear I shall not agree to live here one more hour. Had I known you intended to deal in slaves, I'd not have come in the first place."

Jonathan looked completely bewildered and baffled. "You includin' niggers workin' in the fields? Them whut ain't workin' nohow?"

"Every couple on this plantation who are engaged in the breeding of children must be married."

"Whut happens we changes 'em later? Whut happens we sells off maybe fifty-sixty wenches an' they husbands got no wenches to cover 'cause when the new ones come in, them bucks still goin' to be married to the old ones, an' they ain't goin' to be here."

Sarah had the answer to that too. "You are quite likely legally entitled to divorce them."

He faced her, half in anger, half in continued astonishment. "Got us more'n five hundrud bucks an' wenches. If I got to marry up all of them two by two, I be here 'til next Tuesday."

"That isn't necessary," she said. "Let them take their mates, hold hands and then you may conduct a mass marriage ceremony."

"Sarah, they ain't even goin' to unnerstan' whut in hell I doin', sayin' them words over 'em."

"*We* understand, Jonathan, and that's what counts. I'll expect you to have this accomplished before our evening meal. If it isn't, there will be no evening meal. All activity on this plantation will come to a standstill until you do my bidding. If you still refuse, I shall leave."

Jonathan's shoulders sagged. "Fitz, you heah that? Git 'em lined up fast as you can accordin' to the names I call out. Make 'em hol' hands like they was cou'tin', but don't you grab one of them wenches or you might find youse'f married too."

Jonathan went inside to delve into his sea trunk and find the prayer book, worn smooth from use—though not his. It had been in the family for generations. With this in his hand, open at the proper page, he stood atop the porch steps.

The slaves, standing in pairs as Fitz had placed them, looking on without much expression. A few seemed to think it a game of some sort.

Jonathan shouted, "You, Melbourne, take this woman Resolute fo' you wedded wife? You does! Goddamn it, yo' bettah. Resolute, you take this heavy hung buck fo' you wedded husband? You poor black bitch, you don' know what in hell this 'bout. You an' me, we in the same boat. Neither do I. Tripoli . . . whar in hell you at, Tripoli?"

"He there," Fitz pointed, restraining his laughter with considerable effort.

"One looks like 'nother," Jonathan grumbled. "Tripoli, you takes this woman Phoenix fo' you wedded wife?" He sighed and turned to Sarah. "This poor black bastahd don' know one word I sayin'. How he married legal when he don' know whut's goin' on?"

"Nevertheless, Jonathan, get on with it."

Jonathan gave up. By pairs he intoned their names, shortening the service to a few words until he had joined a dozen of them and then he simply held up the roster of slaves in the ledger. "You bucks whut got they names heah, take the wenches got they names heah, fo' you wives. Same 'bout the wenches. I declare all of you man an' wife. Now git busy and produce plenty good suckers and git 'em started fas'."

Jonathan watched Fitz herd them toward the new cabins which had been built by the first of the slaves. Now this new batch would build for the next coffle, until there were enough. Jonathan didn't intend to stop until he had a thousand slaves hard at work in the fields and in their beds.

"You satisfied now?" he demanded of Sarah.

"As soon as you bring in all the other slaves and marry them, yes."

"Sarah, ain't no call to stop them wukin'."

"I insist, Jonathan."

He knew how obstinate she could be. Jonathan ran down the stairs and called to Fitz. He gave him specific orders that made Fitz roar with laughter, slap his thighs and pummel his father on the back until Jonathan cursed him into not exhibiting so much mirth.

"Your mama thinks we don't mean it, no use in goin' through with it. Now you git them goddamn animals in the rear pasture, but keep 'em separated 'til I gives you the word. Don't tarry none, son. We been wastin' 'nuff time now."

Accompanied by two slaves, Fitz set out for one of the bigger barns. He and the slaves disappeared within. Presently one slave came out leading a cow. He opened a gate and placed her in a small pasture. The other slave brought up a bull, and was having trouble handling him. Fitz emerged and waved to his father on the distant porch.

Jonathan said, "Sarah, you comin' 'long now? Thinkin' you right 'bout marryin' up the niggers, but you goin' to go that far, figger you kin go all the way."

"I don't understand, Jonathan," she said, but she accompanied him down to the pastures. "I do appreciate what you have done so far, however, and I'm most happy that you agree with me."

They reached a point at the fence separating the two enclosed pastures. Jonathan signaled the slaves who promptly walked the bawling cow and the stampeding bull to where Jonathan and Sarah waited. Jonathan opened the Bible and proceeded to read the marriage ceremony in full. Fitz called back the replies. Jonathan closed the book. The two slaves hurriedly leaped the fence after they let go of the animals. The bull pawed the ground, snorted, chased the cow about, caught up with the girl animal and mounted her.

"They married, Sarah," Jonathan said. "Nothin' wrong now, is they? The bull coverin' the cow. We gits a calf and we gits milk, but it'll all taste better 'cause they married."

Sarah turned and walked briskly back to the house. She climbed the porch stairs, slammed the door behind her, went to her room, slammed that door and then sat in the window from where she could see the pastures. The bull was chasing the cow again. She sighed and gave up.

Jonathan and Fitz clambered onto the fence and sat

there watching the bull assault the exhausted cow. Jonathan fished a battered cheroot from his pocket and chewed on it.

"Reckon," he said, "that'll hold her fo' a spell."

"If it don't, nothin' will, papa."

"Time you was thinkin' of settin' out to buy us some good thoroughbred stock."

"Reckon it is, papa."

"Got me some names. Good breedin' farms, all of 'em, but they's one in Kaintucky, close by the border to shorten the travel for you. It's the Meader Farms an' they got Arabian strains I crave."

"Good blood lines," Fitz admitted. "Kinda far piece to drive 'em."

"How else you gettin' 'em here? We drive niggers that fur. Further sometimes. Hosses made for long drives, you don't push 'em too hard and you gives 'em plenty of time to graze. Means you stop early and start late so they kin be at the grass with dew on it."

"When you want me to start, papa?"

"Soon's you kin."

"Nothin' to stop me now. Tobacco's growin' fine. Don't need tendin' much 'til it ripe."

"Then we got to work fast. Wait for it to rain so the leaves won't be so brittle and harvest it quick-like, an' hang it in the sheds."

"Kinda like to be here for that. Reckon I can make it. What you figger in days to git to the Meader Farm?"

"Traveling on a good hoss, an' alone, maybe twelve days. Longer comin' back. An' you'll have to hire some help. Maybe you lucky, you be back in a month or five weeks. No matter, things under control heah. Your mama's content an' Nina, she takes good care of her."

"I'll pack tonight and get off 'fore sunup. You givin' me gold?"

"No—letters from a bank in Richmond says I got more'n 'nuff money to cover any sale. Buy all the good hosses you kin git. Best if mos' a year old. We ain't racin' them we buys, on'y breedin' 'em. If your mama wants me to marry them up, we'll git out the book agin. Few words don't matter none, she happy."

"Needs a map."

"Git one next town you ride through. Mind your manners, son. Don't object none you bed down with a few gals, but don't let one of 'em snag you. Plenty of time for that yet."

"I be ridin' so hard, no gal's goin' to get a rise outen me, papa. On'y one thing."

"Whut's that?" Jonathan chewed reflectively on the battered cheroot and ejected a stream of tobacco juice at an unwary grasshopper that came to light below them.

"Never did bust up Hong Kong and his wench. He shore got no balls lef', but she say maybe she work him up, she have time. He don't want to leave her anyway. Buck's smart an' willin'. We give his wench to some other buck, Hong Kong, he ain't goin' to put his heart into this heah plantation no more. Not if you whups him."

Jonathan nodded. "Got lots of sense for a young 'un. Reckon you ain't so young no mo'. I leave Hong Kong whar he is."

"An' watch out for Nina. Plenty young bucks watchin' her like she ready."

"Any buck comes near her, I hauls him up and whups him good. They knows it. I tol' 'em."

"I'll tell mama now. I takes the black stallion, you say so. He's strong an' fast and rides easy."

"Take any hoss you wants. Jes' bring back a herd o' likely lookin' stock and we in business, son." He sniffed. "Any bucks 'round heah?"

"Don't see none."

"Kinda gits that musky smell. Knows it's in my mind, but I smells somethin'. Times I smell it in my sleep."

"Don' have no meanin', papa. Shore go away 'fore long."

Fitz slid down off the fence and walked, long-legged and eager, to the house. He was being sent alone to buy horses. There was no greater indication that his father now considered him a man. From now on, he'd walk proudly. He wished there had been some way he could have told his father how grateful he was, how lucky. Jonathan would have scoffed and thought him not tough enough should he render all the thanks he felt.

Sarah had a hundred instructions on how he should conduct himself. She'd heard the Kentucky families were highly social-minded and far above the people who tolerated tobacco-raising and slave-breeding plantations.

He found it most difficult to break the news to Nina and made up his mind the best way to do so was treat her as a nigger and let it go at that. Even better, tell her nothing. After all, why should he?

Chapter Six

HE SLEPT fitfully that night, and fought off an urge to visit Nina, who now slept in the big bedroom downstairs. Long before dawn he crept into the kitchen and kicked Calcutta awake.

"Git your black hide down to the stable an' tell Marseilles to saddle up the big black stallion and have him ready in ten minutes."

Calcutta counted on his sleepy fingers. "Stable . . .

Marseilles... black stallion... ten minutes... yassuh, massa, suh."

He stumbled off into the before-dawn darkness. Fitz looked for something he could eat on the way, packed a large portion of baked ham, some drumsticks, biscuits which he first buttered. He wrapped all in a piece of paper, carried it to the porch and let himself out. He walked down the drive toward the road and met Calcutta, and an even more sleepy Marseilles leading the stallion.

There was a little light to see by, but Fitz ran his hands down the horse's legs, stroked his rump, then his mane. He was satisfied the horse was well curried, therefore most likely watered and baited. He tied the sack of food to the saddle, sent Calcutta to the porch to fetch his few spare clothes and essentials. He packed these.

"I be waitin', massa, suh, yo' gits back," Calcutta said, trying to appease Fitz in the event he'd done something wrong.

"You grows grass ten feet long from your ass, you wait," he said.

He vaulted into the saddle, settled himself and realized this was the longest and most important mission he'd ever undertaken. He kicked the horse lightly and cantered down the drive to the road. There he rode on at an easy gait, took the fork to the west and was on the road to Lynchburg. In two days, if nothing went wrong, he'd be there. He looked forward to it for he understood it was a fair to middling big town.

He rode on into the advancing dawn, feeling strong and well, sensing the responsibility thrust upon him. Half an hour later, he missed Nina, but put her out of his mind with thanks to his own wisdom in not letting her see him off. That would have been worse. He knew he must one day give her up, but there was no pleasure in the idea. He was only turned nineteen. Time for a man to start looking for the woman who would bear his children, grace his household and comfort him in his aging years. It might even be that somewhere along this journey, he'd meet such a girl. What would happen between himself and Nina then? He didn't know, and young as he was, found it simple to leave that to future circumstances.

He found Lynchburg not worth more than an overnight stay. There he bought more food to carry him along, and a map showing the route to the Kentucky border. He spoke to few people, told no one of his mission. There were many highwaymen on the roads these days, and if word reached them that a stripling boy was on his way to buy a herd of breeding horses, they'd assume he carried much gold and waylay him.

Fitz tapped the derringer he carried in his hip pocket and felt a little better. He was in a spirited mood to take on half a dozen highwaymen should they care to stop him.

He made Roanoke on the fourth day and knew he was doing well. Here he found an older city, with carefully tended streets, a clean hotel, a fine restaurant and a score of whorehouses which tempted him until he realized he'd waste his money. Riding all day petered a man.

Radford had a small, badly run inn, but he was compelled to stay there over night. On the tenth day he saw the hand-painted sign consisting of a plank of wood nailed to a tree, attesting that he was now passing into the sovereign state of Kentucky.

Some had warned him about the Black Mountains, but he found them anything but formidable because there was a clear and fairly good route through their passes.

On the thirteenth day he stopped his tired horse and looked down onto the green swards of the Cumberland valley. He'd never seen anything as beautiful—except in

Virginia. It had been a relatively uneventful journey, a lonely one too, but it gave him much time to think. To plan and consider how his life was going to be.

He made up his mind that he was too young to marry. That he would hardly do so until after his father and mother were dead. That might be a long, long time, he realized, because they were both healthy. He did amend that decision to consider marrying when his father turned the operation of the plantation entirely over to him. At any rate, it wouldn't be for a long time, so his plans centered mainly on the success of the plantation itself and the possibility of sending his own horses to some of the best racetracks.

It was a wonderful and productive life he looked forward to. If it had to be alone for a long time, he still had Nina, whose body drew from him all the passion he contained.

There was no difficulty in locating the Meader Farm. It was known all over Eastern Kentucky and the first town where Fitz made his initial inquiries set him on the right road to the farm.

He knew it was large and very prosperous, confined solely to the breeding of thoroughbreds which sold for as high as ten thousand dollars, a price that staggered him somewhat until he learned that only once had that figure been paid—for a three-year-old that had won every race she was in.

The household consisted of Elbert Meader, twice a state senator and now being talked of as a future governor. His wife, Shirley, was known for her graciousness and her elaborately formal dinner parties. There was an eighteen-year-old daughter named Benay. Oddly, Fitz couldn't learn much about her and he decided she was probably a buck-tooth, bashful type who never did get around.

The Green County Inn at the county seat was four miles from the Meader Farms and, in Fitz's opinion, a likely place to stay over until the morning when he could arrive at the Meader mansion at a reasonable hour and at least make some sort of an impression by being better dressed and cleaned of all the trail dust and dirt.

He'd heard from enough places along the route through Kentucky, usually in a most casual fashion, that the Meaders were people of great wealth who adhered to all the social graces. They were eminent, influential, and, probably, snobs who could give Bostonians lessons in the art.

Therefore, he turned his horse over to a slave for cooling, watering, a rubdown and feeding. The innkeeper was a corpulent man of about fifty with sideburns that ran down the full length of his face and somehow made him resemble an overgrown monkey, like the ones Fitz had seen in Africa. He was a garrulous man, especially with those who rented his best accommodations, ate his best food and drank his liquor.

There was a room off the main entrance which was supplied with a bar, tables, chairs and a fireplace alive with embers though the weather was far from cold. There were a dozen people about the tables, talking, drinking and arguing. Fitz preferred to lean against the small bar while he drank his bourbon neat.

"So yo' got your eyes set on Meader hosses, have yo'?" the innkeeper said. "Best stock in all Kaintuck'. But they don't come cheap, young fella. 'Bout the most 'spensive hosses they is."

"That's the kind I'm lookin' for," Fitz replied.

"You'all evah meet any o' the Meaders?"

"No, but I heered tell they be uppity sorts with all their fancy balls and dinners an' all."

"One thing ever' goddamn woman in Kaintuck' looks fer all her life is to git invited to the Meader's mansion. They's looked up to, them folks, but whut in goddamn they got to be looked up to, I cain't say."

"Whut's the matter? Don't they pay they bills?"

"Sho' they does. I said they was rich. And friggin' snooty, yo' ask me. Ride in to church ev'y Sunday in they grand carriage. They come walkin' down the aisle like they doin' God a favor. An' Sattiday night they been whorin' and fuckin' like nothin' yo' evah heered tell of."

"Now that don't seem hardly likely," Fitz argued, "they be so rich and so holy."

"Don' know how 'tis in Virginny, but I sho' kin tell yo' how it is in Kaintuck'. Think on it real hard an' yo' cain't blame them none. Not much, leastwise. 'Round here, farms are a day or two apart, yo' want to visit. Folks come an' they stays. When they starts out, they ain't seen nobody in weeks an' when they gits to the Meaders, they ain't seed nobody either. So they all kinda lonely and the young kids kinda horny . . . not havin' been laid in weeks. Don't count the wenches. I talk about screwin' humans."

"Now that's real interestin'," Fitz said. "Open 'nother bottle, my friend."

It was promptly uncorked and the innkeeper accepted a hefty portion of the whiskey, so new it still possessed the tang of the still.

"Bucks'll be bucks, wenches'll be wenches and don't make no difference they human or black."

"Whut you're sayin' is folks visitin' the Meaders are real welcome."

The innkeeper guffawed. "Sho' are. Now I don' say Missus Meader, she spraids for anybody. She so fuggin' high-nosed, don't think she could git her laigs apart. But Sam Meader'll bed down with anybody, any color, any age. Never think so, yo' looks at him."

"Whut about the daughter?"

"Benay . . . that's her name. Kinda crazy one, reckon. Well now, I guess she came in here maybe two-three years ago. She like her mama, snooty and keepin' her laigs crossed, but she got randy cousins and she got uncles who get kinda big 'round the crotch they see even a bitch dog in the heats. Heered tell cousins who fornicate, sometimes gits theyse'ves a two-headed sucker. Don't believe it none. It was true, whole county'd be full of 'em. This here the goddamdest screwin'est county in the world, an' I reckon I done my share."

"He an honest man, this Mistah Meader?" Fitz asked. He was far more interested in that than Meader's sexual prowess.

"Cain't say nothin' agin him that way. Keeps his word, pays his bills an' don't reckon he stabs any of his friends in the back. Likes him, on'y one of the whole crew I do. Like to show my nuts to the gal, but reckon she used to so many, mine wouldn't in'trest her."

Three young men had tied up their horses outside and now invaded the inn. They were about Fitz's age, well-dressed, soft-handed and soft-bellied. They swaggered and strutted as they pulled back chairs and sat down, with a loud hail to the innkeeper.

"See the one in the middle?" the innkeeper said. "That be Gerald Allen, cousin to the gal Benay. Horny bastahd. Cain't keep his hands off'n any gal."

Gerald Allen was not as tall as Fitz but stockier. He had raven-black hair, combed straight back. His eyes were dark brown, his jawline square, but still there was a softness about him. The other two were so much like him they could have been brothers. Fitz doubted any of them had done a lick of work in their lives.

"Them two buckaroos with him are Edwin Buford an' Cort Putnam. They both no damn good. Folks rich like the Meaders. Not as much, but rich."

"Goddamn yo' hide," Gerald Allen called. "Does we git service or don't we?"

"They gits service down they goddamn necks they ain't keerful," the innkeeper said. He picked up a damp towel and went to the table where the three youths sat. He ran the rag around the table top and took their order for corn liquor. Fitz studied them intently, seeing in them what he himself some day would like to be. They had poise, they talked animatedly and they seemed to be well-educated. Their clothing showed better taste than Fitz recently possessed, and no doubt they were easier around girls.

Fitz signaled the innkeeper to give him a full bottle of bourbon. He carried this over to the table and set it down.

"My compliments, gentlemen," he said. "I'm Fitzjohn Turner from Virginny an' I craves to sit down with you-all."

The three acted as if they were astounded, but Gerald Allen suddenly smiled and covertly winked at his companions. "Sit, friend. Mighty glad for your comp'ny. Ain't every day we gits us a drinkin' fren' who stinks of his hoss."

Fitz felt his face color a bit, but he decided to stick it out. He uncorked the bottle and poured the drinks. As he poured his own last, Gerald jiggled his elbow so the whiskey spilled on the table.

"You-all nervous?" Gerald asked. "Or ain't you-all steady in the comp'ny of your betters?"

"Kinda think that's it." Fitz retained his temper. "Got me a reason for askin' your permission to sit. Lookin' for the Meader Farms an' I reckon young gen'mun like you, sho' knows where it's at."

"They don't hire white boys," Gerald said.

"Lessen' we makin' a big mistake an' you got nigger blood," Edwin Buford said.

The third man joined in the fun of teasing the stranger. "Caint always tell. A mustee sho' looks white 'nuff, an' you waits to heah him talk 'fore yo' know he's niggah. You niggah, boy?"

Fitz grinned and drank his whiskey. He poured another glass. Gerald shoved his now empty glass for a refill. Fitz topped it, but when Gerald reached for it, Fitz nudged it to one side and then held it over the edge of the table and spilled the contents on the floor. He corked the bottle, arose and returned to the bar.

"Reckon you got plenty niggah blood in yo'," Gerald called out loudly. "Leastwise yo' got the manners of a nigger."

"Takes nigger blood to recognize it," Fitz said calmly.

Gerald leaped to his feet and came forward with long strides that slowed perceptibly as he neared this young giant who regarded him with considerable humor evident on his face.

"By God," he said, "I got me a mind to make yo' eat them words."

"Why sho'," Fitz said, "glad to obleege. Anytime, suh, and right now's a fine time, I reckon."

Gerald backed off. "Don' yo' lay yo' hands on me, nigger. You got nigger blood. You ain't denied it. You lay yo' hands on me an' I see yo' whupped at the post in the square."

"I got nigger blood in me, I lets you whup me 'til I peeled. Reckon we bettah go outside so's we don' wreck this gen'mun's place of business."

Gerald backed away. "I wouldn't dirty my hands on yo', suh. Wouldn't desiah to punish yo', suh, yo' bein' ignorant and mighty crude. Don' know no bettah, reckons."

Fitz was sorely tempted to throw him across the room, a feat he was perfectly capable of, but this man was related to the Meaders and there was little sense in antagonizing the man from whom he wished to buy blooded horses. Fitz decided to let it go. He turned around and attended to his drinking. Gerald hooted, his friends laughed loudly, but none of them approached Fitz. Which was just as well. He couldn't have withstood much more.

He did realize, with considerable satisfaction, that his way of life was certainly better than theirs. It never occurred to Fitz, nor his father, to insult anyone. These three young bucks were courting trouble and they'd get it from Fitz, in the event he discovered that Sam Meader would refuse to do business with him.

The innkeeper joined him. "Yo' evah see sunabitches like them befo', suh? Here yo' are, mindin' yo' own business, wantin' to ask a civil question, buyin' them a whole bottle o' corn—yo' owes me for two now, suh—and then gettin' yo' se'f insulted like that. Figgers you cain't be a fightin' man."

"Don't fight them related to someone I want to do business with," Fitz said. "Mr. Meader race many of his hosses?"

"Sam Meader drinks all the corn he kin hold, he wenches 'roun' and 'til ten years ago no gal was safe. He horny as a man kin git, and havin' all that money, he take whut he wants. Settled down some now an' he don't believe in gamblin'. Won't sell a hoss to folks who mean to race 'em. Won't race none hisse'f and he got some o' the bes' hossflesh up there yo' evah did see. Plenty hoss racin' in Kaintuck', but not with any o' Sam Meader's critters."

Fitz yawned. "Reckon I bettah git some rest. Rode more'n twenty-five miles today. Please to sen' up hot water. Lots of it. Fo' breakfuss anythin' you got."

He settled for the two bottles of corn, left one half full, carried the other to his room. There he drank some of it while slaves carried up large vats of steaming water to fill the tub. Fitz climbed in and luxuriated in it while the stiffness from riding left him. He was disappointed, however. He'd been hoping that he might meet someone his own age whom he might cotton to and become friendly with, but if those three bucks were an example of what Kentucky turned out, Fitz would be glad to get back to Virginia.

He slept well, long and hard, to awaken refreshed and ready for his first visit to Meader Farms. He dressed very carefully, having had his clothes pressed as soon as he'd arrived. He knew very well that his dark gray trousers fitted him with the tightness demanded of the day's fashions. His burnt orange frock coat was the work of a fine tailor and his ruffled shirt came from Boston where men's fashions were often made. His boots were highly polished, his top hat of dove gray satin.

In the dining room, the innkeeper whistled sharply at the sight of him. "Mist' Turnah, suh, reckon you mo' gent'mun than them three bucks. That's whut they weahs in Virginny?"

"Mostly in Boston and New York," Fitz said. "I'm eatin' fast this mornin'. Wants to git out to the farm, so have my hoss saddled and ready."

"Yes, suh, I will. After yo' lef' last night, Gerald Allen asked me questions 'bout you, suh."

"Anythin' I told you was fine to tell him," Fitz said. "Reckon he kinda laughed some you told him my papa and me was in the slave breedin' business."

"Folks hereabouts—them like the Meaders—they don't much 'spect slave traders or breeders. Buy they stock, dickers with 'em, cheats 'em they think they git away with it, but they have no truck with 'em."

"The po' slave traders and breeders," Fitz grinned. "Whut you want to bet Sam Meader be glad to do business with me?"

"You got plenty of gold, he'll do business. Money makes men like him kinda fergit the man he deals with ain't no blue-blooded gen'mun. I wish you good luck, suh."

Fitz settled his bill, found his horse ready and he rode out of town down the road to which he had been directed. It was an easy ride to the Meader Farms and he was properly impressed when he arrived. The mansion was bigger than his father's, the estate around it had far more shrubs and trees, but the grass wasn't as green or thick. The drive leading from the road to the house was dirty and dusty. Meader could have learned a few things about a house and estate by spending a little time at Wyndward.

There were two slaves, both young wenches, in a section of a garden where a white girl in a wide-brimmed hat bent over the flower bed. The hat obscured her face. Gerald Allen lolled on the ground nearby, watching Fitz's approach, his face devoid of expression. Once he said something to the girl and she looked up, but quickly lowered her head again. Fitz pulled up and dismounted. He removed his hat and bowed ceremoniously.

"Ma'am, I lookin' for Mistah Sam Meader. If you will kin'ly direct me. . . ."

She raised her head now and Fitz looked into the bluest eyes he'd ever seen in all the world. Below the hat were strands of blond hair plastered against a perspiration-moistened brow. She had an even, lovely mouth and a small nose, a firm chin. She was the loveliest creature Fitz had ever met.

"One of the servants will guide you, suh," she said.

Gerald spoke up. "Bettuh find out yo' papa want to see him, Benay. This here man and his papa be slave breeders an' traders."

"We won't want any slaves, suh," she said. "We got plenty, and if we need more, we get them from New Orleans."

"I'm buying, not sellin'," Fitz said. "Not slaves either. I come to look over your papa's hosses."

Gerald laughed. "I suppose you think you can afford a dozen or so?"

"Aimin' to buy me fifty, maybe more," Fitz said gently. "Please, ma'am, if you will kin'ly ask your servant . . . ?"

"Amanda, take him to Mistah Meader right now, y'heah?"

One of the slaves came forward promptly and began walking in the direction of the house. Fitz bowed before the girl again. "My respects, ma'am." As he turned away, he kicked Gerald's ankle and immediately and profusely apologized while Gerald grasped at the aching member and massaged it.

"Clumsy idiot," he said.

Fitz nodded. "Reckon I am, suh. Always fallin' over somebody's feet."

He followed the maid, not looking back. Benay Meader watched him until he entered the house.

"Interesting man," she said. "Handsome too."

"Cousin Benay, he's nothin' but a dirty slave breeder and talkin' crazy talk 'bout buying fifty hosses. I calls him trash, Cousin Benay. Plain trash."

She nodded slowly. "That he may be, Cousin Gerald, but he a handsome buck. I intend to invite him to stay for dinner."

Gerald jumped to his feet. "Cousin Benay, yo' mama will skin yo' alive. A slave breeder at her table? You crazy?"

"They tell me I am sometimes," she admitted. "But I nevah saw a man who bothered me so much."

"Git him outen yo' haid. He cain't even speak nice, and he's got no manners and he don' know the difference between a gen'mun an' white trash. Yo' pa send him out in ten minutes anyway."

At that moment Fitz stood before the desk behind which Sam Meader sat. He was a ponderous man with hanging jowls, helped none by a sagging neck. His eyes were bulbous enough to indicate some bad sickness and his face was flushed red.

He hadn't invited Fitz to sit down. "Now, son, this heah's a big farm. We sells our animals four-five at a time. I gits from five hundrud to five thousand. . . ."

"Wants fifty, they good-blooded," Fitz said casually.

Sam Meader's aplomb was crushed. "Fifty—whut yo' talkin', son? Yo' got that kin' money?"

Fitz presented the letter from the bank. Sam Meader stared at it and gasped. "This says yo' an' yo' pappy got a million and a half dollahs in the bank?"

"Got that much an' more in a Boston bank too," Fitz said casually. "Reckon you want to sell me fifty hosses, suh?"

"Reckon," Sam Meader said slowly. "Shore reckon."

He got up and walked out of the room. Fitz heard him bawling for someone named Faustine. When she answered, it was in a low, cultured voice, partly natural, mostly cultivated, and he realized Faustine was Sam's wife. That meant she was the girl's mother. Fitz would be on his very best behavior.

At the foot of the stairs, Sam Meader dropped his voice to a whisper. "Young buck in there lookin' to buy fifty thoroughbreds."

"He crazy, Samuel? You never sold fifty horses at one time . . ."

"Faustine, he got a bank letter says he and his papa got a million and a half in Richmond and he say more'n that in Boston. Now we ain't turnin' 'way that kin' money. He ain't as much a gen'mun as Gerald or some of Benay's other fren's, but with that lettah, he got bettah manners'n any man in Kentucky. I wants you to invite him to stay fo' dinner and fo' the night. Long as he wants. Million and half . . . three million . . . you evah hear so much money?"

"I shall invite him," she said, "but I shall probably be sickened by his lack of manners. I refuse to lower either my dignity or the rules of my household for him."

"Damn yo' rules of the house. Man's got all that money, he makes the rules. Now yo' jine me, Faustine. Yo' make that boy jump when they's no need, I ain't goin' to stand fo' it. Don't care if he eats with his feet."

She flounced away from him, but she went into the other room and presented herself before Fitz who promptly arose and gave her a courtly bow.

"Miz Meader, ma'am. Your servant."

"How did you know me, suh?"

"I had me a look at this house, I met your husband

and I knows right off you jes' got to be Miz Meader. Takes an uncommon woman to run a house like this, an' an uncommon lookin' one to grace it."

Faustine lowered the icicle slightly. "Thank you, suh. I have learned that you desire to buy some of my husband's horses, so large a number of them that you will need considerable time to inspect them. Therefore, I shall be honored by your presence at our dinner table and I would be happy if you could manage to spend the night."

"The honor is mine, ma'am," he bowed again.

"Good. My husband will take you out to the stables. . . ."

Fitz said, "Reckon I kin find them, ma'am. Likes to look 'round some. Admires you farm, I do."

"As you wish," she said. "The farm and the house are yours, suh."

Fitz didn't wait for Sam Meader to get back. Undoubtedly he was changing clothes for a long spell of work and inspection in the stables. Fitz wanted to see them without Meader's help and, if possible, talk to some of the people working there. Especially if there was a smart slave or two. He could learn much from them and he wanted to know all about the horses—and he wanted to learn what he could about that girl with the saucy eyes, the somewhat bold manner, and the beautiful face.

As he made his way across the grounds toward the farmland and the extensive stables, he saw the girl still at work in the flower garden, but she didn't look up. Gerald did and came to his feet quickly, showing his amazement at the audacity of Fitz heading alone for the stables.

A score of slaves were working hard rubbing down horses, currying them, a few were being cooled. Apparently, they were exercised at the small track nearby rather early in the morning. Fitz sauntered along. Some of the slaves raised their heads to see who this stranger was, but most kept their heads down as they were supposed to.

Everything was spotless. There was no sour odor of unwashed horses or dirty stalls. This portended the same fine care which would be extended to the animals. Fitz was attracted by one jet stallion, nervously twitching while a slave held him. Two others were running brushes across his haunches. Fitz had never seen such a brutally big and beautiful animal. Two or three years old, he judged, and he'd likely be the sire of many a fine racing horse.

The animal, restless enough with these slaves whom he knew, promptly raised his forelegs and reared back to lash out at this stranger who approached so confidently. Fitz scampered out of the way of those powerful legs and shod hoofs. The animal's breath whistled through its nostrils in anger at this intrusion, and it continued to kick and attempted to bite while the slaves let go and dodged out of the way.

Fitz considered going in and trying to hold the horse down, but before he could do so, a tall, muscular buck dashed out of a stall and made a dive for the black stallion. He seized him, held his head down, spoke soothingly and caressed his head with a tenderness he might have used on a woman. In moments, he had the stallion quieted. Two of the other slaves led the horse to its stall. The big buck started to turn away.

"Jes' a minute," Fitz called out.

The black turned and scrutinized Fitz. The dark eyes held a look of quiet insolence, but his tone was polite as he said, "Yassa, massa, suh."

"I liked the way you handled that hoss. Whut your name?"

"Themba, massa, suh."

"Skittish hoss, ain't he?"

"Nevah been gentled, massa, suh. Ain't nobody could gentle him."

"I could," Fitz said, and he saw the frown of worry on the slave's face. "An' I don' mean with a whip or spurs. Ain't no hoss won't respond to kin'ness, Themba. Reckon you know that as well as me."

"Yassa, massa, suh." He began to turn away.

"Come back here," Fitz said sharply, and the slave turned about once more and stood there, his eyes even with Fitz's. This was no ordinary nigger, Fitz could see. He was as black as he could be, but his features were finely wrought. The nose was thin, not flattened. The forehead was high, the hair straight and not woolly. His mouth was sensitive-looking and his eyes were filled with an intelligence no slave should exhibit, but this one wouldn't have been able to hide it.

"Yassuh, massa, suh."

"I'm heah to buy fifty-sixty thoroughbreds. Wants to know the best of the lot and I reckon you know 'em better'n Mistah Meader."

"Please don' ask me that, suh. Massa Meader he doan like it nohow, a slave talk up his hosses."

"All right, Themba," Fitz said understandingly. "You in charge of the stables?"

"Yassuh, massa, suh."

"Likes it 'round heah?"

"Yassuh. Likes it real good, I does."

"Likes the hosses too, don't you?"

"Reckon I likes hosses better'n anythin' in this worl', massa."

"Reckon you'd like to see these hosses you raise run in a race."

The black nodded eagerly, forgetting himself again. "Massa, I do raise hosses beat anythin' in Richmond or e'en N'O'leans. Teaches 'em on that track, suh, and they runs fo' me like they runs fo' nobody else, suh."

"I can see why they would, Themba."

"See, massah, suh? Cain't see nothin' like that, reckons."

"Themba, you likes hosses much as you do, hosses goin' to like you and run they haids off for you. Now ain't that right?"

Themba grinned, another serious infraction. He was beside himself with a rarely expressed enthusiasm. "Sho' is, suh. Reckons yo' knows hosses too, suh."

"Some, Themba. Not as well as you. Do you know who I am?"

"Yassah, massa, suh. Yo' the man f'om Virginny."

"That's right. My papa an' me we run a t'bacca and slave breedin' farm an' we set our min's to breedin' hosses too. But we goin' to race 'em, Themba. That's why I got to get me only the best."

"Sho' would like to wuk on a farm like . . ." he stopped and his face turned icy while his eyes glowed with hatred. "Reckon I gits on with my wuk."

"You can leave when I give you permission to leave, you black imp. You likes it, papa and me raise hosses to race, but you don't like it we breed slaves like you. Ain't any your goddamn business whut we raise an' you got no call to git yourse'f all stirred up. Now I wants you to walk with me and point out the best hosses. I'm buyin' an' I don't care none whut they costs, long's I git good stock. Git, now, show me every goddamn hoss in these stables."

"Yassuh, massa, suh." Some of the hatred went out of his eyes, though his face remained stern.

He began exhibiting the horses, ordering the boys to bring them out, sometimes to walk them. A two-year-old filly was brought to the track and raced for Fitz's pleasure. By now Sam Meader had joined him and after a while Benay Meader sauntered up, obviously prepared to flirt outrageously with him. But he gave her the barest nod and turned his attention back to the animals. Benay, completely ignored, pouted childishly.

"Well, suh," Meader asked unctuously, "whut do you-all think of my animals, suh?"

"Likes 'em, suh. 'Bout ready to dicker."

Meader was delighted. "I can assuah yo', Mistah Turnah, yo' won't find any hoss you buys from me blemished in any way. Breeds 'em and raises 'em right."

"That slave Themba mighty good with hosses."

"He's half hoss hisse'f, suh. Times I thinks he talks to 'em, but he's an uppity black. Cain't handle him easy. Whupped him two-three times, does no good, on'y marks him up, so's he's harder to sell I wants to rid myse'f of him, which I think about plenty."

"Shame to let him go, he so knowin'," Fitz said.

"Papa," Benay thought it time to begin her small campaign. "Papa, you goin' to sell Lily?" She turned her lovely, cool and openly appraising eyes on Fitz. "Lily's my own precious mare, suh."

"My daughter, suh," Meader said.

Fitz bowed. "Wouldn't think of deprivin' you, ma'am. Don't worry none 'bout it."

"I thank you most respectfully, suh." She curtsied slightly.

Fitz turned away from her. It required an effort, but he managed. "Mistah Meader, suh, whut about that black stallion? One with all that dander?"

"Finest hossflesh on this farm," Meader assured him, "but uncontrollable. Absolutely uncontrollable. Bashed in the haids o' two o' my slaves. Tol' 'em to be keerful that hoss, but they got no sense an' they got they haids busted open like a pumpkin. Ain't nobody kin tame that beast."

"I'll buy him," Fitz said, " 'long with the other'ns or separate. Likes that animal."

Meader was figuring what fifty or sixty of his horses would bring and the amount was astronomical in relation to ordinary sales. He could jack up the prices considerably with this boy, who was so naive. Therefore, Meader thought he could make a grand gesture, instilling into the boy a sample of the Meader Farms generosity which might help to conceal its greed.

"Son," Meader said, "I make yo' a present of that hoss. No price will be quoted, suh, not one penny accepted. From here on that animal is your'n, even if you don't buy a goddamn hoss at all."

"Well, thank you, suh," Fitz bowed. "That's right generous. Now we start pickin' 'em out. Goin' to be a hard job, suh. They's all fine animals."

So they toured the stables, examining each horse. Meader brought with him a ledger containing the pedigrees. They talked prices, and Meader found this young man could drive a hard bargain. He almost rued the fact that he'd given him the black killer horse. He'd intended to try and put him to stud, though he'd likely kill the mare in the process and, if it didn't work out, shoot him.

Benay, completely disregarded, had left them long before, but though she didn't know it, Fitz had watched her graceful retreat, the sway which made the triple flounce at the hem of her skirt dance prettily, adding to the femininity of her hips. In his mind, he'd rather well undressed her and was sure beneath those clothes he'd find a lithe, shapely miss who could probably charm him out of his wits.

Meader led him back to the house and into the office. Benay managed to reach the spinet in the ballroom before they entered and she was playing softly, strictly for Fitz's benefit. He walked on by as if the musical instrument made no sound.

Gerald, who slouched in a chair listening to her play, growled an oath. "That lout wasn't doin' business with yo' papa, I'd beat his ears off just to teach him how to be polite."

"Cousin Gerald," she said, "you-all couldn't beat the ears off'n a butterfly. Stop you damn braggin'."

"One thing you admit, I'd be better in baid than him.

Bet you gits him in baid, he don't even know whut to do."

"That mighty fresh talk foah a gentleman," Benay said sharply.

"Whut's eatin' yo', Cousin Benay? Yo' knows how much yo' like the way I lay you. Seems to me yo' cain't git enough. Wears me out so I don't wonder I cain't beat the ears off'n a butterfly."

She gave a rebellious toss of her head and headed for the door. As she passed, he reached out to make a grab at her thigh. She angrily punched at his hand, making him wince.

It was time for dinner by the time Fitz and Meader finished with the papers transferring sixty-six horses with their pedigrees over to Wyndward Plantation. The sixty-sixth was gratis, the black killer horse. Fitz made out the bank draft for one hundred and sixty-five thousand dollars. Meader rubbed his hands, unable to conceal his enthusiasm for the deal.

"Near bought me out, suh," he chortled. "But I gets me mo'. Yo' papa in need of mo' breed hosses, yo' send fo' me, suh. Pleasure to do business with you-all. For a young man, yo' mighty good shakin' a man's price down."

Fitz didn't believe he'd shaken the price down at all. Each figure had been so inflated that he merely had to suggest what the more evident value was and Meader readily agreed. It was, however, a highly profitable deal on both sides. Fitz was sure his father would approve every horse.

Fitz went to his room on the second floor and found a tub of hot water waiting. He climbed into it after he shaved. A body slave, not more than fourteen, came rushing into the room.

"I comin' fas', massah, suh." He gasped for breath. "Fo'gits to tell me they does, I got me a mastah heah. Does the bes' I kin fer yo', massa. Ummm . . . um . . .

them fancy clo's, suh. Nevah seed anythin' like that befo'."

"Shut your black mouth," Fitz thundered severely. "If I want you talkin', I say so."

"Yassah . . . yassah . . . I's sorry, suh."

"Whut you standin' there for? Git to work on them shoes or I'll put 'em on an' warm your ass for you."

The boy grinned and fell to work. The clothes closet contained a shine kit consisting of a whitish oil, some sooty-looking paste and several flannel rags. Whatever the stuff consisted of, it did raise a high polish.

"That's better," Fitz said. He had his pants on, his shirt was properly tight. He sat down and stuck out his legs. "Now put 'em on."

The boy knelt and shoved a shoe onto Fitz's bare foot. Fitz pulled his leg back and kicked him on the shoulder. "Whut's the matter with you? Cain't you see I ain't got my stockings on? Now you puts 'em on, real straight too."

The boy nodded wildly, took the stockings from the dresser, knelt again and hauled them on. Then he pulled the shoes on, spit lightly on each and rubbed the surface some more with his hands.

He stood by watching with vast interest while Fitz arranged his starched cravat. Then he held the coat which Fitz's father had called splendiferous, brushed off his shoulders industriously, raced to hold the door open. Fitz sat down.

"I ready to go, I tell you to open the do'. You knows a slave named Themba?"

"Yassah, massa, suh. I knows Themba I does."

"He got hisse'f a wench?"

"Don' wench none, suh. Massa Meader, he give Themba wenches, but he don' pester 'em nohow. On'y likes hosses, not folks, suh."

"He a mean boy he wants to be?"

The eyes rolled whitely. "Yassah, massa, suh. He real

mean. Don' care none he kills a man in a fight. Us'n is skeered o' him, we is."

"That big black stallion. He killed two slaves?"

"Yassah, they do be tol' they don' go in his stall, but they go an' he kick they haids off, yassah. We got three crips out'n him too. Busted laigs. He a bad hoss, suh. I hopes they kills him, I does."

"Now open the door," Fitz said.

The boy scampered to obey and he gave Fitz an admiring glance as he passed by. Fitz let his hand rest on the black wool for a moment and then he went on, telling himself again that he shouldn't show them any sympathy or display any feelings at all. It was a dangerous thing to do, but when he looked back at the admiring eyes of the boy, he didn't think he'd done much harm.

Faustine was waiting for him at the foot of the stairs, rather impatiently, he thought, and he wondered why. He couldn't have known that Faustine had taken special pains with her appearance this evening and she'd made, in her mind, a delightful spectacle coming down the curving stairs so grandly, only to find that Fitz wasn't even out of his room yet.

"Your arm, suh," she said, not unkindly, for she was considerably impressed with his clothing. Her experienced eye noted the rolled collar and M-notched lapels of the coat, knew it was expensive and certainly far more up to date than the suits worn by her husband and the three young men invited to dinner.

Fitz bowed, held his arm for her and escorted her into the dining room in as stately a manner as she could have desired. The others were already at the table. Sam Meader rose awkwardly and half-heartedly as his wife was seated.

Benay regarded Fitz with open curiosity and much interest. When he bowed in her direction, she smiled and nodded. Clarissa, Benay's cousin, perhaps a year or two younger than she, dropped her eyes shyly when

Fitz bowed in her direction. She was a pretty girl, though she seemed frail and inordinately bashful. Even now, her cheeks were pinkish from the no more than called for attention by Fitz. She was the type of girl he could pass over swiftly, and he did so.

Cousin Gerald, along with Edwin Buford and Curt Putnam, his drinking companions who'd been with him at the tavern, were also present and regarded Fitz with some degree of tolerance and humor, a fact which he didn't miss in his quick scrutiny of the trio. He was rather surprised later to learn they, too, were cousins.

Benay, however, fascinated him completely. She was lovely in a pale blue dress of some gauzy material that set off her blond loveliness. The neck of the bodice was cut low enough to show off her lovely swan-like neck and her slender shoulders. The waistline was sashed widely, emphasizing her dainty figure, or was she that tightly corseted? Fitz believed he could enclose her waistline with both hands and wondered if the opportunity would present itself. Had she dressed up especially for him, or did she make a practice of looking as exquisite as this every day? Her hair was center-parted with curls falling over the ears and at the back of her head. She was devastatingly beautiful. He could scarcely take his eyes off her and turn his attention to the dinner.

The first course was a sauteed fish, caught in nearby fresh waters only hours ago. This was followed by roast pheasant, the feathers somehow stuck back on the browned carcass. The main course was roast piglet, three of them, each complete with an apple held between distended jaws.

Sam Meader carved, using the knife liberally and cutting off substantial chunks without much regard to the edibility of the serving. For himself, he sliced the heads off two piglets and scooped the brains from their skulls, which he cracked as if they were large nuts.

The performance for Fitz's benefit wouldn't be long

in coming and probably would have started already except that Sam Meader couldn't help but boast of the deal he'd just concluded. He choked on a large chunk of meat and held up his hand in a signal that as soon as his mouth was sufficiently cleared, he was going to say something.

"Our distinguished guest," he said finally, "near bought up Meader Farm stables. One hundred and sixty-five thousand dollahs, he spent. Faustine, my dear, did you make sho' the Madeira was our best?"

"We have none better."

"Ah," Gerald said, "then your guest must know all about wines, Aunt Faustine."

"Knows nothin' much 'bout 'em," Fitz admitted. "On'y thing, I likes all kinds and I drank them in twenty ports 'round the world. Had the best Madeira in Barcelona. Had mighty fine po't wine in Lisbon and they got some fancy wines in Africa."

"Have you been to all those places, Mistah Turner?" Benay asked with renewed interest.

"Yes'm, been to more than that, I reckon. Lost count."

"How interesting," Clarissa said, unexpectedly. "Cousin Gerald, have you evah drunk Madeira in Spain? Cousin Edwin, you evah drunk po't in Lisbon? Cousin Curt, you evah been to Africa? I reckon Mistah Turner a much traveled man."

"Been ever' place my papa's ship go."

Gerald saw his chance and pounced. "What cargo did your father's ship carry, suh?"

Fitz smiled. "Don't—'zactly 'member that, seems. . . ."

"I didn't think you would. I suppose your father was a noted sea captain, of course, and the ship a sturdy, fine ship."

"My papa could have been commodore of a fleet if he wanted it. Liked whut he was doin' better. The *Wyndward* was his ship. The second fastes' clipper in the world."

Gerald shrugged that off. "But I asked about the cargo . . . was it something you're ashamed of, Mistah Turner, suh?"

"Nothin' to be 'shamed of. Tryin' to think whut we carried on our way to Africa. Comin' back, of co'se, we carried nothin' but slaves."

"Ah," Gerald said, "you and your father were slave importers."

"Reckon you'd call it that. Reckon papa brought ten thousand of 'em heah."

"Ain't slave tradin' a low kind of business, Mistah Turner?"

"Reckon so, you want to call it that. Cain't be too low, seein' all you folks keep slaves. They got to come from somewhere. They don't walk over from Africa."

"Mistah Turner," Benay said, "my cousins are tantalizin' you. I don't think there's anythin' wrong in carryin' cargoes of slaves."

The wispy Clarissa gave a low moan and brought a hand to her lips. "I'm sorry," she said. "but such conversation at the dinner table makes me quite ill."

"Tush, Cousin Clarissa," Benay said half angrily, "if you can stand and watch a slave cut by a whip until he mos' bled to death. you can stand about slavery tradin'. Now stop that foolishness, you heah?"

Clarissa looked properly chastened and began eating again. Her appetite resumed quite normally and she dug a serving fork into a large chunk of rib from one of the piglets.

Gerald glanced at his two male conspirators. They were up to something and Fitz waited in silent amusement for them to begin.

Gerald said, "Speakin' of slaves, Uncle Samuel, you-all been studyin' on this heah Missouri Compromise, suh?"

Sam Meader looked blank. "Not's far as I knows, Gerald."

"I'm tellin' you we Southerners don't do somethin'

real quick, we goin' to have trouble with the No'th. This heah Missouri Compromise a new law sayin' no slaves in Missouri."

"That right?" Meader laid down his knife and fork, wiped his chin of grease, and sucked his teeth. Anything to do with slaves was important to him, having served in the state legislature.

"Ain't right," Fitz said casually.

Gerald bristled. "You sayin' I'm a liar, suh?"

"Now whut's they to lie about, you say no slaves in Missouri. You just don' know whut you talkin' 'bout, Mistah Allen.

"An' you do, suh?"

"Reckon."

"I don't like your attitude, suh. You callin' me a know-nothin', but you cain't even speak English."

Fitz found the opportunity he'd been waiting for. The one he'd baited for Gerald to nibble at and Gerald had promptly fallen into the trap neatly. Fitz placed his knife and fork across the plate, as he'd been instructed to do since childhood. He looked up and spoke in the perfect Bostonian diction his mother had so painstakingly taught him. If he never used it again in his life, all the study and the turmoil of the lessons, was now worthwhile.

"I beg your pardon, sir," he said. "You happen to be mistaken. I don't question your veracity, Mr. Allen, but I do object to your carelessness in collecting facts. Missouri sought to have legal slavery. The North and the West were against it and interfered with the spread of slavery to this new state. But finally the arguing parties reached an agreement—a compromise as it were—which was what the final document was called. A compromise in that Missouri was admitted to the Union as a slave state, but it prohibits slavery in the Louisiana Territory North of Arkansas, so that now we have a clear line between the slave states and the non-slave states."

Benay sat with her lovely chin resting on the palm

of her hand, her eyes adoring him. Sam Meader had started to lower the serving fork toward another morsel of piglet, this now being the third and last head, but the fork remained poised. Faustine sat in perfect wonder at this young man. Clarissa was openmouthed. Gerald and his two friends sat in stony silence.

Fitz went on, just as smoothly. "In not too many years—my father believes five or ten at the most—no more slaves will be allowed to be imported. However, slaves are a most necessary part of the economy of the South. Therefore, if no slaves can be imported, we must raise our own. That's why my father gave up conveying slaves here, and is now concentrating upon the breeding and raising of slaves so there will always be a steady supply. They'll be better slaves too, more intelligent, healthier, better bred, and happier because they haven't been torn away from their own land and brought here forcibly to all the strangeness that is American. I'm sure you follow me, ladies and gentlemen."

"Whar in the goddamn hell yo' learned how to talk like that?" Sam Meader demanded.

Fitz said, "I was educated by private tutors in Boston and I attended Harvard for a brief time."

"Then whut you speakin' like a Southerner for?" Clarissa found her voice.

"Because, ma'am, I am a Southerner. My father has always been of the South and his father before him. We owned one of the first plantations in Virginia and we hope we'll own the last one hundreds of years from now. My mother is a New Englander, bless her heart. She no more understands slavery and the South than Mr. Allen understands the Missouri Compromise. My father loves her as dearly as she loves him. Now, Mr. Allen, you were speaking of the Missouri Compromise, I believe."

Benay threw up both hands and roared with laughter. Then she jumped up, ran around the table, bent over

Fitz, tilted his head back and kissed him on the lips. Everyone at the table saw the kiss, but not the fact that Benay's darting tongue went on an exploring expedition with Fitz's mouth.

"He's precious," she gloated. "He made utter fools of all of us. He's so far cut above us we should bow our heads in shame. If I ever doubted you to be an ignorant bastard, Cousin Gerald, I certainly do no longer. Not after this encounter with your better. Now please, mama, stop gawking and ring for dessert. I want brandy in my coffee, and I want a cigarette. Damn the graciousness of the South. If we were more like this young man, we'd go further than we have. No reflection on you, papa, 'cause you've done well, but Cousin Gerald and Cousin Edwin and Cousin Curt are poor, lazy trash. That's what they are. Plain trash!"

There was a scraping of chairs. The three young men departed without a word and went upstairs. Clarissa knew she could have joined the revolt, but the coming of dessert was too much of a temptation. Sam Meader decided he didn't want the last piglet's head. Faustine retained her dignity and rang for dessert, gave instructions to the servants and when the lemon dainty was placed on the table, she served it, the maids passing the dishes around. Coffee was brought, a decanter of brandy set before them. Faustine and Clarissa asked to be excused and Fitz quickly helped them with their chairs. He sat down again. Benay changed her position at the table to sit next to him. He rolled her a cigarette, let her lick the paper, wound it tight and handed it to her. He tilted one of the candles and she puffed contentedly. She also poured a large measure of brandy into her steaming coffee.

"Mistah Turner," she said, "you're a very unusual young man. I like you."

Sam Meader cleared his throat. "Fitz, you watch out for that gal. She eats you alive, yo' lets her."

"I might consider it," Fitz said, retaining his Boston speech. "It might very well be a pleasure. In fact, I think she'd make a mighty sweet morsel herself. I haven't told you before, but you're an extremely beautiful girl, Benay."

"Thank you, suh." She flicked her eyelashes at him.

"Reckon," he said in a deep Southern drawl, "you-all's the mostes' wanted gal in Kaintuck'. Reckon thar be boys standin' in line waitin' yo' favors, ma'am. Reckon I bettah git myse'f on the tail end o' that line."

"Move you'se'f up to the front, darlin' Fitz," she countered. She looked up. "Papa, ain't you-all got lots o' money to count? Go 'way. We's sparkin'. Cain't you-all see that?"

Sam Meader patted Fitz on the back. "Goodbye, my friend. When she spits you up, let me know and I'll make the herd ready for travel."

"You an' me," she told Fitz, "might find it warm an' pleasant in the garden, don't yo' think so, Mistah Turner, suh?"

"Reckon," he said, "but first there's this here brandy to drink and this here coffee which is mighty good. Walkin' in the garden kin wait some."

"Why, suh," her eyebrows came up to arch in pretended indignation, "ain't you horny yit?"

He grinned, eyed her meaningfully, and drank some of the coffee. "Been horny since the first minute I laid eyes on you, ma'am. But ain't you kind of direct?"

"Sho' am," she sighed. "It's my big failin', suh. The way I am, I git mo' no-accounts an' lose mo' good ones . . . reckon you-all better teach me to be a Boston lady."

He cackled. "Mama would teach you all right. Maybe she will."

"You mean that, Fitz?" She was suddenly serious.

"Well, you come to Wyndward Plantation, reckon she will."

"And would you tell me why I'd go to Wyndward Plantation, suh?"

"Hell," he said, "I wouldn't want my wife living in Kaintucky while I'm in Virginia. I got juice in me, but it don't stretch that far."

She howled with glee and kissed him half a dozen times. They finished their coffee, after adding more brandy to it, and then they walked out into the garden. His arm was around her waist now and he knew her slimness was natural. His mind told him she was as innocent as she tried to pretend otherwise. She was spirited and wanted to shock him. He'd never known anyone like her before. No one as beautiful, as intelligent, as daring, and as natural.

"Back there," she said presently, "you mentioned my being your wife. Were you proposing to me, Mistuh Turner?"

"Whut you think?"

"Well now, it's hard to say. You've known me only a few hours and I don't know you any better. But then, you're as impetuous as I. Could it be that we've fallen in love?"

"Don' know," he replied honestly.

"Well, what do you feel about me, Fitz? Tell the truth."

"Likes you better'n any gal. Got me a big need to take you to bed. I won't 'cause I knows you ain't that kind, but the need is there. It gits stronger, I jes' got to marry you."

"Maybe," she said softly, "you will."

"Reckon you could wait five-six months?"

"I don't want to wait five or six minutes, but I will. Fitz, this is crazy! Here we are planning to be married and we don't know anything about one another."

"Knows you're sweet an' pure, Benay. Knows you couldn't be more beautiful. Knows I wants you somethin' fierce. . . ."

"Fitz, dear Fitz, in five or six months we'll be surer. It is best to wait. I'll write. I'll tell you what's in my heart, because my love for you will grow so much every day I'll just have to write it down or my heart will burst. I love you, Fitz. From now on, I'm yours. I mean that in every way except that I won't bed down with you. I'm not that kind of a girl."

She came willingly into his arms and this time her lips met his sweetly and not with the impulsive abandon she'd displayed at the dinner table. His hands caressed her face, slowly, wonderingly, adoringly.

"I tried to flirt with you today, Fitz. I wanted to tease you, get you worked up. Least, that's what I thought, but know now I wanted you soon's I laid eyes on you. I love you."

He sighed. "Good to hear you say it right out, only makes it harder to wait. Don' want to, but reckon we kin wait. I git back to Wyndward, 'bacca crop be gittin' ready for harvest an' curin'. Come winter, first suckers be here. Got us least fifty wenches knocked up. House ain't big 'nuff for you an' me, so I gits papa to add on. Then we plants the spring seed, the hosses be quieted down and breedin' too. There be six-seven weeks I kin stop worryin' 'bout the plantation and that's when I'll come for you."

"Fitz, I'll be waitin'. You know I will."

"Knows it," he agreed. "You mind now, I go down and see the hosses gittin' ready so we kin leave first thing daylight. Don't forget I'm comin' back for you, Benay. I sweah I will."

She kissed him and let him draw her hard against him, thrilling to the swelling pressed so urgently against her. She kissed him with an outrageous abandon, then drew her head back.

"Take care now, y' heah? Won't be up to see you off, Fitz. I couldn't stand it. Come back to me . . . soon's you can. Makes no difference how soon, I'll be here waitin'. Goodbye, my love. For now, goodbye."

She kissed him lightly this time, turned and fled. She ran straight toward the house. It was amazing, she thought, how far they'd walked without being aware of the distance.

"Cousin Benay," Gerald hissed from behind a wall of thick bushes.

She looked about. Fitz had long since disappeared into the darkness. She hurried behind the bushes and Gerald drew her to him roughly, while his hand explored her breasts and then grabbed handfuls of skirt, seeking to reach beneath it.

"Stop it," she said angrily. "You always act like I'm nothin' but a wench to pleasure you."

"Cousin Benay, you sho' pleasured me 'nuff and sho' not like no wench. Whut that big lout say to yo'?"

"He asked me to wait for him. He's comin' back in the spring."

"Well fo' Chrissake!" Gerald threw back his head and howled, and she hastily clapped a hand over his mouth.

"Whut in hell you laughin' at, Gerald? His papa got three million dollars. They got a big plantation, growin' bigger all the time. Think I goin' to let him get away from me?"

"Benay, you gone crazy? You aimin' to marry that lout?"

"Lout? Cousin Gerald, was you sleepin' at the table when he told you 'bout the Missouri Compromise? You ever heah a man talk like he does? He's ten times better educated than you or me. He's twenty times the man you are. I reckon it'll take some woman for a man like him, but reckon I'm the woman."

"Won't work. First place, he won't be back. You think they ain't got hot an' pretty gals in Virginny?"

"Million of 'em, maybe, but he saw me first and I saw him first. 'Sides, I like him. I likes him one hell of a

188

lot more'n I like you, or any of my other goddamn cousins."

"Benay, it's a long time to next spring. Whut you goin' to do 'til then?"

"Reckon you know," she said more warmly.

"Reckon. Tonight?"

"I feel like it. Rather it be him, but I screwed that boy and it be last I see of him. He don't know us cousins. He don't know uncles go to baid with aunts... and not the ones they're married to. Heard tell last week, the Saltsoners got theyselves a baby with a head big's a punkin, and no wonder. Baby's papa and mammy are brother an' sister."

"Come to my room," Gerald said. "Be waitin', Cousin Benay, an' I bigger'n that lout aims to marry yo'. I bigger'n two of him."

She hooted at the very idea and fled back to the house. Gerald made his way there by a less direct route, just in case Fitz stumbled across him.

Fitz had gone to the stable area where sixty horses had been run into a corral so they could be quickly roped for the trip to Virginia. Some of them would be used to carry pack. He'd rented ten young bucks from Meader to help him drive the horses, and they were busily engaged with their wenches so they might stand the long journey better.

"Massa, suh," a soft voice came out of the dark.

"Who that?"

"Themba, massa, suh."

"Cain't see you. You're blacker'n the night. Step out."

The slave came forward diffidently, his head lowered as it should be.

"Whut you want? Why ain't you wenchin'? Your master give you permission to roam?"

"Naw, suh, massah, suh."

"Then git to hell where you belong."

"Massa, suh, I craves to ask yo' somethin', suh."

"Well . . . what is it?"

"Wants yo' to buy me, suh."

"Be damned," Fitz said. "Heer'd you want no truck with any slave farm."

"Don't, suh. Thass whut I got ter say, suh. But yo' runnin' hawse farm too, suh. Yo' buyin' best hawses this heah farm got. I raised 'em, I trained 'em. I wants to go with 'em, massah, suh."

"What in hell makes you think I want you?"

"Don', suh. I beggin' yo', suh. Takes me. I breed you hawses, I births 'em. I good as a vet, I is. I gits 'em ready so you kin race 'em and win. Yassah, you kin win."

"Whut makes you think your master sell you anyhow?"

"Don' know, suh, 'ceptin' you rich and yo' pay him he sells me, an' any other nigger he owns."

Fitz studied the dim form in the darkness. He knew that Themba was an exceptional nigger. A smart one and, perhaps, a dangerous one, but he did know horses and he loved them. A man like him would be a decided asset.

"Git you black ass to yo' cabin," he said tartly. "Ain't no nigger tellin' me whut I aims to do. You mine, I peel you down."

"Yassah, massa, suh," Themba said, but there was no disappointment in his voice. Somehow he knew Fitz would buy him and he was gleefully content.

He walked slowly back to the house, feeling that his life was suddenly complete. There was nothing missing. Benay would grace the plantation at Wyndward as no other woman in all of Virginia. With her there as his wife, they could bring the mansion to life. In his mind's eye, he could visualize it glittering with light, the doors open to all quality folk, with elaborate dinners and formal balls which would be the talk of the county.

Back home there was Nina, and he missed her with a fierceness he didn't know he possessed. She could still be his, covertly or openly, depending on Benay. His mother and Benay were bound to get along, for, while Benay could be wanton and mischievous—which would delight Jonathan, no doubt—she could also be the kind of lady Fitz's mother would fully approve. Benay was smart, observant, quick to catch on.

Nothing lay in store for him now except happiness and success. He thought about raising his own family and relished the idea. Wyndward Plantation was not something that would last for only the lifetime of his father and himself. It would nourish and support generations of his bloodline.

He entered the house, found it very quiet, but upon investigation he saw a light in Sam Meader's office so he went there and found Sam seated at his desk, his feet on it, chair tilted back. A long glass of corn and water looked almost frosty in his hand.

Sam rotated the contents of the glass and it made small noises. "Ice," Sam said gleefully. "Last year's ice, my boy. Got us'n a fair size pond half mile beyond the house an' I has the slaves harvest me a shed full of ice. You pack it in straw, pack it real hard, an' it keeps good right through August an' mayhap into September." He shouted for a houseboy who answered promptly and was dispatched to make two more. "Plenty ice," Sam ordered. "Nev' min' it ain't much lef'. Turnah heah, a favorite guest. Sho' is, leavin' all that money."

Fitz laughed. His mood was carefree and joyous tonight. "Thinkin' 'bout leavin' a little more."

"See 'nother hoss looks like good stock?"

"Ain't a hoss, Sam. I want to buy your slave Themba."

Sam considered the problem for a few seconds. "He's a right good hand 'round hosses. Yo' don' git niggers as good as he is fo' train' and breedin'."

"I knows that, but you got other'ns heah who kin handle whut's left of your stock. We got nobody at Wyndward, and got to git a man quick. You don't want to sell him, I'll hire him like I hire them ten bucks goin' to keep herd on the way back."

"He's a fancy nigger. Would you go to three thousand?"

Fitz said, "Soon's you git the papers ready, it's a deal, suh."

"Get 'em ready tonight. Ain't nothin' to transfer a nigger. Got to warn yo' he don't take orders good. Too goddamn independent to suit me, but a young 'un like you kin handle him."

"I'll handle him."

The drinks were brought. Fitz enjoyed his and had another while Sam Meader wrote out the transfer of ownership for one slave named Themba, warranted as sound of limb and without undo scars from the lash on his back.

"Had to whup him two-three times," Sam recalled. "Couldn't git him settled down. 'Members now—I whupped him good and he nevah made a sound. Nevah begged, an' fainted 'fore he howled like the others do. Kinda skeered of him, sometimes. Looks at me like in his mind he's thinkin hard 'bout killin' me."

"We'll cure him of that," Fitz promised. He made out his papers ordering the Richmond bank to honor another draft, this one of three thousand. Idly, Fitz wondered what his father would say to the spending of all this money. But he had instructed him to use all he needed and Fitz didn't consider he'd squandered any.

"You got any plans 'bout my daughter?" Sam asked out of the blue.

"Told her I'd come back in the spring and marry her, suh. Subject to your approval, an' Missus Meader, 'course."

Sam drank a great deal from his glass. "Don' know whut to say. Got no objections. 'Course not, you bein' able to support her good as me. You come of a good family an' you educated like I ought to be, but ain't."

"I kin make her happy, suh."

"No doubt . . . no doubt. The question is, can she make you happy? She's an independent gal. You ain't goin' to pin her down, son. She got a strong mind of her own and she uses it. She kin be nice an' soft as a house kitten, and she kin turn into a mountain lion faster'n you kin say it. You'll have to have plenty of sap to keep up with her. Reckon she could wear a man down she had a mind to."

"I don't think she can wear me down," Fitz assured him. "This here corn mighty hefty, suh. Findin' trouble keepin' my eyes open and my brain clear."

"That's jes' the time fo' one more." Sam yelled for the house servant. While they waited for the drinks they talked horse breeding, tobacco raising, and the operation of a slave farm. Sam Meader hadn't made his fortune by luck. He was a shrewd, sharp businessman and Fitz respected him for it.

They finished the last drink rather quickly, for the alcohol was working on Sam too. He was the first to succumb. He rose unsteadily and grinned. "Goo'night, boy. You hurries back, y'heah? Benay ain't one fer waitin'. Faustine goin' to kick me outen my own baid she smells my breath tonight."

Fitz was actually woozy, but he remained in the office for a short time and read the documents concerning Themba. He wasn't sure if he'd made a wise move. Sam had demanded an atrocious price for a buck, even a prime one like Themba. Certainly the slave would be worth it because of his knowledge of horses, but again Fitz had that weird feeling Themba was someone who might complicate things at Wyndward. He couldn't see how, called himself an idiot for even wondering about it and, with the papers folded and placed in a pocket, he made his way up the stairs. When he reached the landing, the house servant snuffed out the downstairs candles.

Fitz moved along the corridor, walking lightly to make his steps soundless. His hand was on the knob of the door to his room and in the act of turning it, when he heard the sharp click of a latch. He looked up to see a door open and Benay step into the hallway. She had no awareness of him until she turned around. As she did so, the light blue flannel robe she wore swirled open so that he saw she was naked beneath it.

"Oh!" She uttered a sharp little cry at sight of him, but as quickly recovered her poise and moved up to him. "If you'd been here a few minutes earlier, you could have joined my cousin Gerald and me in our evening prayers. We have prayed together since we were children."

Fitz brushed her aside, strode down the corridor and opened the door of the room she'd just exited. Gerald was in the bathroom, completely naked and engaged in washing himself. The bed was in complete disarray, attesting to a healthy tussle having taken place in it.

Gerald stared at him, speechless. His flushed features paled as he regarded Fitz, whose first impulse was to beat Gerald to a pulp. But his anger wasn't such as to blot out reason. Benay had been a willing party to this liaison with her cousin and Fitz knew his anger should be directed toward her. He turned and left the room, slamming the door behind him. It helped to rid him of some of the rage surging through him.

In the hall, Benay blocked his path. Her eyes and her smile were bold as she said, "Do you like our way of praying, Fitz dear?"

He pushed her aside with such force she struck the wall and cried out in pain and surprise. He entered his room, closed the door and immediately began throwing his things into the carpetbags. He spent half an hour at this and then, with one bag under his arm, clutching another, he walked out of the room. There was no sign of Benay.

He made his way downstairs in the dark, left the house, but this time closed the door quietly, not wishing to disturb Sam or his wife, at the same time cursing himself for having been such a fool as to believe in the innocence of Benay.

He made his way to the corral and the stable area. He found a slave sleeping in an empty stall and kicked him solidly in the ribs.

"H'ist youse'f outen there and go find Themba. Then wake up the niggers goin' with me. An' git the herd ready. Have my hoss saddled and the mules for the niggers. You gits all that done 'fore sunup, I gives you a silvah dollah. Now git!"

Fitz dropped his baggage on the ground. His mind was in a whirl. No wonderful dream had ever exploded into nothingness as quick as his. He damned Benay, damned Gerald and wondered why he hadn't killed the man, and, as quickly, he knew. Benay's father certainly knew her. Hadn't he done all he could to dissuade Fitz from coming back?

And Benay had even attempted to brazen it out. She'd actually laughed at him. He knew she regarded him as a fool. And misery flooded him at the thought. He cursed himself for an ignoramus, for having passed up the opportunity of taking her as Gerald had. He'd probably have her clear out of his system by now, had he done so. She was nothing but a common whore, screwing her cousin an hour after she'd promised to wait for the man who had honored her by respecting her body and asking her hand in marriage. Fitz kept telling himself he was lucky to get out of that one, to have found out in time what she really was. But deep within himself, he knew he still wanted her. She was everything he desired in a woman. He cursed himself for the thought and he cursed her as he wondered how many of her cousins she'd lusted for and pleasured herself with. Perhaps uncles as well. He was well rid of her, damn her soul, damn her beautiful, desirable body.

To calm down, Fitz began walking with long and angry strides, not caring where his legs took him. He needed to simmer down and quickly. It would take a level head to start the herd and see to it the bucks were taught the ticklish job of driving sixty-five spirited horses a distance of almost four hundred miles.

Someone was laughing. Fitz stopped to listen. It was after midnight and he could hear the voice of a woman, high pitched, half insane, but alternately laughing and giggling. This couldn't be Benay, in one of the sheds spreading her legs for another man. Or could it? There was no one else on the farm except Faustine—who was very likely fast asleep—certainly, it would be Clarissa, that shy, blushing, quiet little mouse with the enormous appetite. Fitz recalled the way she'd wolved great mouthfuls of food at the table.

The shed was easy to find, for there was candlelight in one window. He approached it, stopped just outside the door. The feminine voice was intense now, urging something, demanding it, and Fitz heard the sharp crack of a whip and a low moan from a male. He opened the door slowly and silently, not knowing what to expect, but startled into frozen silence by what he saw.

In the center of the room stood a buck. He wasn't more than fifteen, but well-developed. He was stark naked. He had his legs spread apart as far as they would go and permit him to retain his balance. His manhood hung low and his penis was erect and huge.

Standing before him was little Clarissa. She held a short whip in one hand. With the other, she had bared her breasts and was fondling one of them, shaking it at the buck. She pulled up her dress, made a little jumping step to spread her legs and arched her belly at him. No doubt what the slave could see was naked.

She cut at him with the whip again. "You-all wants

me," she said in a low monotone. "You'all wants to git on top of me an' ride me like a mule. Yo' keep that big black thing o' your'n right up theah or I thrast the black hide offen yo'. Wants me . . . show me yo' wants me. Then you comes and takes me. So I kin see yo' hung. Firs' by the heels while my uncle whups you so no skin lef'. Then he hangs yo' by the neck and while yo' kickin' up theah, I'll be laughin'. Yo' wants me . . . yo' know yo' does, and yo' got big pleasurin' fo' me, yo' black son of a bitch. Come an' git me so's I kin tell yo' massa yo' rapes me. Come on . . . yo' half a grown animal or ain't yo'?"

The slave's erection had rapidly dwindled and Clarissa raged about it until she saw the pop eyes of the slave looking, not at her, but behind her. She whirled about, dropping her skirt as she did so, but not in time to conceal her nakedness. She suddenly threw the whip to one side, but she didn't close the opening of her dress so that her breasts were still bare. Without looking around, she said, "Git outen here, nigger. Git—an' don' come back or I'll have yo' hide. Git, heah me?"

The slave picked up his shirt and pants and fled, breath hissing from his throat, eyes still rolling wildly. Clarissa moved toward Fitz with a slow smile. He suddenly realized she was quite lovely and there was nothing shy about her now.

"Wants you to rape me, Mistah Turnah, suh. Wants it real bad I do. Firs' thing I see yo' I say 'fore he leaves, he's goin' to pleasure me an' I goin' to pleasure him like he never knew befo'. How yo' feel 'bout it, Mistah Turnah, suh?"

"Feel like it be a good idea. Whut was you tryin' to do with that buck?"

"Goin' to tell yo', Mistah Turnah. Thinks you-all will understand. I likes bein' pleasured real good. Cain't seem to git 'nuff of it, but all I got to pleasure myse'f with are my goddam cousins. They's good at it, and more'n willin', but I gits skeered I git knocked up. Don' even mind that so much, but skeered I birth a monster. Nothin' 'round heah for cousins to bed down. Nothin' fo' papas an' daughters, and mama's an' sons to do it either. All they thinks about 'round heah is hosses an' screwin'. I ain't skeered o' gittin' knocked up by you, suh."

He drew her to him and shoved his face down against her small, ripe breasts. She did something with her dress and it slid to the floor.

"I sees them bucks git hard, it gits to me," she explained, while she nuzzled the side of his neck. "Ain't nothin' like whut I gits with a man like yo', but better'n nothin'. Better'n birthin' a baby with three laigs. Yo' goin' to pleasure me right here, Mistah Turner?"

"Right here," he said half insanely. "It's just the right way to leave this goddamn farm."

Chapter Seven

JONATHAN TURNER, as saturated with sweat as any of the slaves, worked in the fields of tobacco as his father had done before him. The operation of raising this difficult crop came back to him much faster than he had anticipated. He'd been a boy when he was last exposed to the tricks of growing a fine grade of leaf.

He was elated at the success of his crop. Transferred from the cold frames, the seedlings had taken hold firmly and well in the rich soil. They'd grown fast and, in a matter of two or three more weeks, would be ready for harvesting to begin. Some of the plants looked mature now. He was trying to grow light tobacco which meant that he did little topping of the plant and only pinched off the seed head. Had he wished the usual dark, heavy tobacco, he would have trimmed the higher leaves so there'd be few, and those left would grow into large leaves that became dark and strong as well as aromatic. There was room for both kinds, but the bright was in shorter supply, brought the best prices, so Jonathan was devoting himself to that variety.

The curing sheds were ready, fashioned out of logs from the forest clearing and loosely matched so that air could get through the many chinks, purposely left that way. The sheds were sixty feet long, twelve feet high and could cure tons of leaves at one time. Hogsheads were scoured and scrupulously clean. They'd not be needed for some time, but if a blight came along, or an invasion of insects, or an unnatural dry spell, even a severe rainy season, the slaves would be working so hard and long in the fields preserving what they could of the crop that there'd be no time for the hogsheads, and, therefore, it was best to have them ready beforehand.

He wiped sweat off his face with his forearm, looked about to see that the slaves were hard at work and then he walked off the field, climbed the fence and went down to the stable area.

The boy he'd christened Marseilles was no great shucks and while he'd grown into a sizable buck in the last few weeks—or so it seemed to Jonathan—he wasn't too bright. Marseilles was having trouble with a chestnut mare Jonathan had bought in a lot of six riding horses, mainly for use by Sarah who'd always liked to ride. This chestnut was skittish and ornery, not well trained to the saddle.

Marseilles was using a whip industriously on the plunging animal until Jonathan called to him to stop it. Marseilles ducked his head.

"Ain't no way to gentle this hoss, massah, suh. She jes' ornery an' evil. Cain't make her mind nohow."

"Then let her wait until my son gets back. He knows how to handle horses better'n I do. 'Stead of fussin' with her, keep the stalls cleaner, you black imp, or I'll haul yo' to the whuppin' shed sure."

"Massa, suh, yo' tells me gentle this hoss an' I tries, thass all."

"Don't sass me back, heah?"

"Yassuh, massa, suh. I ain't argyfyin'."

"You're talkin' too goddamn much and you ain't payin' proper heed to whut you're doin'. Tells you whut, I come by here next time and there no improvement, you goin' straight out to the fields. Now put that hoss away and do some wuk. Whut the hell you think we doin' 'round heah?"

As he spoke, he watched the distant edge of the woodland. He thought he'd seen something and, a moment later, he knew he hadn't been wrong. Someone was riding casually along the rim of the forest.

"Your mistress ridin'?" he asked.

"Yassuh, massa, suh. Mist'iss an' Nina go ridin'."

"When they gits here, tell 'em I'm in the house."

"Yassuh, I tells 'em."

"An' you tells yourse'f you goin' to do bettah or I skin you."

"Yassuh, I 'members, I does. Yassuh, sho' does, massa, suh."

It had been weeks since Jonathan had heard from Fitz and then only a brief letter written at Meader Farms stating the contemplated price of sixty-five horses—all thoroughbreds. Not a word about Sam Meader or any of his family, nor about the journey. In letters, Fitz was inclined to be cryptic, but it was, nevertheless, quite evident that his journey had been successful. Sam figured, roughly, that Fitz would be home in eleven more days unless he encountered flooded streams or impossible passes or any of the countless impediments placed in the way of a traveler on horseback, to say nothing of a man with a large herd of horses to control and lead.

He shouted for Calcutta. "You gits more useless ev'y goddam day," he told the worried boy. "Ev'y time I goes near the kitchen, you roastin' yourse'f near the stove. Whut kinda blood you got, makes you so cold?"

"Dunno, suh. Don't know nothin' 'bout that, but I ain't slothin'. I sweahs that, suh. Massa, suh," he added hastily.

"Well, git me a tall rum and water. An' I wants it now, not tonight."

Calcutta scooted away. Jonathan heard Nina and Sarah enter. Sarah said something to the slave and she answered brightly and then pattered up the stairs. Sarah walked into Sam's office and sat down.

She'd lost weight since she arrived and she looked younger and far less severe. When Jonathan's drink was delivered, she thought she'd have some Madeira and Calcutta went scooting willingly. He liked Madeira's sweetness more than anything else in the world and he planned some day to drink all he could hold, get himself stinking drunk and find him a wench to pleasure. He was old enough. If the massa didn't know it, Calcutta did.

Sarah sipped the wine. "I wonder where Fitzjohn is about now."

"On his way, Sarah. 'Nother ten days . . . thereabouts. Don't worry none 'bout that boy. He's growed."

"I am worried about him though, Jonathan. Nina's in love with him. Did you know that?"

"Reckon so, way she looks at him."

"Is he in love with her, do you think?"

"Fitz . . . with a nigger? Now, Sarah, you know better'n that."

"She's a most unusual colored person. I can't even call her a nigger, though I've certainly gotten used to calling the others by that name, and they don't seem to mind."

"Why should they? They gets good food, a good cabin, clothes, somebody to pleasure with. They cain't ask for more'n that. And—they is niggers, ain't they?"

"If they were free. . . ."

"Sarah, I don' told you 'bout manumitted niggers. They good for nothin'. They better off slaves. All they do is hang 'round corners an' beg. Known some of 'em to come back to their master who set them free an' ask to be made a slave agin. They's stupid, they don't know anythin', Sarah. We's got to do they thinkin' for them."

"Yes, I've changed my opinions of them since I got here. You were always right. I remember when you came to talk to my father about cargo and you told me you were a Southerner and you believed in slavery. I wanted to be rid of you then and there, but I just couldn't let you go. So I took you slaves and all. I was terribly afraid you owned a number of them and I was delighted to learn you had none and that your father's plantation had been abandoned years ago."

"Cain't run a plantation 'thout slaves, Sarah. We has to pay all that he'p an' we go broke nex' week. They's costly as 'tis. Costs a heap of money to buy 'em and more to keep 'em. Soon's we git us a good crop of suckers comin', I feels better."

"Enough of the women are certainly pregnant. What I dread is to find Nina swollen with child. I would know very well that it must be Fitz's, because Nina has no truck with any of the other blacks. If she were white, Jonathan, I would very much approve of her as a wife to Fitzjohn."

"She's a uncommon wench, all right. Agrees to that, but reckon we got nothin' to worry 'bout. 'Course you knows Fitz is a grown man now, and he got the feelin's an' urgin's of a young man, Sarah. Reckon it possible he's pleasured hisse'f with Nina."

"I'm not even shocked," Sarah said. "She's a sweet girl and I'm very fond of her."

"Don't git too fond o' her. Set a bad 'zample."

Sarah smiled. "She speaks our language quite well. And with almost a Boston accent."

Jonathan regarded her humorously. "You talk like you regard her like she your daughter."

"Perhaps I do," Sarah admitted. "Perhaps because I sense her love for Fitz and since I love him too, we have that in common. She loves to hear me tell about his childhood. And I listen to her tell of hers."

"This climate sorta mellowed you, I think."

"Yes," Sarah admitted. "Except I don't believe I'll ever be able to accept the idea of slaves. To me, they're as much a part of God as I am. They have as much a right to walk the earth as free as you and I."

"You talkin' heretic now, Sarah. Think Nina have too much effect on yo'. You an' Fitz both. Gits the idea sometimes I ought to give her to a buck for coverin'. Shame to waste such a val'able bloodline."

"Jonathan, if you do, I shall never speak to you again as long as I live. That girl . . . with a black? Why, he'd kill her. I've seen enough of those big bucks to . . . to . . . know what they . . ."

"Whut they's equipped with, Sarah?" Jonathan grinned.

"Well—yes. You're crude, but there's no mistaking what you mean."

"Sarah," he said, "never in all my life I been as happy as now. Got me a strong son, a big plantation, plenty of niggers to work it. But most of all, I got me a wife. Loved you more'n you'll evah know. Weeks I was at sea I near went crazy for longin' for you. Skeered to tell you I was haulin' niggers from Africa."

"I'm glad you didn't," she said. "To understand the need for that, one must understand the need of the South for labor. I can't say I like any of it, but I've grown tolerant of it."

"To tell you the truth, Sarah, I never liked haulin' 'em myse'f. On'y way to do it was pack 'em in the holds 'til they kin hardly move. Kep' 'em down too, so they wouldn't mutiny. Knew whut would of happened they evah got loose with some smart buck to boss 'em. They'd slit our throats, ev'ry one of us an' then they'd try to sail the ship and wind up on the bottom just like we'd be."

"Horrible," Sarah shuddered at the thought.

"That's the right word," Jonathan agreed. "Stink got so bad I kin smell it yit. Times I think it crawled into my skin and stays theah to haunt me. Sometimes I smell it in my sleep and I wake up like I been shot."

"It's a foolish idea," Sarah said comfortingly. "I never detected any odor of them on you. It's not in the house. I confess the Negroes smell rather badly after working in the fields."

"They cain't he'p it. That don't make them stink any less you cain't blame 'em. Keeps 'em clean as we kin. Sarah, you knows whut Fitz went to Kaintucky for?"

"Why, a herd of thoroughbred horses."

"I'm aimin' to train an' race 'em."

"I see."

"Reckoned you wouldn't like it, not being a gamblin' woman."

She thudded the base of her wine glass against the desk. "Who said I'm not a gambling woman? I gambled in marrying you, a man I hardly knew. A clipper captain who was gone for months at a time. Jonathan, if you'd continued to operate the *Wyndward* . . . the clipper, I mean . . . I think I'd have gone mad of loneliness for you. All those endless days and years turned me into a recluse. I didn't want to go out. In my thinking, I grew more and more bitter. I resented seeing those about me leading normal, happy lives. I resented Fitzjohn not having a father at home. To get even with you, I brought up our son as a Bostonian. I insisted he speak only our brand of the English language because I hoped it would make you angry. I wanted you to be angry with me because then I'd know you were in love with me. Oh, Jonathan, you did give me a time of it and I paid you back in full with my meanness."

He chuckled. "Nevah for one minute thought you stopped lovin' me. Nevah questioned the way I felt 'bout you, either. Look whut I did? Took the boy in hand and had him talkin' like me in two weeks. You mad 'bout that?"

"No. Fitzjohn's proud of you. He's determined to be like you and I don't mind. I'm happy too. I know this is the life for you now and I'm enjoying it. More and more, I'll grow accustomed to your ways and before very long I'll . . . be talkin' like yo', suh, an' bossin' 'round them niggahs like they nevah bin bossed befo'."

Jonathan roared with laughter and pleasure. He had Calcutta bring more rum and another glass of Madeira. He and Sarah sat for two hours talking about the past and finally bringing into their conversation the future, which never had looked brighter.

"Oh my," Sarah said. "I thought I'd bathe and be cleaned up long before now. Thank you for the saddle horses, Jonathan. Your thoughtfulness pleases me."

"Should have had 'em here when you 'rrived. Knows you loves ridin'."

"Jonathan, what about that Negro who was almost killed by our overseer?"

"Whut about him?"

"There's talk going around that you intend to put him with the bachelors and hand his wife over to some other buck."

"Now whoevah talked that way?"

"Nina heard it from some of the slaves."

"They's wrong. My fault 'cause I hired that no-good overseer bastahd. Knew whut he was an' how he treated niggers, but he gits work done and that's whut I was after. You wants it, I'll straighten that out now."

"I think you should. The poor man must be worried sick."

"Obleeged you brought it to my mind," he said.

He first went around to the watering trough, stripped down to his waist and doused himself with water. Wasn't right any more he should walk around smelling like a nigger. He was, in fact, ashamed of himself. There he'd been talking to Sarah about how the hold of the *Wyndward* smelled so richly of the cargo, and he was seated across the desk, stinking right well himself.

He walked around to the stable area to see if Marseilles was slothing. The slave was plying a rake in one of the stables, but he wasn't doing any sweating.

"Massa, suh," Marseilles said.

"What you want?"

"Massa, suh, yo' puttin' Hong Kong wid de bachelors 'count he ain't got no balls?"

"And if I was, whut's that to you?"

"I'm cravin' he wench, suh. Massa suh, please lemme pester her. I git you big suckers outen her, I does."

"She ask you to pleasure her?"

"Naw suh, massa, suh. She sho' din'. Driv' me off like a sick dawg, thass whut she done. I gots to have her, massahs suh. I'm achin' fer her, I am. Gits you fine suckers . . ."

Jonathan clouted him alongside the head as hard as he could with an open hand. The slave staggered and fell. He didn't get up. For one moment, Jonathan thought he saw flaming, undiluted hatred in the popping eyes, but it passed before he could be sure, and Marseilles was again servile and pawing at his feet.

"Massa, suh, I done nothin'. Sweah I done nothin'. Yo' don' wan' gi me Hong Kong's wench, I fin' me 'nother one."

"You stay away from all wenches. The reason you

ain't got one is I don't want no suckers from your juice. Ketch you pesterin' any wench on this here plantation, I'll string you up and give you twenty cuts with the whup and then I cuts you some place else with a knife. Hong Kong, he got nothin' lef' of his balls, but whut you got lef' won't be any more use to you than his."

"Massa, suh, I do like yo' say. I don' pester no wenches. Sweah I won'. Don' wanna git whupped. Don' wanna git my balls cut. Please, massa, suh. I jes' 'bout die I got no balls."

"The only way you keeps 'em is to do like I say an' no mistakes. Now start yourse'f sweatin', you lazy nigger."

Jonathan inspected the stables and was not pleased. He didn't know quite what to do about it. None of the other slaves, barring Hong Kong, could have taken proper care of the area, and Hong Kong was badly needed for his work in the fields. It was a matter Jonathan would have to take up with Fitz when he returned.

Jonathan pushed open the door of Hong Kong's cabin without knocking. His wench, kneeling before a small fire over which she was cooking something savory, looked up and then jumped to her feet. He'd never seen a wench look so worried.

"Massa, suh," she said. "Massa, yo' tell me it ain't so yo' goin' to set Hong Kong in the barn wid the bach'lors."

"Whut you name?"

"Seawitch, suh. Likes it I do. Please, massa, suh. . . ."

"Who tol' you I was goin' to do that?"

"Don' know, suh. Jes' don't know . . ."

"Someone told it to you. Think—who was it?"

"Don' know, suh," she insisted, keeping to some unspoken tradition of not telling on another slave.

"You don' know, Hong Kong goes to the bachelor barn tonight." Jonathan began turning away as if the word was final.

She clawed at his arm, an unpardonable sin. A month ago, he would have had her flogged. Now he merely unloosened her fingers frantically trying to restrain him.

"Marseilles, he say, massa, suh. Marseilles, he say I his wench soon's yo' gits 'round to it. Massa, suh, cain't do 'thout Hong Kong, an' he sick. He near killed."

"You know he ball-less?"

"Yassuh, massa, suh. I knows that real well. Tries to git him up, suh, but they's nothin' lef', they ain't. Jes' . . . nuthin'. . ." She began to cry.

"So it was Marseilles," Jonathan said. "I'll have him hided for that. Now you listen to me. Whut the hell's your name agin . . . yes . . . Seawitch. You listen to me. Long as I runs this here plantation, ain't nobody takin' Hong Kong 'way from you. Ain't never puttin' you out to be covered, you don' want it. You do, you tells me. Even so, you married to Hong Kong. You not jes' his wench. You married to him. An' I makes Hong Kong boss man. He in charge of every goddamn nigger on this heah plantation an' you tells him, Marseilles says one more thing 'bout takin' you for his wench, Hong Kong got my leave to break his black neck. Means it— Hong Kong kin kill him for all I cares."

Her tears dried and she smiled. He had an idea it had been weeks since she had. "Thankee, massa, suh. Nevah fo'gets, I don'. Hong Kong, he nevah fo'gits. We wuks ha'd fo' you. We loves you, massa, suh."

"Good 'nuff," Jonathan said. "You comes to the house tomorrow an' you gits a new dress. Likes Hong Kong, I do, an' sorry for him. Wants his wife to look better'n any wench on this heah plantation. Not runnin' 'round like some stinkin' nigger."

"Thankee, massa, suh."

"An' you feeds him good, heah? He a ball-less wondah, mayhap, but they gits mighty big an' strong, they ain't got any nuts. You wait . . . maphap somethin' grows back. Now don' want to see no more cryin'. You take keer of your husband and we ain't got any trouble 'tween us."

"I takes bes' keer you evah saw, massah, suh."

Jonathan walked out, leaving the door wide open. He strode away from the cabin, swearing mildly with each step. That was no way to handle niggers, but damn it, there'd been nothing else to do. And he intended to have a talk with that horny, lying Marseilles. If he gave any back talk, Jonathan intended to whip him. He was seriously considering the whip anyhow.

He told Sarah about it at the supper table. "You did exactly right, Jonathan," she said. "That Marseilles is lazy and worthless, except that he seems to know horses and can handle them fairly well. I do hope you'll get someone else as soon as Fitzjohn returns."

"Intends to," Jonathan said. "Tol' Hong Kong's wench I nevah busts them up. Tol' her to tell Hong Kong, Marseilles tell anybody she goin' to be his wench 'cause I say so, he kin kill Marseilles fer all I keer. Goddam lucky, I din' kill him my own se'f."

"I'm glad you handled it that way."

"Tol' her—name's Seawitch—you gives her a dress come t'morra."

Sarah smiled warmly. "I have one just right for her. You know, Jonathan, I'm not the only one who has changed."

"Gits more from a happy nigger than a unhappy one. Jes' a matter of business, Sarah. Nothin' else."

"Of course not," she said, humoring him. "Certainly you must not show those poor people that you care for them in any way."

"Cares for 'em 'cause they wuth money. No different than the hawgs, the hosses, anythin' else. They wuth money."

"Yes, Jonathan, I understand," she said.

That night she surprised him by inviting him to bed after sending Nina away with orders not to come back until morning. And, to Jonathan, his world was now as complete as it ever would be. He had it all. Everything there was to be had, including the genuine love of a woman he loved and would devote the rest of his life to. His wenchin' days were over. He'd be as good and devoted a husband to his woman as any Northern bastard.

It rained that night, alarming him somewhat when he awoke. Rain could harm the tobacco leaves unless the sun came out and dried them promptly. He went down to the fields to examine the plants. There were some about ready for harvesting. If need be, he intended to cut the stalks and bring them to the curing sheds at once. He spent all day in the fields, watching with gratification, the sun slowly drying the plants and removing the threat of damage.

By midafternoon he was tired and sweaty. His shirt clung to him, dark with moisture along the small of his back. He wanted a rum and water. He wanted to sit down, perhaps talk to Sarah, now that they'd reached a definite understanding and she recognized his problems. It was good to have her to talk to, especially with Fitz away.

He stopped by the trough again and washed thoroughly, carried his soaked shirt inside and threw it on a pile of laundry. He went upstairs without looking in the office or the drawing room. He changed to fresh clothes after he'd shaved, and he felt much better. Smelled some better too, he reasoned.

Going down the stairs he hollered for Calcutta and the boy scooted to the foot of the stairs to meet him. "You knows whut I wants. Git it and quick now."

The boy bobbed his head and raced off to fetch the rum and water. Jonathan walked into the drawing room. "Sarah?" he called out. "Sarah—where you at?"

For some reason, the silence portended something frightening. Just why he should feel this way, he didn't know, but the fact remained that he did. It annoyed him. He wasn't accustomed to being frightened over nothing more than some silly premonition.

"Whar your mistress?" he asked Calcutta when he returned with the drink.

"I don' know, massa, suh. I ain't seed her."

"When you see her last?"

"Reckon. . . ." he scratched his wool energetically, as if trying to draw out some kind of information in the process, "reckon 'bout hour ago, massa, suh."

Jonathan drank half the contents of the glass in two big swallows and then, clutching the glass, he hurried to the kitchen. Elegant was seated at her table, stuffing herself with some biscuits left over from breakfast.

"You see you mistress?" he asked.

"Suh, I bin sittin' heah waitin' fo' her to come give me ordahs fo' dinnah, suh."

"Did you see her leave the house?"

"Yes, suh. She stop by an' say she an' Nina goin' ridin' and when she come back, she tells me whut for dinnah, suh."

Now thoroughly alarmed, Jonathan finished the drink, left the glass in the kitchen and went racing down to the stables.

"Marseilles," he shouted. "Marseilles, where the hell are you?"

The barns and the stalls were empty. There were no slaves about. Then, by sheer accident, he noticed the stall where that chestnut mare was kept. It was empty. He ran down along the other stalls, looking for that skittish, frisky and unpredictable animal.

He gave vent to a shout of alarm, led out the nearest horse, saddled it quickly. The animal took off at high speed in response to hard kicks. Suddenly, Jonathan realized he didn't even know what direction to take. Sarah did ride down near the forest, sometimes along trails cutting through it, seeking the coolness of the shade. He veered in that direction and kept looking about him.

In his mad haste, he hadn't thought about finding Nina, but then she would have gone wherever Sarah went. The girl had proven to be a natural rider and was allowed the use of a horse so she might keep up with Sarah. Surely that had been precaution enough, but Jonathan was never so worried in his life.

He reached the forest trail and started along it. The shade of the oaks and poplars closed around him and there seemed to be serenity here he'd never known before. His horse was slowed by the twists and turns in the trail. Once he saw fairly fresh hoofprints and he remembered it had rained last night rather heavily. The trail through the forest was hard-packed enough and not very wet, but once he broke through to the other side, the field ahead was a morass of mud—and two horses were grazing where the grass was taller and greener.

Jonathan rose in the saddle to see better. He heard a low moan to his left. He slid off his horse, raced in that direction. Nina was lying on the ground, on her back. Her face was bloodied, her dress ripped to shreds. The amber-colored body Jonathan had intimately known was once more exposed to his gaze, but this time there was no lasciviousness in it.

He knelt by the girl, raised her up. Her eyes flew open and she began to scream and beat at his face until she realized who was holding her. Then she fell back with a deep sigh.

"Nina," he said. "Nina . . . whar your mistress? Whar's my wife? Answer me, nigger gal. Answer me. . . ."

She opened her eyes again and shuddered violently. He got her into a sitting position. He shook her until her teeth clicked.

"My wife . . . Sarah . . . whar is she?"

Nina's wits slowly oriented. She tried to rise, but Jonathan had to help her. Nina looked about, searching for something. Then she pointed and Jonathan followed the direction of her finger. It was no wonder he hadn't seen her right away, for she lay in a pool of mud and it almost completely covered her. He raced to the spot, waded into the four-inch-deep morass and knelt. He turned her over gently, knowing very well that she was dead. He lifted her, carried her to where the grass protected dry ground and set her down. He tore free large handfuls of the tall grass and used it to remove as much of the mud as possible. He was cold-blooded about it now. He examined her for any signs of rape and found none.

Nina crouched down beside him, weeping bitterly. Jonathan turned toward her. "You knows she daid?"

"Yassuh, massa, suh. I knows."

"The horse," Nina said, "no good. Din' want to be rid, reckon."

"It was the chestnut mare."

"Yassuh, massa, suh. When we gits to the stable, the chestnut saddled an' ready. My horse too, so we jes' . . . ride, suh. We gits here an' the chestnut got skittish an' . . . an' . . . mis'tiss fall off."

"Whar we found her just now?"

"Yassuh . . . that whar."

"Why didn't you help her?"

"Massa, suh, aimin' to, but Marseilles . . . he come out of the woods an' he grab me an' he rape me."

"Didn't you tell him your mistress was maybe dying in that goddamn mud?"

"I tells him. I begs him. I say . . . he he'p her, I lets him pleasure me, but he laugh an' say he like me fightin' him."

"He did nothing to help her? Didn't go near her?"

"Reckon he jes' got on me, suh. He hit me . . . I don' know whut happen afta that, suh. I real sorry. I so sorry I think I like to kill myse'f, suh."

"You do and I'll whup the hell outa what's left,"

Jonathan said. "That's the last thing she'd want you to do. Go bring the horses here."

"Yassuh, massa."

She began with a slow walk, realized what she had to do and sprinted to the chestnut. The horse surrendered meekly. She seized the other horse and led both to where Jonathan still knelt beside the body of his wife.

He lifted Sarah and placed her over the saddle of the quieter horse, then he vaulted onto the chestnut and when the animal began to dance, he kicked her in the ribs as hard as he could. The animal quieted down somewhat.

"Git up behind me," he ordered Nina, and she swung onto the saddle like an Indian, wrapping her arms around him. With one hand he led the tame horse carrying Sarah's body, held the chestnut in check with the other and the horse seemed to realize any acting up would be met with pain.

They moved slowly across the field. In the distance, some of the slaves were attracted to the strangeness of the procession and stopped work to look. After a bit, the fields became busy with slaves darting about, either seeking information as to what was going on, or giving it.

In front of the house, Hong Kong appeared first. He whipped off his grimy hat and then bowed his head as he recognized the cargo draped over the saddle.

Nina slid down and darted into the house, leaving the door open. Hong Kong moved up to help, but Jonathan brushed him aside, lowered Sarah's body and cradled it in his arms. He marched into the house. Hong Kong followed at a discreet distance.

Inside, Jonathan carried his burden to their bedroom. Nina must have guessed that's where he'd come, for she had the bed turned down, as if Sarah was merely going to be tucked in for a night of rest. Jonathan laid her down, carefully smoothened her clothing. One eyelid was partly open. He closed it very gently. Then he opened her mouth, pushed a finger into the morass which filled her oral cavity and her throat. He knew the answer now. She'd fallen into the mud face down and, for some reason, she had been unable to get up, or turn over. Perhaps she'd been stunned. She was able to breathe in only the viscid mud which had choked and smothered her to death.

Jonathan straightened up. He stepped back beside Nina. "Whut you told me was truthful?" he asked, knowing very well it was, but he had to ask it anyway for absolute confirmation.

"Yassuh, massa, suh," Nina said through her sobs.

"Marseilles could have saved her, he gone quick to turn her ovah. That right?"

"I tol' him an' I tol' him, but he crazy . . . he say hell with her. He say I mo' impo'tant. I kick an' I scratch an' I yells, but no use, suh. No use . . . he hit me. . . ."

"Listen well, Nina," he said, "this was not your fault. You did all you could. Now I wants you to send Calcutta to find the ca'penter and orders him to make a coffin. Then you gits four bucks to dig a grave, way down back the house near the big oak. You unnerstan' whut I say, wench?"

"Yassuh, massa, I knows."

"Clean her up and put on her purties' dress. I come back we buries her."

"Yassuh, massa, suh. I does it."

"Don' know when I gits back. Goin' to find Marseilles. You knows whut d'rection he run off?"

"No, suh. Aftah he hits me, I don' know nothin'."

"I'll find him," Jonathan said. "I'll find him . . . !"

Hong Kong, with that same strange ability to anticipate what his master might want, had two fresh horses saddled and waiting. He also had a long length of rope in his hand and Jonathan's rifle, which ordinarily would have resulted in swift death to the slave who removed it from the pegs inside the house.

"Wants to go too, suh," Hong Kong begged. "Wants to monst'ously, suh."

"You knows whut happened?"

"I knows."

"Marseilles saddled the chestnut. He knew it was skittish and would throw her. Then he followed them to the woods and when the hoss threw her, Marseilles let her die with her face in the mud. While she died—and all the sonabitch had to do was turn her ovah—he was busy rapin' Nina."

"We ketches him," Hong Kong said angrily.

"We wants him alive an' kickin', y'unnerstan' that?"

"Yassuh, massa, suh. We wants him 'live."

They mounted, Hong Kong trailing behind respectfully until Jonathan signaled for him to ride abreast. "Whar you reckon he run to?" he asked.

"On'y place, massuh, suh, he figgers on gittin' 'way, he goes 'long the road to Spahtan, suh. Li'l town twenny mile no'th."

"Yes, I think so too. Let's go git him!"

They kicked their horses into a gallop and they raced down to the dirt road, turned north and galloped along it. Jonathan cursed himself for not finding out how long it had been since Marseilles began running. He calculated that Nina, being young and strong, couldn't have been unconscious very long and Marseilles must have taken off very soon before Jonathan came upon the scene. That meant he wasn't far. Jonathan signaled Hong Kong to pull up.

"Figger he ain't far," Jonathan said. "Figger he heahs us comin' he dives in the grass. So whut we do—I'm ridin' on like I lookin' for him alone. You rides offen the road, on the grass an' you keeps watchin' me. That black bastahd heah me go by, he think he safe now an' he shows hisself 'cause he goin' to take off the other way. You rides him down."

"Yassuh, I rides him down, suh."

"I don't want him killed."

"No suh, massa, I don't kill him. Like to, but I don't."

Jonathan pointed to the west. "Ride 'longside the road ovah theah."

They parted. Hong Kong, heading into the tall grass, was all but lost from sight. Wisely, he let Jonathan go on well ahead and he scanned the roadside for the first glimpse of Marseilles. He'd be bound to jump out to the clear way along the road and scamper in the opposite direction.

Jonathan rode steadily, not too fast. His eyes were peeled, but he had few hopes of catching Marseilles as simply as that. He didn't think, his mind was too numb. He had but a single objective now—to catch Marseilles. Vaguely, he wished that Fitz could have been here. Jonathan felt alone—terribly alone. There were no neighbors to be sent for, no doctor if one had been needed. The nearest farm was that of Colonel Coldwell and a fast-riding slave wouldn't get there until morning now, be another day before the Colonel could reach Wyndward. Whatever had to be done, it was Jonathan's cross to bear alone.

A shout from Hong Kong alerted him. He turned his mount in time to see Hong Kong leap out of the saddle of his running horse and vanish in the tall grass. Before Jonathan could get his horse into motion again, he saw Hong Kong straighten up and, with one hand around Marseilles' throat, hold him up for Jonathan to see, as if he were a rabbit just killed.

Jonathan rode into the grass, but when he reached the side of the two slaves, he didn't dismount. Somewhat to his amazement, he saw that Marseilles was spanceled. Hong Kong had brought along a pair of wrist cuffs. Hong Kong had likewise looped the end of a long rope around the neck of the terrified slave.

"He got no mo' sense'n a rat, suh," Hong Kong declared contemptuously. "Riz right up soon's yo' go by. Massa, yo' say so, I kills him fo' yo'."

"Alive," Jonathan said. "Much alive. Ride behind. If he falls, pull him up 'fore he strangles on the rope."

"Yassuh," Hong Kong said. He approached Jonathan and handed up the other end of the rope which Jonathan affixed to the saddlehorn.

"Massa . . . massa, suh, yo' don' kill Marseilles. I done nothin'. Sweahs I done nothin'. I on'y po' nigger done nothin'. Don' kill me, massa. Yo' whups me good, but don' kill me, massa, please."

Jonathan didn't reply. He kicked his horse into motion. The rope tightened and Marseilles staggered behind the animal. His wrists were cuffed behind his back, the rope was around his neck and all he could do was run.

Once he tripped and fell. The rope tightened, he was dragged along the dirt road over which they were now riding. Jonathan felt the tug at the rope, but he didn't turn around. Hong Kong rode up, leaned far down from the saddle, secured a grip on Marseilles' wool and hauled him to his feet. Marseilles was screeching once the rope relaxed sufficiently so he could breathe again. Jonathan kept that same steady pace, just enough to make Marseilles run.

That was the way they reached the mansion, up the drive cut through the bowling lawn. When they reached the house, Jonathan dismounted. Hong Kong slipped out of the saddle and stood awaiting orders.

Jonathan said, "You takes him to the tool shed. You drives four heavy stakes into the groun'. You spreads him far as you can 'thout pullin' him apart. You leaves him theah. You tells all the niggers, the buck or wench goes near him, he gits whipped—twenty-five lashes."

"Yassuh, massa, suh."

"Massa, suh," Marseilles pleaded. "Massa . . . yo' ain' goin' kill Marseilles. I good nigger. I done nothin'.

I be bes' nigger yo' evah see, suh. I does anythin' yo' tells me. Whup me yo' wants, but don' kill me, massa."

Jonathan looked at him with steely eyes. He walked away. Hong Kong had shortened the rope still around Marseilles' neck. Now he kicked the slave as hard as he could and drove him toward the tool shed. Groups of slaves who had abandoned work and gathered nearby didn't move except to turn their heads and watch Hong Kong drive the slave with frequent kicks that brought howls from Marseilles.

Inside the house, Jonathan was met by Nina, in her maid's serving uniform. The tears were fresh against her cheeks. It was evident they'd never stopped. Elegant emerged from the kitchen to waddle her bulk up to face him.

"We done washed her good, suh. We done combed her hair and cleaned her toenails and fingernails. We done put on bes' dress we fin' an' box waitin' yo' say to bring it."

"Bring it," he said tersely. Then he mounted the stairs. She lay on top of the covers of the freshly made bed and she seemed to be asleep. Jonathan walked to the window and stood there, looking out, until he saw four slaves approach with the coffin. He bent, picked up the body. There was no expression on his face. He carried her down the stairs. Nina, on her way up, dodged around him. A moment later, she descended to pass him. In that brief space of time she'd stripped the bed of its soft quilt and she hastily lined the plain wooden coffin with it.

Jonathan placed Sarah in it, gestured and turned away while the slaves arranged the quilt and then nailed down the lid. By some agreement, more bucks appeared and, without a word, they carried the coffin to the porch and there they lifted it to their shoulders.

Jonathan walked behind them. In his hand was the Bible he'd used aboard ship so seldom, the companion to the prayer book by which he had married all these slaves because Sarah had demanded it. The remembrance brought the barest trace of a smile to his lips.

His orders had been carried out explicitly. As the procession moved in the direction of the area he'd designated as the cemetery, Hong Kong quietly came from beside the path. He gave Jonathan one crisp nod, indicating that Marseilles was staked out.

It was almost dark when they reached the open grave. The spot had been well chosen—by Nina, he judged— from the way she took over. It required only a few moments to lower the coffin. Jonathan stood at the head of the grave and read the brief ceremonial words that had absolutely no meaning to his stunned mind. All he could think of was that it was so lonely here. No one to see her off, none to weep. It was done almost as if in secret.

He closed the book and walked away, not waiting to hear the thud of the first shovels of earth. Every slave on the plantation stood a respectful distance from the grave and the murmur came from their throats. It grew and grew until it became a chant, a song that welled up until it attained the timber of a great organ.

Jonathan displayed no recognition of this. He walked between the slaves alone. No one followed, not even Nina. He returned to the house. It was empty. It was so damned empty he could feel it. He went into the office, began to call for Calcutta and knew he'd still be at the burying. So he found the bottle of rum himself, picked up a glass at random, went to his office, sat down and began to drink. By midnight, he was unconscious.

In the morning he woke, still seated in the chair behind the desk. Sunlight streamed in, making him blink. His head ached, his whole body ached. He began to stand and then he remembered and sank back again. Nina came in once, studied his solemn face and quietly backed out of the room.

An hour later, Jonathan arose. He walked out of the house. Hong Kong was there, waiting. "Fetch two strong bucks and give 'em long shovels," he ordered. "Fetch a rope for hangin' and fetch the snake. We goin' out to the old elm, way the end of the corn field."

"Yassuh, massa, suh. I fetches 'em."

"And bring Marseilles."

"Yas, suh, he ready fo' bringin'."

Jonathan walked very slowly toward the lone, half-dead tree with its bare and arching branches. He paused as he neared it to study the tree itself and select a branch. This done, he waited until the two bucks with the shovels appeared.

He stamped the earth to indicate the spot. "Wants a hole straight down, three feet higher'n you haids. Round hole . . . straight down."

They seemed to know exactly what he demanded, though neither could remotely guess the purpose of such a hole. They fell to, working rapidly. They were strong and agile, and the hole gradually grew deeper and deeper until it became necessary to send for a pail in which the dirt could be hauled out by the buck deep within the earth.

It took a long time, under a hot sun, but the bucks never slackened their work. Jonathan had seated himself against the trunk of the tree. Marseilles, his neck ringed by the rope, his hands spanceled behind him, groveled on the ground, his eyes rolling wildly. He called to Jonathan, pleading with him, begging him, imploring him. Making rash promises, calling himself a bad nigger. All through it, Jonathan sat unmoved.

The slave was finally hauled out of the deep hole. Jonathan walked over and looked down into it and was satisfied.

"Shuck him down an' tie him by the heels," he ordered. He gestured to the two sweating bucks who'd dug the hole. "Grab onto the end of the rope and haul him up.

I wants him swingin' an' you keeps him that way."

Hong Kong picked up Marseilles, now tied at the ankles and carried him to a spot exactly under the tree branch. He dropped him like something tainted. He threw the rope over the lower branch, four muscular arms yanked at it and Marseilles went sailing upwards to hang there, head down, suspended directly above the hole in the ground.

Jonathan picked up the long blacksnake whip. There was neither gratification or rage betrayed on his face. There was nothing. He swung the whip and Marseilles screamed as it cut half an inch into the flesh around his back. The whip sang again, Marseilles screeched and begged that it be stopped. Jonathan swung the whip ten times by deliberate count. Marseilles was quiet now. Conscious, but so wracked with pain he was unable to scream. His naked body rotated slowly, like some ugly thing left on a gibbet.

"Run fetch water," Jonathan ordered. "Sluice him down."

Slaves brought four pails of water from a nearby pond and they doused him with it until he began to moan and incoherently plead his case.

The force of the water had caused him to start turning somewhat wildly. Jonathan steadied him, then he stepped back and signaled for Hong Kong. The big buck approached and stood beside Marseilles' still swaying body and looked sorely puzzled. Marseilles had been properly whupped, not enough certainly, but punished. Hong Kong could not guess the significance of the ten-foot-deep hole so painstakingly cut out of the earth.

Jonathan looked at the two slaves holding the end of the rope which ran around Marseilles' ankles, went up over the branch and into their hands.

"Lower him slow," Jonathan ordered.

The pair didn't move. Hong Kong suddenly realized what it was about. He hurried over to the pair and kicked one of them. They began to lower Marseilles. As his head disappeared below the surface, he too realized what was in store for him.

Jonathan moved up to the side of the hole and stood there until the slave's head was supported by the bottom of the hole and the rope slackened. Hong Kong lay flat, reached down and untied the rope. Marseilles was moaning, his body struggled feebly.

"Breathe dirt," Jonathan spoke. "As you made her breathe dirt, breathe it yourse'f."

Hong Kong picked up a shovel. He leaned on it, oblivious to Marseilles' half smothered cries, until Jonathan walked slowly away in the direction of the house. Then he looked down into the hole.

"Yo' sho' headin' in the right d'rection, Marseilles. Sho' 'nuff aimed whar yo' b'longs."

He threw the first shovelful of dirt into the hole and Marseilles screeched, finding strength in the last few seconds he had of life.

Jonathan trudged slowly across the field. He found himself slightly off course and changed direction toward the front porch. He raised his head and glanced at the empty tobacco fields. He stopped and stared. Calcutta, on the theory that he'd be needed for preparation and delivery of drinks, had left the scene at the elm tree much against his personal desires. He drew abreast of Jonathan, who had resumed walking.

"Why ain't they in the fields?" Jonathan asked sharply.

"It Sunday, massa, suh. It Sunday."

"Oh!" Jonathan said, and kept on walking. He cleared his throat and spat. He could smell the slave ship again. It seemed to permeate his nostrils to a point of almost making him ill.

Epilogue

FITZ, dusty and tired from his long journey, complicated by sixty-five spirited horses and ten slothful slaves held in check only by Themba, listened to his father's story.

"Work has to go on, Fitz," Jonathan said. "Got us this plantation goin' at last, way it should be."

Fitz drank the rest of his rum and water. "Goin' to say goodbye to mama. Be back soon."

Outside, he found Hong Kong waiting, his hat in his hand. "Come along," Fitz said. "Show me whar my mama buried and whar Marseilles stuck in the ground."

"Massa, suh," Hong Kong fell into step with him, something he should not have done, "this heah new nigger yo' brings, he goin' to boss me, suh? Gots to know 'cause he actin' like he overseah."

"His name is Themba," Fitz said. "He'll be in full charge of the hosses and the stables. That's all. You still oversee the plantation."

"Yassuh, massa, suh. Long's I knows."

Fitz stood at the foot of his mother's grave. It had been covered with wild flowers and he knew the slaves must have done that. He bowed his head for a moment, and then walked away rapidly, Hong Kong guiding him to the far end of the corn field where the sunken and ragged edge of the hole betrayed where Marseilles had died.

"Wants you to take all the niggers you need, find the

biggest rock they be 'found here, roll it over the hole an' leave it there. Wants every nigger to know whut it means."

"Yassuh, massa, suh. I does it."

Fitz returned to the house, called to Calcutta to bring him and his father another drink and then he sat down opposite the desk behind which his father still sat, slumped in his chair.

"Got us'n the best hosses in Kaintuck'," Fitz related. "Paid high for 'em, but they's worth it. Bought us'n a new nigger too. Big buck who'll make a fine black stud, but more important, he one smart nigger 'round hosses an' he crazy 'bout racin' 'em. Only thing, he one smart nigger 'bout too many things."

"I jes' buried me a smart nigger, head first," Jonathan said. "Let this new one know that. How were the folks in Kaintuck'?"

"They be the greediest I evah saw, papa, and the mos' uppity. Cain't git over it. They has fine manners an' all, but they bed down with they own relatives and anybody else they kin get they hands on."

Jonathan eyed him shrewdly. "Takes it you liked one of 'em."

Fitz nodded. "Name of Benay. Her papa is the man I bought the hosses from. Mos' beautiful gal I ever saw, papa. Pure too, I reckoned, but I was wrong. Cain't he'p thinkin' 'bout her. Go to sleep thinkin' 'bout her, I do. Knows whut she is, but that don't matter seems."

"You aimin' to go back and fetch her?"

"Times I'd like to kill her. Times I'd like to die without her. Don' know whut I do, papa."

Jonathan said, "Whut you needs is some wenchin' and Nina she been pantin' like a bitch in the heat. You needs dreenin', boy, and she's here to pleasure you."

"Been thinkin' 'bout her too. Misses her 'bout as much as I do Benay. Maybe she'll be 'nuff, papa. I aims to find out—right now."

225

He strode out of the house, feeling the effects of the two drinks, feeling also an uncontrollable desire for Nina. He hadn't even seen her since his return, and he was pleased she'd stayed out of the way until after he'd been told about his mother.

He found Nina near the stables, talking to Themba. Fitz experienced a sudden wave of anger at that big handsome buck. He called to Nina. She turned, came running as fast as she could and went into his arms without regard to Themba or anyone else who watched.

"You back, massa, suh," she cried happily. Then she lowered her eyes and went limp in his embrace. "I cry fo' yo' mama, massa, suh. Loved her, I did."

"She's dead and gone," Fitz said. "We got to live and I got me sap saved up for weeks. Come on, 'fore I takes you right here."

She smiled again, let go of him and when he began walking with his long strides toward the house, she trotted along in his wake, where she belonged.

Themba watched them. His face was composed. There was nothing new in this. He was well aware of what Fitz wanted of Nina, but Themba's eyes glittered in a way Fitz would have found interesting—and dangerous.

There was a rebellion being slowly seeded all over the South, though not even the slaves were aware of it. In the North, the first stirrings of the Abolitionists were being fanned into small flames that could not help but grow because of what it had to feed upon.

A way of life, gracious and charming on the outside, of white pillars and magnolias, had not yet betrayed the shallowness which lay beneath the quiet and pleasant facade. There were still years of slaves and whips, of garden parties and wenches raised for pleasuring their masters, for bearing offspring to work the fields. But the decay had started, beginning like a tiny spot of disease too small to be noticed or felt, but which would grow until one day it would be visible for all to see.

When that day came, a way of life would end, a way that could never return, but before it did, the sickness, now so small, would feed and nurture itself on the strength of the master and the weakness of the slave.

PART 2
Master of Wyndward

One

THE CURING SHEDS, sixty feet long and twelve feet high, were rapidly filling with tobacco. At Wyndward Plantation, the harvesting was done by stripping only mature leaves from the three extensive fields of plants. In this way the tobacco harvested was of a finer quality. Smaller tobacco farms were unable to afford the luxury of this slow method of harvesting, but Wyndward now had eight hundred slaves, most of whom worked in the fields. Labor therefore was no problem, and young Fitz Turner, who now all but ran the plantation for his father, always harvested this way.

The leaves were brought in after being taken from each prime stalk, five or six at a time. They were then inverted and hung on sticks suspended from the beams running across the top of each shed. The sheds were built of hand-hewn lumber, set loosely in place so air could circulate.

Now the tobacco hung there to be air-cured, during which a chemical process began to darken the leaf and change its composition. Soon female slaves would be assigned to build small fires on the floor of each shed and allow the smoke to circulate and help cure the leaves. Finally the tobacco would be taken down and packed into hogsheads that held from six hundred to a thousand pounds. The leaves would be pressed down hard and left to cure.

Fitz, and his father Jonathan, had made a study of

growing tobacco, and instead of using a six-month period of time for ripening, they planned on eighteen months. By then the leaves would have fully fermented, and the result would be a Virginia rivaled by none.

Slaves in relays brought in the leaves while the wenches hung them carefully. One buck, toting a bulky sheaf over his shoulder, was soaked with sweat. He was naked to the waist as all of the bucks were, and his black torso glistened. To him, this was a monotonous work, back and forth, back and forth. It was no great physical strain, however, for which he was grateful. Cutting sugar cane in Louisiana could kill a man in five years. This simple chore gave him time to think about one of the wenches who'd just arrived in a coffle brought by a Richmond slave trader. He was thinking that he'd like to cover her, and he was trying to make up his mind whether or not he'd be whipped if he asked Massa Fitz for her.

He stepped hard on a small, sharp stone, and the pain shot up his leg and it buckled under him. The sheaf of leaves skidded to the ground, some of them landing on top of the slave as he sprawled out.

Instantly, there was another buck beside him, a towering, ebony black, possessed of sharp eyes and an obvious intelligence. Unlike the others, he wore a clean cotton shirt, a better grade of pants and his feet were encased in shoes—which was unfortunate for the buck who had fallen.

The big buck, who was in full charge of the farming part of this two-thousand-acre plantation, was named Hong Kong, perhaps a bit facetiously by Jonathan Turner, who owned Wyndward. Jonathan had been the captain of his own clipper ship and he'd brought more than ten thousand slaves into the country. Because his first hundred plantation slaves were fresh from Africa and without names he could remember, he had instituted the device of naming all bucks after ports of call and all wenches after ships.

So this huge buck was Hong Kong, and he rather liked the name. He didn't like slaves who were so clumsy they fell over their own feet. He kicked the fallen man soundly in the ribs.

"Git up, yo' no-good bastahd," he said calmly. "Git up, nigguh, or I drags yo' down to the whuppin' shed and gives yo' ten."

The slave struggled to his feet and bent over to pick up the tobacco leaves. Hong Kong kicked him as hard as he could in the buttocks and the slave fell forward on his face. He struggled to his feet and resumed picking up the leaves, careful to keep his buttocks aimed in the other direction. Hong Kong strode down the shed, checking the way the leaves were hung, watching the wenches threading the tobacco on the sticks. They were working industriously now. As soon as he left the shed, they'd taper off and begin their everlasting gossip. He didn't know what they had to gossip about unless it was the performance of their men on the cornstalk-stuffed mattresses.

Hong Kong no longer had the slightest interest in sex. He was a eunuch, having been turned into one by the savage reprisal of a white overseer whom Jonathan Turner had hired when the plantation first began operating. Hong Kong remembered that day very well, when he'd been strung up by the heels, his legs pulled apart. The overseer had used a specially made club, smashing it down between Hong Kong's legs. Hong Kong had only vague recollections of Fitz Turner whipping the overseer and breaking him up into a mewing, crawling mass of shattered human flesh.

From the day Hong Kong was able to walk about again, he'd been made black overseer and placed in full charge of the fields. Another buck named Themba had control of the barns and stables where he spent much of his time training race horses which were the second money crop of this sprawling and successful plantation.

The third crop was pickaninnies—suckers. The wenches had been covered by their bucks even before the plantation opened for business and now the birthing cabins were jammed.

The plantation lay between Richmond and Lynchburg and was owned completely by Jonathan Turner. Wyndward Hall squatted atop a plateau with a rolling lawn stretching down to the dirt road half a mile below. It was pillared, had a rambling porch and a gallery. It was painted white and sparkled in the sun.

Behind the house were the stables where almost a hundred specially bred thoroughbreds were kept. There were work horses and common riding horses too.

The plantation had been named Wyndward after the clipper ship which had made all this possible. Jonathan had been its captain and while his cargo had consisted of material goods when he left the States, on his way back it had always been slaves. He'd become rich from the trade, which had been his aim, for he wanted a plantation in Virginia second to none. Slaves bought in Africa for paltry sums sold right off the clipper for four hundred dollars or so each, in big lots, no questions asked and no examinations made. Slaves at the vendue table sold for six or seven hundred. An exceptional buck brought nine hundred, and a good wench whose breeding qualities had already been demonstrated, seven-fifty.

Wyndward Hall was reached by a drive paved with fieldstone. Beyond the drive was a bowling green stretching almost as far as the eye could see. At the rear of the house were the separate buildings used as kitchen, bakery, dairy, curing sheds, storehouses, cold spring and the rather elaborate outhouse which was divided into two sections with a door for each. It looked like a miniature cottage with overhangs, a random roof, two chimneys to accommodate the round pot-bellied stove in each segment. A stone walk, beneath a narrow arcade, made visits to the outhouse protected in all manner of weather, though the womenfolk would rarely make the trip without an open parasol over their heads. The residence of the former owners, still standing, was to be turned into a guest house.

Wyndward Hall itself was square and uncompromisingly plain, as befitted the residence of a captain of a clipper ship. Four double chimneys rose above the slanted roof and accommodated eight fireplaces, one for each room in the house and each fireplace large enough for a tree trunk. One thing Jonathan remembered about his boyhood, the winters were cold.

Jonathan had been lavish in building and furnishing the house. He had wanted his wife, Sarah, to be pleased and contented here, and she had been during the brief period she'd occupied it. The inside of the house was as opulent as the exterior was plain, from the moment one entered the large reception hall with its chandeliers and sconces which decorated the walls and gave off warm glows of candlelight. The hallway was carpeted in a rich gold-colored rug which followed on up the winding staircase, graceful as the arching of the clipper *Wyndward* in a mild sea.

There was a ballroom which also served as the drawing room. Here again was a feeling of quiet wealth in the massive furniture, all upholstered except for a row of gilded cane-back chairs to be used when the room was converted into a ballroom. The floor was covered with a large oval rug, varied in color, woven tightly and expertly. Around it, mahogany flooring had been polished to a brilliancy which made all the furnishings stand out in bright reflection.

The fireplace was framed by a mantel of white marble, with two enormous andirons holding up massive logs, ready to be lighted. The side windows were mullioned, hung with pale draperies over filmy curtains. The draperies were edged with gold fringe, and tied back with thick, golden-threaded cords, heavily tasseled. The tables held oil lamps with glass shades.

The dining room, rather bare for the sake of practicality, had a long table and twenty heavy chairs. There was a bedroom on the first floor, spacious and nicely furnished. One room was fitted like an office, with a long table and a large desk with a high-backed leather chair behind it. There were walls of mostly empty bookshelves, and a brightly polished spittoon done in what looked like gold plate.

There were four upstairs bedrooms. For the master, Jonathan had had duplicates made of every piece of furniture in the bedroom he had shared with Sarah in their Boston home. It had been his hope that it would lessen her resistance to coming to Virginia to live. Sarah was a strong-willed woman and at the time she came, she'd had no idea that Jonathan had acquired most of his wealth in the slave cargoes he'd brought back from Africa.

Wyndward Hall was the seat of a vast farming enterprise built up over the years by Jonathan's labors. Its two thousand acres were located seventy miles west of Norfolk, not far from Richmond and plenty close to Lynchburg and Petersburg. All prime land—three money crops, as Jonathan would proudly state. Tobacco, pure-blooded horses and niggers.

To one side of the stables was a hard-surfaced race track, a mile in circumference, where the horses were often clocked. Everywhere one looked, slaves were busy. Jonathan Turner's carefully planned scheme was to breed slaves for sale. While the breeding went on, the slaves worked the fields. Thus one money crop supported and aided a second money crop. The horses were a sideline, but now it appeared likely they might become the greatest moneymaker of all.

Jonathan Turner sat on the porch, rocking idly. He was a tall, lean man, with considerable breadth of shoulder and rather long arms. His muscular brawniness was exceptional in one so tall and slender-waisted. Though he was only forty years of age, his face was deeply lined and leathery from his years at sea, making him seem much older. He was not highly educated, but he was smart and clever. On a small table beside him was an almost-empty glass of Barbados rum and water. Jonathan surveyed what he could see of his property, land, buildings, animals, and slaves. There was so much of everything, and it was going to make him even richer. But he was also a lonely man. His blue eyes, which used to be so bright with the urgency of living, were now watery long before their time and he was even prone to admit he felt old beyond his years.

He could be proud of his son, though, and his watery eyes held a hint of pride as Fitz approached the porch casually, with a long-legged stride. He was slim, tall, strong as the best buck nigger. Handsome too, Jonathan decided, even if his white shirt and pants were dark with sweat. The big floppy-brimmed straw hat kept the sun off fine, but it didn't keep a man from sweating or turning the color of deep bronze.

Fitz was as tall as his father, but filled out more, which meant he was heavier and even better proportioned. His light brown hair was almost golden in hue, from having been bleached by the sun. His eyes were blue-gray; his chin, aggressive. There was something of his mother in his mouth which was soft, not as thin-lipped as that of his father. He'd been named Fitzjohn as a compromise between his mother who'd wanted him called Fitzgerald after her family and his father who'd wanted him to bear his own name. Jonathan still resented the compromise, but felt it was better than Fitzgerald which, in Virginia, would have made him sound like some fancy-named nigger.

"Calcutta!" Jonathan yelled. "Git out heah."

The houseboy scuttled from the kitchen to the porch

and stood before Jonathan, waiting his orders. He was about seventeen and attired in knee-length white cotton hose, short pants buckled just below the knee, a white cotton shirt and a white coat.

"Two glasses this time. My son's comin' an' he looks like he could handle a dozen. Git the water from the springhouse. If it ain't cold, I kicks yore black ass so you won't sit down fo' a week."

"Yassuh, massa, suh." Calcutta gathered up the empty, hurried back into the house, paused in the hallway long enough to tilt the glass and drain what few drops were left. Then he raced out to the springhouse. He wasn't really afraid of his master. He was used to the constant flow of threats, but he didn't think his master exactly meant them. Not now, anyway.

Fitz removed his hat, shook the sweat off the band, and dropped it on the porch as he sank into a chair. "Hot's hell, papa. Good fo' the crops, though. Corn comin' real fine. Wheat goin' to make some prime grain, reckon."

"Ever'thin's comin'," Jonathan said. "Hosses, suckers an' 'bacco. Ever'thin' 'ceptin' me. Jes' got no juice any mo'. Don' give a goddamn whut happens."

"Long as we keeps makin' money," Fitz grinned.

His father laughed. "Reckon. Whur in hell's that no-good nigger with our drinks?"

"Likely runnin' back from the springhouse 'bout now, papa. He ain't shiftless."

"Not when you watches him."

Fitz lifted his long legs and rested the heels on the porch rail. "You ain't sleepin' well, papa, lessen you gits pow'ful drunk. Hears you movin' 'round half the night. Been months now mama was killed. Time you was gittin' over it."

Jonathan looked at him bleakly. "Knows that, son. Jes' don' understan' it. Keep thinkin' about her. Bringin' her down here from Boston was a mistake."

"Do you think she'd have stayed there after you gave up slavin'?"

"Maybe not. Don' rightly know. Lots o' things keep me 'wake. Way she died . . ."

"I knows."

"That sonabitch Marseilles give her a devil hoss, knowin' damn well she'd be throwed. An' when it happened, Marseilles was waitin'. Even guessed whur it would happen. Nevah tol' you the whole story, did I?"

"Reckon not," Fitz said. He'd heard it a dozen times, but his father seemed to gain some magic release of tension when he told it again. Before he could begin, Calcutta appeared, balancing a tray with two drinks on it. He set them down very carefully, backed away, waiting to be told he could go, or be kicked in the slats for some reason he wouldn't fathom.

"Git," Jonathan ordered. "In fifteen minutes bring two more, an' bring 'em sober, y' heah? You stinks o' rum I goin' to break you ass good. Did it once. Kin do it again."

"I don' drink none, massa, suh. Sweahs I don'. Knows bettah I does, massa suh."

"Beat it," Fitz growled. Calcutta did a fast spring, almost letting the door slam, a sin Jonathan was punishing rather harshly of late, as if he couldn't stand the sound of it.

Jonathan drank deeply. "Sarah had yo' wench Nina ridin' 'long like she used to do, an' Marseilles he waitin'. Give yo' mama that mean hoss nobody ride. The hoss got skittish in the mud and mama fell off. She landed on her face in four inches o' mud and choked to death. Marseilles ripped the dress off'n Nina and rapes her, while his mistress drowned in the goddamn mud, an' all he has to do is turn her over. But he too busy screwin' Nina so your ma, she died."

"The slaves keep mama's grave real nice and fresh with flowers, papa."

"They liked her. Ever'body did, soon's she began to fo'git 'bout the No'th and started actin' like a so'thern lady."

"You notice the big rock I had Hong Kong roll on top of the hole where you stuck Marseilles?"

"Noticed it. Reckon that's a good idea. Ain't a nigger won't think whut happened to that sonabitch. I strung him up by the heels and whupped him with the snake. I cut him good. Then I had him lowered head first into a ten-foot-deep hole and filled it in. He died eatin' dirt too."

"That part keepin' yo' 'wake, papa?"

"Hell no! Whut's one nigger? Cain't he'p thinkin' 'bout your ma. Ever'thin' goin' so good and she content at last. So'm I. You know whut I mean, son?"

"I knows, papa."

"I makes up my min' day she got kilt I ain' nevah gonna do no mo' wenchin'. Meant it too. Even thought mebbe I don' smell that rotten stench no mo'. Mebbe wouldn'a wuked though 'cause I sure keep smellin' that goddamn hold in my ship whur I kept the niggers chained. Pow'ful stink. Like it's got into my nose and won't go 'way. Smells it in my sleep, I do. Reckon I ain't good fo' much any mo'."

"Needs mo' time. 'Nuff wuk keepin' them books anyhow. Birthin' house full. Gittin' so we sho't-handed, all them wenches knocked up and ready to pop us suckers."

Jonathan nodded. "Bes' I send somebody for the veter'nary to come stay heah 'while. Don' want to lose any o' them suckers. Wurth two hundred dollahs first breath they take. Wants to keep 'em breathin'."

"Good idea, papa. I send for him soon's you say."

"Bettah do it tomorra, son. Cain't take no chances. 'Nuff die anyhow 'fore they gits big 'nuff to sell."

Fitz took a pull at his glass. "Not on this plantation," he declared confidently. "We wuks 'em, but not too hard. We feeds 'em bes' any nigger gits anywhur. They got they solid cabins for when winter comes an' they be snug. Figgered you was wastin' money goin' to all that expense for a few hundred niggers, but I sees now it pays off."

"Known that a long time. My papa had a plantation too an' he showed me how to run one. Whur in hell that nigger?"

Fitz lowered one leg and stamped the foot on the porch floor. "Calcutta," he bellowed.

The houseboy came rushing out. "Think you gittin' deef," Jonathan complained. "Holler my haid off 'fore you drags you ass out heah. Two more drinks an' you sloth an' I whups you for breakfuss."

Calcutta hurried away, not worried any more. Talk of being whipped was just talk. When Master Jonathan whipped, it was for a very good reason—it wasn't any trivial matter. Like the first time he tasted the master's rum and got drunk.

"Nice sittin' heah," Jonathan said. "Lookin' out oveh all. Easy talkin' heah. Never did know all about that gal you met in Kaintuck when you bought our race hosses."

"Benay?" Fitz sighed. "Benay Meader. Pretties' gal I evah saw, papa. Smart too, on'y she din' know how to cool down her hots. She talks like a real lady, she does. Curtsies an' smiles, an' laughs kinda low. Hear her yit. Asked her to wait fo' me."

"Knows the rest, son."

"Don' ache me to talk 'bout it, papa. Sure figgered me as a man then. Got thinkin' I had all I wanted, an' then she came outen her cousin Gerald's room, naked's a jes'-born sucker under her wrapper. Said she an' Cousin Gerald been prayin' ev'ry night since they children. Cousin Gerald was a-prayin' at the washstand, cleanin' up his goddamn juice, an' the bed look like they wrastles in it fo' hours. Jes' walked away from her, I did. An' no goin' back." He closed his eyes in painful memory.

"Sure does miss her and want her, papa, but I ain't marryin' no cousin-screwin' whore."

"Ain't much 'tention paid to it heah, son. Done all the time. Heered o' it when I jes' a boy. On'y thing eyah bothered me, I din' have no cousin to screw."

"I gits over her," Fitz vowed. "Like you, papa, I needs time."

"You wench, Nina, she he'ps, reckon?"

Fitz nodded. Calcutta came bustling out with two more drinks. He set them down, collected the two empty glasses. Fitz waved him away without a word and Calcutta disappeared to sit by the door in the kitchen and wait for the next summons he knew would come soon.

"Drinkines' massas evah did see," he remarked as he settled down on the floor.

The cook, enormous, blue-black, named Elegant by Jonathan, walked over and slapped him smartly across the face. "Yo' talks 'bout yo' massa, yo' talks nice o' yo' don' talk nohow. Whut's the mattah wid yo', nigger? Don' yo' knows yo' oney a goddamn black suhvent? Wants a whuppin' yo' does."

Calcutta rubbed his smarting face. "Massa don' whup me. Massa, he loves me, he do. Whut yo' hit me fo', Elegant? I din' do nuthin'."

"That why yo' gits slapped—'cause yo' does nuthin'. Now keep yo' mouth shet, heah? Or I shets it fo' yo'."

On the porch, Fitz sipped his drink, consuming it steadily and doggedly, as if he too, craved forgetfulness in its numbing effects.

Before it turned dark, Nina appeared to announce supper was ready. She was slight of build and narrow-hipped. She had finely chiseled features, lacking the large teeth, thick lips and sloping forehead of the Negro. Her small, shapely nose hadn't even the hint of a flare-out at the nostrils. Her mouth was small, thin-lipped. Her cheekbones high and her hair straight, with a reddish tinge through its darkness as if it had been lightly touched with a feather dipped in dye. Her legs were fuller, not the spindly ones of most African girls. Her ankles were slender, her thighs slim and firm. Jonathan's opinion of her was that she was too flat-assed and too meagerly tittied to give Fitz a sucker.

She was an extremely attractive girl, yet she was as much a slave as the others. One drop of Negro blood made that person a Negro without any chance of appeal. Those who were white enough to pass, did so whenever possible. Those who could not, lived a life of hell. The men were made pets of, to serve white mistresses or perform lewd acts for their masters. The girls were brought at high prices to become white men's women and then to be sold again, passed on to others, until they were either dead or dying of disease before thirty.

Nina had been brought over in the slave cargo of Jonathan's last voyage. Jonathan himself had deflowered her, and Fitz had fallen in love with her, as much as a white man could. She'd come of Arabian stock, her mother part of the harem of a prince. That made no difference when she was kidnapped and sold to Jonathan as part of the six-hundred-and-fifty-slave cargo.

Nina was intelligent and gay-spirited, and she loved Fitz with a strange devotion. She knew her place, but relished the fact that he cared for her above anyone else. When she didn't share his bed, she slept on the floor at the foot of it. While Fitz's mother lived, things had been different, but Nina managed to find Fitz's bed often enough to satisfy him—and herself.

As she turned away, Fitz let his hand casually caress the sleek lines of her buttocks. She gave him a quick smile, as if to assure him that when he wanted her, she'd be ready for him.

They went in to dinner. It used to be a pleasant meal, with Sarah Turner supervising. Now that she was dead, it seemed the two men only wanted to bolt their food and get away from the table, as if they could see her ghost sitting there in disapproval of their manners which had grown careless with no white woman around.

After supper, Jonathan went to his office on the first floor and attended to the book work. Often he did it over and over, not to correct any mistakes, because he was meticulous in his handling of it, but to pass the time and keep his mind occupied. Nights were the worst for him. It seemed to him now that he'd hardly known Sarah. He met her in a seaport town near Boston. Her father was an importer-exporter and Jonathan would solicit his trade for the voyages East. Jonathan carried a general cargo then. He took no cargo on his way back, save the human one packed in the hold until the very hull of the ship reeked from the body sweat, the excrement, the vomit of ten thousand seasick slaves chained to the hold.

He'd married Sarah after a few days' courtship. She was then staid, fussy, domineering, not given to any great passions, but she had birthed Fitz. His voyages were very long, there was little time between them. During the years he kept this up, while his fortune grew and grew, Sarah educated their son. Fitzjohn, a name composed partly of her maiden name, partly of Jonathan's name, was educated to be a Boston gentleman. He'd even gone to Harvard. He could, when he wished, speak flawless Boston English, but when he went on his first voyage with his father, he lapsed into the indifferent speech his father affected. He liked the slowness of it, the softness of it, after the clipped Bostonian style. Besides, he knew it pleased Jonathan to hear his son speak like him.

Then Sarah had consented to move to Virginia and become mistress of this plantation. She'd arrived with strange ideas about slaves, but she slowly adjusted and the kind of family life Jonathan had dreamed of became a reality. Then she'd been killed, soon after she arrived, in a stupid, cruel, heartless way. It almost seemed as if she'd never been here at all, except for the grave which the slaves always kept decorated with flowers.

Before it was quite dark, Fitz strolled casually to the stable area. He saw Themba, a slave he'd bought from Sam Meader in Kentucky, thrust a ragged-looking newspaper page under the box on which he'd been sitting. He was a big man, very black, with finely wrought features, high forehead, straight hair. His mouth was sensitive; his eyes, intelligent.

He was different from the run-of-the-mill buck for another reason. He was an expert in the training, breeding, and care of thoroughbreds. For that purpose he was priceless. But Fitz didn't quite trust him. There was something about this slave that bothered him. Not in an irksome way; nor in any manner to frighten him. It was more as if he were being warned to watch the man, to consider what he did and examine it. As now, with the newspaper page Themba had tried to hide.

"Whut you got theah?" Fitz demanded.

"Nothin', massa, suh. I got nothin'," Themba replied humbly.

"Give it heah," Fitz ordered. "Come on . . . give it heah or I sen' you back to Kaintuck."

Themba produced the ragged, crumpled page of a Richmond newspaper. It contained a few advertisements, part of a story about the new river steamboats and several political cartoons.

"Whut's in this heah paper? You gits to read it?"

Themba smiled thinly. "Cain't read, massa, suh. Cain't read nuthin'. Pleasures me to look at the pitchers, suh. Wish'n I could draw like that."

Fitz threw the page aside. "Whut about that big black stallion I bought from Mistah Meader? The one ev'rybody say cain't be tamed?"

"Massa, suh, I thinks I kin tame him, but he a sonabitch an' like to kick me to bits. Cain't make him do

245

nothin', an' I crazy 'bout hosses. Mos' like me too. This 'un like to kill me, he do."

"Thinkin' we bes' shoot him."

Themba sprang up quickly. He whipped off his hat, which he hadn't done up to then. "Massa, suh, please don't do that. He good hoss, on'y cain't unnerstan' yit. He do, an' he be the fastes' hoss evah. Faster'n that lil' mare yo' clocked yestiddy."

"She did pretty well. Time we set her against some opposition."

"Yo' means racin' her, suh? She ready! She's sho' ready. Reckon ain't no hoss in she class kin beat her, massa, suh. You wants I gits her in shape?"

Fitz nodded. "Reckon 'bout time."

Themba hesitated a moment. "Massa, suh, kin I say somethin', please, massa, suh?"

"Whut is it?"

"They's goin' to be racin' in Richmond come two weeks."

"How you know that?"

"Yo' members last coffle that Mistah Briggs he bring heah to try an' sell yo' some? He have one buck I knowed an' he tol' me."

"I'll see whut I can learn," Fitz promised. He idly scooped up the page of newspaper before he turned away. He was still carrying it as he vanished into the approaching gloom. Themba didn't move. He kept looking at Fitz's dwindling form and his forehead was wrinkled in deep worry.

Fitz stopped by the cabin of Hong Kong and Seawitch, his wench. As was customary, Fitz merely opened the door and walked in. There was no need to knock on the door of a slave's cabin. Hong Kong was seated before the fireplace, for the evenings were getting chilly. Tallow candles flickered on an upended keg. Seawitch, an exceptionally intelligent wench, dropped the pan she was washing and, with her man, faced Fitz respectfully.

"How things with you, Hong Kong?" Fitz asked.

"Jes' fine, reckons. Jes' fine, massa, suh."

Fitz smiled for Seawitch's benefit mostly. "Your buck sure make a fine overseer. Bes' ever had, an' 'preciates it. My mama lef' plenty dresses an' shoes . . . things like that. You come to the house tomorrow, Seawitch, you tells Nina whut you wants. Two dresses, shoes. Leave some fo' nex' time. Wants you to be best lookin' wench heah."

"Thanks you, massa, suh," she said, highly pleased.

"How it go with Hong Kong?" Fitz asked casually. "Knows he ain't got much lef', but you able to git anythin' up yit?"

"I wukkin' on it, massa, suh. Like you say, ain't much lef', but I keep wukkin' an' prayin' some."

"How you stan' not bein' pleasured?"

"Stands it fine, massa, suh." She looked at him with fresh worry. "Massa, suh, yo' ain't fixin' to turns me oveh to some buck . . . ?"

"Tol' you once, I ain't nevah goin' to bust you and Hong Kong up. Ain't goin' to tell you agin."

"Yassuh, massa, suh." Seawitch bobbed her head happily.

"Massa, suh, kin I talks to yo'?" Hong Kong asked.

Fitz nodded and walked out, knowing that whatever Hong Kong wished to talk about was none of his wench's business. They paused in the darkness outside the cabin. There were no other cabins nearby and no slaves were lounging about to overhear.

"Wants to talk 'bout that Themba, suh."

"Whut 'bout him?"

"He mighty good wid them hosses."

"Bes' I ever see," Fitz said.

"He smart nigger, massa, suh. Don't like him, an' wants no truck wid him. He lookin' to talk to Nina, he do."

"You seen him with Nina?" Fitz asked harshly.

"No suh . . . not fo' pleasurin' I din', but she go by an' he talks. Likes her he do. Kin tell."

"Themba lays a finger on her, you gits to whup him twenty lashes, Hong Kong. He covers her an' I kills him."

"Yas suh, massa, suh. I don' like makin' trouble, but you my massa an' I loves yo' way yo' treats Seawitch. Yo' wants him whupped, I whup him. Fights him, yo' say so. Kills him, yo' say so."

"He's a fancy nigger," Fitz said. "He too valuable to kill. Don' even wants to scar him up with the whup, but I will he don' leave Nina alone."

"Yassuh, massa, suh. Reckon that fair 'nuff."

Fitz looked off into space. "Whut Nina do, he talk to her?"

"She walk fas', massa, suh. She don' say nothin'."

"Gittin' in the last of the 'bacco in the first field tomorrow?" Fitz thought it time to change the subject.

"Gits it all in 'fore we quits terday, suh."

"Good. Git the bucks busy in the second field. Low leaves comin' to harvest by now. Git us'n a good crop."

"Bes' land fo' it, massa, suh."

Fitz nodded and walked away. It was not customary nor wise to bid a slave goodnight, nor unbend to him in the slightest degree. Hong Kong was an exceptional black and invaluable, but he was black and a slave. There were no exceptions.

Fitz strolled back to the house. Calcutta, peering out of the windows set beside the door, admitted him with one of his grins and a quick bow. Fitz ran his hand over the boy's wool, roughed him up a bit and went on. Calcutta closed the door, locked it and shivered in his delight over being petted.

Fitz sat down before his father's desk. Jonathan didn't greet him. He was slowly growing glassy-eyed with rum, but he never fumbled his speech no matter how drunk he became. He sat there looking at Fitz, guessing his son had something to tell him and waiting until he did.

Fitz scanned the crumpled page of the newspaper before he threw it into the fireplace. "Themba says they fixin' fo' a hoss race in Richmond in two weeks, papa."

Jonathan nodded. "You wants to run one o' the hosses?"

"The little mare's ready. Clocked her and she ain't goin' to be easy to beat."

"Then we races her. How Themba heah 'bout it?"

"Say when Mist' Brigg's coffle pass through last week, he knows one of the slaves and talks to him. Tells him 'bout the race."

"Goddamn Briggs oughta keep he goddamn coffle 'way from our niggers."

"Did, papa. Themba lyin'."

Jonathan looked interested. "Whur he heah 'bout the race then?"

"Ketched him lookin' at a Richmond newspaper, papa. On'y one page, but it say 'bout the race. Papa, that nigger kin read."

"We sells him cheap nex' coffle come by," Jonathan decreed promptly.

"Cain't, papa. We needs him. Won't be no racin' we don' have him."

"Keep your eyes skinned he near," Jonathan advised. "Mayhap we shuck him down and give him a taste of the whup."

"Thinks he run, we do that. Don' want no runners from this heah plantation. Bes' we do is nothin', but like you say, skin yo' eyes an' watch him close. Reckon I step out a bit fo' some air befo' goin' to baid."

Fitz went out onto the porch before Calcutta came out of his doze to spring from the kitchen and reach the door first. Knowing he was too late, Calcutta went back to sleep. Fitz stood at the top of the porch steps and looked out into the darkness. He was being plagued by the memory of Benay Meader. Out there in the nothingness of the dark he could visualize her, blonde, tall, slender and lovely, with the bluest eyes he had ever seen in this world. Even thinking about her brought a reaction and he suddenly had need of Nina. Just as he turned to go back into the house, he heard a branch snap somewhere in the darkness.

"Who that?" he called.

There was no answer. He hadn't expected one, but at least whoever watched knew they hadn't quite gotten away with it. Some slave, wondering what it was like in the big house, he presumed. He wasn't worried. He went in and bounced up the stairs to his room. Nina was there, seated beside the window looking out. She jumped up when he entered.

Fitz went directly to her and seized her roughly. She didn't object. She was more than willing, and he kissed her hard and long until he was seething with desire for her.

He sat down while she quickly removed his clothes. Always she took care not to touch his flesh as all slaves must take care. She did manage to keep him highly aroused, however. He slipped into bed. She walked past the window, pulling up her dress as she did so. She glanced out into the night once and then came into the bed for his caresses. His hands closed around her full, ripe breasts with their hard nipples. She had no odor, as wenches usually did. The only smell about her was a faint feminine one. She washed every night before he came to the room so that she would always be ready for him if he wanted her.

His eagerness was not to be contained however and, before long, he rolled on top of her, penetrated her and quite involuntarily he said, "Benay!" He felt like a fool afterwards as he lay on his back, wondering if he was going to be able to sustain another bout with Nina tonight.

She lay on her side, watching him, her eyes still flashing the fires of her passion. "Massa, suh, why you say Benay? Whut that?"

"Thinkin' 'bout name of a hoss. Nothin' you worries you lil' haid 'bout, Nina. You see somethin' outen the window 'fore you crawled in?"

"No, suh, sees nothin' out theah. I pleasure yo' good tonight, suh?"

"Never failed me yit, Nina. Nevah once. You the bes' lil' piece I evah had. Goin' to keep you handy 'til you die. Reckon we kin still do this we gits old and shaky?"

"You keeps me, we shore do it, massa, suh. I ain't nevah goin' to be old. Mayhap I gits wrinkled an' lame, an' my skin hangs offen me, but you in baid I be good's I am now. Cain't he'p it, massa, suh. I loves you, I do."

"Reckon so," he said, and drew her to him again. He was lucky to have her, but he still thought about Benay. That blonde, heated-up bitch Benay, whom he never wanted to see again, and missed profoundly.

Two

THE TOBACCO CROP was almost entirely harvested. Most of the stalks had been cut and the fields would now be allowed to rest. Before too long, winter would descend on the plantation and much of the work outside would be curtailed. There'd be plenty to do in the sheds, however. There was always clean-up work, and there were fifty new cabins to be built. Jonathan wanted a thousand slaves on the premises before spring, and that did not include the bumper crop of suckers now almost ready.

In the sheds, the curing fires burned slowly on the floor, each watched by three pregnant wenches, on the theory that all three wouldn't fall asleep at one time. They were swollen and moved slowly, so this was fine work for them. Jonathan watched his wenches with pride. The original fifty were almost all pregnant, about half of these in the same stage of pregnancy, because they'd been covered at the same time.

On the last night of Jonathan's final voyage, he'd selected fifty prime bucks and fifty wenches, matching them well. He'd chained all fifty bucks to the deck and then handed each a wench to be covered right then, on the spot. It had been one riotous night for the crew, and timed well enough because by the next evening they'd all be ashore in Norfolk where there were enough whorehouses to go around. There'd never been such a mass covering in history, Jonathan judged, and laughed whenever he told of it.

The main work of the year was at an end so the slaves were permitted a little more leisure time. This was Jonathan's way of running a slave-breeding farm. You didn't work them to death, you fed them well. You refrained from whipping them, but always held the threat of it over their heads. Now and then, one would require a few lashes, But Jonathan didn't use a snake on them. Such a whip scarred their backs permanently, made them harder to sell, and sometimes turned an otherwise placid slave into a rebellious one. Wyndward Plantation was, therefore, without the blemish of a runner. Probably no other farm, slave-breeding or plain crop-raising, could boast of such a record. To Jonathan, it was a simple matter of good business. Feeding the slaves cost a pittance, letting them take it easy didn't stop production, and if it did cost him something in the way of added profits from the crops, it was more than made up in the value of the healthy pickaninnies who would soon be screeching and running around the place in droves.

When Fitz returned from an inspection trip through the curing sheds, he found his father seated on the porch as usual, drinking rum and water. He'd been consuming formidable quantities of it lately. The row of barrels was going down as fast as if five men were working on them instead of two. The enormous supply of it which Jonathan had brought in on his final voyage was depleted to the point where an order had been sent for more to be imported. Fitz did think about purchasing some cane in Louisiana, having it transported to the plantation and building a still, but Jonathan vetoed the idea.

"You gits niggers wukkin' 'round a still, boy, an' you askin' for trouble. They ain't like us white folks. They gits stinkin' drunk an' 'bellious. Cain't handle it like we kin."

He set his glass on the little table beside him with hands that shook so badly, the glass toppled over, spilling its contents on the floor.

Fitz seated himself on the porch beside his father. Calcutta had been trained to watch for Fitz's return to the house, and, at the first sign of him, run to the springhouse for cold water, return to the kitchen to mix the rum and water and be back on the porch by the time Fitz had reached it, ready for his first drink of the day. It would be Jonathan's tenth or fifteenth. The seventeen-year-old houseboy was in the habit of draining the dregs of each glass. There was always a little left that had become too warm for Jonathan's palate. As a result, Calcutta was usually in the mid-stages of drunkenness by nightfall. He thought he successfully concealed its effect on him so that nobody even remotely guessed his condition.

"Boy's gittin' to be a regular drunk," Fitz mused.

Jonathan shrugged. "Don't hurt him none, reckon. Make the poor sonabitch fo'git he black."

"Reckon we bettah start fixin' things so we kin go to Richmond for the races, papa."

"Leaves that to you. Jes' git that stagecoach I bought, ready. Be sure to grease the wheels an' springs. Las' time I near shook the piss outa me."

"Richmond's a good piece," Fitz observed. "Sixty miles or so. Don't much like the idea of walking that mare all the way. She gits tired out 'fore the race begins."

"Ever'body walks they hosses theah. How else you figger on gittin' them to Richmond?"

"Don' know, papa, but I sure got to think on it."

Jonathan was watching a slowly advancing cloud of dust along the road. "Reckon we got comp'ny comin'."

"Who it be?"

"Reckon the veter'nary, Doc Parker. You sent him word to git up heah befo' the wenches start sheddin' them suckers like they goin' to do mighty soon now."

"You pays him 'nuff, reckon he stay and watch things while we go to Richmond?"

"I'll see whut he says. Goin' anyway. Craves me the pleasure o' seein' one o' my hosses win. You aimin' to bring bettin' money, son?"

"All I kin, papa. We raisin' hosses to make money and that's the on'y reason you trains hosses fo' racin'."

The cloud of dust was turning through the plantation gates now and parting sufficiently to reveal the outlines of a buggy. Presently it slowed and then stopped and after a few seconds the dust settled while an almost perfectly round blob of a man climbed down. Two slaves were racing from the stables to take charge of the horse and buggy and to be of help if the doctor carried any luggage. It turned out he had four pieces of it, a leather bag for his instruments and three carpetbags for his clothing. It looked as if he intended to make a career of Wyndward Plantation.

He trotted his ungainly way up to the porch, this short, round man with the beet red and sweaty, dust-streaked face. He shook Jonathan's hand soundly, as befitted a man of science who was about to render his skills for a price. He thumped Fitz on the back and dropped into a chair. He'd barely warmed its seat before Calcutta appeared with the tray rather well slanted. He bobbed about, collecting the two empty glasses, setting out the three full ones. Dr. Parker drained his in a single swallow, during which he somehow managed to keep his throat wide open while the stream of strong liquor simply flowed down and splashed into his stomach. Calcutta stood there, gaping in frozen astonishment and admiration.

Jonathan delivered him a straight kick in the buttocks and Calcutta scuttled away for another drink. Dr. Parker patted his belly and sighed.

"Don' git myse'f rum 'round heah lessen I comes to visit Wyndward. Now yo' tells me yo' got plenty wenches knocked up and birthin'."

"Birthin' damn soon," Jonathan said. "Last count was 'bout thirty-five."

"All at the same time?"

"Papa gave a mass coverin' party," Fitz explained with a laugh. "All got knocked up the same night."

"I do declare, that might be a good way o' handlin' things, suh," Doc said approvingly. "Real easy on the vet, all that wuk at one time."

Fitz said, "Wants you to look at a big black stallion we got. Ornery critter, kick hell outen anybody who gits near 'nuff. Kin you tell if a hoss is crazy, Doc?"

"Reckon that be kinda hard to do, suh. Ahhh . . ." He accepted the drink straight off Calcutta's tray. "Fetches me 'nuther one, boy," he said. "Mighty dry ridin' through all that goddamn dust."

"You 'zamines the stallion soon's you git finished with you nex' drink, Doc?"

"Sho', Fitz, yo' wants me to. Easier to tell a nigger's crazy 'cause you ask him and he kin answer, bein' an animal whut kin talk. Hosses is diff'rent. All the crazy ones kin do is kick an' bite."

"Then this one is sho' crazy," Fitz commented.

"How long you reckon it take to birth thirty-five suckers?" asked Jonathan slyly.

"Cain't say. The good Lord pops 'em when it's time they pop. Maybe three . . . four a day. Gives me time to 'zamine yo' racin' animals too, suh."

"Figger me an' Fitz, we goin' to Richmond fo' a day or two. Means you stays here in charge, Doc. Somebody has to stay and bein' you got all that birthin' to 'tend. . . ."

Doc didn't fall for the guile. "Reckon I be in charge you gone . . . two weeks or so . . . I gits paid fo' the birthin' an' fo' the 'zamination, an' fo' handlin' this heah big plantation, an' nigh onto eight hundrud niggers. Got to get me ten dollah a day, Jonathan."

"Kinda steep, ain't it?"

"Don't reckon so, bein' all whut I got to do, suh. An' yo' gits to give me privileges 'bout yo' rum barrels too."

"You gits ten dollahs a day for being a vet, you drinks up fo' dollahs wuth o' rum. We split it. Eight dollahs an' the rum."

Doc thought about all those lovely barrels which he'd seen often enough. His mouth watered at the thought. He nodded slowly, giving in because he was a man who sought pleasures in the world more than financial gain.

"Pick o' yo' wenches, suh?" He wanted some additional concession.

"Pick hell," Fitz broke in. "You touches my Nina an' you goin' to holler more'n the birthin' wenches. We got one . . . jes' one . . . whut got no buck yit. You gits her and no other'n. You got to unnerstan' that, Doc."

"She young an' frisky?"

"She virgin," Jonathan said. " 'Nuff gal theah to pleasure you fo' two months an' we be back in less'n two weeks."

Doc stuck out his flabby hand. "A deal, Jonathan. A bargain fairly struck. I gitten the wust o' it, but bein' a gen'man, I gives in 'cause yo' my fren'."

Fitz arose. "Time we looks at the stallion, Doc."

"Soon's I gits me the drink I ordered. Whur that black boy at? Be comin' right down, Fitz. Yo' go' 'long."

Fitz thought he might as well. Doc might want a fourth drink and it wouldn't stay daylight forever. He walked down to the stables. The fast little mare was being groomed by Themba. The slave stopped work to doff his cap, but he didn't turn his gaze downward like the others.

"We leavin' tomorra," Fitz said, "for Richmond, and we takin' the mare to race."

"Thass good, massa, suh. I gits her ready and I cares fo' her all the time. . . ."

"Who said you were comin'?"

The black face lost its grin and grew somber. "Yo' ain't 'tendin' to leaf me heah, massa, suh? This mare, she know me. She do whut I say."

"I'll think 'bout it," Fitz said. "Got two worries. Hates to walk the mare all that fur. Knows all the hosses gits walked to Richmond, but got me one didn't walk that fur, got me a fresher hoss."

"Yassuh, massa, suh, yo' right."

"Come on," Fitz ordered and headed for one of the barns, walking ahead of the slave. He let himself in and approached a large wagon with high-staked sides used in hauling corn husks from the fields. Fitz examined it, studying the wheels, the shafts and the sides.

"Reckon we kin make do," he said. "Kin hitch two hosses to this heah wagon. Kin build up the sides so they stronger. We fills the bottom with lots o' hay an' we walks the mare into it and ties her fast. We rides her all the way to Richmond. She gits used to ridin', she like it fine."

Themba's eyes glittered in pleasure. "Massa, suh, that

sho' goin' to wuk. We don' let others'ns know we rides the mare an' she win easy an' yo' bets 'nuff, you gits plenty o' money, suh."

"When I wants yore advice, I'll ask for it," Fitz said harshly, though the idea of keeping the freshness of the mare a secret was a fine one. He studied the wagon again and gave Themba precise instructions as to how it should be readied.

Outside, in the late afternoon sun, he expressed another problem to Themba, because this problem was also the slave's. "Been lookin' roun'," he said, "but we ain't got a buck or a boy light 'nuff to ride the mare. We gotten to find us one in Richmond, no tellin' whut we gits, but reckon there no other way."

"Massa, suh, been thinkin' 'bout that myse'f, suh. Yo' likes to know whut I thinks?"

"You do too goddamn much thinkin' round heah, Themba, but go 'head. Whut you think of?"

"Massa, suh, they be no law says jockey gots to be a boy. That so massa, suh?"

Fitz didn't know what he was getting at, but he was certainly going to listen to any ideas.

"None's I knows of. Why?"

"Yo' evah see yo' wench Nina ride, suh?"

Fitz should have clouted him for saying Nina was his wench, but it was the truth and everyone knew it. Besides, he had an idea Themba was on to something. He knew what was coming next and the idea intrigued him mightly.

" 'Fore you gits heah," Fitz said, "my mama show Nina how to ride. Knows she kin."

"Done let her ride the mare day 'fore yestiddy, massa, suh. She beg me and beg me. Done clocked her roun' the track. Fastes' that lil' mare evah did run, massa, suh. Like she like Nina an' do she biddin' real good."

"Nina or the mare bust they necks," Fitz said sternly, "an' you gittin hided down 'bout now. Go fetch Nina."

"She comin', massa, suh."

Fitz looked around. Nina was trotting briskly over the lawn in their direction. The thought occurred to him that it had been all prearranged. When Fitz would appear at the stables and be talking to Themba, Nina would then come at once.

Fitz waited until she'd regained her breath somewhat sternly. "Nex' time you rides, you lemme know firs', y'heah? Bust your goddamn neck and I git madder'n hell."

"Yassuh, massa, suh. I tells yo' nex' time," she said with a big smile, showing she wasn't at all impressed with his warning, which only went to show Fitz that it's impossible to make a pet of a nigger and expect strict obedience.

"Themba," he said, "you finds you a nigger 'bout Nina's size an' you gits his clothes you got to shuck him down right there. Make it fas', heah me?"

Themba didn't quite know what the order was about, but he could do nothing but obey. Asking questions was strictly forbidden without the consent of the master and, in this case, it wouldn't have been wise. So Themba went off, trying to remember what boy was built like Nina.

Fitz said, "Nina, you likes this heah buck Themba?"

"No, suh, don' like him nohow."

"Been seein' him, ain't you?"

"No, suh. On'y 'cause I likes to ride. Yo' mama she learn me how. 'Fore I was sold to yo' papa in Africa, suh, I used to ride. They's got good hosses whur I come from. I on'y a lil' gal, but I knows how to ride 'fore yo' mama learns me 'bout how it do in this country, suh."

"Knows what a hoss race is?"

"Yessuh, massa. I knows."

"Evah ride a race?"

"On'y fo' fun, suh. In Africa."

Fitz rubbed his face and suppressed a grin. What he had in mind would give him a vast amount of pleasure.

"Thinks you could ride that mare in a real race? In Richmond?"

Her face lit up, causing delightful sparkles in her eyes. "Yo' takin me to Richmond, massa, suh? Oh, I craves to go to Richmond, massa, suh. I does anythin' I gits to go they."

"Stay away from Themba or you go no place, y'heah? You belongs to me, nobody else."

She took advantage of her closeness to Fitz to place a hand gently on his arm and look up at him seriously. "Massa, suh, I knows I yours. Likes it that way. Themba, he scare me. He so big reckon he kills me yo' tells him to cover me, suh."

"I won't ever tell him to do that. Whut's the matter with him? Kin have all the wenches he likes. He a prime buck, but they tells me he don't pester no wench nohow. He half woman, maybe?"

"No, suh," Nina said firmly and flatly. "He all man, massa. But he look at no wench. . . ."

" 'Ceptin' you."

"Yas, suh, 'ceptin' me. Cain't stop him, massa. Don' know how."

"I'll stop him he lays a hand on you."

Themba's return prevented any further talk about him, though Fitz wouldn't have cared much. He stopped only because of Nina. Themba apparently had some luck because he was carrying a handful of raggedy clothes.

"Git in one o' them stalls, shuck down and put on the pants an' shirt," Fitz told Nina.

She took the men's clothing rather distastefully, but she obeyed him. In a few moments she reappeared. Except for her hair, she could pass for a boy. Her figure was slim enough, her breasts were not heavy nor too large. If necessary, they could be bound flat, though Fitz doubted it would be. He snatched the cap out of Themba's hand, jammed it on Nina's head. It was much too large but he arranged it so it sat on top of her head and she obediently pushed her hair up beneath it. Now she did look like a boy.

"Goddamn," Fitz gloated. "You sure a fine lookin' boy. Whoee . . . this goin' to be some race. Sure is. Themba, you knows whut to do 'bout the wagon. An' bettah run the hoss . . . wait! You bring the mare out now and we'll see how Nina handles her 'round the track."

Themba was no longer surly. The one thing he liked was to race a horse he'd raised and trained. At the Meader Farm where Fitz had bought sixty-five blooded horses and Themba as well, the slave had raised and trained them, but Sam Meader refused to let any of them race. Now, at last, Themba thought he had a chance to see what his horses would do against competition.

He walked the mare back, a sleek, light brown thoroughbred with a good bloodline behind her. She seemed as eager as Themba. They led her to the track where Themba opened the gate and Nina led the horse onto the track itself. Themba disappeared for a few moments and returned with an old clock. It would do for timing purposes. Nina mounted the animal as smoothly as any trained jockey. On the horse, in the small saddle, with her knees raised almost to her chin, she looked exactly like a boy. Not only that, Fitz thought, but like a white boy. Fitz began looking forward to an interesting and happy time in Richmond. There were rules about taking wenches into hotel rooms, but surely none against a jockey sharing quarters with the owner of the horse he was going to ride.

Themba looked steadily at the clock. Fitz noticed how completely the big slave took over when he had the opportunity, and he did it so slyly as to be all but unnoticed. Fitz decided not to call him on it this time.

"Now!" Themba shouted. Nina kicked the horse into motion and used the crop to get more response out of her. They went around that track in a streak of speed, a run as fluid as that of a fast moving stream. Nina rode expertly.

"Whut's the time?" Fitz asked Themba after the horse and rider had flashed by and Nina was standing in the stirrups to slow the horse down.

"Two minutes," Themba gloated. "She does it in two minutes."

Fitz knew it would be less than that if properly checked because that ancient clock Themba used wouldn't be reliable.

"Massa, suh," Themba said, "I gits to go? Please, I does gits to go?"

"You drive the wagon with the hoss in it an' you in full charge. Pick four otheh bucks to go 'long. Be ready tomorra' 'bout ten."

"Yassuh, massa, suh; I be's ready. Sho' will. Gits to see my horse run. Been a'waitin' so long . . . so long."

Nina brought the mare to the gate and turned her over to Themba. Her silky hair had escaped the confines of the cap.

"We gotta cut off Nina's hair, massa, suh," Themba said, covering the animal with a blanket. "Cain't let her ride with that long hair. Give us 'way right off."

"I decides that," Fitz said, his voice cold. " 'Bout time you stopped tellin' me whut we s'posed to do 'roun' heah."

"Yassuh, massa, suh," Themba said. "Jes' so I kin goes."

"You goes you min' yo' manners," Fitz said. "Now go walk the horse. Cool her off."

"Yassuh, massa, suh."

Fitz watched Themba walk away with the animal in tow, knowing his swift obedience wasn't due to any change on his part, but rather that he wanted desperately to watch the mare run in the race. He was right, though. Nina's hair would have to be cropped, and he hated to tell her because he knew she was proud of it.

She reappeared from the barn where she'd gone to get her dress and they walked back to the house together. Her eyes sparkled with the thrill of the ride and the knowledge that she'd pleased her master.

Jonathan and Doc were still sipping their drinks, but they paused to gape at Nina, wearing the boy's clothes.

"This heah," Fitz said with pride, "our new jockey."

"Nina! For chrissake!" Jonathan exploded. "They rules agin' gals ridin' in a race in Richmond, Doc?"

"Nevah heerd o' one, but then gen'men in Richmond takes they racin' serious. Reckon they ain't no law agin' it, they sho' make one if you win."

"She kin get away with it," Fitz insisted. "We cuts her hair short."

"Nina," Jonathan ordered, "turn sideways."

Nina obeyed and Jonathan shook his head. "She tittied up too much, Fitz."

"Massah, suh, I binds down my titties, I do," Nina said. "Looks like a boy sho', yo' lets me try. 'Specially with my hair cut off."

"Whut yo' think, Doc? You bein' a vet an' all."

"Lookin' at her sideways, I gits me a big desire to take her to my baid. Frontways, reckon you could call her Tom an' git away with it, nobody starts feelin' 'roun'."

Fitz patted Nina on the buttocks and sent her to dress. "Gits you real fancy ridin' clo's we gits to Richmond," he told her. He sat down beside his father. "We startin' in the mornin', papa, it all right with you."

"Fine with me, now we got us a good man to oversee. Reckon it 'bout time for supper. Or do you fancy drinkin' more, 'fore eatin', Doc?"

"Drinks 'fore supper 'an after dinner and the same fo' breakfast and suppah an' in between. You might say I a steady drinkin' man, 'specially I gits this rum. Mighty good for the soul, Jonathan."

When Nina announced supper, they were ready for it. As always, Nina hovered behind Fitz's chair and anticipated everything he required. The other two men shifted for themselves, for all of Nina's attention was glued on Fitz.

Nina busied herself lighting the candles as soon as they had finished eating, and then she retreated to the kitchen for her own meal. Calcutta was slothing more than usual these days, for he was getting fat, both from drinking too many remnant rum and waters and because whatever was left on the supper plates was scraped off for him. Lately, Jonathan had left most of his meal. Elegant, the cook, refused to serve leftover scraps to Nina —or to herself, for that matter—and she and Nina dined on white folks' food served on china plates, not tin or cracked dishes.

They heard the commotion down near the stables, just as Fitz, his father and Doc did. Fitz seized his hat, jammed it on and went racing in the direction of the loud whinnying of some horse in severe pain and anger.

On his way to the scene, he saw a stableboy squirming about in the dust while Themba was trying to catch the big black recalcitrant stallion Fitz was sorry he'd bought. The horse, more than sixteen hands high, was a mass of brute strength and in a complete rage. He reared up and made serious attempts to kick Themba into the ground who, in turn, avoided the animal only by quick dancing steps.

Before Fitz could prevent it, the stableboy on the ground leaped to his feet and picked up a length of two-by-four laid aside for use in building a corral.

He swung the length of wood and caught the horse alongside the neck. Themba screeched at him, but the stableboy was as insanely angry as the horse. He swung the makeshift club again and opened a wound on the left flank of the animal.

Themba, occupied in trying to hold the horse and at the same time escape the hoofs, had no chance to turn his attention to the stableboy. Fitz did. He seized the club, held back for another blow, tore it free of the boy's grasp and clouted him hard on the point of the jaw. The stableboy flew backwards and dropped.

In the near darkness, it was hard to evade the maddened horse, but Themba finally had him. He talked softly, stroked the muzzle of the quivering animal, eased him gently toward his stall.

"Tie him to the hitchrack," Fitz ordered, "'til Doc Parker gits heah. That hoss hurt bad. Whut happened?"

"Don' rightly know, massa, suh," Themba said. "Heerd the hoss a-nickerin' an' then he screeches kinda so I looks out an' I sees this boy pullin' an' yankin' on him."

Jonathan and Doc were on their way. Fitz walked over to the stableboy, trying to rise up from the ground. Fitz kicked him soundly in the ribs.

"On your feet, you nigger," he shouted. "Whut fo' you try to kill this hoss?"

"Din' try to kill 'im, massa, suh. Sweahs I din' try to kill 'im. He tryin' ter kill me, he do."

"You're a goddamn liar. See you myse'f hittin' him with that piece of wood. Now whut's the truth? You gittin' whupped, boy, but how many lashes you gits depends on how many lies you tell."

"Massa, don' whup me, please. Ain't nevah been whupped. Hates that hoss, I do. Tries to kill me ev'y time I goes neah him and Themba he say I gots to curry 'im and 'noint he hoofs with oil. I tries, massa, suh, but that goddamn hoss waitin' to kill me."

"Did Themba tell you to take him out of his stall tonight?"

"Naw, suh. But the hoss, he kick me ha'd this mawnin' and I been hurtin' all day so that hoss he oughta be huttin' jes' like me. So I goin' to scare him some. That's all, massa, suh. On'y scare 'im."

"You goddamn near killed him. Themba, you got that hoss tied?"

"Yassuh, massa, suh." Themba shot a baleful glance at the shaking stableboy as he approached.

"Wants you to go to the house an' tell Calcutta—the houseboy—to gits you the strap. He know's whut I means. Fetch it heah."

Themba hurried in the direction of the house, taking off a battered hat which had replaced his cap, a gesture of respect to Jonathan and Doc as he passed them. Jonathan joined Fitz while Doc went on to examine the injured horse.

"Say he don' like the hoss an' tries to kill him," Fitz said disgustedly.

"Naw, suh, massa, suh, I don't try to kill him. Naw, suh, on'y scare him. He bad devil. Hates 'im, I do. Hates 'im so much I wish he daid."

"He dies you bettah start feelin' you neck 'cause it goin' to change when a rope goes 'roun' it," Jonathan said. "That hoss wuth mo' than you. He a thoroughbred, you a plain nigger, don' know nothin', and not wuth much more."

Doc joined them. "Reckon I got to sew up the cut in his flank and he got 'nuther'n on his neck, but not so deep. Git me half a dozen strong bucks to hold him while I fetch my tools."

Themba returned with a length of thick cowhide, wide enough and supple enough to be a paddle that could hurt. Fitz flexed it several times while the frightened stableboy regarded it with rolling eyes, alight in terror.

"Themba, fetch six big niggers to hold the stallion while Doc sews him up. Bring back spancels fo' wrists an' ankles. An' git you black ass back heah quick."

Themba rushed away. In a few moments the bucks appeared, some pulling on their britches because they'd already gone to bed. Doc told them what to do. Themba returned with the shackles. Fitz got behind the stableboy and kicked him in the tail.

No further words were spoken. The stableboy marched

ahead, his steps slowing every now and then, but he increased his pace when Fitz delivered another kick. They were going to one of the tool sheds. Themba got the door open, rounded up tallow candles and lit them.

Inside the shed were four wooden stakes driven into the ground. The last time a slave had been ironed to them was when Marseilles, the slave who'd been responsible for the death of Fitz's mother, had been staked there before his lashing and execution the following day.

"You knows whut to do." Fitz gave the stableboy a hard shove toward the stakes. The boy fell to his knees to plead again. Themba grasped him by the hair, hauled him between the stakes, turned him on his belly and bent down to affix the spancels. When they were in place, Fitz ripped the boy's shirt off his back and then pulled down his pants as far as he could get them.

He proffered the strap to Themba. "He gits ten an' you make sure they sting good. He killed that stallion I'da used the snake on him, an' cut him to pieces. This time he gits the strap, but he feels it mighty pow'ful."

Themba held the strap in his hands. "Massa, suh, I cain't whup no nigger. Hates whuppin'."

Fitz said, "You whups him, ten strong lashes or I do it an' when I finish, I'll iron you down an' give you twenty. Take your choice an' no more argyments."

Themba nodded. "Yassah, massa, suh. Ain't cravin' to be whupped an' reckon this heah nigger gits whut's comin' to him. I gives it to him good, massa, suh."

He stepped back and swung the strap. It made a slapping noise when it hit, followed by a screech from the stableboy. Themba swung it again. Fitz cursed him, took the strap from him and swung it the way it should be swung. The stableboy's screech was twice as loud and so was the slap of the strap.

"Seven more," Fitz handed Themba the strap, "an' they all sounds like that one or you gits it right on your black ass, an' you stays home, 'stead of comin' to Richmond."

The threat of being left behind removed all of Themba's reluctance. He swung seven more times, all of which were harder than the blows Fitz had inflicted. When it was over, the stableboy was beyond screeching and could only moan.

Doc came in, followed by Jonathan. He knelt by the boy and moved a candle closer so he might inspect the boy's back. His finger poked at some of the outsized welts, bringing more moans, to which Doc paid absolutely no attention.

"Heerd 'bout this heah strap," he said to Jonathan. "Ain't cut the skin nohow. Cain't see any blood 'tall. Sho' raised welts, but reckon when they goes down, they won't be a trace of the whuppin'."

"It hurt too," Jonathan said proudly.

"Yo' don' have to tell me that, suh," Doc said with a grin. "Heerd him yell louder'n the hoss when I sewed him up."

"The stallion goin' to be all right?" Fitz asked.

"Reckon. Be some time 'fore you kin ride him."

"Ride him," Jonathan jeered. "Ain't no man kin ride that brute. All he good for is to knock up as many mares as we kin git under him. Themba, you fetches a pail of water and douse this heah moanin' nigger 'fore you unchains him. Reckon all this runnin' 'roun' made me kinda thirsty. How 'bout you, Doc?"

"I always thirsty," Doc said with a laugh. "Ready when you are, suh."

They departed before Themba returned with the pail of water which he promptly hurled at the stableboy. Then he released him, pushed him to the shed door and kicked him out.

"Themba," Fitz said quietly.

"Yassah, massa, suh?"

"Whyn't you crave to whup that boy 'til I said I wouldn't take you to Richmond?"

"Don't 'zactly know, suh. 'Fraid I don' 'zactly know."

"You laid it on good when you got reason to. But jus' carryin' out orders, you held back. Wants to know why."

"Don' 'zactly . . ."

"I heerd you say that. I wants the real reason."

Themba didn't raise his lowered head. "I bin whupped. 'Nuff to make a man die, it is, massa, suh."

"Seed the scars on yore back. They's from a snake. Don' use no snake heah 'cept special times. Strap ain't as bad as the snake. Niggers got to be whupped, but we try not to hurt 'em too much. So why you didn't give it to him good?"

"Reckon . . . don' know, suh. . . ."

"You knows goddamn well why an' you tells me, Themba. You tells me now."

The massive head came up and Themba seemed to stand straighter. "Reckon, suh, doan like whuppin's, thass all. I'se a nigger and I gits whupped, but it don' seem right lessen' the nigger awful bad."

"Kin you read, Themba?"

The big buck's eyes widened. "Massa, suh, I ain't nevah bin to no school, no suh. Cain't read, cain't write and cain't spell. Nohow! I'se nuthin' but a po' nigger, massa, suh."

Fitz nodded. "I takes your word fo' that this time. Won't again, I asks you. Lyin' niggers wust of all, Themba."

"Yassuh, they is."

"That's all. Snuff the candles."

"Massa, suh, I gits to go wid the little mare to Richmond?"

"You gits to go. You whupped the stableboy good so you goes, but nex' time you don't do whut I says, you never gits 'nother chance to see one o' your hosses race."

"I be good nigger, massa, suh. Sweahs I will."
"You bettah, you know whut's bes' fo' you."
Fitz walked out and made his way back to the house.

Three

THE CARAVAN was a short one, but it got a late start because of the reluctance of the mare to climb into the wagon, or stay there without trying to kick it to pieces. Fitz gave Themba the credit for quieting the animal, and during the entire journey Themba rode with the mare.

"That buck sure got hisse'f a way with hosses," Jonathan commented. He and Fitz rode in the stagecoach Jonathan had purchased when he first arrived at the plantation. Nina, her hair cropped close, rode on the high seat with the driver. Four young bucks, for use in grooming the mare and tending the other horses, trudged along behind or, sometimes, ran, to keep up until Fitz realized that was slowing them down, so the four bucks were then allowed to ride. One pair was assigned to the stagecoach top; the other two rode with Themba and the mare.

They made two overnight stops in small towns. Before they reached each one, the mare was urged from the wagon and walked, so that no one could pass the word that the racing stable from Wyndward Plantation was carried by wagon to conserve strength.

In each town, small as it was, they found the private jails where slaves could be locked up and fed. The inns where Jonathan, Fitz and Nina stayed were none too clean, the food universally bad and the prices high. Not that it bothered Jonathan or Fitz, for they were wealthy, free to spend whatever they wished.

Wenches were not allowed, so Fitz sought out a clothing dealer in the first town and bought trousers, a shirt and a short black coat in small sizes for Nina. Dressed in these, she could easily pass as a white youth. She was possessed of no negroid features and she was arrogant enough to hold her own among whites.

She slept with Fitz each night, wildly amused at the idea of breaking the white men's rules. Everything interested her, and she was like a child. Fitz couldn't remember when he'd loved her as much—always keeping in mind that this was not the same kind of love he would have for a white girl who would bear his children. Yet, if Nina were taken from him, he was sure he'd grieve as much as his father now grieved for Fitz's mother.

There was something wrong with this attitude toward slave girls and Fitz knew it, but firmly erased it from his mind every time it came up. Slaves were slaves and had to be treated as such, he kept reminding himself. The slightest exception would only create trouble. The rules were to be followed, and so long as Fitz was helping run a huge plantation where the blacks were absolutely essential, he would abide by them.

They timed it to reach Richmond in the afternoon. The night before, Jonathan sent one young buck ahead on foot to reserve the necessary room at the Exchange Hotel on Franklin Street, and to arrange the space for the slaves in the private jail adjacent to the Odd Fellows Hall, where the largest and best-run slave mart held auctions.

"Heah's you pass," Jonathan told the young buck. "You runs you haid off and gits to Richmond firs' thing in the mo'nin'. You stopped fo' a runaway, you shows 'em this pass. You goes into the hotel by the back do' an' you mos' polite you talks to the white folks. Then you goes to Fairchild and Loomis near Odd Fellows Hall and you hires space fo' all the niggers we totin'. Kin you understand that?"

"Yassah, massa, suh. I kin do it."

"See you does. Each nigger gits one silver dollah to spend an' time to spend it. You handles this right, you gits two bits extra."

The slave went racing off. That extra two bits would keep him on the move even in the face of invitations from any wenches he happened to meet along the way.

Late the next afternoon, they halted to rest the animals and to pasture them while a fire was started and chickens, purchased at a farm, were plucked and spitted. The slaves ate the same food now, because there was no provision for cooking anything special for them. Chickens at twenty cents each were not considered a luxury.

Jonathan was in a good mood anyway, and decreed that nothing but the best would satisfy him and his entourage. Fitz believed this was the first time Jonathan had been able to forget the tragedy.

Themba now walked the mare, heading the procession so that the horse didn't have to breathe any of the brownish dust kicked up along the road. Nina, seated beside the stage driver, looked like a boy. Much to Fitz's surprise, she'd made no protest at having her locks shorn. Jonathan was beside himself with the idea of racing his own horse. His enthusiasm was no whit less than Themba's.

They came into view of Richmond, a city of nineteen thousand people, nine thousand of whom were slaves. They saw the domed capitol atop an imposing hill, from where there was a fine view down the James River and over the business area. Their slaves, all of whom had arrived on the plantation directly from Africa, were overwhelmed. They'd never seen anything like this.

The City Hotel, the St. Charles Hotel, the churches, the tobacco factories—Jonathan counted twenty during an inspection tour—the stores and the offices of slave traders and professional people—all were impressive.

On the streets off the main square were rows of private jails where slaves would be held and fed for a maximum of forty cents a day. There were stores where they could be outfitted in cheap clothes so they'd be more presentable when offered for sale.

Jonathan left the slaves to put up the horses and vehicles. Themba immediately led the mare to a stable where he would bed down to watch over the horse until the time of the race.

Checking in, Nina wasn't even remotely suspected, though Fitz had to caution her about betraying too much excitement. The races had brought crowds to jam everything, from hotels to restaurants and, as Jonathan opined, every goddamn whorehouse worth a visit.

The streets were either dusty or muddy, depending on the weather. Right now, they were very dusty. Once checked in, they left Nina to unpack. Jonathan surveyed the slaves who'd accompanied him. After stabling the horses, they'd returned to sit outside the hotel and wait. They were tired and dirty and they wore their plantation clothes.

"Goddamn iffen I goin' to be seen with niggers lookin' like that," Jonathan said. "Takes 'em all to the store near Odd Fellows Hall, Fitz, an' buys 'em the bes' they got. Shoes too. Then you gives 'em a silver dollah and turns 'em loose. They been wukkin' hard fo' us so let 'em find they some wenches. You buys Nina a jockey outfit an' gits a coat of some color you favors an' we makes that the colors of Wyndward Plantation an' stables."

"Sure, papa," Fitz said. "Thinkin' of buyin' me somethin' fancy too."

"Jes' whut I aimin' to do 'fore I looks up the best whore in town. Wants to make an impression. They's always bettah they thinks you a rich gen'man."

While Fitz summoned the slaves and led them to a store specializing in slave clothing, Jonathan visited the best shop in the city and placed himself fully in the hands of the tailors. By working all night, they would have his clothes ready before the race and they would be in the full tradition of the southern planter. There would be a large hat, in this case white straw. He'd wear tight pants, a long black coat, a low-cut waistcoat, polished boots, heavy gold seals to set off the waistcoat and a cane with a solid gold head.

This duty done, Jonathan engaged the tailors in their opinion of the fanciest gal in town, then happily sought out the whorehouse recommended.

He was in a holiday mood, tempered only by flashes of a past that still hurt. He still had the memory of the stench of the slave hold on his ship, which seemed to have become a part of him. It had been nearly a year since he'd even seen the ship, tied up at Norfolk, but the stink persisted even here in Richmond. Jonathan knew it was all in his mind, but that didn't soften the imagined smell nor the memory of the stinking holds.

Fitz, meantime, had outfitted the slaves in fancy clothes. Skin-tight pants, white ruffled shirts, new hats, and he gave them the privilege of selecting a coat of any color they liked. He insisted they cram their splayed feet into shoes. None had ever worn them before and they minced about in a gay, somewhat painful frame of mind. He sent one of them to relieve Themba and send him here for outfitting.

Themba was more selective. The pants were the same, but he asked for permission to buy a shirt somewhere between pink and orange in color. It had a wide collar and a button at the throat. He selected a long coat of dark purple and a medium-sized straw hat. He slipped into shoes without protest and didn't seem annoyed by the feel of them.

Fitz regarded him approvingly. "You sure ain't goin'

to find no nigger looks good as you, Themba. They goin' to be a whole line of wenches clawin' one another to git at you."

"Yassuh, massa, suh," Themba agreed. It was the first time Fitz had seen him actually happy away from his horses. Maybe, Fitz thought, he'd misjudged this black. Maybe he's not dangerous at all, and it seemed unlikely he could read. In a forgiving and somewhat conscientious frame of mind, Fitz gave him two silver dollars.

"The other niggers got one dollah, Themba, but you in full charge an' it only right you gits mo'."

Themba bowed his head. "Been wukkin' as a slave since I be nine and this the firs' time I evah gits to have a dollah in my hand. Now I got me two dollahs."

"We wins the race, Themba, and yo' gits five silver dollahs."

Themba raised his head and looked Fitz full in the face. "Massa, suh, don' need no five silvah dollahs fo' me to wants to win the race. We wins an' thass all I keer 'bout."

"Yo'll git the money. Yo' gits a chance to talk to other niggers whose mastahs racin' tomorrow, listen all yo' kin 'bout they hosses."

"Yassuh, massa, suh, I does."

"Go 'long then," Fitz ordered.

Fitz visited another tailor shop where he bought himself a new outfit, but not as somber as his father had chosen. Fitz's waistcoat would be a pale blue, his long coat a light lavender, and he decided to make lavender the colors for Wyndward Stables. He didn't dare bring Nina for a measuring or fitting, so he had to rely on some measurements he'd taken of her figure. He was assured the knee-length pants, the long stockings of pale lavender, the white shirt and the glossy lavender short coat would not only be acceptable for a jockey, but practical as well.

This done, Fitz roamed the streets, as interested as all

the other visitors. He dropped by the stable to find a disgruntled slave watching over the mare. It seemed that Themba had ordered him to spell the guard over the horse, and the slave still had his money and a barely repressed desire to spend it.

The private jails and barracoons were jammed with slaves. The traders and auctioneers were going to be busy tomorrow, before and after the race. Whenever any event brought people in from the surrounding cities and countryside, the traders were hard at work. A horse race was especially profitable because so many of the sports would use their slaves for betting purposes and, invariably, lose them. Some would be sold, some would go to the coffle of the winners.

By eight Fitz was tired. It had been a rapid and exhausting journey. He was in no mood to find a woman. He had one, all to himself. An astonishingly good girl with a superb figure and a vast desire to please him.

He was rather conscious of, and embarrassed by his trail-dusty clothes as he walked through the hotel lobby which was now jammed with well-dressed men and women in bright gowns, scented with perfumes imported from France.

So he proceeded directly upstairs to find Nina sitting by the window, as she usually did when she was alone, watching the gaiety on the street below.

She jumped up when he entered and rushed to him. He enveloped her in his arms, but the desire was not yet beginning to peak, so he stood with her by the window after he gave a hard yank on the cord which led downstairs and would summon a hotel servant.

"We's stayin' two-three days," he said. "Cain't walk you 'roun' tonight, Nina, but tomorrow after the race, you goes whur I go. Ruther have you 'long as a pretty gal, but you got to be a boy. Bought you the bes' racin' clothes you evah did see. An' 'fore we leaves, you kin buy any dress you likes. Las' day, you kin weah the dress and be a gal. Gives you money to spend cn yourse'f . . . all you wants."

"Massa, why yo' treats me so good? I ain't nuthin' but a nigger."

Fitz chuckled and patted her on the behind. "Yo' sure is, Nina, but they ain't many like you. Pleasures me fine, does all yo' kin fo' me. Likes yo', an' I wants yo' happy."

"I is, when yo' is." She snuggled up to him until they were interrupted by the hotel servant. Fitz ordered him to have hot water toted up for a bath, and while it heated, a table should be brought, along with a meal of the best the hotel had to offer.

While they ate, a relay of slaves carried huge vats of steaming water to fill the tub. Fitz took his bath first. Nina scrubbed him down, somewhat lasciviously toward the end. When he stepped from the tub, she promptly removed her clothes and luxuriated in the same water, gleefully smelling the perfumed soap Fitz had sent up.

"You goin' to smell good tonight," he grinned at her. "You don't stink nohow. Mos' niggers musky as hell, but you smells like a white gal. Bettah, I reckon, some of them I smelled."

Her slim, slight little body, still warm from the bath, pushed up against him. "Wants to pleasure yo', massa. Needs to, I does. Yo' so kin' to me. Does whut yo' asks."

"Two things you got to do, Nina. Pleasure me good tonight and win the race tomorrow."

"I does both, massa. Yo' waits. I does both."

She had to hurriedly dress before the slaves returned to remove the bath water. While they did, Nina looked out of the window again and Fitz read a newspaper he'd bought in the lobby.

The uniformed hotel servant, bossing the water-toting slaves, approached Fitz respectfully. "Massa, suh, I gits to as' yo' a question?"

"What do yo' want?"

"Yo' is Massa Fitz Turner, massa, suh?"

"That's my name. Why?"

"Lady an' gen'mun asts me yo' is. I ain't sho'."

"Who were they?"

"Don' know, massa, suh. They stayin' heah jes' like yo'."

"All right," Fitz said. He frowned, wondering who in Richmond knew him by name. He'd never been here before. He'd not mixed socially with anyone since his arrival at Wyndward. He shrugged and smiled. Colonel Coldwell, of course. He had a plantation ten miles from Wyndward, he was an old boyhood friend of Jonathan's and Fitz had stayed at Coldwell Hall the night before he saw Wyndward Plantation for the first time. The Colonel wouldn't miss a horse race if he could help it.

Colonel Coldwell wasn't going to miss the race either, but he and his entourage happened to be camped out seven miles away, not having been able to make it by dark.

In the lobby, the hotel servant sought out a prosperous looking, graying man, extremely well dressed. With him was a girl of about twenty, honey-haired, with bright blue eyes and a lovely face. Her youthful figure in a dress of heavy pink silk with silver satin stripes made her the cynosure of all eyes, both male and female. As the servant reported that the man they'd seen hurrying through the lobby really was Fitz Turner, the girl smiled happily.

"Way that boy run out on yo'," Sam Meader said, "thinks yo' rather use a shotgun on his goddamn hide."

Benay Meader fanned herself contentedly. She was the most attractive woman in the lobby and she knew it, relishing the attention she was getting, while at the same time pretending to be unaware of it.

"Papa, I ain't blamin' him none. He asked me to marry him an' right after, I went to baid with Cousin Gerald. Fitz caught me comin' out of Gerald's room.

Told him Cousin Gerald and me prayed every night since we children, but Fitz jes' walked into Cousin Gerald's room an' caught him washin' up. An' not from prayin'."

"Yo' settin' yo' cap fo' him again?" her father asked.

"Papa, reckon I grew up some that night. Way he looked at me, way he brushed past me without sayin' anythin'. Made me feel real bad, he did, an' made me think some too. I ain't bedded with Cousin Gerald or anybody else since then. Don't want to. Only wants to bed with Fitz. I loves him, papa. I wants him real bad, He don't know it yit, but he will."

"Yo' could do worse," her father agreed. "His papa got more'n two million last I knew. An' that boy kin' talk like a preacher he wants to. Nevah heered a boy talk so good."

"Papa, he went to college in Boston. He's smart, an' he's handsome, an' I gets him. Nevah wants anybody else long's I live."

"Bettah find out how he feels 'bout it," her father cautioned. "Way I see him, he's as strong-willed as yo', Benay. Ain't goin' to fool him none. Now heah comes Major Apperson—Charlie Apperson. He an old fren'."

"Nevah heard of him, papa."

"He got the best race hosses in Virginny. Wins these heah races mos' ever' time. Now yo' be nice to him. Figger on sellin' him some o' my stock."

Major Apperson was a stocky man of about fifty, a forceful sort of person given to walloping friends with good-natured, back-pounding slaps that sent them reeling as he passed by. He drank hard, he wenched hard, and he bet heavily. He shook hands with Sam Meader and made a sweeping bow to Benay, accompanied by a covetous look that told as well as words how much he'd like to go to bed with this rare beauty.

"Major," Sam Meader said heartily, "been hearin' yo'

got the best hosses fo' the races. Goin' to win, they says."

"Well, might let one go by fault," Apperson said charitably. "Wins 'em all, yo' cain't get any good bets down. Heerd yo' sold a herd of thoroughbreds to this slave breedin' farmer . . . what's his name?"

"Jonathan Turner, suh. Sold him sixty-five fine blood lines."

"He's runnin' a li'l brown mare in the main race tomorrow. Reckon she from yo' stable. She a good animal?"

" 'Members her," Sam nodded eagerly. "Kinda small. She carryin' much weight, she ain't comin' in firs'."

"Sent two o' my boys to look her ovah and they say she in mighty good shape."

Sam shrugged. "They rode her heah, din' they? Three days she been rid. She's tired, Major. Good hoss, but cain't win. Too much agin it."

"Glad to heah that, suh. Bettin's kinda heavy on the mare. Reckon I won't worry none, yo' says so, an' I takin' all the bets I kin git. Figgur' I'll make a killin' this time, suh."

Sam saw an opportunity to better his relationship with the Major and so find it easier to sell him some of his horses.

"Might interes' yo' to know that Jonathan Turner got hisse'f two million dollahs last I knew. An' reckon he a bettin' man. Got a son who'd bet heavy too."

The Major rubbed his face and nodded. "Thankee kin'ly, friend. I'll meet Jonathan Turner an' talk him into bettin' heavy, his hoss agin mine. An' I sends my son to meet Jonathan's boy an' git him to bet. One won't know the other bettin' heavy. Stands to make some good money, suh. I does, an' I buys generous from yo' farm."

"Thass whut I lookin' for, Major, suh. Glad to do business with a gent'mun like yo'. Plans to do some bettin' myse'f. Come along, Benay. . . ."

She shook her head. "I'm tired, papa. Wants to go to

my room an' rest. Wants to be wide awake when the races start. You got friends all 'round this lobby. You won't be lonesome."

Sam Meader had his eye on a buxom woman in a dress with remarkably low decolletage, giving promise of a soft place to lay his weary head—if he could get her into bed—which he thought likely, the way she'd been looking at him so coyly.

Benay went upstairs and unlocked the door of her room. Inside, she sat down to think about it. Presenting herself to Fitz would be the most humbling thing she'd ever done in her life and Benay was not a humble person. Yet she had missed him far more than anyone in her lifetime. She knew how much in love with her he had been, and how hurt he was when she'd grown so careless as to let him catch her all but in bed with Cousin Gerald. As she'd told her father, it was true that since that night, she'd not bedded with anyone, even though the desire had been there more than once. There were even times when she'd considered making the journey to Wyndward Plantation and asking his forgiveness. Fitz was a proud young man, though, and if he'd sent her away, it would have been unbearable. Only that thought kept her from going there. Now they were under the same roof, living in the same hotel. She had but to walk down the corridor, knock, and find him.

Considering the problem seriously, she hesitated. Although she knew very well that she was in love with him, if he turned her away, it could blight her entire life. She wasn't certain she wanted to take the risk. Now, however, there was still another need to see him. That Major Apperson was going to force Jonathan to bet heavily and, through Apperson's son, approach Fitz and get him to bet huge sums as well. Benay had a fierce desire to see that this man she knew she loved not be cheated. Whether he accepted her or not, she couldn't stand by and let this happen.

Benay lit all the candles in the room, arranged half of them on the dresser so she might touch up her face with a little powder, a touch of rouge and enough French perfume to, she hoped, enchant him. She fussed with her hair, decided she looked attractive enough, and then, before she could change her mind, she walked out of the room, down the corridor and knocked on his door.

Fitz, lying on his back with Nina snuggled close to him, was resting before he attempted another interlude of sex. The knock on the door annoyed him, but he supposed there was nothing he could do but answer it.

"You git in the bathroom an' stay theah," he told Nina. "Don' want nobody to know you ain't a boy. Git!"

She fled in all her alluring nakedness to the bathroom. Fitz slipped into his shirt and trousers before he padded to the door. He lit a candelabrum and held that as he opened the door to stare in utter astonishment at the girl who'd haunted his waking and sleeping moments so much. With the shock of seeing her, came the onrushing and bitter memory of Benay emerging from her cousin's room. His face showed no sign of the emotion he now experienced, nor the desire to seize her, to take her.

"Kinda 'sprised," he said without other welcome.

"Fitz, I saw you pass through the lobby and I had to talk to you. Can I come in . . . please?"

He thought of Nina in the bathroom, but so long as Benay didn't see her, it hardly mattered. Besides, he was curious why Benay had looked him up. That it was for a serious reason was plainly evident on her face.

"You kin' come in, you likes," he said. He closed the door and set the candelabrum on the dresser. Then he lit other candles. Benay was looking at the mussed bed.

"You ain't alone, Fitz?" she asked in a worried voice that pleased him tremendously.

"Hotels so crowded got to sleep with the boy who

282

goin' to ride papa's hoss tomorrow. He hidin' in the bathroom. He kinda shy—'specially he ain't wearin' any clothes."

Benay saw the boy's clothing draped over the back of a chair and felt vastly relieved.

"Fitz, first of all, I ask your forgiveness for the way I acted when you were a guest in my home. I didn't mean for that to happen. I didn't want it to happen, but . . . I suppose there's no excuse. I'm headstrong and I take what I want. Reckon you could have no use for a girl like me. That ain't the whole reason I came, just to talk about myse'f and say I'm sorry. Fitz, there's a man named Apperson—Major Apperson—here. He always wins all the races. He's been worried 'bout that mare you got entered, but papa says the mare cain't win 'count of she bound to be tired and she too small to carry much weight anyway."

"That mare goin' to win," Fitz said flatly.

"Fitz, there's always a chance she won't. Major Apperson is goin' to taunt your papa into bettin' heavy while Apperson's son talks you into bettin' heavy too. Figgers they kin git rich on what they win."

Fitz nodded slowly. "I'm obleeged, Benay. Much obleeged."

"Is that all?" she asked. "Just obliged for my telling you this?"

"Thass all," he said.

"Very well, Fitz. Guess I cain't blame you. But I didn't want you to be tricked. One more thing, I've seen many of the races where Apperson runs his horses. They get behind, his jockeys got orders to win no matter what, short of shootin' down the hoss looks like it goin' to win. You warns your jockey 'bout that."

"Obleeged agin, Benay." He walked to the door and held it open. She paused just before she left the room.

"You're a hard man, Fitz. I'm goin' to tell you now I'm in love with you. Didn't know it 'til after you left, and then I missed you so much I knew. I don't blame you for feelin' like you do, but a man should be able to forgive one transgression."

"One?" he exploded. "I heers you screwed every man jack who stayed overnight in your house. One? Be on'y one, maybe . . . maybe . . . git outen heah, Benay. Don' come back. Beholden to yo' fo' warnin' me, but not that much."

She didn't move. "You did love me and you still do, Fitz. I can tell. When you think hard about this . . ."

"Whut in hell you think I been doin' since I lef' your papa's farm? You think I fo'got? Tried goddamn hard to, but I 'members, on'y I 'members you comin' outen that room an' knowin' whut you did in theah."

He pushed her gently into the hall, closed the door and noisily locked it. Then he walked slowly back to the bed, snuffing the candles on his way. He crawled into bed and pounded a pillow with his fist until he groaned and lay back.

Nina crept from the bathroom to slide into bed beside him. She had heard everything and her heart was broken, though she'd known this was bound to happen some day. She moved up close to him, she fondled him, but there was no reaction and then she realized it had finally happened.

"Loves that gal, yo' does," she said unhappily.

"Hates her goddamn guts," he said ferociously.

"Yo' hates her so much, yo' pleasures me now, suh. I feels yo' cain't pleasure anybody agin tonight 'ceptin' her."

Fitz grabbed her and threw her out of bed. She bounced on the floor. He pulled the covers over him. Presently, he heard her crying, softly. He sat up.

"Nina, git in heah. Whut the hell you think? Man cain't pleasure yo'? Yo' come and see how much I kin pleasure yo'. An' stop that goddamn bawlin', y'heah?"

She climbed into bed gracefully and he held her in

his arms, but even before he felt the enticing warmth of her, he knew it would be no good.

Nina said, in a whisper, "Yo' gots to marry a white gal, massa. Yo' gots to, or you cain't have no suckers. But I heah to pleasure yo' jes' like befo'. Knows yo' loves me too an' I satisfied, yo' is."

"Shut up," Fitz said gently. "Go to sleep."

"Yassuh, massa. Yo' sleeps too."

"Nina—you heerd whut that gal say 'bout the race?"

"I heahs."

"Maybe ought to git me a real jockey."

"Massa, suh," she sat bolt upright, the bed covers sliding down, making her more enticing than ever to Fitz's eyes. "Massa, I rides that mare an' no boy goin' to jog me off, suh."

"They's ridin' fo' big money," Fitz warned her. "Ain't nothin' they won't do to win. You does exactly whut I says, an' you gits to ride."

She hugged him in glee. "I does . . . anythin', massa, suh. I ain't skeered."

"They shoots off a pistol to start the race. You hears the gun, you gits that mare runnin' fas' as she kin run. You kicks her and you whales her with the crop an' she stays out front all the time. You in front an' they cain't ketch you, ain't nobody kin git near 'nuff to throw yo' off, an' you wins."

"That mare mos' fas' she starts off, massa. She rested fine. She don' slow down. I wins. I sweahs, I wins."

He hugged her in his own glee, but he went to sleep without indulging in any more sex with her. She remained awake a long time and finally crept out of bed, gathered up her clothes and pulled them over her when she lay down at the foot of the bed.

As she saw it now, she might as well get used to it.

Four

FITZ'S new garments and Nina's jockey costume were delivered by midmorning. He let her unpack them and marveled at the reverence with which she handled everything, hanging Fitz's clothes in the closet and spreading hers out on the bed. She was visibly overwhelmed with the silky sheen of the jockey shirt and her hands caressed the fabric tenderly. The tears that glistened in her eyes were brought on by the emotion of the moment, and when Fitz told her to try on the outfit, she let out a cry of delight.

"Ain't nevah seed nuthin' like this befo' in my whole life," she said. "Massa, does I look real good, suh?"

"Jes' one thing wrong," he judged. "When I gits a look at yo' titties tryin' to bust they way outen that shirt, I gits to feel like pesterin' yo'. Shuck down to yo' waist."

He tore one of the sheets off the bed and ripped it into fairly wide strips. He held the end of one against Nina's back, rotated her while he bound the strip of cloth around and around, pulling it so tight she squealed and then had trouble breathing. But when he was done, and she replaced the shirt, she was flat as a prairie.

"Don't git me no hard-on lookin' at you now," he said seriously. "Reckon yo' sho' look like a boy. Got to walk like one too—take big steps. Stay even with me and step right out." He seized her hand and they practiced in the hotel room.

Then he had Nina lay out his new clothes, over which a number of slaves had sweated all night long to make ready. He stripped down to the buff and put on the clothes while Nina clapped her small hands in approval and acted in no manner a slave should, but Fitz never gave a thought to calling her on it. He was as excited as she.

Always, in the back of his mind, lurked the memory of Benay's brief visit. It felt like a mighty weight on his shoulders. He was grateful for the upcoming race, for it would take his mind off her and he prayed that they wouldn't meet again.

"Massa, suh," Nina said, "yo' the mos' splendiferous lookin' man I evah seed."

He preened before the somewhat wavy mirror. "Don't mind admittin' it myse'f," he grinned.

"Massa, the white lady sees yo' now, she goin' to come runnin'."

He whirled to face her. "Mind yo' own goddamn business, Nina. Don' want that gal. Don' want to evah see her agin all my life. Hates her. She a devil with a beautiful face. Ain't goin' to see her agin. Nevah."

The very vehemence with which he shouted the words were proof enough to Nina that he loved the white girl and that he would, one day, see her again and then things would change. She sighed, having adjusted herself to it some time ago. But it would be hard to accept anyway.

A hammering on the door announced Jonathan, who entered with a flourish, garbed in his new outfit. His face beamed approval as he regarded his son.

"The ladies sho' goin' to eye us, boy."

"Papa," Fitz said, "somethin' mo' important than that. Heerd some folks like to bust us. They plannin' to git us to bet real heavy and then win the race."

"Shore 'nuff?" he asked. "How you knows that?"

"Sam Meader heah, papa. Benay heah too. Las' night

she heerd her papa and Major Apperson talkin'. They fixin' to dump Nina she look like she wins."

"Holy hell a'mighty." Jonathan looked at Nina. "She a boy? She sure ain't no gal. Got nothin' to swing." He grinned lewdly. "Had me one las' night, boy, an' she could swing 'em 'roun' her neck, she have a mind to. Don' know why I likes 'em fat, but they pleasures me real good and dreens me complete."

"Told Nina when the race starts, she to git that mare runnin' fas' as she kin, right off. Git ahead and stay ahead an' then they cain't ride her down or whutever they does."

"Thinks yo' kin do it, Nina?" Jonathan asked.

"Yassuh, massa, suh. I does it. I ain't skeered none, an' the mare, she do whut I say."

Jonathan sat down on the unmade bed. "Reckon she kin handle it at that, son. How come this heah Benay tell yo' 'bout it?"

"I don' know, papa. She mad, 'cause they fixin' to cheat us, reckon."

"You figger she's after yore hide, son?"

"Tol' her to git the hell 'way from me an' stay 'way. Hates her, papa."

Jonathan nodded slowly. "Knows that kin' o' hate. Burns hot, it does, an' gits too hot it ain't hate no mo'. I hopes you thanked her kin'ly for warnin' us."

"Yes, papa, I did. 'Fore I threw her out."

"Well, got us'n more to do than worry 'bout this heah gal," Jonathan said. "Nina, you stays in this heah room, mind. Don' want nobody gittin' to bump yo' li'l ass an' feel yo' a woman. Cain't hide ever'thin' you got so plenty of. Son, reckon we want to git cheated real bad, we goes to the slave auction at Odd Fellows Hall. Bes' auction they is, an' Major Apperson bound to be theah. Let's give the po' man a chance to trim us."

"I'm ready now, papa," Fitz said. He turned to Nina. "Wenches come to fix the room, yo' stays away from 'em. Go in the bathroom an' close the door. 'Member, they thinks you is white an' they goin' to steer cleah lessen you tell 'em not to."

"I stays way from 'em, massa, suh. Sweahs I will."

"Come on then," Jonathan said. "Got us work to do. Ain't much time 'til the race. Town's so crowded you have to step keerful or you kick somebody. Reckon that whorehouse made five hundrud dollahs las' night. Comin' an' goin' all the time. Bought me my woman for the whole evenin'."

Fitz paused at the door. "Nina, sends you up breakfast. Eats at the table like a white boy. Mind now."

"Yassah, massa, suh. I be white as I kin."

Jonathan and Fitz walked briskly down the corridor to the stairway. "Whut goin' to happen yo' marry some white gal?" Jonathan asked. "Nina real smart nigger an' goddamn pretty too."

"Ain't thinkin' 'bout gittin' married, papa."

"This gal Benay, reckon she kin change yo' mind, son. Ain't nevah laid eyes on her, but don' seem to me like the kin' of gal what gives up easy."

"Papa, I know I git married some day and have a family. Gots to, we want our name to go on. But if I does, Nina got nothin' to complain 'bout. She cain't ever marry me and she knows that. But I takes care o' her the rest of her life. I pleasures her and pesters her, I in the mood for it. Gal I marry don' like it, hell with her."

Jonathan nodded. "Reckon yo' kin keep up with two gals 'thout no trouble. Nina, she bein' nigger, yo' bats her one she gits jealous. Yore wife, bein' white, yo' cain't bat her, but yo' sure as hell kin tell her she don' like whut yo' do, yo' move in with Nina. That'll shut her up."

"Goddamn it, papa," Fitz said angrily. "Tol' yo' I ain't marryin' anybody now. Bes' yo' shut up too."

"Yore in love all right," Jonathan grinned. "Sure is,

289

gettin' touchy like that. Wants to meet this heah Benay. Don't like her papa none, even if I nevah met him, but that gal sound like she be real good to have 'roun' in my old age."

"How much you goin' to bet?" Fitz asked desperately, to change the subject.

" 'Pends on how nasty Major Apperson gits. Real sassy an' I calls him on anythin' he offers and raises him."

"Whut 'bout me?"

"Half whut I got yours. Do whut yo' likes. But don' do it cheap, son."

"Won't," he promised. They passed through the lobby with Fitz jerking his head in every direction, hoping for a look at Benay, but there wasn't a sign of her. They entered the dining room and all during the meal, Fitz hopefully anticipated her appearance. After breakfast, they strolled along Franklin Street as far as Fifteenth Street where the three-story Odd Fellows Hall was located, a building erected on the side of a hill so that its first floor was partly basement, partly ground floor. Here, out of respect for the prominence and importance of the area, the street was cobblestoned for six blocks. This flat-roofed building was one of the largest in Richmond—and one of the busiest.

The area was already crowded, for here only the best of the slaves were offered for sale. The usual crowd of hangers-on, present only to see slaves stripped, blocked the entrance. Jonathan elbowed his way through them roughly. Those who turned to challenge him decided against it when they saw his tall, husky son following in his wake.

Most of the auction rooms were filthy, with dirty floors and walls. They were provided with crude, rough benches to seat the bidders who invariably expectorated every few moments on the floor.

Odd Fellows Hall, however, was maintained on a high scale. Things were reasonably clean, the vendue table was large and backed by a screen. The slaves sat on long benches awaiting their turn and the bidder had wider planks to sit upon.

Jonathan and Fitz unceremoniously shoved a couple of men they categorized as cheapskates further along one bench and seated themselves. The sale had not yet started.

Once again, Fitz found himself looking for Benay, not that women came to these places very often, but he recognized the fact that if Benay had wanted to come, she'd be here. Jonathan was eyeing the row of slaves who would be auctioned off first. They'd be the primes, the best of the lot. Mostly unmarked, sound in health, young and able.

"All I needs to do is look at a likely bunch o' niggers an' I begin thinkin' I wants 'em," Jonathan said. "How many we got on Wyndward now, son?"

" 'Bout eight hundrud, reckon."

"Craves me to buy a hundrud more. Fifty bucks, fifty wenches fo' matin'."

"Papa," Fitz reminded him, "time we gits back maybe forty, fifty more birthed since we lef'."

"Small fry got to grow. Takes time. You mind herdin' a coffle back?"

"Ain't much to it, papa. When you think Major Apperson finds us?"

Jonathan said, "Look to yo'se'f. See that big man, pow'ful lookin' man, but all fat? That's Major Apperson and the fancy lookin' boy 'side him, his son. He'll git to us soon's he thinks the time is right. Boy looks like he half-woman to me. See some fancy niggers goin' on the table and I make you a bet the Major's son is fixin' to buy him a couple."

"Sure like to bust him," Fitz said yearningly. "Take ev'ry dollah he's got. Papa, you aimin' to buy a hundrud niggers take all day. We got the race. . . ."

"Son, one thing yo' got to learn 'bout Richmond

Trader heah doan sell no trash on the vendue table at Odd Fellows Hall. On'y the bes' git this far 'cause on'y heah will the prices be paid fo' prime stock. You takes mighty few chances buyin' heah. In the other markets, I wouldn't buy a nigger 'lessen he shucked down and got hisself looked at ev'y goddamn pore he got."

The auctioneer, resplendent in white pants and a white-frocked coat out of respect for the moneyed buyers who were sure to be here today, took his place on the platform and raised his arms for quiet. The buzz of conversation died away.

"Gentlemen," he said in a sonorous voice affected for the occasion, "I'm goin' to sell yo' this mornin' some as likely lookin' niggahs as yo' evah seen put up. They are sold fo' no fault an' ev'y one of 'em is wahanted. Yo' won't see a single lot of 'em heah, yo' won't want. Are yo' ready to begin?"

Two boys were marched onto the vendue table. They were overdressed in cheap short pants, thin yellow shirts and secondhand coats trimmed with faded gold braid. They were obviously twins and the way they stood there and simpered it wasn't hard to guess what use they'd be put to.

"Fi' hundrud dollahs fo' each." It was the Major's son bidding.

Jonathan said, "Fi' hundrud fifty each."

Fitz gave him a startled look. "Whut in hell you goin' to do with that pair, papa? Yo' ain't so hard up. . . ."

"Not me," Jonathan grinned. "Jes' makin' trouble fo' the Major. Gits him mad an' he gits reckless and thass whut we lookin' for, boy."

"Six hundrud," the Major's son called in a falsetto.

Jonathan blithely raised it fifty and the next bid was for eight-fifty. Jonathan promptly subsided. The auctioneer, who believed he had something going, regarded Jonathan somewhat balefully.

"Yo' finished, suh? Yo' lettin' these two likely bucks

go fo' the pittance o' eight hundrud and fifty dollahs?"

"Bucks?" Jonathan exploded with laughter. "Yo' calls them bucks? I lookin' fo' niggers to wuk, not to suck. Let the gen'man bids so high have 'em. Likely kin make more use outen 'em I kin."

The Major jumped to his feet, all two hundred and sixty pounds of him, quivering with rage.

"I don't know who yo' are, suh, but I takes mighty serious offense whut yo' says 'bout my son."

"Start the biddin'," Jonathan said in a tired voice.

The Major sat down. He really didn't want to tangle with this man, and anyway, there was hardly anyone present who didn't know what his son used these fancy niggers for. It was the bane of the Major's existence, but it was there, the boy was his son, so he could have what he liked.

The auctioneer signaled and a tall, fine-looking, coal-black buck walked onto the vendue table. He knew he was the best of the lot, that he'd fetch a high price and he was proud of it.

"Eight hundrud an' fifty dollahs," the Major called out. It was obvious no one intended to bid until he was through. The Major had a reputation for pushing the bids too high and then dropping out, as Jonathan had done with the pair of fancies.

"Thousand," Jonathan called languidly.

" 'Leven hundrud," the Major bellowed.

"Fifteen hundrud," Jonathan said.

"Sixteen . . ."

"Hol' up, theah," Jonathan said. "Mr. Auctioneah, suh, this buck looks prime. If the nex' forty-nine prime as him, line 'em up an' I bids on the lot."

"Fif . . . fifty . . . yo' said?"

"That's whut you heerd, suh. Askin' on'y the right to 'zamine this one, and you wahants the other forty-nine as good as he, or near to it."

"Yes, suh." The auctioneer looked nervously at the

Major who always bid for the best ones and seemed now destined to take only the tag end of the lot.

"He's your'n 'zamine," the auctioneer said, after he'd waited for some comment from the Major and none seemed forthcoming.

Jonathan walked up onto the stage. He stood before the buck, looking him straight in the eye. "Whut yo' name, boy?"

"Tabete, suh."

"Who yo' masta?"

"Massa Quinlan, suh. He done die."

"How old you?"

"Twenny, massa, suh."

"Who raised you?"

"Massa Quinlan, suh. I was birthed on his fahm, suh."

"Anythin' wrong with you'?"

"No, suh, nothin' I knows of. Nevah been sick in my life, suh."

"Open yo' hands."

The slave obediently extended both hands, palms up. Jonathan ran his fingers across the callouses. They were heavy and hard, indicating a man who really worked. Jonathan felt of his neck muscles, his fingers prowled for growths or lumps. He gestured and the buck opened his mouth wide. Jonathan shoved a forefinger all the way to the back teeth, testing each tooth for firmness or decay. He walked around behind the slave.

"Shuck down," he ordered.

The slave removed his thin shirt, lowered his pants and stepped out of them. Jonathan saw no marks of the whip on his back; it was clean of scars. In obedience to his order, the slave bent over, spread his buttocks to show he had no hemorrhoids. Jonathan went around to face the man again, ran his hands down his legs, feeling the sinews. This was an exceptional buck. He'd be a fine black stud for Wyndward. Jonathan hefted his testicles, looked for signs of disease.

"Takes him," he announced as the buck pulled up his pants. "Prime nigger. Whut I wants. Now fo'ty nine mo'."

"Sight unseen?" the auctioneer gasped.

"I looks 'em ovah, suh. They's any ain't prime, you gits 'em back."

"Bids open fo' fifty prime bucks," the auctioneer announced.

"Thirty thousand dollahs," the Major shouted.

Jonathan was on his way back to his seat. "Fifty," he called without turning around. He sat down beside Fitz.

"Fifty-five," the Major announced. He was red-faced with anger now and determined not to let this stranger get the better of him. Not before this crowd. If he bid too high and found he couldn't swing the deal, the auctioneer would quietly take back those he couldn't pay for. He'd better, if he wanted any more of the Major's business.

"Seventy-fi' thousand," Jonathan said casually.

The Major sat down. Jonathan grinned at Fitz and winked. Then he stood up. "Mr. Auctioneah, suh, I craves fifty wenches fo' these heah bucks to cover. Bids fo'ty thousand 'thout lookin' at 'em, pervided I kin send back them as ain't good."

"One . . . two . . . and three . . ." the auctioneer smacked a fist into his other palm. "Sold to this gen'mun . . . name of . . ."

"Jonathan Turner, suh. Yo' sends the bucks an' wenches to the bes' barracoon in town. You feeds 'em good. Wenches too. Yo' steps 'roun' to my bank when you likes, an' the money be waitin'."

The Major jumped up and made his way to the aisle on which Jonathan had been sitting. Jonathan was now on his feet, ready to leave. The Major held out a flabby hand.

"Suh, if I'd knowed who yo' was, I wouldn't bid 'gin

yo', suh. Mattah o' courtesy from one hoss lover to 'nother. Understan' yo' racin' a li'l mare this afternoon. Yo' got a notion she kin win?"

"Got more'n a notion," Jonathan said. Fitz had by now drifted away, seeing the Major's slender son at the back of the hall. "The mare'll beat anythin' you got runnin', Major."

"Wants to make a small bet on that, suh?"

"How much?" Jonathan asked.

"Up to yo', suh."

"Hundrud dollahs," Jonathan said promptly, knowing the Major intended to drive it up as high as he dared.

The Major shook his head. "Suh, that there bet's nothin' short o' bein' disgustin'. One hundrud dollahs, the gen'man says. Big sport, this man who buys slaves by the hundrud. Find that purchase bust yo', suh?"

"Yo name it," Jonathan said good-naturedly.

"I suggests somethin' in the neighborhood o' say . . . ten thousand."

There were murmurs of astonishment that such an amount could be bet on a horse race. The Major looked about for approval.

"Might make that twenty-five," Jonathan said as casually as he had bid.

The Major hesitated. Such an amount would make a serious depletion in his bank account, but he was going to win. If not fairly, then by letting his jockey take care of the rider on the mare. The Major hadn't bothered to tell Jonathan that he had three horses entered in the same race.

"Well now," the Major said magnanimously, "reckon we got us'n a sport aftuh all. I takes it, suh."

"Go higher you like," Jonathan offered.

"Wouldn't take that much 'vantage, suh," the Major said. "Twenty-five thousand it is, suh. An' may the bes' hoss win."

"She will," Jonathan grinned.

At the back of the hall, Fitz let the Major's son push his bet up to twenty thousand. Fitz accepted it, wrote out the IOU and handed it to a man handling the bets. There was nothing left to do now but run the race.

Jonathan proceeded to the bank to make the necessary arrangements for transferring the price of the slaves from his account. When he reached the hotel, he found Fitz giving Nina last-minute instructions.

"Papa," he said, "Nina say the hotel niggers got no idea she a gal. They's pretty smart, these big city niggers, so reckon she kin get away with it."

"Fo' forty-five thousand dollahs she goddamn well bettah get away with it. Heerd tell at the bank that there be no rules with the race 'ceptin' Major Apperson makes his own sometimes. He fin's out we run a gal fo' a jockey he surer than all hell goin' to say that agin racin' rules, they be any or not."

"Cain't back out now," Fitz said. "The Major's all hot air anyhow, papa. Folks heed him 'cause they used to it, but we don' have to. C'mon, Nina. An' 'member to walk 'side me an' like a man. See you at the race, papa."

Themba had the mare saddled and ready. He barely identified Nina at first approach because she kept her rather long peaked cap well down. Fitz rubbed his hand against the ground and dirtied her face slightly. That helped too.

"Mare's 'bout as ready she evah will be, massa, suh," Themba declared. "She do like Nina say an' we wins sho'."

Fitz looked from the stable area up along the flat ground over which the race would be run. There was a starting post, a shaved-down trunk of a tree as the guide. The horses would line up. At the sound of the starter's pistol, they'd streak over the grassy course in a straight line to where another post had been erected. The distance was about a mile. Nobody was really sure, because it had been measured only by guess, but it was accurate enough and had served many a horse race.

"Yo' mounts an' rides up to that line all the way to where yo' sees them folks in a crowd," Fitz told her. "Yo' don't talk to nobody. 'Nother jockey speaks, you don't answer. Make it look yo' don' heah him. The gun goes off, yo' kick this mare fast as yo' kin. Nina, they set to knock yo' outen the saddle they gits the chance, and they 'nuff of 'em to do it."

"I knows, massa. They ain't goin' to git a chance."

"You rides like hell an' don' look back. Iffen them others ketches up to yo', drop back. Don't want yo' hurt."

"They ain't ketchin' up," Nina said grimly. "I sweahs they ain't, massa."

"Then mount up," he ordered. "They's gittin' in line already. Hell of a race—they needs a track, not just to run over goddamn grass."

Themba gave Nina a leg up. She looked small, wispy on the back of the mare, but she handled the animal well. Themba was giving her soft-spoken advice to which she listened attentively. It was not a slave's prerogative to do this, but Fitz wisely kept out of it.

She certainly looked like a boy, though Fitz, knowing every inch of that supple body, had some strong doubts she'd get away with it. With Themba leading the mare, they walked to the forming line. Fitz beckoned Nina and she leaned out of the saddle.

" 'Member now, yo' gits in front an' stays theah. No matter whut. An' if you cain't, drop back fast. Nevah mind yo' lose. There be other races comin'."

"Massa," she said, "I wins. Gots to."

Themba led the horse in line. It stood there, diminutive in contrast to the others, just as Nina was small, even compared to the boys riding the other horses.

Fitz joined his father. Major Apperson wasn't far off, surrounded by those courting his favor. Jonathan chewed on a thin, black cheroot, but other than that he displayed no signs of nervousness.

The starter's gun was raised now, the horses well into line. Fitz began to tremble in excitement. He'd never realized just how exciting it was to have your own horse in a race where many thousands of dollars was at stake.

The gun went off and the start was perfect. All nine horses seemed to spring forward at one split second and they were all on even terms. Before they'd covered fifty yards, Nina was out front. Bending low, her face practically against the mane of the mare, she used the crop intermittently, but never harshly. Fitz had some doubts about that method of winning a race, but Nina and Themba knew the horse better than he, so he relaxed.

Fitz doubted that Major Apperson suspected anything was afoot, and it was now apparent that he had a speed horse running. A roan horse capable of very fast running for half the length of the track, but once in front this was the horse that could block Nina.

"Mare's fresh," Jonathan commented. "That's whut's goin' to count."

"That roan doin' mighty good," Fitz said in a worried voice.

"Not good 'nuff," Jonathan declared confidently.

And it seemed he was right. At the halfway mark, the speed horse was breathing on the mare's tail but not gaining and, as the race progressed, the speed horse lost its stamina and began to drop back. Three-fourths of the way, Nina was ahead by two lengths and increasing the distance steadily. When she pounded over the line, she'd stolen the race.

Fitz yelled himself hoarse and waited with great impatience while the horses trotted back. "Papa, you see that? The Major nevah had a chance. Reckon that lil' mare bes' as good as they come. An' Nina bes' goddamn jockey I evah saw."

"Hell," Jonathan grunted, "this the firs' race you evah

saw too. Sure, Nina and the mare go good together, but I'm worryin' whut the Major's goin' to do now he lost all that money. We wasn't the on'y folks he bet with. Reckon he lost damn near eighty thousand dollahs an' he ain't lettin' that go 'thout raisin' hell, he kin find a way to do it."

"We won, fair an' square," Fitz said happily. "Whut kin he do?"

"He finds out our jockey a gal, he goin' to make some rules of his own. Don' fo'git, the Major's mo' impohtant in Richmond than yo' or me, son. He kin have his way he wants it—an' has somethin' to stand on when he makes his complaint."

Fitz said, "Bes' we move over close to him so maybe we kin fin' out he plannin' somethin'."

"Good idea. Sashay oveh 'thout his seein' us, you can."

They managed to get within earshot of the Major to stand behind him, mixed with the crowd. The Major was unduly red of face. Sam Meader was trying to console him. Benay, who stood at his side, barely concealed her triumphant joy.

"Sold Turnah that hoss," Sam Meader said. "I had her she nevah run like that."

"Well she sho' run like that today," the Major said sourly. "Nothin' else had a chance."

"Whut you goin' to do about it, Major?"

"Don' know yit . . . but I be watchin' that jockey. Got me a notion they's somethin' wrong with him. Cain't figger it, but somethin'. . ."

Benay trained her eyes on Nina, still astride the mare some distance away. Suddenly Benay quietly left the side of the Major and her father, then moved viftly through the crowd.

The Major watched the mare and her rider approach. He gave a snort of amazement. "Mistah Meader, suh, take a look at the jockey. Evah see a jock sittin' on a beam that wide? Evah see a jock built so little? Sho' they's all little, but not like this one."

"Sees a jockey." Sam Meader squinted at the horse and rider. "Thass all I sees, suh."

"Reckon that there's a gal sittin' that hoss. Ain't no gals evah rid in a race befo'. You evah hears of one?"

"Nevah. But whut kin you do about it, Ma or?"

"I kin claim the race wasn't fairly run. That's whut I kin do. Firs' I got to make sure it's a gal. Then I goin' to raise more hell than yo' evah did see. When I gits through, that sonabitch Turnah goin' to owe me the bet."

Nina kept her head down, though she would have loved to raise it and sit erect and proud in the saddle. It was necessary, however, to conceal her features.

"You . . . on the mare!"

Nina heard the whisper. Had it come from a male throat, she'd have been paralyzed with terror, but this was a woman speaking. She lifted her eyes sufficiently to scan the people nearby and she saw Benay signaling frantically. Apparently Benay wanted her to follow. Nina didn't know why, and she had no orders to do anything except ride the horse to the winner's place before the judges, but there was something about Benay's face that warned Nina she'd best cut out and trot down toward the row of sheds where the horses were prepared for the race. It was a natural thing to do. The watering trough was there.

Fitz and Jonathan saw Nina cut away. "Whut in hell she doin'?" Jonathan wondered.

"Mare's thirsty?" Fitz asked, also in complete dismay at this odd turn of events.

"How she knows the hoss is thirsty?" Jonathan demanded. "Whut difference it make anyhow? The judges waitin', the hoss could wait fo' a drink."

"Don't know, papa, but reckon we kin trust Nina. She shore goin' to be my pet from now on."

"Gots to git us a boy to ride," Jonathan said. "We gits trouble they fin' out. Maybe no rule agin a gal ridin', but like I said befo', Major Apperson he makes his own rules."

Fitz relaxed. "Kin see the water trough down theah. Nina gittin' off and the mare's drinkin'. Thass all they is to it, papa."

"Let's move up. The Major's headin' for the judges an' I reckon he got a complaint of some kin'."

"Be a hell of a thing we lose all that nice money, papa."

"Don' min' the money so much, but our hoss won. Thass whut counts with me."

The Major, with Sam Meader to back him, stood before the judges and spoke loudly enough for all to hear.

"I protest the race, gen'men," he said. "Protests it 'til we gits a look at Mistah Turnah's jockey."

The judge who seemed to carry the most weight was thin enough to be scrawny, with a white beard and long white hair setting off his frail figure, but he had a sonorous voice and an authoritative one.

"Major, yo' protests an' we wants to know on whut grounds, suh."

"Don' know yit, but I wants to talk to the Turnah jockey."

"Whur the winnin' hoss and jock?" the judge demanded, looking about vainly.

Jonathan pushed forward. "Judge, suh, reckon the jock rid the hoss down to the waterin' trough. Leastwise, saw the mare drinkin'."

"Winnin' hoss has to ride straight to the judges' stand," the Major bellowed.

"Who says so?" Jonathan inquired blandly.

"I do."

"Yo' kin show me the rule, Major Apperson, I concedes the race."

"They is such a rule, suh."

Jonathan grinned at him. "They ain't no rules wrote down anywhur, suh. Racin' needs 'em, I agrees, but they ain't none now an' you cain't show me none. So reckon we jes' pass that by, Judge."

"Git yo' hoss and rider heah," the Major demanded. "Then we settles this." The Major had the impression that Jonathan was stalling, which meant he had something to hide, and hoped to talk his way out of the situation. The Major didn't intend to give him an opportunity to do so.

"Keep yo' pants on," Jonathan grumbled. "They's comin', the hoss slackens her thirst."

"That hoss and jock ain't heah in fi' minutes," the Major said, "I declare this here race as not countin'."

Jonathan said tartly, "Reckon I got somethin' to say 'bout that, suh. . . ."

Fitz jiggled his elbow. "They comin', papa," he said nervously.

Jonathan peered over the heads of the crowd, now consisting of about everyone at the event. His jockey, astride the mare, was riding casually in the direction of the judges' stand. If Nina was concerned about anything, she didn't show it.

Jonathan bent his head in Fitz's direction. "Oh, Lawdy," he whispered, "less git to hell outen heah fas' as we kin run."

"Cain't," Fitz said firmly. "Got to see they don' hurt Nina none."

"Reckon we do," Jonathan sighed.

"Papa, if they no rules wrote down, how they goin' to say a gal cain't ride?"

"'Cause, son, we won a point ovah the Major and the nex' one goes to him. The judges know him an' they don' know us. We win one point, he wins one, and that'll be fair 'nuff far as this crowd thinks. But we lose the race an' the money."

The horse and rider came to a stop before the Major

and the judges. Major Apperson seized the jockey's leg and yanked him off the horse. The jockey, caught by surprise, fell. The Major pulled him to his feet, propelled him toward the judges' stand.

"This heah a gal," the Major shouted in triumph. "Claims this jock a gal an' I claims no gal kin ride...."

"Git your goddamn hands offen that jock." Fitz elbowed his way closer. "Don' keer you own the whole goddamn city, take yo' hands offen the jock, Major."

Major Apperson conceded that much to this young giant who looked capable of eating him alive, but he intended to profit by it.

"Reckon din' mean no harm to this gal," the Major apologized with an ironical bow in the direction of the small figure wearing the colors of Wyndward Plantation. "Wants yo'-all to see how my touchin' this heah gal riles this heah young man whose papa owns the hoss. I got one thing in mind, gen'mun. Claims this heah jock a gal. Claims she is, my hoss won the race. So all we gots to do is have this heah jockey shuck down. Right heah, front o' ev'ybody."

Fitz grabbed his father's elbow. "Don' say nothin'. Don' do nothin'."

"Cain't figger whut in hell I kin do 'cept run," Jonathan grumbled.

The Major said, "Boy, if yo' is a boy... start shuckin'."

The jockey made no protest, peeled off the colorful jacket, unbuttoned the shirt and shed that. The boots came next, followed by the pants. Then the long peaked cap was removed. It was a boy, about the same size as Nina, but certainly not the same build. For some unexplained reason, his penis was tumescent. The boy was totally unembarrassed. He, like Nina, was at least three-fourths white, and had the same fine features instead of broad negroid ones.

"You says that ain't no boy?" Jonathan roared in his

glee. "You evah see a gal wearin' one o' them, gen'mun? And so goddamn big? Major, I craves your apology and I wants the money you owes me."

"We'll see 'bout that," the Major thundered, still carrying his bluff. He needed moral support and he looked around for Sam Meader, but he had vanished.

Sam had left abruptly the moment he had a good look at the jockey. He hadn't progressed ten yards before he met Benay.

"Papa," she said, "if you tell the Major that boy belongs to you, I sweah I'll tell him you been workin' with Jonathan Turner."

"Benay, whut in hell you do?"

"Nevah mind, papa. What I did, might get me a husband—the one I wants."

"The jockey was a gal," Sam cried. "You switched that trainin' rider o' mine fo' the gal."

"Major Apperson don't know that, papa, he still do business with you. Jonathan Turner thinks you helped him by lettin' your boy change places with their gal. So he does business with you too. You got nothin' to lose, papa, if you keeps your mouth shut."

Sam said, "Feels sorry, I does, fo' that boy yo' got yo' mind on. Reckon they goin' to be one boss on that plantation and it won't be the boy or his papa."

"You'll do as I say then?"

"Whut else kin I do?"

"Good. Now go back and listen to the Major bust his heart while he pays Mistah Turnah all that nice money."

"Reckon I feels better now. The money sort o' stays in the family."

"My family, not yours." Benay patted his cheek affectionately. "Scoot now, 'fore the Major starts wonderin' where you went to."

Benay strolled down to the sheds. Nina, dressed in the clothing of the boy who had substituted for her, looked forlorn until she saw Benay's face.

"Yo' is smilin'," she cried happily. "I wins the race, mist'iss?"

"You won it, Nina. Fair and square too," Benay said. "Wish you could have been theah. Made the boy shuck down and he stands theah lookin' like a buck ready to cover a wench. Reckon he seen you shuck down to change clothes with him."

Nina laughed as no slave should have. When she suddenly realized that, she sobered quickly and bent her head.

"Mist'iss, whaffo' yo' do that fo' Nina?"

"Not for you," Benay said frankly. "Thinks you know what I mean."

"Fo' Massa Fitz?"

"That's right. I'm goin' to marry him, Nina."

"Yes'm, reckon yo' is."

"Reckon you're his wench, Nina."

"Yes'm, I his. Nevah been nobody else's."

Benay sat down beside the copper-skinned girl. "Nina, I know well as you that I'm talkin' to you as another woman and not as a slave. It won't always be that way, but you can help me and I can help you. Tell me, do you love him as a slave or as a woman?"

"Loves him, I does, thass all I knows."

"Has he ever said anythin' 'bout me?"

"Reckon."

"You don't want to tell me. That's how it should be, Nina. I know how much he must trust you. Of course, you know that he can never marry you."

"Yes'm. Knows that."

"He'll have to marry some day so he can have white children."

"Yes'm."

"You'll have to give him up then."

"Yes'm," Nina said, with strong reservations which she kept to herself.

"I want to be his wife. If I do marry him, I shall

want you for my personal servant. Would you mind?"

"No'm. Likes it, mist'iss."

"Good. You know I can't talk to you like this in front of anyone else, not even your master."

"I knows."

Benay reached out, placed a hand beneath Nina's chin, tilting her face upward. "Why, you're almost white. And you're the prettiest wench I ever saw. You're also very smart, Nina."

"Mist'iss, I be jes' 'nother nigger, yo' say so."

"Even if I should have you whipped?"

"Yes'm."

"I think you want me to marry your master."

"Does, mist'iss."

Benay breathed a long sigh. "Why?"

"Massa, he call yo' name when he . . . sleeps."

"But I'll be takin' him away from you."

"Cain't he'p it, mist'iss. Knows he wants yo' an' I wants him happy, I does."

Benay said, "Nina, if I marry him and move to Wyndward, you shall never want for anything as long as you live."

Nina risked a smile. "Feels good, I does, mist'iss. Likes yo', I does."

"Good. Now go back to Fitz. Tell him what happened, you a mind to."

"Yes'm, mist'iss, I tells him."

Nina pulled on the beat-up cap she had received in exchange for the jockey peaked cap. She walked lithely toward the thinning crowd and easily picked out Fitz, whose head towered above anyone nearby.

"Nina," he said, "whut in hell happened? Whar that boy come from?"

"Mist'iss Benay, suh, she knows whut's goin' to happen, an' she fetches me down whar we cain't be seed. The boy, he belong to her papa. Knows how to ride, he does, and he 'bout my size so we changes clothes . . ."

Jonathan arrived in time to hear the last of it. "Nina, did he change his clothes while you changed your'n?"

"Yassuh, massa, suh."

"He was lookin' while you shucked down?"

"Yassuh." She turned a delightful pink under her normal bronze-colored skin.

Jonathan roared with laughter. "Nevah could figger why that boy looked like me when I starts pesterin' one o' them fat whores. Nina, whutevah yo' wants, yo' gits. Fitz, you sees it she buys anythin' pleases her eye while I go an' collect all that money."

"Sure, papa."

"An' you gives Themba a double eagle an' you gives that boy used to belong to Sam Meader ten silvah dollahs."

"Used to belong?" Fitz asked.

"Bought him fo' three thousand from Sam Meader jes' now, son. Give him a name when we git back. Reckon Meader wants me to think he switched the boy for Nina. Knows bettah, but Sam he likes to think that way, don' mind none. Reckon 'fore long he related to me anyway."

"Papa," Fitz said, "I tol' you, ain't figgerin' on marryin' Benay. Don' like her. Hates her. Don' want to see her I kin he'p it."

"Yes . . . I knows." Jonathan patted him affectionately on the shoulder. "You does whut you thinks best fo' you, son. But yo' change your min' 'bout Benay, reckon I won't cry none."

Without another word, Fitz began walking rapidly in the direction of the barn where the horses and wagons were kept. Nina tagged along behind him, looking so much like a boy no male even cast an eye in her direction. They passed by the shed where Nina had exchanged clothes with the boy. Benay stood not far from the watering trough, lovely in a promenade dress of blue muslin with three rows of pink lace at the hem. The sleeves were cuffed with lace as was a ruff at the neckline. Her matching bonnet was heavily plumed and her parasol was tilted far back so that Fitz wouldn't possibly miss her.

He looked directly at her and gave one quick nod of thanks for her part in the substitution and the defeat of Major Apperson. Then he moved right on without a faltering step. Nina, trying to keep up, looked back over her shoulder. Benay was twirling the parasol in what looked like sudden pique, turning into anger. Her color heightened at Fitz's grudging acknowledgment of what she'd done, but she managed a smile for Nina. Nina wanted to wave, to reassure her somehow, but there was nothing she could do. Should Fitz see her offering any sort of encouragement to Benay, he might consider whipping her.

All Fitz wanted to do was get back to Wyndward Plantation and see about the training of more race horses. Nothing had ever excited him as much.

Five

THE RETURN TRIP was made in good time, despite the fact that they were herding a coffle of a hundred slaves. The fifty bucks, chained in groups of ten, walked behind the rest of the caravan. The fifty wenches occupied wagons, three new ones, which Jonathan had been compelled to buy.

Fitz was morosely quiet all during the journey. He successfully argued against staying over at Colonel Coldwell's farm, on the grounds that the situation at Wyndward might require their presence.

"All the wenches droppin' they suckers," he argued. "The 'bacco, mayhap not dryin' good. Whut's Doc know 'bout 'bacco? Themba been 'way too long from the hosses. Reckon we best git right 'long, papa."

"Son," Jonathan said, "she ain't goin' to ketch up with us. She a lady an' reckon she won't chase you. Thinks you made a mistake 'bout her. Seems like she just right to be mistress of Wyndward, and the house shore needs a mistress."

"Tol' you, I hates her. Shut up, 'bout her, y'heah?"

"Jes' passin' the time." Jonathan rocked with the moving stagecoach. He wiped sweat off his face and neck with a huge handkerchief. "Whut Nina buy?"

"Dress an' a hat, an' shoes an' some fancies she weahs under all that. I bought her some sweets, an' a bracelet too, 'cause she sure won that race."

"Whut Themba do with all his money?"

"Don' rightly know, papa. Got hisse'f somethin' 'cause he totin' a heavy bundle he comes back to the barn."

"Well, whut you think 'bout horse racin'?"

Fitz lost all his moroseness. "Papa, we goin' to make Wyndward the bes' racin' stable in the whole goddamn country. We goin' to buy an' breed an' raise hosses like nobody evah seed befo'. Likes racin' mos' of all."

Jonathan looked out of the coach window at the thick wooded area through which they were moving. The coolness from the tree shade felt good. He pulled off his boots and relaxed.

"Cain't say I blame you, son. Likes it myse'f. Racin' goin' to be mos' as big as raisin' niggers an' 'bacco 'fore long."

"Goin' to be bigger, papa. Whut we got to do is git them to build a round, hard track like we got on the plantation. Got to have rules, an' veter'naries to see the hosses are of good bloodlines an' no mavericks rung in.

Reckon take ten years to fix it all, but I goin' to see it gits done."

"But without Benay?"

"Goddamn it, papa, you got to bring her into it ev'y damn time we talks?"

"Jes' askin', son. Reckon we be back in 'bout an hour or so. Plenty time 'fore sundown. Wonder how Doc did?"

"He kept his red nose outen your rum barrels, reckon he got us plenty of suckers waitin'."

"Well," Jonathan rested his head back against the black velvet cushion, "won our firs' race, got us'n our firs' crop of suckers, got us'n our firs' crop of 'bacco curin'. Had a good year, son. Mighty good yeah . . . reckon . . . for the worst yeah I evah had in my life."

"I knows, papa. Knows you still feels bad 'bout mama. Reckon bein' in Richmond he'ped some."

"Reckon. Goin' to tell yo' the truth, son. I goes upstairs with this fat whore an' I shucks down, but I cain't raise it 'nuff to stick in a glass o' watah. That whore she wuk on me, but take 'til near mornin' I gits ready fo' her. Then I gits dreened out after the second time. Gittin' old, or gittin' so I don' care none 'bout wenchin'. Figger nex' time I git me a skinny one. Mayhap there be a difference. Don' reckon so, but wuth tryin'."

They grew silent then, weary from the long journey and content to doze or think their private thoughts. When the coach made its turn under the wooded arch bearing the name of their plantation, they lost all fatigue, cast aside all other thoughts except those connected with Wyndward Plantation.

The great house, gleaming whitely, looked like a haven of all imaginable delights. The house slaves came running. Behind them tottered Doc, his face redder than ever, but his smile one of genuine welcome.

Hong Kong appeared to take charge of the new coffle. Themba ordered his crew to care for the horses, and personally led the little mare to its stall where he lavished on her all the oats and straw she could wish for.

The stableboy, who'd belonged to Benay's father, stood to one side, sharply eyed by Calcutta the houseboy, whose jealousy showed plainly in the scowls and grimaces he directed at the newcomer. Obviously, it was an attempt to frighten the strange boy.

Jonathan said, "Doc, how'd it go?"

"How many suckers?" Fitz asked, being more practical-minded.

"Ever'thin' goin' fine, reckon. Slaves bin good-natured. Cook makin' me fat's a hog ready fo' slaughterin'. On'y complaint I got 'bout this heah Calcutta. He the mos' lazy, slothful boy evah did see."

Jonathan said, "Knowed that for some time, Doc. Calcutta, git you black ass oveh heah."

Calcutta obediently moved toward him, keeping his head down.

"See the new boy I bought?" Jonathan asked. "Makin' him a houseboy jes' like you. He goin' to show us how slothful you are, an' you don' git runnin' this heah boy takes you place and you goes to the fields with the rest o' the niggers. Mind now . . . an' you gits whupped firs'."

"Sweahs I runs, massa, suh. Sweahs I runs faster'n this heah new nigger. Runs fas' I kin. Brings you rum an' watah right now, suh. Watah nice an' cold from the springhouse, massa, suh."

"Don' stand theah talkin' 'bout it. Git it, you no-good black bastahd."

"I goes, massa, suh, I goes real fas', I does."

He tore off in the direction of the house. Fitz spoke to the new boy. "You goes in the house an' fin's the cook. Her name Elegant. You tells her you new houseboy an' git you'se'f some vittles."

The boy took off faster than Calcutta, obviously already trying to prove he was the better man. Fitz looked at Doc.

"Asked you befo', how many suckers, Doc?"

"Thirty-eight. So far, thirty-eight. Whut you feedin' them bucks, Fitz? They was three sets of twins an' goddamn near ev'y sucker big an' healthy. On'y four died."

"Well now," Jonathan said, "got us'n a good crop, then. Obleeged, Doc."

"Ain't been gittin' much sleep. Suckers start bein' born at two in the mornin'. I tells the wenches to cross they laigs, but it don' always work so I has to git up and he'p 'em some. Got a few lef', kind o' slow gittin' they suckers movin' 'roun'."

"You stay 'til the las' one gits borned," Jonathan said.

Fitz nodded agreement. "Doc, thinks you an' me have us a look in the birthin' houses. Likes to see this crop o' niggers."

"Sho', Fitz, don' blame yo' none, this bein' yo' firs' crop."

They walked in the direction of the slave quarters about a quarter of a mile from the house. Jonathan was too weary to join them. He walked onto the porch and sat down in one of the rockers, tilting it way back so he could get his feet on the porch rail. He hadn't even bothered to go inside. There was nothing there for him anymore. He hated the lonely feeling the house gave him unless Fitz was around.

Calcutta, dripping with sweat, rushed out with a tray with three full glasses of amber liquid. He looked about for the others.

"Leave 'em," Jonathan said. "Drinks 'em myse'f they don' git back. When they does, you keep yo' eye peeled and yo' git drinks fo' them soon's they set foot on the po'ch."

"Yassah, massa, suh. Don' like the new boy. He eatin' like a hawg, suh. Don' reckon he good houseboy nohow."

"Effen he had one laig and half an arm, he'd be better'n you. Git the hell outen heah."

Jonathan leaned back, drained the first glass without

stopping and waited for the alcohol to seep into his brain and numb him a little. He'd never thought coming home to an empty house could be so bad. He finished his second drink and picked up the third when Calcutta came dashing out.

"Hoss comin', massa, suh."

"Where?" Jonathan asked.

Calcutta pointed to the road over which Jonathan had traveled only half an hour before. He saw a cloud of red dust.

"What it be?" he asked.

"Massa, suh, got us'n a man on hossback."

"Think it's a fish ridin' a dog, you stupid nigger? Who's ridin' the hoss? Kin tell?"

"Naw, suh, cain't tell nohow. Gots to wait. . . ." Calcutta's jaw dropped. "Massa, suh, reckon that theah a lady comin'?"

"Shore 'nuff." Jonathan smiled widely. "Fetch more drinks. Fetch a whole goddamn tray of 'em an' do it fas'. Wants 'em time the lady gits heah."

Calcutta raised a cloud of dust of his own. Jonathan began to rock and hum contentedly. He'd never seen this girl in his life, so far as she was aware, though when she finally slid out of the saddle and walked toward him, he remembered having admired her in a truly lascivious way in Richmond. Now Jonathan arose and removed his broad hat to bow formally as she came up the stairs, her riding crop in one hand, the other holding up the skirt of her riding habit.

"Yo' mighty welcome to Wyndward Hall, ma'am."

"I am Benay Meader and you are, of course, Fitz's father."

"Reckon I knowed who you were soon's I saw it was a lady ridin' up. Sit down, Miz Benay, and make an old man happy fo' the firs' time since I took Major Apperson's money 'way from him."

Benay laughed gaily and with far more abandon than

he had ever seen in a southern lady. "I never laughed so much in my whole life. Nina tells you what happened?"

" 'Bout the boy?"

"Co'se I didn't see him when he shucked down 'fore the judges, but in the shed, he was peekin' at Nina. By the time her titties jumpin' round, the boy gittin' himself all big, 'sides bein' bug-eyed."

"Nevah fo'gets it in my life, Benay."

She began to remove her gloves as Calcutta dashed out with more drinks. She accepted one, tasted it, downed half of it quickly.

"Rum," she said in a pleased voice. "Don't often get this, suh."

"Cellar's full and more comin'," Jonathan said.

"You know why I'm here, Jonathan?"

"I knows."

"Well, what do you think of my chances?"

"Benay, he's eatin' his heart out fo' you. All the way home he sit there jes' thinkin', and he don' have to tell me whut 'bout. Says he hates you, and he knows he's lyin'."

"What 'bout you, suh? How do you feel 'bout me?"

"Feels fine. You a nice lookin' gal. Go further'n that. You beautiful. Bes' looking gal I evah did see an' that includes Fitz's mama. Loved her, I did. More'n I kin say, but for looks she couldn't touch you. You a real south'n breed o' lady."

Benay set her glass down, leaned over and kissed him on the cheek. "I think I'm really in love with you, Jonathan, and using Fitz as an excuse to come here and live."

"One thing," he cautioned her. "Knows whut made Fitz mad when he livin' at your papa's farm. Reckon that happens agin, that be the end to it."

"That was the last time, Jonathan. Never cared much before I met Fitz. Reckon not even then, 'til I saw him ridin' off. Like to break my heart, it did. Papa wasn't goin' to Richmond this year, but I thought Fitz might be there so I talked papa into goin' 'til he couldn't stand it no more and we set out. Fitz is a proud boy. Reckon his pride stands in the way of his need for me. Because I know he needs me as much as I need him. Reckon he'll send me away?"

"Cain't rightly say, but he does, an' you go, reckon he start after you soon's you out of his sight."

"I hope so. I'm scared, Jonathan. I'm awful scared."

"Jes' sit theah an' don' move. Sees him comin' now. Jes' give him the time of day, ladylike, an' let him do whut he's goin' to do."

"You wants me here, Jonathan, as his wife?" she asked.

His gaze was steady, his nod firm. "Reckon so, Benay. Knows a lady I sees one. Knows why whut happened did happen. You an' me, we're alike. Wants you heah, but up to Fitz."

"I know that," she said.

He picked up his glass and entered the house. Fitz, in serious conversation with Doc, didn't raise his eyes until he reached the porch steps, or if he did, only glimpsed the figure in the rocker and thought it to be his father.

Now he came to a stop and literally gaped at her. Doc, wisely, continued on after giving Benay a low bow. As the door slammed behind him, Fitz began to climb the stairs. Benay sat quietly rocking, doing nothing, as Jonathan had advised.

"Whut . . . how . . . whut in hell you doin' heah?" Fitz asked.

"Good afternoon, Fitz."

"How'd you git heah, I said?"

"I rode behind your coffle. I stayed close enough so that I knew I was safe."

"You jes' . . . slep' on the ground . . . ?"

"There's a good blanket tied to my saddle."

He removed his hat and suddenly tossed it into the

air and leaped toward her. Before she was out of the chair, he had her in his arms and he covered her face with kisses. She laughed breathlessly, then sombered as their lips finally met with the firmness of love. They held the embrace for a long, long time.

She drew her head back as he smoothed her hair gently. "Reckon you lookin' at the bigges' fool in the world, Benay," he said.

"Tell me," she said quietly, "in the kind of English you and your mama spoke."

He smiled. "She'd have liked you, Benay. She'd have loved you. Of course you met papa. I don't have to ask how he felt. In fact, I wouldn't have to ask how any man felt if he looked at you. I loved you back there in Kentucky. I loved you dearly, or I wouldn't have been hurt by what happened. . . ."

"Fitz, I have no explanation, no excuse. . . ."

He placed a finger against her lips. "Nothing happened, Benay. I was a jealous idiot. I ate my heart out all those days traveling home. I wouldn't let myself hope you'd be in Richmond and then, when you came to me, I hated you all over again because of my damn pride. That's a Boston pride, Benay, and there's none worse. What I should have done was show some southern temper and hauled you the hell away from your father's farm that night. Will you forgive me?"

She smiled and placed her cheek against his. "You're a gentleman, my dearest Fitz, even if you do come from Boston."

"I've asked you to marry me a thousand times in my mind. Will you, Benay? I sweah I'll be good to you always."

"I know that. Of course I'll marry you."

"When? When will you marry me? How soon?"

She moved out of his arms and sat down. "Fitz, it's a long journey to Kentucky. Papa's still in Richmond and we could get word to him. He'd come, I'm sure.

And try to sell your father more horses. Mama couldn't stand the trip. We can be married here as soon as you can get someone to perform the ceremony."

"Sends to Maynton . . . sends a nigger tonight. Preacher be here day after tomorrow."

"That will be fine," she said quietly. "Fitz, I want to be part of this plantation. . . ."

"Shows you all 'roun' tomorrow. You see anythin' you wants changed, tell me."

"There's only one thing I ask. That you give me Nina as my personal maid."

"She yours. She was mama's. Mama trained her good too."

Benay raised her voice slightly. "Jonathan, you can come out now. He asked me."

Jonathan stepped onto the porch grinning, mostly at Fitz's half-dismayed discomfiture. Jonathan kissed Benay in a fashion that made her eyes pop, but she said nothing. She shook hands with Doc and then more drinks were sent for, using both boys this time, and they discussed in brief detail the plans for the wedding. It would, of necessity, be simple because there were no near neighbors to come. A boy would be sent riding fast to Richmond for Sam Meader. If he didn't arrive in time, Benay said she didn't mind. He could visit for a few days so he could return to Kentucky and reassure Benay's mother that she was in good hands at Wyndward.

Nina heard it all too. She'd gone to the room assigned her and changed into one of her new dresses, but as she preened, she saw Benay riding up. Nina removed the new dress, put on her uniform to help serve supper and went down to the kitchen.

"Who dat good lookin' woman come to visit?" Elegant asked.

"Yo' new mist'iss," Nina said. "Massa Fitz goin' to marry her soon's he kin, reckon."

"Po' chile," Elegant sympathized. "Yo' was boun' to

lose him some day. We's niggers an' we doan birth no white chillun. If we does, they still niggers. Man's got to have a family. Cain't have it with no wench."

"I knows all that," Nina said. "Knowed it for a long time, but that don' make it any easier for me to let him go."

"Let him go? Chile, he be in yo' baid, in no time. Soon's mist'iss gits knocked up, he come to see yo'. Wrong time of month for her, he come to see yo'. Nothin' to worry 'bout. Nothin's goin' to change much. I knows white folk."

Nina had no reply. It was still too early to set the table so she drifted out the back door and wandered down near the stables. She stopped to pet the little brown mare. As she passed the stall of the black stallion, the animal began to kick viciously and scream at her. She moved faster. She was afraid of that horse; it was the only horse she'd ever known in her life that affected her that way.

Themba sat on a wooden box, tilted so that his back rested against the wall of the barn in which he maintained his quarters. He was whittling idly on a piece of wood. The knife was shiny and new. Slaves were not supposed to carry knives of any kind.

"Whar yo' git that?" she asked him boldly.

"Bought it. Got me a double eagle an' I buys it. Knows I ain't s'pose to have it, but don' care. Wants it, belongs to me, I keeps it."

"Seem to me yo' lookin' fo' trouble, Themba."

"Trouble comes, I here to say howdy. Long's it's trouble fo' the white folks. Comin' fo' me, I runs."

"Yo' black," Nina reminded him severely. "Yo' a nigger an' yo' a slave. Trouble come, it come fo' you, not the white folks. Why yo' talks hard agin 'em? They treats yo' good."

"Likes 'em awright, reckon. Far as white folks go, they fine, but they white folks an' I hate 'em fo' that."

"Themba, yo' crazier'n that black stallion. Massa goin' to shuck yo' down and whup yo' good."

"Been whupped. Kin stan' it. Why yo' carin' fo' them? Knows new mist'iss come. Massa Fitz, he kick yo' the hell outen he baid now. Yo' pleasures him long time. Whut's it git yo', Nina? Not even a suckah?"

"Whut's the matta with yo'? Talk like yo' fixin' to run."

"Not me," Themba said with a shake of his massive head. "Knows bettah. Man runs, they sen's word an' white man who stops 'im, gits two hundrud dollahs. Then they whupps the runnin' man 'til he near daid— 'fore they hangs him. Themba nevah runs, but Themba git away from heah some day. When Themba go, he walks 'way an' ain't nobody kin stop him."

"Won't listen to yo' talk like this," Nina said.

"Themba arose and laid a hand on her arm gently. "Wants to show yo' somethin' yo' don' tell nobody. I means nobody."

Nina was intrigued enough. Themba had a great deal of money in Richmond and it had bought far more than this clasp knife with its red handle. She followed him into the barn. He climbed a ladder to the loft where he slept and kept his things. Nina scrambled up after him.

Themba dug his long arms beneath the hay and pulled out a wrapped package. He removed the cord and opened it slowly and reverently. He displayed to her what the package had contained.

There were five school books, a map of the world, two pens, a bottle of ink and drying powder. He'd bought a box of writing paper and several old newspapers.

"Themba," Nina said softly, "yo' learnin' yo'se'f to read an' write. Niggers git whupped fo' that."

"Tol' yo', ain't skeered o' no whuppin'. Aims to read an' write good's a white man. Aims to study 'til I reads them papers an' knows whut in hell goes on. My massa, 'fore I comes heah, don' min' I reads. Kin read now.

Whut I wants, I kin talk bettah." His voice took on a lower range, as if to add that quality to his demonstration. "Right now, Nina, I can talk good."

"Wha' fo'?"

"Yo' think niggars allus goin' to talk like we does, we gits free?"

"Free? Yo' thinks massa goin' to manumit yo'?"

"Don' want that. Wants to walk 'way from heah 'thout that. Jes' walk 'way."

"Yo' crazy, Themba. I skeered o' yo'."

"No need fo' that. Time comes I makin' yo' my wench. Treats yo' good as massa an' don' marry no white woman."

Nina laughed lightly. "Think I be a wench to a crazy buck?"

Themba's eyes were hot with ambition. "Talk up No'th 'bout settin' us all free. Heered no'thrun gen'man tell my ol' massa 'fore I comes heah. Say cain't keep men fo' slaves an' don' mattah they's black. Knows it goin' to happen."

"Themba, yo' sho' crazy, but likes yo', 'cause you kin' to hosses an' yo' he'ps me win the race. Won't say nothin' 'bout whut yo' talks."

"Craves to pester yo', Nina. Ain't pestered no wench yit on this heah fahm, but craves to pleasure yo'." He held up his hand. "Don't git mad. Won't do it 'til yo' comes an' say yo' wants to be pestered. I heah, waitin' 'til the day comes. 'Twill. Knows that."

Suddenly Nina wanted to be as far away from this man as possible. "Reckon gots to git the table ready, Themba."

"You mad?" he asked.

"No . . . I ain't. No ways."

"Yo' come back to see Themba?"

Nina gave him a coquettish smile. "Mayhap I comes. Reckon won't fin' yo' 'cause they sho' hangin' yo' they heahs yo' talk this way. They fin' yo' books they goin' to whup yo' good."

Nina fled from the barn and hurried back to the big house. She was worried about Themba. She couldn't help but like him. For all his huge size, he was gentle and kind. Most bucks would have lured her into the barn, raped her and dared her to tell. Themba acted as if he could wait. That he believed this wild talk of walking away free some day. She respected his desire to learn how to read and write. Had Jonathan's wife lived long enough, Nina would have received that much education, for Sarah, Boston bred, didn't believe in slavery as Jonathan or her son did. Nina now could write a passable letter and, if she wished, talk as well as Themba when he was demonstrating his prowess.

But when a slave sought better things and educated himself, he was not going to be a good slave and, sooner or later, his secret would be found out. No white master could then do anything but flog him half to death. One inflexible rule was that no nigger must ever receive an education. Nor was he allowed to attend church or any public meeting unless there was a white man present to be sure no gathering of slaves resulted in talk of freedom or rebellion.

Most of the slaves, especially the field hands, were content enough. On this plantation they were far better off than roaming the streets as free men, without work, without money, without anyone to care for them. Here they had tight cabins, all the food they could eat. They worked, but they weren't driven. Massa Fitz and Massa Jonathan beat none of them unless the slave himself made this necessary.

Themba was too ambitious. And ambition and slavery did not blend and never would. She vowed not to tell anyone about Themba. If he had these crazy dreams, they helped to soften his destiny. Even give him hope, which was another alien feeling to a slave.

Nina reached the house, ran a comb through her short hair and washed her hands. Then she went to the kitchen.

Six

BENAY AND FITZ were married on September tenth in the presence of Jonathan and Sam Meader. It had taken a week to bring a preacher to the plantation, so there'd been enough time also to send for Sam and her clothes. The ceremony was brief. Afterwards, a case of expensive madeira was opened, toasts were drunk, a keg of rum was brought up. Jonathan and Sam believed madeira a little too rich for their blood and preferred rum. The preacher decorously drank madeira and was gloriously drunk before Sam or Jonathan gave any indication that the rum was working on them.

Fitz was still overwhelmed by Benay's blonde loveliness and considered her the loveliest creature he had ever seen. Her swanlike neck and slender shoulders showed to perfection in her gown. A white satin bow called attention to her dainty waistline and the candlelight seemed to be reflected in her honey-colored hair which was center-parted with curls falling over the ears and at the back of her head. He repressed with difficulty the urge to gather her in his arms and rain kisses on her lovely mouth, small nose, firm chin.

Nina moved about, busily serving, helped by Calcutta and the boy Jonathan had purchased from Sam Meader. He was eager, willing and fast and Calcutta was hard put to it to keep up with him.

Fitz, self-conscious about the whole business, sat on a horsehair sofa beside Benay and made what conversation he could in order to suppress the strong desire to take her upstairs now. Not that her body was unfamiliar to him, for on the first night she spent under his roof, she slipped into his room and crawled into his bed. She'd even locked the door against the possibility of Nina showing up.

She'd been all the woman Fitz had dreamed of and more. She was possessed of a certain knowledge that made her practiced and quite wonderful. Each night after that, she came to him, and each night he went to sleep satisfied and more in love with her than ever.

Now they were married, and he had to sit here like a damn fool, making conversation. "What's the stableboy's name? The one papa bought?" Fitz asked.

"His name Mobuza, but papa called him Moses for short," Benay said. "He's a good boy and willin'."

"Sees that. Rides good too."

"Why did your papa say he goin' to change Moses' name?"

"Always does," Fitz said with a grin. "Reckon he must be 'bout runnin' outta names 'cause he hasn't given Moses a new one. Maybe he forgot. I evah tells you how he gives ev'y nigger a new name?"

"Nevah did," Benay said thoughtfully. "But most of them sounds familiar. The bucks anyway."

"Reckon you read much you heard 'em all before. Papa loved his ship and loves all ships. Loved to travel to all parts of the world. So when he settles down heah, he names all the wenches after ships he knew or heard of an' liked, an' all bucks after po'ts o' call. Only name he never changed is Themba. Reckon he nevah thought of it."

"Glad he didn't," Benay said. "I kinda likes the sound o' it."

"Jes' so you don' like him," Fitz said meaningfully.

"Don't never need to worry 'bout that," Benay said, giving him a sharp look. "You worry you married me?"

"Been mayhap, fo'ty minutes we married. Ain't sorry yit," he grinned. "Ever'body on this plantation married, yo' know that?"

"The slaves?" she asked.

"Mama come down heah from Boston an' papa matin' the bucks an' the wenches. Mama say that ain't right lessen they married."

"Fitz," she said in astonishment, "do you mean a preacher was brought here . . . ?"

"No white preacher marry them, an' they ain't no nigger preachers I know of, so we told that to mama an' she says papa a ship captain an' he own this plantation an' it jes' like a ship, so he kin marry them. Thass whut he done. Named 'em, married 'em an' tol' 'em git to they cabins an' git busy making him suckers."

"Imagine that!" Benay said. "He did that for your mama! And I thought he was a stern and uncompromisin' man."

"Fixed mama, he did. Got a bull on one side o' the fence, a cow in heat on the other an' he reads outen the book, marryin' them. Then he has the bull turned loose and whut that bull done to that cow. Sweahs that old bull knew he was married."

Benay laughed. He ordered her another glass of rum and water, for she too had abandoned the sweetish madeira, though the preacher was raising his glass whenever enough strength returned so he could do so.

"Got everythin' I wants now," Fitz said. "Had mos', but reckon a wife mo' impohtant than all the rest of it together. Loves you, Benay. Sweahs I never raises my voice or my hand to you. Sweahs whatever you wants, you git. We rich . . . don't know how rich, but they's plenty. 'Bacco crop will be sold next year after it seasons. Hoss crop come sooner'n that, and ev'y likely pony goin' to see whut he kin do on our track 'fore we sells him.

Sucker crop take longer, but when it comes, in ten-twelve years, we richer than evah. Papa figgerin' on sellin' three-fo' hundrud niggers a yeah soon's they full growed."

She touched his cheek tenderly, making him blush because the others were watching. "Don't care a whit how much you got. All I wanted was you, Fitz. I ain't like my papa."

Before dark, they loaded the preacher onto his buggy and turned the horse in the right direction.

"Preachers be prayin' men," Jonathan observed, "so he kin pray his way home, reckon. Me, I'm too goddamn old an' too drunk to pray, an' your papa, Benay, he's drunker'n me. Reckon we call it a day an' I goin' to lie awake all night wishin' it was me in your baid. Craves me a grandson. Git busy."

Nina waited in the room which had been assigned to Benay, to help her change into her nightdress. Nina hadn't cried much. She'd wiped a few tears as she stood in the kitchen door to watch, but she'd been wept out days before. She knew that Benay had spent every night in Fitz's room. One week, and Nina was lonely already. She hated sleeping alone in her room downstairs, even thought it was as luxurious a room as any slave ever had.

The fact that she adored Benay made it a little easier to bear. Had she been some domineering, lazy slut of a woman, Nina would have been completely heartbroken.

She had a tub of hot water ready when Benay arrived. She assisted in disrobing her, in scrubbing her and setting out the long, voluminous nightdress and the all-encompassing wrapper that went over it.

Benay said, "Nina, I wish he was two men."

Nina applied a brush to Benay's thick hair. "Mist'iss, I ain't cryin' no mo'. Knows I kin nevah marry him no mattah whut, so I been prayin' he gits a fine wife an' yo' is whut I prayed fo'. Reckon he happy, I be happy.

Jes' don' wan' him or Massa Jonathan to tu'n me ovah to some buck. Kills myse'f they does that."

"Don' worry 'bout it, Nina. Maybe I'll do a little praying that a nice man comes along for you. One as white as you and as clever and smart."

Nina smiled. "Yas'm, sho' like that, but it ain't goin' to happen."

Nina hurried then so that she wouldn't be in the room when Fitz arrived. Benay, alone, walked to the window overlooking part of the plantation. By night she could see little, but her mind had registered every building and every cultivated field. She knew what was out there and she made up her mind that she was going to be worthy of all this, that she had much to make up for and she would, until Fitz was entirely happy, and the past which she knew he remembered was erased from his mind.

She snuffed all the candles save one which she placed on a small table beside the bed. She sank onto the soft mattress and when Fitz entered the room, she held out her arms to him.

Fitz moved toward her, but by a route all the way around the foot of the bed to the open window. He stood there, peering intently into the darkness for a few more moments before he sat down on the edge of the bed, still dressed, Benay had lowered her arms and sat up, wondering.

"What is it, Fitz?" she asked, sensing his worry.

"Mistah Frisbee jes' came by."

"Who's he, Fitz?"

"Owns a plantation 'bout fo'ty miles no'th. Mos' big as ourn. He say his niggers rebelled. Killed his wife an' his two children . . . sliced they haids clear off, he say. Burnin' an' rapin' wherevah they goes."

"Are they comin' this way?" she asked in sudden fear.

"Don't rightly know, Benay. Hell of a thing cain't

go to baid with my wife on our weddin' night, but reckon be bes' I looked 'round some."

"Are you worried about your slaves?"

"No, not much. Treats 'em good, but cain't ever tell."

"Be careful, dearest. Be very careful."

"Aimin' to." He grinned to inspire some measure of confidence in her. "Seein' this my weddin' night, like I said. Now you jes' lie quiet. Won't be long an' nothin' to worry 'bout. Runnin' niggers nevah head south. They go no'th to git out of the slave states."

She pulled his head down and kissed him warmly. "Hurry back, Fitz. You know why."

Fitz nodded and promptly left. Downstairs, his father and Sam Meader were ramming shot and powder into every gun they possessed. Fitz picked up a rifle, dumped shot into his pocket, along with a small powder horn.

"Won't head this way," Sam Meader grumbled. "Why' hell they goin' south when they knows they's freedom in the No'th?"

"Niggers," Jonathan argued, "don' know no'th from south, Sam. They git free, they jes' go. They comes heah, we shoots 'fore we asks questions. You be keerful, Fitz. Sure don' want the job of consolin' yo' widow on her weddin' night."

Fitz walked out, the rifle under his arm. It was one of the new Hall flintlocks, a revolutionary change in firearms, for the charge could be inserted in the breech with no ramming down of powder, wadding, and ball.

He moved silently through the darkness, pausing now and then to listen. He walked down between the rows of slave cabins, each one exactly like the next. He heard no sounds of anyone being awake, though he knew that if the escaped slaves were here and were being given shelter, every black would be as quiet as death.

He went around to the stables and inspected these. A horse nickered, drawing him toward that stall, but the animal was merely restless and didn't seem to have been alarmed. Fitz turned back toward the house. He found nothing, not a trace of the murderous slaves, but he had an eerie feeling that wouldn't pass off. There were even times when he thought he was being watched, but attributed that to his natural nervousness. After all, on a nuptial night, a bridegroom should be doubly fearful of any danger which might come to his bride.

As he left the stable area, he didn't see the shadow move very lightly in his direction. Nor did he see the skulking man suddenly seized around the throat, with a hand clapped against his mouth and strength enough applied to lift him from the ground so his feet would make no scuffling noises.

After Fitz was far enough away that he'd not likely hear any whispers. Themba set his prisoner down, but kept his hand over his mouth.

"Yo' bes' quiet now or I busts yo' neck. Knows who yo' are, but I ain't agin yo'. Goin' to let go now. Don' make any noise."

He removed his big hand. The escaped slave gave a long exhalation of relief.

"Done figgered I was gone. Yo' says yo' a fren'?"

"Thinks yo' crazy, but I a slave too an' I a nigger. I yo' fren'. How many mo' 'roun' heah?"

"Be'leven, countin' me. Be hidin' so's I can call 'em."

"Whut yo' aimin' to do?"

"We burns an' kills an' we rapes they white mist'iss. We comes heah to fin' any white woman fo' rapin', chillun fo' killin' an' white men to git they haids chopped off."

" 'Leven crazy niggers goin' to own the worl'," Themba said disgustedly. "Needs 'leven thousan'. . . ten times 'level thousan'. Yo' hangs now, they ketch yo'."

"Knows that, an' we goin' to kill an' rape all we kin fo' they ketches us."

"They's one white woman heah. Got herse'f married today."

The slave grinned broadly. "Sho' be a weddin' night we gits to her."

"Be a wench theah in the big house," Themba warned. "Lay a hand on her an' I kills yo'. She mine."

"Reckon they knowed we comin'?"

"Saw the young massa with a rifle, din' yo'?"

"Din' see me, an' none o' the niggers wid me."

"He did, an' yo' floatin' yo' way to heaven by now. Yo' wants to git 'em, yo' bes' do it quick."

"Reckon so. Thinks they's plenty whites lookin' for us now. Yo' comin' 'long?"

"Yo' thinks I crazy as yo'? They goin' to hang yo' no mattah whut, but I ain't done nothin' an' I don' wants to hang. Don't tell the others yo' talk to me. Don' wants one of 'em say I he'p."

"Keeps it real quiet. Yo' heah them white folks a'yellin', yo' come an' git yo'se'f coverin' that white woman who jes' married. Ain't nobody goin' to tell yo' did, 'cause we ain't goin' to let none o' them live."

"Maybe," Themba said. "Mayhap I does."

Themba faded into the night and sought his loft in the barn. He was highly pleased with himself. Even if the eleven niggers didn't burn the house and kill everybody, they'd raise plenty hell. Themba could stay on the sidelines and enjoy it.

In the house, Fitz locked the door, sped to the kitchen and made sure that was also bolted. He hurried back to where Sam Meader and his father were laying out the arms for defense.

"You see any rebel niggers out there?" Jonathan asked.

"No, papa, but got me a feelin' they's heah. Kep' thinkin' I bein' watched. Don' know I'm right, but thinks we bes' git all sides o' the house covered and ev'ry damn gun in the house loaded."

"Got seven, all told," Jonathan said. "You take three, Fitz, I take two an' Sam two more. I covers the side; Sam, yo' watch outen the back do'. Fitz, take the front.

Sing out you even thinks you sees or heahs anythin'."

"Wish that goddamn posse git heah quick," Sam Meader said. "Reckon they be close, Jonathan?"

"Cain't tell. Sure cain't 'pend on 'em. Up to us, them niggers come. No tellin' how many they is so shoot straight an' shoot to kill."

Fitz gathered up his guns, surplus wads, balls and the flask of powder. At least he could load quickly, far faster than with the old ramrod method of setting the ball.

Fitz raised a window just enough so he could poke the rifle barrel through. Then he settled down to wait. He wished it would be daylight soon. Waiting for niggers, blacker than the night itself, wasn't the easiest task in the world, nor the safest; for those niggers were murdering rebels.

Half an hour went by and there was no sound. Fitz wondered how Benay was taking it, and he also found himself wondering about Nina, who slept in the room just off the kitchen. He was half tempted to go there and reassure her, for she was certainly being kept awake by the commotion of loading all the guns.

Something moved. Fitz kept his eyes trained on the spot. A branch seemed to bend forward slightly, but there was no breeze.

"Papa," Fitz whispered hoarsely, "they's heah. Git ready."

A dim form stepped from behind that bush. Fitz drew a bead on the man, but held his fire. It could be one of their own slaves, prowling about because he was unable to sleep. Then he saw the second form, and then a third, and he knew they were closing in.

He watched the first man draw closer. He was holding some sort of weapon—it looked like a cane-cutting machete. Fitz gently squeezed the trigger. The slave screamed as he was hurled backwards by the force of the heavy ball. A second man darted for the bushes, the third headed for the porch. Fitz killed him as he took his first step up the stairs.

Fitz heard either his father or Sam begin shooting. Fitz kept his eyes on the darkness while he reloaded the two guns. There was a flash of fire amidst the brush and one man came rushing forward carrying a torch. They were going to try and burn the house over their heads.

Fitz's bullet hit the slave in the face. He fell down, with the torch dropping beside him. It rolled up to his body and set his clothes on fire. He didn't move. He didn't cry out. He was beyond the pain of the flames. In a few moments the smell of scorched flesh could be detected.

Fitz heard a wild yell from the rear of the house where Sam Meader was on duty. Then he heard a door open. Fitz swept up two guns and rushed to the kitchen. The rear door was wide. Outside, fire was beginning to lick at the shrubbery around the house. If it got going, the house was going to burn.

Sam Meader had known this. He'd gone out into the open to try and quell the flames. Sam was there now, knocked to his knees by two big blacks. One of them had a machete raised. Before Fitz could bring up a gun, the machete tore Sam Meader's head off. The rest of his body seemed to collapse slowly while a fountain of blood shot upwards, illuminated by the fire.

Fitz shot the man still holding the machete. The second began to run. Fitz hit him in the thigh, and sent him sprawling. Fitz saw buckets of water on the floor, waiting for the morning dishes. He seized one, rushed out, dumped it on the burning brush, returned for another and got the fire out with that one.

The slave he'd wounded was crawling away. Fitz went after him. He caught up with the man, stopped beside him. The slave looked up, terror-stricken, while Fitz swung one rifle by the barrel and hit the slave's skull until the blood ran.

He whirled about as another raced up to him, carrying a short-bladed knife. Fitz still held the rifle by the barrel and he swung it again, meeting the onrushing slave as he came within reaching distance of the rifle. The slave went down and stayed there.

Jonathan's rifle cracked followed by a screech and then at least five or six slaves went racing at top speed to get away from this plantation as fast as they could. One of them was the leader who'd spoken to Themba. He was limping from a sprain suffered when he'd fallen. It would slow him down. He was looking for Themba to take him in and hide him.

As he neared the stables, he drew a knife from his belt and held it ready. He was eye-rolling scared. This hadn't come off the way he'd planned. No telling how many were dead back there, but he didn't intend to add to their number.

Themba stepped out before him. The slave didn't lower the knife. He wasn't trusting anyone now.

"Tol' yo' it wasn't no use," Themba said. "Bes' thing yo' kin do is run and keep runnin'."

"Got me a hurt laig," the slave protested. "Cain't run no mo'. Wants yo' to hide me."

Themba looked around quickly. "Reckon yo' don' git hid quick, they's goin' to fin' yo' sho'. Walk to my barn. I watch an' make sho' nobody come."

The slave nodded and moved toward the barn. Themba moved too, silently, and with deadly purpose. He leaped lightly, wound an arm around the slave's neck, getting his head under his armpit. With his other hand he knocked the knife out of the slave's grasp. Themba braced himself, thrust one leg forward, bent slightly and gave a sharp twist. With the slave's head locked under his arm, Themba moved, but the head and neck didn't. There was a sharp crack, no other sound. The slave went limp. Themba dropped him and backed off. After a moment, he approached and kicked the slave in the ribs as hard as he could. There was no movement, no cry of pain.

Someone was coming in his direction. "Massa, suh," Themba called. "Massa, suh . . . I heah!"

Fitz came first, rifle ready. He approached the dead man, knelt beside him, half raised the man and saw the head loll limply in any direction he tilted the body.

"Yo' killed him, Themba?"

"Busted he goddamn neck, massa, suh. He got a knife an' he say he goin' to kill ev'ybody on the fahm so I busted his neck, I did."

"Good. You see any more of 'em?"

"Heerd 'em, massa, suh, runnin' fas' they kin. Don' know whut's goin' on, but I skeered o' this nigger 'cause he have a knife."

Jonathan joined Fitz. "See Sam?" he asked.

"Saw him git his haid cut off," Fitz said. "Killed the nigger who done it. Got two of 'em back theah. 'Live, I reckon. Cain't say how many we killed. Themba got this 'un."

"Four . . . five . . . daid, rest of 'em won't come back, I reckon. Les' git the two still breathin'."

The whole plantation was awake by now. Nina stood on the front porch and Benay was at the upstairs bedroom window. Fitz waved to both of them.

"Don' come out," he said. "Nina, git yourse'f inside, heah?"

They found the two living slaves, one of them with a badly bleeding thigh. The other one lay on his back, his face smeared with blood. He was moaning slightly. Themba had followed them and Hong Kong appeared out of the gloom. Fitz said, "Themba, you Hong Kong, drag these niggers down to the whuppin' shed. Spancel 'em good. Then sit theah an' watch 'em. They no-good niggers. They kill my wife's father jes' now. They gits away from you, takes it out on yore hide."

On their way back to the house they checked three other blacks to make sure they were dead.

"Them Hall rifles sho' kills a man daid," Jonathan observed. "Mighty straight shootin' with 'em too. Gits me mo' soons I git to Norfolk or Richmond."

Somewhere in the night distances they heard the baying of dogs, followed by several shots.

"Reckon the posse heah," Jonathan said. "Tell Nina to light ev'y candle in the house. You an' me, Fitz, we bettah git us a couple o' niggers and have Sam's body carried down to the graveyard. 'Fore Benay sees it."

Fitz found the slaves and gave the necessary orders. Somewhat gingerly, the torso and the head were picked up, placed together on a large piece of tobacco field netting doubled and redoubled. Fitz walked slowly back to the house as the body was being carried in the other direction.

Jonathan sat on the porch steps, one rifle across his lap, one on either side of him. The house was aglow with candlelight now. Fitz went in, laid his rifle across a table, threw his hat onto a chair and marched up the stairs.

Nina, standing at the foot of the stairs, watched him and felt his sorrow too. She quietly slipped back into her own room. Elegant was there, huddled in a corner and shivering visibly. Calcutta and Moses were somewhere in the kitchen, well hidden.

Benay stood in the center of the bedroom waiting for him. Her face, in the light of half a dozen candles, was ghostly white.

"I know what happened," she said. "I heard . . . my papa call out and I heard you . . . he's dead, ain't he?"

"Yes'm," Fitz bowed his head. "Saved us from bein' burned out, he did. Don't reckon I'd done it way he did. Saved us all an' no question 'bout that."

She sat down slowly on the edge of the bed. "Is it . . . over?"

"Mos'," he said. "Heerd a posse roundin' up whut's left of them. They heah soon now. Bes' I go down and settle it for good."

"Be careful," she begged. "There may be more of them hidin' somewhere...."

"No, they's all gone. No more, heah. I'll come back soon's I kin."

Ten minutes later, a posse of seven men appeared, riding up the road to the house. Behind two of the riders, slaves were being dragged by ropes around their ankles. They didn't mind, Fitz saw, when the posse pulled up. Both were dead. They did have a live one, however, on his feet with a rope around his neck. If he stumbled, he'd have choked, so he'd been careful not to fall, although it would have been a less painful way for him to die.

"Did the bes' we could, suh," the leader of the posse said. "Bastahds too goddamn black to see at night 'an so many of 'em the hounds got theyse'ves mixed up. My name's Ira Wilkins, suh. Rest o' the men from Frisbee's Plantation."

"They killed one o' us," Jonathan said. "We shot four and we got two prisoners spanceled an' waitin'."

"Back on Frisbee's plantation, they killed ev'ybody. Rapes the missus, they did, an' cut the haids offen the children. Was 'leven of 'em when they started to run. Countin' whut you killed, suh, an' what we killed, an' only them three lef', guess we got 'em all."

"Les' finish it so we kin go home," a member of the posse begged. "No sense wastin' time."

"Firs', our whuppin' shed," Jonathan said. "Be good 'nuff to follow me."

He led them to the shed where the two prisoners were chained, with Themba and Hong Kong in attendance. The third slave was hurled into the shed to fall beside the two manacled blacks. He started to get up. Themba kicked him in the face and he fell flat.

"Shuck 'em down," Jonathan ordered.

All three were kicked to their feet by Themba and Hong Kong. The one with the wounded leg screeched as he tried to remove his pants, blood-clotted to the wound. Hong Kong grasped the pants and yanked them free. Blood spurted. Hong Kong tripped him neatly, tied his ankles to a pair of stakes driven into the ground so that the slave's legs were almost pulled out of their sockets. Hong Kong slipped a length of rope through the handcuffs, pulled it tight and leaned back to keep it rigid. Themba took down the blacksnake whip from its wall pegs and slowly unrolled the ugly length of it. For ordinary whippings a leather paddle was used, but in extreme cases like this, the snake was more effective and it didn't matter if the slave's back was covered with welts and deep slashes. Ordinarily, that would bring his price down when he was sold, but these three would never be sold again.

Jonathan nodded and Themba put his full weight into each of the twenty lashes. He hated these three for nearly spoiling everything by premature action. When a rebellion was begun it had to be by more than eleven ignorant niggers. Themba didn't resent the rebellion, only the carelessness with which it had been handled. He was glad he had something to vent his anger upon.

With each lash, blood gushed out of the slash, which sometimes penetrated all the way to the bone. Themba finally untied the man, rolled him over and left him half conscious, moaning weakly.

The second rebel was whipped severely. The posse, Jonathan and Fitz stood by, their faces grim and without a shred of mercy showing.

After the third man was whipped, Themba and Hong Kong dragged them out of the shed and down to a spot below an oak, with a heavy lower branch some twelve feet off the ground.

When the trio lay beneath it, Themba went off to procure three ropes. On his way back with them, he fashioned a noose in each one. Neither Themba nor

Hong Kong had been given any orders. They knew exactly what to do.

Now they summoned four more slaves, husky-looking ones. The ropes were placed around the necks of the feebly protesting prisoners, the other end thrown over the branch. Two slaves manned each rope, braced themselves and waited for the signal.

Jonathan walked up to the three and stared down at them for a moment. "Pull 'em up," he shouted.

The ropes whizzed across the branch. Each slave was hoisted to his feet as the ropes tightened, and then off them to swing in the air until their struggles ceased and their bodies were limp. It was just dawn when the last jerk announced that the final rebel was dead and the rebellion quelled.

The posse declined the offer of drinks. They were weary from many hours of the chase and wanted to go home. Fitz and Jonathan walked slowly back toward the house. Themba and Hong Kong took charge of burying the slaves and Hong Kong sent a burial party to prepare a grave for Sam Meader. He would lie beside Sarah Turner, a woman he'd never met.

Jonathan said, "On'y way to do it, son. Don' like killin' them po' ignorant sonsabitches, but cain't help it."

"They got whut was comin' to them," Fitz said in a dull voice.

"Themba busted the neck of one of 'em," Jonathan marveled. "Done good. Reckon we give him 'nother double eagle. He be the richest nigger in Virginny, but he earned it."

"Wonders why Themba not even scratched," Fitz mused. "Wearin' a nice white shirt an' no dirt on it. 'Sides, the buck he killed was totin' a knife. Saw it on the ground 'side his body. How come Themba didn' git nicked?"

"Don' know. Don' care long's he killed the rebel. Near

time fo' breakfuss. I goin' to have four-five drinks o' rum."

Fitz gave him a thin smile. "Got myse'f married today. Bride waitin'. Now her papa killed. This goin' to be a hell of a seedin' day, papa."

Seven

THE BURIAL of Sam Meader next morning was attended by a weeping Benay. Jonathan was there, also wet-eyed, and full of rum, along with Doc who cried openly and was plainly drunk. Fitz stood by, his features expressionless, as Themba and Hong Kong lowered the nailed-shut casket. Unlike the time when Fitz's mother had been buried here and the slaves turned out to sing and chant, not one appeared, except for Themba and Hong Kong who were under direct orders to be on hand.

Fitz didn't know whether they stayed away out of a sense of shame, or because they were in a rebellious mood themselves, inspired by the murderous rebels who'd swept over the countryside. More stories had reached the plantation about the depredations of these escaped slaves.

It became evident, however, that the Wyndward slaves had not been influenced by the rebels and it really was a sense of shame that kept them from attending the services. That became even more evident after the funeral was over, for, later in the day, Fitz and Benay walked to the cemetery to inspect the new grave and found it heaped with field flowers.

"I want something done for them," Benay said. "No one asked them to do this. I want them all to understand that we appreciate it."

Fitz nodded. He was strictly against the idea, and he knew he was enduring for the first time the exercise of privilege that Benay would be bound to exert from time to time. Fitz was firm in his belief that slaves should be extended few favors, and these very small, for fear they'd come to expect too much and be disappointed when greater favors were not forthcoming. He knew very well that a dissatisfied slave, a frustrated one, has in him the seeds of revolt.

"Reckon we gives 'em tomorra off and we sets out a picnic for 'em all. I got to ask papa, y'unnerstan'."

"He'll agree," she said. "I know he will."

Jonathan saw no harm in it and the decree was issued. In the morning, the smokehouse was raided, succulent hams, sides of bacon, smoked turkeys were taken down. Vegetables were prepared by scores of willing workers, every kettle and pot that could be found was put to work. By midafternoon the picnic was on, noisy, quarrelsome, gay and, as Jonathan commented, profitable. Young bucks were taking wenches into the woods by the score.

Benay, on the other hand, was unapproachable. Fitz could sympathize with her and did his best to console her when she was in one of her frequent fits of sorrow over the loss of her father. When he slipped into bed with her, however, she turned her back on him.

Not out of the lack of loving him, which Fitz couldn't have withstood, nor did she blame him in any way. It was simply that her bereavement had left her sexually shallow. She was ashamed of it and said so in her forthright manner. All Fitz could do was tell her it would pass. Benay even got into the habit of taking sleeping draughts.

At the end of the third week, Fitz lay sleepless beside

her as she snored lightly in her drugged condition. He was reluctant to touch her, to try and awaken her, but his need seemed great. Finally, he slipped out of bed, tiptoed from the room, down the stairs to Nina's room close by the kitchen. He opened the door softly, closed it and the latch made a snick that brought Nina sitting upright.

"Be quiet," Fitz warned her. "Push over some. Ain't aimin' to fall outen the baid we gits goin'."

She seized him in a tight embrace and felt his desire pressed against her. Womanlike, she understood why he was here, what his needs were, and she took care of them in a way that left Fitz gasping for breath.

"Yo' comes when yo' needs me," Nina whispered. "I here, waitin', massah, suh. I yo' wench 'til I dies. Loves mist'iss, I do, but loves yo' too, massah, suh."

Fitz drew her to him. "Shut up an' git busy," he ordered. "Wants all I kin git tonight so's I kin stan' it for the next few days."

Fitz made two more of those sporadic trips to Nina's room before Benay's grief finally subsided. They were preparing for bed and Benay poured her small portion of water, opened a packet of the sleeping drug, but with an impatient gesture she flung it away and rushed to Fitz, wound her arms around him and all but carried him to the bed. That night Fitz rediscovered the prowess and skill of his new wife. She was as wanton as he'd hoped she'd be, and as cooperative as he'd judged she would be. She offered no excuses, simply gave herself to him in a night of lovemaking such as he had never known.

In the morning, the house seemed to shed its aura of mourning. Benay came down to breakfast, smiling and gay. She assumed command of the household servants for the first time, supervised the house and arranged meals for the day. Wyndward Hall seemed suddenly to come to life.

The flowers on both graves had long since faded and there were no more, for the fields were barren of them and the grass was turning brown and sear. There was a crispness of late autumn in the air. Slaves were plying their axes and saws, storing up firewood for the mansion and for their own cabins. Whole sections of the wooded area were cleared, the stumps burned and pulled, and more land made ready for spring planting.

Additional cabins were being built for the new coffle Jonathan had brought in from Richmond, and he planned an extra row of them for another hundred bucks and their wenches so the population of the slave farm would rise to a thousand. That meant, roughly, three hundred or more suckers a year being born. He had no worries about overpopulation for in another year he would sell off many of the adults.

It became a winter of hard work because the snows were deeper than usual and Jonathan's plans grew more and more extensive.

"If this keeps on," Benay told him one evening, "you'll be the richest man in Virginia."

"Reckon I be damn close now," he said with a grin. "Aims to git richer'n that."

It was a splendid opportunity for a talk. Fitz was at the stables, trying to determine what to do about the same black stallion that was kicking his stalls apart. She and Jonathan were in the downstairs room he called his office. Jonathan, primed with food and rum, was in an expansive mood.

"Jonathan," she said, "if you be so rich, how it happen you-all walk the floor night after night?"

He sighed. "Figgered Fitz told you, but seein' he didn't, I will. First off, I'm a lonely man."

"Then why don't you get married again? You sure ain't old, and there're sure lots of women who'd accommodate you, suh."

"They already does—an' I pays 'em for it, Benay.

No, I couldn't marry again. Not go through all that. It ain't the only reason I walk the floor."

"If you'd like to tell me, mayhap I could help," Benay suggested. She wasn't being inquisitive and Jonathan knew it. Otherwise he'd have promptly cut her off. He had a vast admiration for the beautiful woman his son had married.

"Ain't a damn thing you kin do. 'Preciates your offer though. Came about this way. For more years'n I like to remember, I hauled thousands o' slaves here from Africa. We jammed 'em in the holds, five hundred bucks at a time. Now five hundrud prime males take up lots of room and I was after the biggest payin' cargo I could cram into the ship. So we chained 'em in the hold, shoved agin one 'nother 'til they ain't got even room to puke— which they did whenever the ship rolled an' that was most o' the time. Could'nt let 'em loose to take care of theyse'ves so they pissed ag'inst they neighbor's rump and they crapped the same way."

"Reckon you was no different than any other ship's captain."

"Lots o' ways I was better'n most. Brought 'em on deck once a day for a hosin' down. Fed 'em good, gave 'em limes so they wouldn't get sick. But after ten thousand of 'em being chained below, the hold fetched up with a stink I ain't ever forgot. Smells it in my sleep, smells it in my rum, in my seegars, in every damn thing I do. Smells it here, smells it in Norfolk an' in Richmond. Kind of like I be crazy, knowin' it's in my haid. Won't go away."

"Give it time," she said. "That's all it needs—time. You watch these suckers grow, see your mares come to foal, watch 'em race, auction your tobacco in Richmond . . . it'll go away, Jonathan."

"Reckon," he agreed, but he didn't believe it.

"Do you think Fitz is satisfied with me?" she asked,

mainly to change the subject. If he dwelt upon it too long, he'd only get worse.

"Why wouldn't he be? You're eve'thin' a man could ask for, Benay. On'y thing, I reckone it gits lonely heah, never seeing no other woman 'ceptin' the wenches."

"What would you say if I planned some parties for the spring?"

He looked up with interest. "Sarah was plannin' that 'fore she died. Bes' thing you kin do. Co'se, folks got to come from a long way off an' we puts 'em up for the night. Maybe a few nights. Means lots of work. First off, you gotta fix up the old house for the guests to sleep in."

"It'll pleasure me to do it," she assured him. "I jus' wanted your approval."

"Likes the idea real good. How does Fitz feel 'bout it?"

"I haven't asked him," she smiled. "He won't mind. Long as I have your permission, suh, he'll go along with it. First, I write to mama and ask her for the names of friends she knows hereabouts. I'll send them invitations. First off, maybe won't be so many, but these folks knows other'ns an' next time we have more. Ain't no sense havin' this big, beautiful house we don't make some use of it, Jonathan."

"It's your house," he said. "You do whut you likes."

So that winter she planned and she wrote letters, received many replies and set about refurbishing what would be the guest house. Toward spring she was ready to put her social season into being.

Down at the stables, Fitz had his own problems. The black stallion had demolished two more stalls and Fitz was torn between the idea of destroying this beautiful ornery beast, or building a stall so strong it would withstand all the abuse the stallion could give to it.

"Themba," he said, "you gits the wood-cuttin' niggers to saw you boards five inches thick, an' have the carpenters make this heah stall with lots o' room. I aims to lock up that sonabitch hoss 'til he weakens from no exercise. An' then we takes him out and we runs him. We gits a saddle on him or I'm aimin' to shoot the black sonabtich."

"Yassuh," Themba agreed. "Done all I kin an' he chews at me ever' time I git too close. An' kicks the boys I send in to curry him."

"He needs time to do some thinkin'," Fitz said. "We gives him the rest o' the winter an' a little more'n that."

"I makes him mind, 'thout beatin' him to death," Themba assured Fitz. "Ain't nevah had to kill a hoss, massah, suh. Ain't aimin' to do it now."

"I tells you to kill him, that's whut you do," Fitz said harshly.

"Yassah, massa, suh. You tells me, I do it."

Fitz walked slowly back to the house. He wasn't too well pleased with Benay's plans for several large soirees, but he could understand that she might be lonely and so he offered no objections. Fitz was too wrapped up in the plantation to spend much time indulging himself and he knew what these extended parties could mean. Folks who came traveled so far, they always stayed awhile—and expected their hosts to do the same when their positions were reversed. So far, no mention of their taking the time to travel to other plantations had been brought up. When it was, Fitz was going to put his foot down. He couldn't afford the time.

With the coming of spring, activities picked up in tempo until the plantation was again teeming with action. Fields were plowed and made ready for the tobacco seedlings which had to be grown inside, in frames, until the tender plants were strong enough to be set out in the fields. Wheat was planted, corn began to come up readily. Early flowers bloomed, the birthing houses were busy and the first crop of suckers were beginning to creep and crawl about. It was a happy plantation and Fitz aimed to keep it so. He knew what other slave breeders were doing and he would have no part of half starving the blacks, clothing them insufficiently, housing them in dirty barracoons and working them to death. Those farms were lean of progeny, rife with rebellion and hate, and the slaves reared there never brought a very good price. Every one of those raised on Wyndward was prime.

The price of slaves kept rising, there was much talk that laws would soon be passed, stopping all importation of slaves. That meant young bucks and wenches would be at a premium, and just about the time the Wyndward suckers would be full grown the demand would be even greater and the prices would peak. The future of the plantation had never looked so good.

About midspring, everything seemed to be in order, so Fitz announced plans to tote the first tobacco crop, now pressed into hogsheads, to Norfolk. The auction there was going to receive the best tobacco ever grown in Virginia.

"Figger 'bout time you got to the city," he told Benay. "All those soirees comin' up, you needs plenty clothes an' this'll give you time to have 'em made. Needs us maybe fifteen wagons to tote the hogshaids, an' we ride in the stagecoach papa bought."

Benay cried out in delight and threw her arms around his neck. "Fitz, if you only knew how I been waitin' for you to say that. I got so many things to buy I sweah I goin' to bankrupt Wyndward Plantation."

"Sure take a lot to do that. Aims to git thirty thousand dollahs for this 'bacco. Reckon that much'll put a few rags on yore bones."

Nina, hovering in the background as she always did, looked woebegone. Fitz grinned at her, over Benay's shoulder. "Reckon we takes Nina too?"

"Why, of course," Benay said. "I wouldn't think of going anywhere without her."

"We leaves 'bout three more days," Fitz said. "Soon's I know the crop comin' an' the weather holds out."

"Suh, massa, suh." Nina came forward.

"What you want?" he asked her.

"We gits to race the little brown mare agin, suh? You lets me ride him, suh?"

"Oh no," Fitz said with a laugh. "Themba, he trainin' Moses. That boy you changed places with. Don't want to go through with that agin. He a good jockey. Nex' time, mayhap, we don't git so lucky as last."

Nina was disappointed, but not enough to overcome the excitement of making a trip all the way to Norfolk this time.

It required almost a week before the necessary wagons and dray horses could be assembled. Hong Kong picked the slaves who would go along. Two men were needed for each team, to spell one another and, when they reached Norfolk, to handle the hogsheads of tobacco. Much of the journey would be by barge, but it was still a trip that would take three weeks.

Jonathan seemed wistfully sad as they prepared to leave. They knew he wanted to go along, but he realized someone had to remain and take care of the plantation. It was also time that Fitz learn how to handle the selling of the plantation crops. Once again Nina clambered to the top of the stage to sit with the driver. Benay excitedly kissed Jonathan. Fitz shook hands with him gravely and then signaled the procession to roll. Doc was occupied at one of the birthing cabins and didn't see them off.

It was monotonous and tiring until they reached the dockside where they would transfer everything to a river barge and float down to the city. The barges were a popular means of travel and their decks were fitted with fine cabins. The passengers were mostly gentry, along with their servants. There was a great deal of gambling, but Fitz didn't feel in a class with the suave men who shuffled cards as if they'd been born with a deck in their hands.

"Me bein' raised in Boston," he explained to Benay, "I be a greenhorn, tanglin' with them gamblers. Saves my bettin' for when I races our hosses. Then I know whut I bettin' on."

Benay agreed that was wise. She had come to respect his judgment more and more, and she grew prouder of him with each passing day. From her, he drew a deep, constant satisfaction in bed and out of it. She was beautiful, she knew how to conduct herself, she attracted more attention than any other woman on the barge and when they reached Norfolk, she turned heads by the score.

Fitz found accommodations for himself, Benay and Nina at the Union Hotel. It was convenient for doing business and for locking up the slaves at Whitehurst's Slave Jail, almost directly across the street. Small cubicles were provided for personal servants in the hotel, and Nina was given one of these.

Fitz had to return to the dock to supervise the unloading of the hogsheads of tobacco. He took along four slaves who would be assigned to guard the crop now rolled into an auction warehouse. In the next few days, he hoped to sell it all.

"While I'm busy down there," he told Benay and Nina, "you tend to buyin' whatevah you likes. See Nina gits whut she craves too, you got no objections."

"Nina shall have the best uniforms, and a pretty dress, together with all the other things she needs," Benay assured him. "We're goin' to spend a right fancy amount o' money, Fitz."

The next day, Fitz displayed his tobacco crop to a crowd of admiring buyers. The bidding started far above what they were paying for run-of-the-mill leaf, and even Fitz was startled at what the hogsheads were bringing. He was intensely busy all day. At night he was weary, but he accompanied Benay to a theatre performance of Shakespeare, through most of which he dozed. Afterwards, there were drinks and a late supper at the hotel dining room.

Upstairs, many of the purchases had arrived and, despite the hour, he sat admiring the style show. He approved of Benay's selection of clothes, but he was too tired to accompany her and Nina that following evening for a fitting session. Instead, he dropped into the hotel bar and drank bourbon. He wasn't impolite to strangers, but he did nothing to encourage them, so they drifted away. Two passable whores gave him some notice. He shook his head. He simply wasn't interested.

He heard a saccarine female voice call his name and turned to see a young woman of short stature framed in the entranceway, smiling enticingly at him. He frowned in puzzlement as sudden recognition escaped him. Her dark curls touched the sallow flesh of her bared shoulders, and her gown, though of the latest fashion, did nothing to heighten her appeal. She wasn't the type to turn male heads, even though there was open invitation in her eyes. Then he remembered and he thought of the last time he'd seen Clarissa Wareham. One hand had held her dress up to her neck as she exposed herself to a young Negro buck. She'd ordered him to drop his pants and she was making rude gestures to arouse him. When her words and gestures caused his penis to erect, she would lash him with the whip she held in her other hand, at the same time daring him to rape her. It had been in one of the barns at the horse farm operated by Benay's father.

It happened the same night Fitz had seen Benay boldly emerge from the room of her cousin Gerald. Fitz, angered and disgusted, was getting ready to leave the farm in a hurry. But he was fascinated by Clarissa, a cloyingly sweet type of girl, as she exposed herself to the buck so she could watch his tumescence rise and fall. When she became aware of Fitz, she sent the buck away in a hurry and then, without hesitation, let him possess her as she wanted to be taken.

He knew what she was, outwardly sickeningly sweet, but inwardly a bitch of the first order, inspired by sadism and an unholy regard of the sex act. But she was Benay's cousin. He couldn't ignore her, which was his first impulse. He left the bar and walked to the lobby. She rushed into his arms and, despite the people around them, kissed him with considerable abandon.

Then she assured everyone nearby of the propriety of it. "Cousin Fitz, am I evah s'rprised to see you heah. An' wheah is yo' charmin' wife?"

"Hello, Clarissa," he said. "Whut brings you to Norfolk?"

"Now you see heah, Cousin Fitz, they got a nice dinin' room in this heah hotel an' they serves ladies madeira an' sherry. Ain't you agoin' to take me fo' a drink and some supper so we kin talk?"

He smiled tolerantly as he escorted her to the dining room. She insisted on a table well back near the potted plants. There she sipped her madeira while Fitz bolted straight bourbon poured from a bottle he'd ordered. She was trouble and he didn't quite know how to cope with her.

"Benay's mama, she near died she got Benay's lettah sayin' Sam been killed by runaway niggers. She's keepin' the fahm goin' pretty well, I reckon. Not that she has to, with what Sam left."

"I'm glad o' that," he acknowledged. "I asked, what brought you to Norfolk."

"Oh—that. Well, suh, Benay wrote her ma she was comin' heah 'bout this time o' the yeah. She say you haulin' yo' 'bacco crop to sell. Well, me an' Benay, we gits along real fine and I missed her, so I jes' came down heah and waited 'round, knowin' if you came, you'd check into this hotel. Been heah foah mizzable days waitin'. How soon Benay comin' back?"

"I don't know for sure," he told her.

"Reckon they's time fo' you an' me to kinda lay in baid fo' a while, Fitz? I sure ain't fo'got how pow'ful you are with a gal. Ain't nevah fo'got that night."

"Clarissa, I'm married now."

"Pshaw, whut difference that make? Reckon you got 'nuff to satisfy two women. I'm cravin' it, Fitz."

He shook his head and damned the luck that had brought them together. "I'm too damn tired."

"Now you ain't tellin' me yo' is too tired to lay in with me, Fitz, 'cause I know you be lyin'. Craves you, I do, real bad. Craves you so much you don't come with me right now, I'm aimin' to tell Benay whut you done that night you ketched me playin' with that nigger. On'y I ain't goin' to tell 'bout the nigger, on'y whut you did to me. Benay goin' to be real mad, I tell her, Fitz, and all you got to do is cool me down some, an' she never knows."

He bolted two drinks, arose and walked toward the exit. She followed him and caught up while he paid the waiter. He took her by the elbow, whisked her across the lobby to the stairs, went up them, asked her the location of her room and proceeded there with Clarissa noisily panting at his side.

He accepted the key, unlocked the door, let her go in first. He didn't light any candles, merely whirled about, enveloped her in his powerful arms and began disrobing her while she squealed and fought playfully.

He picked her up and dropped her on the bed, climbed aboard and in thirty seconds she lay breathing so hard, the air wheezed through her throat. Fitz rolled off the bed and got dressed. It didn't take long. He hadn't removed anything but his pants.

"I'll tell Benay you're heah," he said. "You tells her whut we done that night in Kaintuck, an' whut we done heah tonight, and I sweah I wrings yore mizzable neck. Means it, Clarissa. This was the second an' the last time for us. You 'members that or you'll wish you wasn't borned."

He closed the door behind him. She hadn't said a word. He went down to the bar, armed himself with another bottle and damned Clarissa. When Benay came through the lobby, with a package-laden Nina at her heels, Fitz hurried out to intercept them.

"Oh, Fitz," she exclaimed, "wait'll you see what I bought."

"Wait 'til you see whut's in the hotel lookin' for you. Cousin Clarissa."

"She's here?" Benay cried in glee. "Oh, Fitz, I've been wantin' to talk to somebody from home. Where is she?"

He gave her the number of the room and Benay fled to the staircase. Fitz led the way to his own room with Nina following. Nina set the packages carefully on the floor and then stood by for orders.

Fitz said, "You look as tired as me. Benay starts spendin' money, she sure weahs ever'body out. You git whut you wanted, Nina?"

"Yassuh, massa, suh. I gits more'n I should. Mist'iss so good to Nina. 'Mos' as good as yo', massah, suh."

"Go to bed." He dismissed her, not unkindly, but definitely. She gathered up her things and left immediately. Fitz wished he'd brought a bottle to the room with him. He was ill at ease. The unexpected appearance of Clarissa upset an otherwise smoothly functioning family relationship. She was a bitch and he knew it. She was capable of far more trouble than he could bear and she was so loaded with passion she was sometimes unable to control herself. As tonight, when she'd demanded he satisfy her.

He didn't want Benay to ever find out what had happened that last night at her father's farm. He'd put on his act of indignation at finding the evidence linking her with her cousin, and it wouldn't do if she discovered that, moments later, he'd taken another of her cousins into the hay. Benay was properly respectful of him because he had been indignant. She never forgot for an instant that she'd been in the wrong. Once she knew he'd slept with Clarissa that same night, she might change. He wasn't looking forward to it.

Two agonizing hours went by before Benay returned to their room and when she opened the door, he held his breath, lest she accuse him of doing the same thing he'd called her for. But she was gay and laughing and very, very happy.

"Clarissa's such a meek little thing," she said. "Fitz, she's skeered of you. She says every time you come near her, she starts shakin' 'cause she think you 'bout to rape her."

Fitz stifled a groan. "The day I rapes her, she the on'y woman lef' for five hundrud miles 'round."

Benay touched her cheek to his. "I know that. I told her she was being silly. Fitz, it was so nice to see her again, to find out about mama and the farm."

"Reckon it was," he admitted.

"I asked her to come and stay with us for awhile. Don't be mad at me, Fitz. She's the only friend I got."

Fitz thought that if that were the case, Benay was completely friendless. "Don't bother me none, she wants to come for a few days. She ain't got dresses for the big party next week, you better buy her some. Reckon she'll stay that long?"

He was wondering if she intended to stay the rest of her life. It would be like her to blackmail him into that, and to arrange that he visit her from time to time. Fitz didn't quite know what he'd do about her if that happened.

The following day, he dispatched Nina to the barracoon to have them get the slaves ready for the journey home. They were to report to the docks, where the wagons and horses were put up, early the following morning. They were to be given clean clothes, a silver dollar each and turned loose for the day and night.

"You tells 'em, any man who shows he been drinkin' too much cawn goes on the vendue table 'fore we leaves. Any buck git hisself locked up, he stays theah 'til he rots for all o' me."

"I tells 'em, massa, suh. I tells 'em good," Nina promised.

"Tell Clarissa to be ready 'fore dawn," he said to Benay. "Wants to git an early start an' they's a barge leavin' 'bout then. She still aimin' to come 'long?"

"More than ever," Benay assured him. "She's goin' to be grand company for me, Fitz. Mayhap there'll be someone at the soiree she can grab. Clarissa ain't bad lookin'. She dresses up, she real pretty, but she too damn shy."

You should know the real Clarissa, Fitz thought.

Eight

THE JOURNEY HOME was uneventful. Clarissa was her outward sugary self, ever so grateful that Fitz was permitting her to spend a few days at Wyndward Hall which she craved so to see. Now and then he caught an avaricious gleam in her eyes, but apparently she'd not confided in Benay so far.

Clarissa used a heavy scent of lavender that had a tendency to choke him in the hot confines of the stagecoach by which they'd made the last part of their journey.

Behind the stage trailed the large wagons, and sometimes Fitz wondered if Benay had brought back more goods than he'd brought to market in the hogsheads which had crowded the wagons.

Jonathan was the first to greet him, with Doc in the background. Apparently, Doc was making this plantation his life's work. Fitz didn't mind that—he was very good around animals and slaves, besides being company for Jonathan. It was Clarissa Fitz worried about. Even more so when she quickly kissed Jonathan after Benay introduced her. Clarissa did it on tiptoe, as a little girl might, and her kiss was feathery light—while quite by accident she pushed very firmly against his waist. Nobody could say she'd deliberately begun a campaign to seduce him and no one could say she hadn't—especially Jonathan, who looked at her curiously.

Then the two women rushed into the house. Clarissa's exclamations of delight as Benay showed her about drifted out to them. Fitz accepted a thin black cheroot from his father, lit it and sat down on one of the porch chairs.

"No trouble gittin' fo'ty-two thousand fo' all that 'bacco," he said. "Goin' to be a better money crop than ever come 'nother year or two. An' they told me we got prime leaves, aged jes' right, and the biddin' heavier an' faster'n at any other lot."

"Wait," Jonathan gloated, "till we sells our firs' crop o' niggers. But that's good profit for our first year, son."

"Talked to some folks from Richmond and Norfolk too, 'bout racin' hosses an' how we needs a real track. They goin' to see Richmond gits one first an' then Norfolk. Hosses goin' to pay off jes' like niggers an' 'bacco, papa. Dunno whut in hell we does with all the money, but it's fun makin' it. Doc, I got you a case o' rum . . . black as a nigger's ass, this is. Strong as a buck too. Mayhap make you grow ten inches you drink 'nuff of it."

"Kinda likes some o' that myse'f," Jonathan grumbled.

"Two wagons full," Fitz grinned. "Wine too . . . 'nuff for the party Benay goin' tuh give."

"Whut 'bout this heah gal Benay brought back? Son, she kiss like a virgin and squirm like a whore. Cain't figger whut she is."

Fitz laughed. "Reckon you figger her 'bout half o' each an' yo' be right. You wants her, papa, she's yours."

Jonathan chuckled. "Heah that, Doc? My son's mighty gen'rous. On'y thing makes him that way, he got two women now 'na keeps him dreened. Reckon I be dreened for good. Doc, you know anythin' to he'p a man who kin think hot, but got nothin' to pleasure a woman with?"

"One thing," Doc said in his best professional manner. "You takes somethin' like that Clarissa who jes' come heah, an' you strips her down to she ain't wearin' nothin' an' then you starts makin' love to her. Nothin' happens then, time you got yourse'f a cane an' a long white beard. She a likely lookin' heifer."

"Ain't sayin' I won't try it, ain't sayin' I will," Jonathan told them. Inwardly, he dreaded the moment he did and found that nothing happened. He didn't mind humbling himself before some whore, but with this slim, fragile little girl, he'd be mortified unto death.

Clarissa, however, gave Fitz little trouble. With Benay, she entered wholeheartedly into the plans for the first social event of Wyndward. That meant much work. The makings of decorations, a thorough housecleaning that kept eight wenches busy, and the two houseboys, Calcutta and Moses, were on the verge of constant collapse.

Elegant grunted at the suggestions for the half-dozen formal dinners, the suppers, the breakfasts, and then proceeded to organize the menu as she saw fit. Which turned out to be a good thing because she knew more than Benay and Clarissa about what to serve.

Fitz and Jonathan were occupied with the starting tobacco and the constant checking of the stables to find the best horses for racing. Themba kept the track on the plantation busy, using the smallest bucks he could find for riding. Moses, the jockey who'd wear the plantation colors, was working as a houseboy at the moment, because none of the others were sufficiently trained to handle that kind of work.

Benay was in full charge now and, from her mother's teachings, knew how to turn out a fine social event. She and Clarissa had a gown for every day and a dozen in-between ones. Nina kept them ironed and ready. Fitz and Jonathan were forced into wearing formal clothes and two tailors came from Lynchburg to fit them in the latest style.

On the day the first of the guests were to arrive, everyone on the plantation felt so tired they guessed, mournfully, that the affair would be a disaster. Then the carriages began to roll up to the door and the fatigue and nervousness vanished. Benay was the gracious hostess and Clarissa moved about, making herself useful and attractive, especially to the men.

Fitz seemed stuffily formal at first, but after Jonathan and Doc smuggled him out to the spring house where half a dozen male guests were already swigging rum and spring water, Fitz drank his share and loosened up.

The first night, dinner was comparatively small, for half the guests had not yet arrived. But it was a lively evening with music and dancing and Fitz found himself enjoying it.

Jonathan was mostly glum. Those who knew about Sarah could sympathize with him. Others were quickly apprised of his recent loss. Gradually, however, Jonathan joined in, the rum and Clarissa's liveliness having their desired effect in lifting his spirits.

Plantation work was suspended and the slaves set to caring for the horses and carriages, toting the luggage, helping in the kitchen, setting up long tables for picnics to be held during the daytime. They had to haul cords of wood for the fireplaces because the evenings were still cool, and the kitchen stoves consumed kindling by the cord as Elegant and half a dozen helpers swarmed about with all the cooking to be done.

In the late afternoon, while Benay and Clarissa led the womenfolk on an inspection tour of the gardens and the plantation, the men rocked contentedly on the porch, served by Calcutta and Moses, who were in and out of the house so often they frequently bumped into one another.

Calcutta, who slowly grew drunk from all the leavings in the countless glasses, was staggering and serving unsteadily while he grinned tipsily and swayed as he extended the tray.

"Goddamn boy needs a whuppin', that's whut he needs," Fitz growled.

"By tomorrow," Jonathan chuckled, "he'll be so sick a whuppin' might even feel good, 'cause it'd make him fo'git the misery he's goin' to have. No harm done an' reckon ev'body gittin' a good laugh outen the boy. Fitz, you fetch me a bottle of rum. Don't let him see you do it."

Fitz got the bottle and Jonathan waited until Calcutta reeled back into the house for more drinks. When he returned, he served them and then passed the tray around for the empties. Jonathan had poured his empty glass half full of straight rum.

"Water ain't cold 'nuff," he growled at Calcutta. "You fetches fresh spring water, y'heah?"

"Yassuh, massa, suh." Calcutta bobbed his head, his eyes on the generous leavings in Jonathan's glass. He managed to get the screen door open, entered the hall and set the tray down. He picked up Jonathan's glass and drained it.

"Whoooeee!" he cried softly. "Sho' ain't cold 'nuff."

Elegant watched him pass through the hot kitchen and shook her head. "That boy's goin' to fall down he don' stop drinkin' whut they leaves in the glass. Reckon he ain't sober fum sunset 'til mawnin', what with all the drinkin' goin' on."

Fitz dragged a rocker over beside his father. The dozen men on the porch were smoking their cheroots, drinking their rum and talking about horses.

"Got 'em all interested in racin'," Fitz said. "They goin' to spread the word, papa, an' soon ev'body will be goin' to any race they kin git to. Means we gits us the kind o' tracks we want an' they gits excited 'nuff, they sure buys our hosses."

"Might's well make some profit outen the party," Jonathan agreed. "Costs 'nuff, way Benay handled it, but she knows bes' an' don't you call her on whut she spent. Makes no mind how much 'tis."

"Knows that. Got some bad news now. Remember that Major Charlie Apperson we won all that money from in Richmond? He's comin' tomorrow. Nobody asked him, but he comin' anyway. They ain't no soiree 'round heah 'thout he there."

"Cain't do no harm," Jonathan said. "Mayhap we see a chance to take a little more money from him. That'd make the party real good. Yes sir, surely would. Whur that no good nigger?" He raised his voice. "Calcutta... whur in hell you at?"

Calcutta appeared, walking as if on a tightrope. His tray was laden with full glasses, part of which had slopped over the tray. It was at a crazy angle with all the glasses bunched up near the tray's lowest point. Calcutta mumbled something, started to bow and present the tray to Jonathan and then he gently collapsed on the porch, spilling the drinks, and promptly went to sleep.

"Jonathan," someone called out amidst the laughter, "you sho' treats yo' houseboys right, suh. That 'un ain't goin' to wake up fo' two days."

Fitz called two bucks standing by in case more guests arrived. They picked up Calcutta and toted him to the back of the house where they deposited him behind a bush.

Fitz and Jonathan wedged their chairs closer to the group. They were fully accepted now, and respected as well. Matt Lawton, who lived only thirty miles west, appreciated the efforts of his host, and he was repaying it in part.

"Major Apperson," he said, "is comin' heah, suh, to make trouble he gits a chance. Ain't nevah stopped hatin' you 'cause you beat him fair an' square that last race. Busted him like he never been busted befo'. Had to mortgage some of his land, he did. Man like him keeps lookin' fo' a chance to git back. You kin consider that a friendly warnin'. Ain't none of us here don't know about it."

"Obleeged," Jonathan nodded. "Been my pleasure to take the Major's money once, mayhap I takes it again. Don't know how yit, but we waits a chance."

The ladies returned with the waning sun and presently supper was announced. They sat around the long table, which would be extended further in the morning for the additional guests. It was a lavish meal, as they all were, but the best ones were being saved for the following evening when there'd be a banquet and more dancing.

In the soft candlelight, the interior of the house looked fresh and lovely. There were early flowers everywhere. New gimcracks decorated tables and walls, all purchased by Benay in Norfolk.

Clarissa did her best to flirt with the men, but she wasn't having much success because everyone was tired and too sated with food and drink. The men, with cigars and brandy, fell to talking about tobacco and corn, slave prices, and the growing politics in the North that were becoming ever more and more critical of the slave holders.

By nine, everyone had retired to the guest house. Even Clarissa begged to be excused. Elegant sat in the kitchen fanning herself industriously and wondering how white folks could eat so much. Nina was busy cleaning up in the dining room. Fitz and Benay left the house for a brief walk in the sultry spring evening.

"Dear Fitz," she linked her arm under his, "do you have any idea how much I'm in love with you? All through this, you've been so good. You never complained once."

"Whut's there to complain 'bout?" he asked. "Sides, I gits riled, I looks at you and fo'git whut I'm riled 'bout. Mighty proud, I am, Benay. Heerd 'em talkin', not knowin' I was close by, an' they all say you splendiferous, sure 'nuff."

"I'm glad they said that, because I want you to be proud of me. Tomorrow there'll be more than thirty people heah, Fitz. Mayhap fo'ty. They comin' 'cause they heerd tell 'bout Wyndward. Next time they'll come 'cause they likes us an' not just to see whut we got heah."

"Been told Major Apperson comin'," Fitz said.

"That man . . . him? Fitz, I didn't invite him."

"Knows that. Heerd he gits no invite, he comes anyway if the party impohtant 'nuff. Reckon he lookin' to make us trouble, he kin."

"If he spoils this party, I'll kill him," Benay declared. "Daid!" she added with emphasis.

"Papa an' me, we lookin' for another way to take some o' his money. Don't trust him none, but he a guest in our house, we treats him like one."

"Papa used to tell me he's a mean, ornery man who gits his own way an' he don't care much how he does it, Fitz. He's comin' heah 'cause he's still mad and he goin' to do somethin' to embarrass us."

"It's a nice night, Benay, so let's fo'git the Major and jes' walk an' talk a little. Been meaning to ask you . . . we married now kinda long time. You plannin' we goin' to have a family?"

"Reckon we don't have to worry 'bout that, Fitz. Ain't sure yit, but ask me mayhap nex' week."

He stopped and stared down at her. "You knocked up? That whut you tryin' to say?"

"I'm not sure. I think so. I wasn't goin' to tell you 'til I was, but you asked me just now an' that's what I got to say 'bout it."

"Glory be." He hugged her tightly. "Been waitin' fo' that. Papa he goin' to jump clear outen his skin he heahs 'bout it."

"Don't tell him 'til I'm sure," she begged. "Jonathan's mopin' 'round too much. We tells him and it ain't true, he's goin' to feel bad."

"Part of it is that goddamn clipper ship," Fitz said. "He keeps smellin' it. I tells him over and over agin, they ain't no smell, but don't do any good. He gits a grandson, he sure goin' to fo'git that damn ship."

"I'll do my best," she promised.

They turned around and strolled back, not saying much, each busy with thoughts of the change that would be made if there was a child born to Benay.

Nina waited for them and opened the door as they crossed the porch. Fitz grinned at her. "Wants you to take mighty good care of my wife, Nina. Extra keerful eve'ythin' you does 'round her. She knocked up, reckon."

Neither saw Nina's smile fade rapidly and the moisture in her eyes threaten to flow over. She said, "Yassuh, massa, suh, I takes keer o' mist'iss."

Fitz had to have a drink on the strength of the news. Benay and Nina went upstairs together where Nina helped Benay undress. She laid out her nightclothes and Fitz's long nightgown, working quietly, not looking directly at Benay.

"Nina, will you take care of my child if there is one?" Benay asked.

"Yes'm, mist'iss, I takes mighty good keer."

Benay grasped her gently by the shoulders. "I know

how you feel, Nina. Ain't that blind I don't see you love him too, but it cain't be. You a nigger. Don't make no difference you don't look like one. You think'n' right now, it's you should be knocked up, 'stead of me. But it wouldn't be right."

Nina nodded. "Knows that, mist'iss. I sweah I keers fo' yo' baby like it be my own. Long it his'n too, I be happy. Wants he should have a son, I do. I cain't give him one. reckon wants you to do it more'n anyone else."

Benay said, "Nina, I'm goin' to ask Jonathan to manumit you. You goin' to be free. I don't think o' you as a nigger any more'n Fitz does. You goin' to be manumitted soon's I kin git Jonathan to agree."

"Likes that, I do," Nina admitted, "but Massa Jonathan he say no, don' make no difference to me. I stays if I slave or free."

Benay touched her cheek, brushing away a solitary tear that coursed its way across her flawless bronze skin. "Goin' to find you a man," she said. "No buck. Got to be a mustee 'thout much nigger blood, like you. An' you goin' to marry him, like white folks git married. You wait an' see, Nina."

"I waits," Nina said, but she could have told Benay there was no other man for her. She'd be content here, to live out her life among them. Sometimes the need for Fitz was great. He hadn't slipped into her room now in some weeks and she missed him, but she also understood. She went about her duties again, but made certain to be gone before Fitz came upstairs.

Nine

MAJOR APPERSON arrived the following noon with two carriages and a wagon in his entourage. His baby-faced son was with him, but not his wife. No one clearly remembered seeing her anywhere the Major went, and there were some who thought she was an illusion.

The Major had brought half a dozen slaves to cater to his whims and his needs. The two young bucks who'd been sold to the Major's son were among them, indicating that while the Major might get along without satisfying his carnal desires, his son was not so inclined.

"Mistah Turner, suh." He shook hands with Jonathan. "It's mighty nice o' yo' to invite me to yo' pahty. Took the liberty o' bringin' 'long my son an' a few niggers to wait on us. Mrs. Apperson begs yo' understandin', ma'am." He bowed to Benay and let his eyes travel from her face to the low, revealing decolletage. "Miz Apperson, ma'am, is failin' some. She a frail woman, but an understandin' one, and she wants fo' me and our son to have us a fine time."

"I'm sorry to hear she's ill," Benay said, forcing a politeness difficult to assume. "Please excuse me now, Major. So many things to do . . ."

"Hurry back," he said with the exaggerated manners he believed to be very smooth. "Mistah Turnah, suh, I understan' yo' serves a hell of a fine rum drink and I craves one, you be so kind."

Jonathan summoned Moses, the jockey turned houseboy. Apperson looked at him intently, but didn't say anything, not being sure if he had been the jockey. His ego wouldn't have permitted him to bring up the subject of his loss anyway.

Major Apperson smacked his lips loudly after his first sip of rum. "Mighty satisfyin', suh. Warms me clear down to my balls, it does. You still got that mare whut won all my money, suh?"

"I still got her," Jonathan said.

"Been brought to my 'tention yo' and yo' son been urgin' the construction o' new race tracks. In favor of it, suh. Been tryin' to git that done fo' yeahs, but nobody listens. 'Tween us, we'll git our tracks this time, suh, an' I'm lookin' to the day when I can git back my money."

"Any time," Jonathan said. "Hoss racin', card playin', bettin' on the weather, don't matter none to me. Yo' a bettin' man, so am I."

The Major nodded appreciatively. "See 'bout that later on, suh. Does crave yo' permission to put on a little treat fo' all these kind folks. Brought me 'long a big buck whut got the biggest pecker in the worl'. Brought 'long a wench. She virgin, an' 'tween she an' the buck, we sho' see some real lovin'. Makes the gal squeal like she bein' reamed out. Co'se, yo' folks be agin that, I spancel the buck and tie him down."

"Reckon it ain't more'n mos' folks heah seen befo'," Jonathan said and hoped that was the truth. He, himself, was not averse to watching one of these exhibitions. He'd seen them all over the world, but that had been a long time ago. Properly performed, such an exhibition might just restore his juices which he feared were dried up.

"Then set yo'se'f fo' the damndest screwin' match yo' evah did see, suh."

"When the dancin's over," Jonathan stipulated. "So them whut don't wants to see it, kin go to baid. 'Specially the womenfolk."

"Why, shucks, suh, they's the one like it mos'."

The Major drifted away to meet some of these people he considered to be old friends. Jonathan noticed that quite a number of them quickly moved away when they saw Apperson coming. Fitz, hearing it from his father, was not much in favor of the exhibition.

"Major's son been shinin' up to Clarissa," Fitz said. "Squirmin' and bowin' all over the place."

"She a bitch in the heats," Jonathan declared. "Las' night she gits me dancin' 'gainst my will. She bats them big eyes o' her'n at me, snuggles up right close and fo' the firs' time in my life, I felt like I gittin' my money's wuth from a whore, right in public. She squirms like she got the itch, she do. Year ago I'd shooed her out back an' give her whut she was cravin', but I sure feels like I used up, son."

"She doin' the same thing to the Major's son," Fitz said. "Gittin' him pantin' like a coon dawg bayin' up a tree."

Later in the evening, after one of the most sumptuous banquets ever served in the state of Virginia, Benay told Fitz the same sort of story about Clarissa.

"Shameful whut she doin', Fitz. Never knowed her to be like this. Oh, I ain't sayin' she turned down any of the boys, but she did it ladylike. Major Apperson's boy gettin' a workout like they on a honeymoon."

"Serve 'em both right," Fitz grumbled. He wished there was some way he could get Clarissa off the plantation. Some day she was going to be angered by him and blurt out the story of what he'd done to her the night he had walked away from Benay. The fact that he'd made love to her didn't matter, but it mattered because of the way he'd treated Benay for doing the same thing half an hour before.

"Major Apperson aimin' to put on a show pretty soon," he warned her. "Got him a big buck whut kin make a wench squeal real loud. You got any objections I tell him to send his damn buck to one o' the sheds to stay there."

"Like they does in N'Oleans?" Benay asked. "Ain't never seen one of them shows, Fitz. You don't mind, I don't, and reckon mos' folks heah seen 'em before."

"Reckon," he said. "Still, got me an idee the Major's up to somethin'. Cain't tell whut it is, but he lookin' like he got three aces up his damn sleeve and cravin' to play 'em."

All the guests were mellowed by wine and rum about the time Major Apperson summoned four of his slaves. They immediately moved furniture back in the ballroom, lining the walls with it. Then they lighted the cleared space in the center of the room with many candles. This done, a tall, huge, heavily-built buck walked in. He was clad in skin tight trousers only, and the bulge at his groin was ample evidence of what this was going to be. The four slaves who'd readied the room took up positions as if they'd done this many times before.

The buck flexed his muscles, showed his strong, big teeth in a wide grin of anticipation. He spread his legs, stationed himself and waited.

The wench was very light and very frightened. She had no idea of what this meant. Where she'd come from, Fitz didn't know, but it was assured Major Apperson had brought her along.

The audience waited in strict silence. Women as well as men knew what would happen and most were eager for it to begin. Benay, however, had some doubts.

"Do you mean that buck is going to . . . to . . . rape that wench right in front of us?"

"Reckon that be the idea," Fitz said. "You wants me to stop it, I will."

"Not if . . . they expect it and . . . want it," she said.

"They expects it an' they wants it. Whut's the difference, Benay. We all knows these niggers nuthin' but animals anyway. They act like animals, it's jes' natural they do."

Benay said nothing more. Clarissa and young Apperson moved up close to where Fitz and Benay stood, though without noticing them. Clarissa was wide-eyed with anticipation and Fitz saw that her hand tightly gripped that of young Apperson.

The wench looked around, sorely puzzled, but all the candles were between her and the audience so she didn't know who or how many were present. The dancing lights and shadows flickered over the scene, making it more eerie than ever. The buck stood there, smiling, not moving a muscles, waiting for the girl to come to him. She was frightened and evidently took him for a friend. She approached him and looked at him appealingly.

She was a small girl. Fitz thought she'd been especially chosen because she was so doll-size. The simple cruelty of the whole thing struck him. That was his Boston influence, but the southern ones were stronger. He began to show some interest in what was about to happen.

The buck suddenly lunged forward. With a single sweep of a mighty hand, he clawed the thin dress off the girl, ripped it so that she stood before him, and the audience, naked. She brought her hands down, vainly trying to cover herself. Her bronze breasts were young and firm and she was a splendidly healthy girl.

There were long drawn out gasps from the audience beyond the candle flames, making the wench look about as if she expected a horde of rapists to descend upon her.

The buck tugged at a piece of rope around his waist. He lowered his pants, kicked them free and stood with his manhood erect, a huge monstrosity of a male organ.

The girl backed away, but when she came close to one of the slaves assigned to each side of the room, she was roughly pushed toward the buck. He wasn't going to wait long. That was quite apparent. The girl gave a sharp cry and backed away again, only to be hurled back at the big man. This time he caught her to him. He tripped her neatly, as if he'd done it many times before in exactly the same way. Then he stretched her on the floor. There were no preambles. He simply slithered on top of her. She screamed this time and then screamed again and again.

Benay said, "Fitz . . . do something."

Fitz moved toward the fantastic scene being played out before him. One of the slaves made a weak pass to stop him. Fitz slammed a fist against his jaw and sent him reeling back. He stepped close to the puffing, panting buck, drew back a foot and kicked him squarely under the chin. The buck fell over on his side. Fitz stepped close again, kicked him twice alongside the head. Then he bent down and picked up the unconscious girl. He thrust her at one of the slaves, who stood uncertainly, holding her in his arms like a baby.

"Nina," Fitz shouted. She elbowed her way to his side. "Have her taken to your room an' care for her. She daid, we goin' to have a hangin' 'fore sunrise. Whur Major Apperson, you sonabitch?"

Apperson approached him with considerable belligerance. "Now see heah, Mistah Turner, suh, yo' knew whut was goin' on. Yo' told me to go 'haid with it. Whut the hell yo' so wukked up 'bout? On'y niggers . . . they ain't human an' you knows it. Ain't no different than a good dog fight, or a bear bait'n' fight."

Fitz walked past him without a word. The candles were being distributed to illuminate the whole room now, furniture was being put back. A disappointed four-piece orchestra began to play chamber music and the guests began to move around the ballroom and the other rooms. No one had much to say about the affair, at least out loud.

"Thank you," Benay said softly.

"That was the Major tryin' to make us look bad," Fitz said. "Reckon he done it too. Them whut wanted to see the rapin' are mad 'cause I stopped it. Them whut didn't want it, thinks I shouldn't have let it start. Got me a mind to hide the Major good."

"That would only make things worse," Benay said. "I don't know how our guests feel about this, but if they're angry because you stopped it, they can go to hell. Did you see Clarissa?"

"Don' want to," he grumbled.

"She grabbed the Apperson boy and near raped him on the spot. Never seen a girl so affected by this. Like she couldn't git 'nuff, standin' there bug-eyed and squirmin' 'round."

Fitz said, "Your cousin kinda crazy-like comes to bucks who got no clothes on. She ever tell you whut happened the night I got mad and walked out on you back in Kaintuck?"

"What do you think, Fitz?"

He took her lightly by the elbow and guided her outside into the garden where they could talk freely. He was in no mind to keep the events of that evening a secret any more. So long as he did, Clarissa could hold it over him, threaten him with exposure. It had disturbed him ever since she came back into his life, but more than that, he was going to become a father in all likelihood, and he wanted no secrets kept from Benay now. Not even if she resented what he'd done, and he couldn't blame her for that.

"I asked you if Clarissa told you whut happened," he reiterated.

"And I asked you if you think she did."

"Whut's that mean?"

"Fitz, if you have something to tell me, even if you believe it'll anger me, it's your place to tell it and mine to hear it. If I say Clarissa told me, you'll never know.

So if you want to tell me, go ahead. You don't have to tell it, you don't want to."

"Still don't make no sense, but don't matter none. I found Clarissa in the barn on your papa's farm that night. She was whuppin' a young nigger boy, teasin' him by showin' him her titties and tellin' him to rape her so she could have him whupped and then strung up. She act like she crazy. I took the whup away from her, sent the nigger packin', and then she turned to me. I was mad. I didn't care if I ever saw you agin, so when she hands herse'f to me, I didn't turn her down. That's whut I did, fifteen minutes after I walked away because you'd done the same thing."

"What else, Fitz?" she asked.

"Clarissa come up to me in the hotel in Norfolk. She say if I don't baid with her, she tells you whut happened. Couldn't stand you bein' told that. I obleeged her, but I aimin' to kick her hot ass offen this plantation come mornin'. I don't like her. She nothin' but a she cat in the heat all the time."

Benay said, "Fitz, she told me what happened that night. You weren't even off the farm before she came runnin' to tell me. An' she told me you raped her in the hotel, but I didn't believe it, knowin' Clarissa like I do, an' knowin' my husband like I do. But I wanted to hear it from you. That's why I asked her to visit us."

"Ain't no use sayin' I'm sorry. That don't do no good. Won't happen agin, that much I kin promise."

Benay was looking off in the direction of the ballroom. "We'll talk 'bout this 'nother time. Your papa's lookin' for you, I reckon. Askin' folks . . . looks like."

"Hell of a party," he said vehemently, and strode off to the ballroom. Jonathan approached him hastily. "Whur in hell you bin? Lookin' for you."

"Been talkin' to Benay 'bout whut happened—and other things. Papa, you mad 'cause I kicked that goddamn buck off'n the wench?"

371

"Woulda done it my own se'f you hadn't. Disgustin', an' most our guests say so too. But the Major, he claim he insulted. He say you near busted the big buck's jaw so he wouldn't be a good fighter any more."

"Fighter? Figgered he wasn't more'n a raper."

"Major Apperson says on'y thing make him happy now, if we lets that buck fight our best man. Hell, Fitz, we didn't raise any fighters. We got no fightin' men."

"He talkin' 'bout bettin'?"

"All whut he lost in the race an' ten thousand besides. Says I'll be a cheapskate I don't bet and let the fight go on. Don't mind that so much, but how the goddamn kin we fight his nigger lessen we gots a man who kin stan' up to him?"

"Themba could do it," Fitz said.

"Find him," Jonathan said. "I'll keep listenin' to that ol' windbag while you looks. Don't waste no time. I be deaf you take too long, or crazier'n that big buck, the Major keeps tauntin' me."

"Don't make no bets 'til I come back," Fitz warned.

"Son, you thinks these folks stand for a fight after whut happened?"

"Fightin' and rapin' two different things, papa. 'Sides, mos' sure would like to see that buck git his brains beat out."

"Reason I kind o' mad, watching the buck rape the wench didn't do anythin' for me. Saw things like that in Algiers, in China and Marseilles. Come to think of it, saw it in New O'leans and in N'Yawk too. Used to send me huntin' the nearest whorehouse, but I jes' an old, no-damn-good man any more. Now you get Themba. I kin watch a fight with pleasure anyways."

Fitz left the house by one of the doors leading to the lawn. He went loping across it on his way to the stables. Themba usually sat outside the barn where he lived, especially when the slaves who worked under him were busy elsewhere. Themba didn't believe in leaving the stables alone for a moment. He was there tonight, whittling idly, as the curls of wood at his feet betrayed. He'd put away the knife at Fitz's approach.

Themba, knowing that knife could get him in trouble, promptly arose and doffed his cap, something he rarely did for anyone, while he tried to crush the telltale wood chips into the ground by standing on them.

"Yassuh, massa, suh," he said meekly. "You lookin' fo' me, suh?"

"You a big, pow'ful man," Fitz said.

"Yassuh, reckon."

"Evah fight 'nother nigger?"

"I no fightin' man, massa, suh. Doan wants to fight no nigger. Doan know how, suh." Themba's face began to show some worry.

"Ain't no need to know how. You jes' start hittin' the other nigger. You kin bite him, kick the balls offen him, bust a laig or an arm, or his goddamn neck. Make no difference how you do it long's you win."

Themba's eyes were big, rolling slightly. "Massah, suh, I knows these heah fights. I don't kill t'other nigger, he kills me. On'y one nigger walks 'way. Don' mind fightin' 'cause I big an' strong, but whut worries me, I gits killed or I gits to be a crip, whut 'bout the hosses? Massah, suh, they mighty impohtant."

"I suppose so," Fitz said. "I can't afford to lose you."

"You asks Hong Kong. He a fightin' nigger, suh. Big's me an' stronger'n me."

Fitz nodded slowly. There was logic to what Themba said. He was needed, and risking his life might create more complications than the plantation could safely handle. Fitz believed there was a certain amount of cowardice in Themba's refusal to obey, but the pressing dependence he'd come to assign to this man discounted cowardice as meaningless in this situation.

There was a light in Hong Kong's window. Fitz opened the door and walked in. Hong Kong's wench was not there, having been assigned kitchen work at the house, and Fitz was grateful for that bit of good luck. What he would order Hong Kong to do was not something he relished doing in front of the woman.

"Wants you to fight a big buck owned by Major Apperson," he said bluntly.

"Fight him?" Hong Kong asked in wonder. He wasn't going to argue the point or seek excuses, but the order startled him because nothing like this had ever happened before at Wyndward.

"Means he aims to kill you, he kin."

"Yassuh, knows that, but reckon take a pow'ful heap o' hatin' to make me kill a man."

"For this buck you sure can find the hate. Major Apperson bring him heah to put on a show. This buck he hung heavy like a bull. Likely near kill any woman he lay down with. So they gives him a little gal . . . smaller'n Nina, and lets him rape her. I don' know she daid or not. Nina carin' for her now."

Hong Kong brought his ham-like hands before his eyes and slowly opened them flat. "I kills him, yo' says so, massah, suh."

"Think you kin?"

"Yassuh, I kin. Was in one o' them fights once an' I won it. Didn' kill the nigger, but I sure coulda I'd a mind to. Got whupped 'cause I din'."

"This one mighty big. Heavy hung, like I said, and that mayhap mean he extra pow'ful."

"I ain't hung nohow," Hong Kong said without bitterness. "Heerd some massas cut they balls off'n some bucks to make 'em strong. That's whut happened to me, massah, suh. When that overseer he bust me 'tween the laigs, I got nothin' lef' to pleasure with, but I gits mighty strong."

"Heerd that happen sometimes. I kin tell you one thing, maybe he'p. This buck, he rapin' the wench when I kicks him on the chin. Reckon I din' bust his jaw, I sure come near to it, so he goin' to have one damn sore face."

Hong Kong's black features lighted up and he displayed large even teeth in a broad grin. "He'ps, massa, suh."

" 'Nother thing. My papa an' me, we bettin' heavy on you. Don' want this fight, but cain't git outen it. Major Apperson wants back the money he lost to us on the hoss race."

"You wants me to fight right now, massa?"

"Might's well git it over with."

"I'se ready, suh."

"Firs' thing, wants you to see the wench he raped. Man gits mad, he fights better an' this goin' to make you mad as hell. Come 'long."

Fitz brought him into the house through the rear. Hong Kong's woman, at work in the kitchen, exhibited some apprehension as Hong Kong passed by without glancing at her. She said nothing and looked away hurriedly.

Nina's room off the kitchen was large, airy and far better than what the average slave was ever given. Nina sat beside the bed on which the girl lay. Her eyes were closed and she was very still.

"How she, Nina?" Fitz asked.

"Reckon she live, massa, suh. Don' rightly knows she will. Don' rightly know she cares she lives. She fo'teen, suh. Thass al, fo'teen. Her name Viney."

Fitz laid a hand gently on the girl's forehead. She winced at the touch, but didn't open her eyes.

"She bleed too much," Nina said. "Stops now but she bad hurt, massa, suh."

Fitz nodded. "Sendin' a boy to bring back the veter'-narv. Mayhap he kin he'p." Fitz suddenly yanked the blanket down, revealing the naked girl. Hong Kong stared at her, saw what had happened to her. Fitz watched the big buck's fists open and close tightly, the only show of emotion he gave.

"You think you kin fight this nigger?" he asked the big black.

"Yassuh, massa, suh. I fights him. Quick's you kin git him ready fo' me, suh."

Fitz gently covered the now-trembling girl. He touched her face again. This time she didn't wince. Fitz led Hong Kong from the room.

Ten

IT WAS AFTER ONE in the morning, but no one slept at Wyndward this night. Fitz had summoned a score of slaves to ready one of the sixty-foot-long tobacco drying sheds for use as an arena. Candles were brought and set up so there was sufficient light for the combat. The guests, still clad in their finery, took up positions to form a ring of ample size.

Major Apperson hadn't appeared yet. He was outside, cussing the absence of his son whom he'd last seen heading for the woods with that hotted-up cousin of Benay's. Apperson's annoyance was twofold—he wanted his son with him during the fight, and he was jealous that the boy had reached the girl first and was probably now enjoying whatever favors she had to give.

He spoke to the towering buck. "Yo' wins this fight an' yo' kills this heah nigger you fightin', I gives yo' two jugs of cawn fo' yo'se'f, an' two silvah dollahs."

"I kills him, massa, suh," the buck declared matter-of-factly.

"Yo' bettah, heah? Yo' lose the fight, might's well let the other buck wring yo' goddamn neck 'cause he don't, I kills yo' myse'f."

"Yassuh, massa, suh. Got no call to fret, suh. Ain't the firs' one I kills."

"Git in theah now, and let's see you murder this 'un."

Hong Kong was already waiting, clad only in trousers. His broad shoulders seemed more massive than ever. His thick neck was rigid with excitement, his biceps bulged as he kept flexing his arms.

The Apperson buck swaggered into the ring, also stripped down. Without orders, both bucks shed their pants, shucking down to their bare skins.

Someone gasped and pointed at Hong Kong's deformity. Fitz had been afraid of that. He could easily see how strong the Apperson buck was and Hong Kong would have serious need of all his own strength and confidence. Jeering comments on his lack of manhood were not going to do him any good. The Apperson buck noticed Hong Kong's lack, and gave a wild laugh which stopped abruptly when Hong Kong suddenly leaped in close and hit him on the nose.

The Apperson black retreated drunkenly while he recovered his wits and tried to stem the flow of blood spurting from his broken nose. Then the pain came and he howled with it and lunged at Hong Kong.

The two men went down with a thump that shook the ground beneath the feet of the onlookers. They struggled, seeking some kind of hold that would enable them to tear one another to pieces.

The Apperson buck managed to get on top, riding Hong Kong and pounding at his face. Then he bent and tried to bite Hong Kong's jugular. He missed, but his enormous teeth closed on the lobe of Hong Kong's ear and ripped part of it off.

Pain gave Hong Kong added spurts of energy and he threw off the big buck. He got to his feet, one hand clapped to his severed earlobe while blood streamed through his fingers from the wound. The Apperson buck was finding it harder to breathe through a broken nose, and his mouth was agape as he sucked in air.

Hong Kong moved in, took a mighty blow to the side of the head to get in one of his own that squashed whatever was left of the cartilage of the buck's nose. Now he could only breathe through his mouth and Hong Kong's fist collided with that, reducing the heavy lips to a bloody mass and knocking out most of the front teeth.

Infuriated, and for the first time afraid of his opponent, the Apperson buck charged in without regard to the punishment he took. Hong Kong aimed one punch at the buck's throat, seeking to break his larynx and thus let him choke to death. He missed. A hand covered his face, the fingers seeking Hong Kong's eyes to gouge them out.

Hong Kong quickly recognized the danger here. He retreated in a backward leap which caught the Apperson buck off balance. His hand slid down across Hong Kong's face, the nails gouging trails of torn flesh and making Hong Kong's head bloody and aching with pain.

The Apperson buck charged, pounded away, weakening Hong Kong gradually by the sheer power of the stomach and chest punches until Hong Kong was gasping as badly as his opponent.

Then the Apperson buck made a mistake. He was hurt, winded, afraid, and fighting like a robot now, seeking only to cause the maximum amount of damage as quickly as possible because he realized he couldn't last much longer.

He brought up a knee to Hong Kong's groin. Ordinarily this would have doubled his opponent over and made him easy prey, but the buck's knee didn't encounter what should have been there. Surprised, and overcome with a fresh wave of terror, the buck used both hands to reach between Hong Kong's legs to tear off what Hong Kong didn't have. Too late the buck realized he'd forgotten that Hong Kong was not equipped to be rendered helpless with this move.

The Apperson buck was bent over in his fumbling attempt to find what he was looking for. Hong Kong hadn't forgotten that the buck had either a sore jaw or a fractured one. He brought up his right knee. Bone cracked. The buck howled and was thrown back. He tripped and fell. Hong Kong promptly hurled himself upon the man. He thrust a thumb into the buck's eye socket, popped the eyeball out to hang from its muscular attachment. He raised his open hand and brought the side of it down against the buck's windpipe. The screech coming from the buck's lips turned to a gurgle. Blood welled out of his mouth.

Hong Kong stood up, lifted one foot with a heel as hard as steel, and brought it down against the buck's face. Whatever was left of it now turned into a gory, mangled mass.

Hong Kong raised the same foot, poised it. He looked around. His own face was swollen out of shape, he could barely see out of one eye. Blood ran down the side of his face and on along his chest from the severed ear. He was seeking Fitz, but everything seemed blurry.

"Massa, suh," he called out. "Yo' wants me to kill him, suh?"

Fitz walked into the ring and took Hong Kong by the arm. "He half daid now. No sense finishin' him off. Be no damn good to anybody any more."

He led Hong Kong out of the shed. Benay, white-faced and trembling, had brought Seawitch, Hong Kong's woman. She gasped at his appearance, but she sensed he was otherwise all right.

"Hong Kong," Fitz said, "kin you heah me?"

"Yassuh . . . yassuh . . ." the words came through enormously swollen lips.

"You the bes' fightin' man I ever did see, but this your las' fight. Nevah again, you understands that?"

"Yassuh . . . ready, yo' wants me, suh."

"Goin' to manumit you an' your wench," Fitz went on. "Goin' to make you overseer for good an' give you a big cabin to live in and a week's pay. For the rest o' your life. Now go home and rest. Ain't 'spectin' you in the fields for a week. More, you hurt that bad."

Hong Kong stumbled off, supported by his woman. Fitz gave a growl of satisfaction. Benay moved up to him.

"That'll settle goddamn Major Apperson for awhile. Got jes' one more thing to do 'bout that gen'mun. Tell you later, Benay. Won't be long."

Fitz knew the likeliest spots around the plantation house where a man and a woman might go for extended lovemaking. There was one behind the springhouse and that's where he found them, on the ground, locked in one another's arms. Fitz nudged the Apperson boy with his foot.

Clarissa got up first, pulling down her dress and trying to arrange the bodice over her ample breasts. "Whut yo' buttin' in like this fo', Fitz?" she asked and added, coyly, "Mayhap yo' be jealous?"

"I sure am," he said. He brushed grass off the Major's son. "Reckon I have a hell of a time keepin' up with this heah buck," he grinned.

"Whut you bustin' in fo' then?" Clarissa asked. "I'm tellin' yo', Fitz, yo' gits me mad, yo' know whut I'll do."

"I knows. That's why I'm here, to do you a favor, Clarissa. Right now Major Apperson huntin' high an' low for you. Says his son got you, he goin' to bust his damn back. Major Apperson's hot for you, Clarissa, an' he say nobody goin' to keep him offen you."

"I'll kill him," Horace Apperson cried out in a thin, unconvincing voice.

"More likely he kill you," Fitz reminded him. "Knows a way out. Reckon the only one, and there ain't no reason why both o' you shouldn't like it."

"Don't trust you," Clarissa said suspiciously.

"Why not? It's me skeered o' you, Cousin Clarissa. You knows what Benay'll do she finds out. . . ."

"Never you mind 'bout that," Clarissa glanced apprehensively at Horace, but the darkness shielded his face and she wasn't sure what he was thinking.

"You kin listen to me," Fitz said. "Both o' you stay right heah fo' ten minutes. Then take that path to your lef' down to the stables. Have a carriage ready by then. 'Fore yo' papa kin find out, Horace, you an' Cousin Clarissa on your way to Lynchburg. Gits theah by mornin'. Finds yo'se'f a preacher an' gits married. Then the Major cain't lay a hand on you, Clarissa, an' he cain't do a damn thing to your husband."

"The Majors kills us," Clarissa objected.

"Cain't do nothin'. Major's older'n he looks, Cousin, an' he a sick man. Cain't live long an' when he dies, ever'thing he got goes to yo' husband. You be rich as Benay and you got yo'se'f a fine husband to boot."

He might be at that, Fitz told himself, provided Clarissa didn't mind if he made an occasional trip to the barn with his twin personal servants now and then.

"Whut you say, Horace?" she asked.

"Reckon I cain't stop my papa takin' you fo' hisse'f lessen we do that, Clarissa. An' papa rich. Mayhap he die pretty soon an' like Fitz say, you be rich as Benay. Reckon we's married we don't have to do our screwin' on the ground no mo'."

Clarissa gave an emphatic nod of her pretty, empty head. "Yo' gits that carriage ready, Cousin Fitz, an' I fo'gives yo' all yo' sins far as I'm concerned." She stepped closer, kissed him on the lips, explored slightly with her

381

tongue and smiled. "Reckon it was fun anyways, Cousin Fitz. Jus' cause I married ain't no reason yo' cain't come to see yo' lovin' cousin now and then, is they?"

"Every week," Fitz promised. If they didn't get out of here soon, the Major was going to find them and Horace was going to learn that his father's rage was aimed at Jonathan and Fitz and he couldn't possibly care about Clarissa at this particular moment.

Fitz had Themba harness one of the carriages. Themba worked quickly because he'd been ordered to do so and when the carriage was ready, he stood by, holding the horse steady.

"Massa, suh," he said tentatively.

"Whut you want, Themba?"

"Heahs Hong Kong near kill that big buck, suh. Yo' ain't mad 'cause I din' do it? Could have, but I keeps worryin' myse'f 'bout yo' hosses. . . ."

Fitz walked away without answering, still puzzled about Themba, wondering if he was a coward or if he'd spoken truthfully. It didn't matter anyway. It was done with. Major Apperson had now lost another enormous sum of money. Fitz didn't think Cousin Clarissa was really going to be as rich as Benay.

He met the pair on his way back and sent them along to the waiting carriage. When he reached the house, most of the guests were outside, clustered in groups still talking about the fight. The huge, beaten buck came from somewhere in the night, staggering and reeling. Unable to sense the presence of the whites who got out of his way, or to see them, because one eye was gone, the other all but tightly closed. He didn't know where he was going, but when his bare feet felt the smooth path beneath them, he sensed that it would lead somewhere, to safety, or to help. He was too dazed to think.

Major Apperson suddenly detached himself from one of the groups and trotted clumsily down the path. When he reached to within a dozen yards of the stumbling black, he drew a gun, aimed it and before anyone could stop him, he fired a bullet into the slave's back.

The buck fell forward without a sound. He didn't move, his tortured body didn't even twitch. Major Apperson stuck the gun under his belt and wiped his hands as if they were dirty. He began to turn away, only to find Jonathan on one side of him, Fitz on the other.

"He belonged to me, suh," the Major complained nervously. "I wants to kill the sonabitch, that my right."

"Nobody denyin' that," Jonathan said.

"Whut you lookin' at me this way fo', then? You mad 'cause I killed him? Whut good he—reckon he been blind. Nevah fight agin and couldn't rape a two-yeah-old after this. Why you lookin' at me this way?"

"You owes me a right smart piece o' money, suh. Knows you don't tote that much 'round, but in my office I gots pens and writing paper, suh. You kin write out a note to your bank for the money you owes me."

"Whut good writin' on paper? I tells my bank to honah yo' draft, suh."

"Better papa brings your draft to the bank, suh," Fitz said.

Major Apperson sighed. "Reckon that's the way yo' wants it, suh."

"That's the way," Jonathan said complacently.

"An' that done, git your niggers to tote the daid buck offen our propitty," Fitz said. "We ain't got no buryin' grounds for your niggers heah, and don' aim to start one."

The Major nodded curtly and led the way toward the house. There he reluctantly and angrily wrote out the order to the bank while Fitz and his father looked on. The Major threw the quill onto the desk, spattering ink. He got to his feet.

"Reckon I don' keer to remain in yo' house, suh," he told Jonathan. "Yo' a gen'mun, which I doubt, yo' fetch yo' bes' hoss flesh to Richmond soon's the track's finished, an' yo' gives me a chance to git my money back."

"Think onto it," Jonathan said.

"Yo' don't, suh, I makes it my business to call yo' onto a field o' honah, suh."

"Fight a duel?" Jonathan howled with laughter. "Yo' wants it, suh, I'll fight you now. With clubs, rocks, fists, pistols, shotguns or swords. You takes yo' pick. It's a nice night fo' it, huh, and I aims to pervide my guests with all the amusements I kin. This duel be the mos' amusing thing happen today. Whut'll it be, suh? Name your weapon."

"There are formalities," the Major said indignantly. "Yo' will heah from me."

Jonathan bowed. "When yo' is ready, suh."

The Major walked into the ballroom, searching for his son. Fitz led his father to one side. "You think he means that?"

"A duel? Fitz, he ain't got no stomach fo' that. Reckon won't heah from him agin. You notice he was mighty keerful nobody but us 'round when he challenged me. The Major's a coward an' a fake. Don' fret me none. Like his son, that's whut he is."

Fitz chuckled. "His son and Cousin Clarissa on they way to Lynchburg to git married. She screwin' him all night an' he so heated up don' know whut in hell he doin'. Don' care so it's with Cousin Clarissa. His papa goin' to be mighty mad come the time he heahs what that fool boy done."

"Serves him right."

"Papa—I tol' Hong Kong we goin' to manumit him and Seawitch, his woman. Tells him we makes him overseer heah for life, and we gives him a big cabin and we pays him a week's wages."

Jonathan frowned. "Don' know I likes that, son. You begin treatin' a nigger that way, they all wants it. The rule is, give 'em nothin', no mattah whut they does fo' you."

"You kin tell any buck on this plantation, he put up the kind of fight Hong Kong did, he git manumitted too. Reckon they be no takers."

Jonathan nodded. "No slave evah made his mastah so much money as Hong Kong did. We manumits him, and Seawitch, pervided nobody knows. I kin make the judge file the papers 'thout tellin' anybody. That way, Hong Kong 'pears like a slave, but when I dies, or somethin' happens to you, then Hong Kong a free man fo' real."

"We gives him the cabin, papa?"

"Lets him build it hisse'f, usin' all the he'p he needs. An' we pays him some, puts more in the bank fo' him and Seawitch. Goddamn, Fitz, you goin' to have me actin' like a goddamn Abolitionist you keeps on."

"Does the best I kin, papa," Fitz said with a smile.

"My mistake in the firs' place. No man buyin' and sellin' slaves, or wukkin' 'em, should marry a woman from Boston. That's whut's wrong with you, son. It's Boston blood."

"Reckon so," Fitz nodded.

They stepped onto the porch just as Major Apperson came striding around the corner of the house, followed by two of his slaves. He looked at no one, spoke no word, but he did pause beside the body of the dead fighting slave and kicked the body half a dozen times while he cursed it bitterly.

His two slaves picked up the dead man and carried him down the path in the wake of their master.

"Reckon comes mornin' the party's over," Jonathan said. "Kind of sorry, too. Kep' me from that everlastin' thinkin'. Fo' a few minutes I didn't smell that goddamn slave clipper. Like livin' over agin, but now it back. That infernal stink seeped into my flesh an' my bones an' won't wash away. Reckon I be crazy, son?"

"Way you handled the Major, you crazy in a way

goin' to make us richer'n ever, papa. That stink in yo' mind. Takes time, but it'll go away."

Jonathan nodded. They were standing on the porch now, observing the groups beginning to break up. Inside, coffee, brandy and little decorated cakes were ready for a light repast before the guests bedded down.

"Your mama wanted this too," Jonathan said. "Wanted it bad, she did. Stink don't make no diff'rence no mo'. Missin' her worse'n the stink. You finds Calcutta, an' he suber 'nuff, send him to my room with a bottle o' rum an' a pitcher o' cold water. Aimin' to drink myse'f to sleep, like I been doin'. On'y way I kin shut my eyes 'thout seein' her so plain I starts talkin' to her. Good night, son. Tell Benay she done real good with our party."

He walked away, bent and aged-looking at forty. He was successful, one of the richest men in the country, and he seemed to have so little to live for.

Fitz swore softly at himself and ran after his father, caught him halfway up the stairs.

"Papa, clean fo'got somethin' mighty impohtant."

"Tomorra, son," Jonathan said. "Keeps 'til then."

"This won't. Benay knocked up."

Jonathan's tired eyes opened wide, his slack mouth assumed its normal contour. He lifted both arms above his head and gave vent to a howl of joy that brought everyone into the reception hall.

"I the happies' man you evah did see," Jonathan shouted. "Friends, Benay, she knocked up. Nothin' in this world ever pleasured me mo'. When that boy borned we goin' to have the bigges', bes' and longest party evah known. All o' you invited as o' now. By damn, I thought it would never happen. Like my son, mayhap, too shy."

Benay, at the foot of the stairs, called up, "Papa, no son of yours could be that way. An' I here to say Fitz ain't. He blushes like crazy, but don't do no blushin' in baid. If our son is like his papa, I'm satisfied."

There was much activity early next morning while carriages were harnessed, brought out, and waited for their passengers. Benay, Fitz and Jonathan watched each carriage pull away, with much waving of hands and promises of more parties, early and often. That it had been an astounding success was evident from each family group. Major Apperson had been the only evil abstraction.

"We made many friends," Benay said. "There'll be a lot more to be made. Jonathan, if you say so, I'll make this the best and the happiest plantation in Virginia—or anywhere."

Jonathan tilted her head back with his finger. "You 'tend to havin' that grandson o' mine, y'heah? That's mo' 'pohtant than a thousand parties, or a million friends. Fitz an' me, we wuk our haids off to fix it so he has ever'thin' they to be had on earth. Jes' knowin' he on his way makes me feel younger an' sprightlier an' makes me come to a decision I been wukkin' on for months."

"Now, papa," Fitz objected, "ain't no call to fret 'bout anythin'."

"Frettin' all I been doin' since your mama died. But she daid now a long time an' I got to fergit bes' I kin. That on'y half of it. Like I said, stink of that ship stays. The *Wyndward* lies tied up in Norfolk. Lef' the ship's carpenter to stay 'board and keep her up some. Tomorra I'm leavin' for Norfolk."

"Aimin' to git rid of the *Wyndward,* papa?" Fitz asked.

"Whut I got in mind, son."

"She'll bring a fancy price."

"Long's that ship afloat, I kin smell her. In my mind—sure it is—but if that goddamn ship goes to the bottom, whut's they lef' to stink? I aimin' to put out to sea, start her afire and watch her go down. Whut's at the bottom o' the ocean cain't stink, even in my mind. You knows whut I'm talkin' 'bout, Fitz? You too, Benay?"

"Reckon that's the best idea you evah had," Benay said encouragingly.

"I gits the stage ready for mawnin'." Fitz gave his approval in that manner.

"Nevah min' the stage. Goin' alone an' takin' a carriage. Ain't no hurry. Reckon I go whorin' 'roun' some. Mayhap buy me a coffle o' bucks an' wenches, they looks good to me. Got nothin' to do heah. You in charge, Fitz, an' you do it all, so I jes' sits and gits older. Sap runnin' outen me fas', but reckon they be ways o' gittin' it back."

Eleven

By the time Jonathan reached Richmond, he was bored to death by the now-familiar trip. He thought about staying with Colonel Coldwell and his wife for a few days, but the idea wasn't tempting enough. He and the Colonel were boyhood friends and the Colonel enjoyed dwelling garrulously upon the past. That was what Jonathan was desperately trying to forget.

The past was good, no doubt of that, up to the time of Sarah's death. Now there was a grandson to look forward to, which made the future even better. At no time did Jonathan consider the possibility it might be a granddaughter. He'd love her nonetheless, after his surprise was over and done with, but for the moment he thought only of a grandson to carry on the plantation.

So it was that the future looked fine. It was true that his mind still dwelt upon the memory of Sarah, but it was easing. Trouble with him lay in the fact that, after her death, he'd moped and left all the work for Fitz. When he returned, he meant to settle down and actively help his son make the plantation bigger than ever.

The stink was what bothered him most and he happily contemplated watching the clipper go down, stench and all. It would never bother him again. If it was all in his mind, what difference that? He thought he constantly smelled the polluted hold of the ship. When it sank, he'd think it impossible to smell it again and that would be the end to it all. The idea had occurred to him before, but not with such magnitude and the necessity for carrying it out, until he heard that Benay was going to have a child.

He checked into the same Richmond hotel he always used. There was a slave auction at Odd Fellows Hall and he went there to be greeted with the utmost courtesy and warmth. Hadn't he bought fifty prime bucks and fifty fine wenches at his last visit? This time he saw no slaves worth the buying so he proceeded to his bank where he deposited Major Apperson's draft, remaining with the bank president until a messenger was dispatched to the Major's bank and returned with the money.

Jonathan spent half a day with the bank bookkeeper, going over his accounts and discovering that he had more than a million dollars on deposit. There was an almost equal sum in a Boston bank, most of it his profits from years of transporting slaves. In Norfolk was an even larger amount. Wyndward Hall was solvent and secure. Nothing but the gravest catastrophe could alter its success.

He ate a solitary supper, though he could have had his choice of friends, for he was quite well-known here by now. The story of Major Apperson's downfall and the savage fight between the two bucks had already circulated throughout the city. There were many who would have liked to hear the story firsthand. Major Apperson wasn't telling any of it. Since his arrival two days before, he hadn't even been seen at any of his usual places. Jonathan wanted no company save that of some knowing, skilled prostitute. There was one in particular—he only knew her as Nell—who could be trusted not to shout all over the city that Jonathan Turner was no longer able to get it up. Nothing would have humiliated Jonathan more. It was getting to a state where he couldn't stand thinking about it.

He had, however, a strong idea this would be soon remedied by the devices he had already planned. A grandson, the sinking of the *Wyndward*, hard work on the plantation—all of that would renew him. But first he had to try a woman.

Nell, he was told, was busy for the evening, but he didn't believe it and believed it even less when his offer of fifty dollars was promptly accepted. Nell was busy only to the extent that she was sleeping off the weariness of her recent labors. She promptly recovered at sight of him, for he was not only a generous man, but incapable of making her work very hard.

"Sho' didn't 'spect you agin so soon, Cap'n," she said with all her false warmth. "Reckon Nell takes real good keer o' yo' an' that's why yo' come back."

"You're pretty good," he admitted. "There was a time when I was too, you 'member rightly. Been feelin' better lately an' wonderin' mayhap it come back to me. The kind o' sap I used to have."

"We kin sho' try an' find out, Cap'n."

"They's a hundrud dollahs for you if you sets my juice runnin' agin."

"I could give the statue down near Odd Fellows Hall a hard-on fo' that kin' o' money, Cap'n. They ain't nothin' I don' know 'bout this. Been my life's wuk, it has. An' enjoys it, I do. 'Specially with a man like you, suh. An' the hundrud dollahs do no harm, suh. Not one li'l bit, suh. Will you kin'ly take off yo' clothes now, so's we kin git down to business?"

He disrobed slowly, looking about the gaudy, cheap room, wondering why the hell he had to come to these places for sex. He could have had that juicy little piece from Kentucky he'd been of a mind to—and if he had what it took. He hadn't dared because if he'd failed and she laughed at him, that would have been his complete downfall.

There were two highly religious pictures over the bed. He wondered if they salved Nell's conscience and then decided she couldn't have a semblance of one, and they were likely meant more for the comfort—or the puzzlement—of her customers.

Until dawn they performed their antics on the bed. There wasn't a trick Nell didn't try and some she invented on the spot. Jonathan tried too, and nothing worked. He was as badly off as Hong Kong, but Jonathan had his testicles and his penis so he had no excuse to offer, or exhibit. He was either too old, or he was sick, or his memory of Sarah yet too strong.

He drank heavily toward morning and finally rested with his head cradled against Nell's ample bosom, after she'd quit trying an hour before.

He lay sleepless for awhile, more and more convinced it was the memory of Sarah responsible for his present horrible predicament. A man, supposedly in his prime, unable to satisfy a woman, let alone satisfy himself. Sarah had been reticent with her favors. When she tendered them she was superb, draining him as no other woman ever had. But she was also Boston straight-laced and hard to arouse. That must have left an impression on him. Now, with Sarah dead these many weeks, her memory was still so strong within him that he couldn't respond to another woman.

Not to a white woman. But a nigger—maybe. While Sarah was alive, he'd bedded down with many of them, usually the golden-skinned kind like Nina. In fact, he had deflowered Nina before Fitz ever laid a hand on her. Laying with a black was different. It had nothing to do with a sense of faithfulness to one's wife. Wives understood this and tolerated it, mainly because there wasn't much else they could do about it.

A light-skinned nigger! Why hadn't he thought of it before? He closed his eyes and fell peacefully asleep. It didn't occur to him that if a black could make the difference, his passion would have been so aroused by now that he'd have leaped out of bed and gone hunting one. Instead, he slept hard and long and awoke with the same idea instilled in his mind, differing only in that a jet black wench might be even better.

"You done you bes'," he told Nell. "Ain't no reason to complain an' I pays you whut I promised."

"Reckon," she said, "they somethin' on yo' mind, Cap'n. You comes heah las' yeah an' I weak for two days after yo' lef'. Sho' din' have no trouble them days, suh."

He gave her the money, lifted her dress and whacked her on the bare behind as he left. There was another house, not far away, where they kept women of various colors. He'd been there before and he knew he'd be welcome again. He ate a hearty breakfast first and then walked to the address. But he kept on going. The closer he got to the place, the less he wanted to go in. He was too well-known here. It would be serious enough if the white whores laughed behind his back, but if the black ones spread the word, he'd never live it down. So he proceeded to the dock area where he made arrangements for passage on one of the fancy barges to Norfolk. Returning to his hotel, he packed his bag, checked out and got aboard the barge armed with four bottles of fine rum. Two hours out of Richmond, he was dead drunk and he remained that way until several hours before they were due to Norfolk.

It was night when they reached the dock. Jonathan hired a carriage to drop him off at a whorehouse he knew of, and to deliver his bags at his hotel.

At least here he wasn't well known. At this black and tan house, he'd been a customer but once, seven or eight years ago, when he wore his captain's uniform, had more hair and less belly. He didn't think anyone would remember him.

He promptly secured the services of a Negress who was as black as midnight, but young, shapely and who knew her business. She asked no questions because while she worked in this whorehouse, she was as much a slave as Nina was back at the plantation. More so, because the hard-earned cash that was paid to her mistress never found its way into her hands. She was given fancy clothes, fed well, not made to perform any menial tasks, but she served any man who came along and had the price.

It was no use. Even here, with a nigger, Jonathan couldn't function. Had Sarah been alive, a visit to this place wouldn't have bothered him. It would not have been on his conscience. A married man was not considered unfaithful if he bedded down with a nigger wench. That's what they were for. At many an auction, a young, light-skinned virgin brought fancy prices because she was desired for more than plantation work or housework. So, if Jonathan failed with a nigger, it was not the memory of Sarah that held him back.

He lay beside the woman, no longer trying. He grasped her wrist, lifted her arm and stuck his nose close to the armpit. He coughed and gagged.

"Goddamn, you sure musky," he said. "Stinks, you do. Now I know whut's wrong an' I knows whut to do 'bout it."

She said, "Massa, don' know whut in hell yo' talkin' 'bout. Don' stink wuss'n any nigger I knows. All niggers musky, suh. Cain't he'p it."

"Knows that," Jonathan declared, only adding to her

astonishment. "But when I smell your stink, I smells the stink of ten thousand niggers?"

"Massa, suh, yo' crazy?" she asked, with an overwhelming curiosity and her right to speak somewhat freely to a man she'd been sleeping with and encouraging all night.

"Been crazy up to now," Jonathan said happily. "Knows whut's wrong and knows how to take keer of it. You a good-lookin' nigger an' you a real fine whore. Mayhap I comes back and shows you whut it's like to be good and raped. For now . . ." he gave her twenty dollars and, knowing the ropes, he added, "you keep this. Stick in your ass if need be. I pays downstairs 'sides this. Nobody knows you got all that money."

She reached down and cupped his manhood in both hands. "Yo' comes back, massa, an' I tries again. I tries ha'd, I do. Loves you, massa. Please come back."

He grinned and left. It was still daylight. He didn't even go to the hotel, but walked briskly to the dock area where ocean-going freighters anchored.

He hadn't seen the *Wyndward* for more than a year now, but there she rode, anchored at the furthest end of the area and far enough out that she couldn't be easily boarded for pillage, or used as a floating refuge for the homeless. Empty now, she rode high in the water, and the barnacles seemed thick enough to render her useless, which Jonathan knew wasn't true in any measure. She was the same sleek, fast clipper that had broken records in her day and could still break them.

She'd been his home for many years and he knew she was seaworthy, even after this long time anchored in the harbor. Tied up to the dock, almost at his feet, was a dory bearing the name *Wyndward*. Probably that meant Lawlor, the ship's carpenter who'd been paid to live aboard the clipper and watch over her, must be ashore. Jonathan climbed into the dory, fitted the oars and pulled steadily toward his ship. His muscles had grown unused to this form of exercise, but it felt good to be on the water again and he didn't mind if his arms felt as if they were being pulled out of their sockets.

He tied up the dory, scaled the ship's ladder and then stood once again on the deck. He made his way to the bridge and stood behind the wheel for a few long moments filled with memories. He went below to his cabin. It was clean and intact. The carpenter had done his work well. The curtains Sarah had insisted be placed at the portholes were there, a little faded, but they had been washed and ironed.

His charts were spread on the map table, his desk drawers stuffed with old and now useless papers. It was like coming home after a long, long absence.

He muttered to himself, went above again and walked toward the hatch covers over the entrance to the holds. They were tightly closed. He bent to open one of them, but hesitated. Te didn't want to smell that awful stench again, yet he knew he had to. He must be sure this was what he kept smelling in his imagination.

He raised the hatch and the stench came blasting up to greet him. It seemed to Jonathan that it had been stored up here so long it appeared to have either grown in bulk or concentrated itself because he'd never remembered it being as bad as this. It was the same stench. It hadn't all been his imagination. This was the abomination that kept him from performing like a man and was slowly driving him into the darknesses of insanity.

He slammed the hatch back, walked to the rail, leaned over it and vomited until there was nothing left in his stomach and he felt torn apart.

He went below again, to his cabin, and searched for a bottle of rum in one of the cupboards. He used to keep a supply hidden there. To his delight, he found several bottles, uncorked one, lay down on the bunk and brought the neck of the bottle to his lips. He drank a great portion of it. Anything to wash out the stench of the hold and the acid of his own puke.

Gradually, as the alcohol took effect, he grew calmer. In half an hour, he was happier than he'd been in weeks. It was over. He knew what had been wrong with him all these months. The memory of Sarah was partly responsible—yes—but mainly it was the memory of this ship and the stench burried in its holds, that nearly drove him mad and rendered him utterly incapable of taking care of a woman. He'd be over that soon. Once this damn ship settled beneath the waves, the ocean would wash the holds clean again and there'd be no stench, nor even a memory of one. Jonathan was absolutely convinced of this. So much so, that he was beginning to feel the faint stirring of desire, something he hadn't felt for what seemed centuries.

He was roaring drunk when he heard footsteps on the deck. He bellowed out a command for the ship's carpenter to come below and be quick about it.

Lawlor, a slim, nervous sort of man, looked apprehensively into the cabin as if he were viewing a ghost. "Cap'n Turner! I knew somebody was aboard 'cause the dory was gone, but I didn't 'spect you, sir."

The Boston accent. It made Jonathan wince with more memories, but the rum was in control and this didn't last but a few seconds. He shook hands with Lawlor.

"You sure kept this vessel shipshape," he said. "Looks like she ready to sail the minute we lift anchor."

"She is, sir. She shorely is. The canvas is all intact, there's nothin' wrong with this ship."

" 'Ceptin' the goddamn stink."

"Well . . . yes. I keep the hatches battened down all the time. Long as they're closed, none of the stink comes up on deck."

"Have a drink," Jonathan invited. "Some of that Barbados rum we used to pick up, 'member? Had a few bottles stowed away, even you couldn't find."

"Sure looked," Lawlor confided with a grin. He'd already been doing some drinking, though he was, by no means, showing the effects of it. "Cap'n, seems a shame this clipper just sit here doing nobody any good. I hope you come back to sell her."

Jonathan shook his head. "Sink her, Lawlor, not sell her. Burn her and let her sink to the bottom with all that goddamn stink in her hold. Maybe kill half the fishes in the ocean, but that's their headache, not mine."

"Sink? Burn her?"

"That's whut I said. Now you go back ashore and buy some oil. Lots of it." Jonathan gave him a handful of bills. "Bring it back here an' we'll sail her out where the water is deep, and let her go down."

"But, Cap'n, this is one of the best clippers ever sailed the sea. She's worth a lot of money."

"Worth more to me she's sunk. Cain't 'splain, Lawlor. No need to anyhow—this is my ship an' I kin do whut I wants with her. I say burn her an' sink her an' remove this ass-stinking ship from the earth. Now you go fetch that oil. Any kind that'll burn will do. Get back here in time to help me hoist 'nuff sail to get movin'. Wants her on the bottom soon's we kin do it."

Lawlor accepted the money and backed away, not at all certain but that he dealt with a madman intent upon destroying thousands of dollars worth of perfectly good shipping. Still, he was the captain, he owned the ship. Lawlor rowed ashore.

Jonathan roamed the deck again, needing the air because he was getting drunk. He tripped over some of the rings bolted to the deck and threw back his head and roared with laughter at the memory of that carnal night.

By the time Lawlor returned, it was growing dark. They hauled up the casks of oil—four of them. Plenty, to do the work. Jonathan let them roll over the deck.

He and Lawlor inspected the canvas and, as Lawlor had declared, it was strong and clean.

"Get some sleep," Jonathan ordered Lawlor. "Tomorrow we hoist anchor and take her out for the las' time. You wantin' to come 'long?"

"Reckon I do, Cap'n. Never saw a ship burn and go down before. There are a few things aboard I'd like, you intendin' to let 'em go down too."

"Take whutever you wants," Jonathan said. "Wish I could tell you to take the stink. Then we wouldn't have to sink this ship. I'm goin' to my cabin and sleep 'til mornin'. See you then."

Lawlor pilfered the ship all night long. Jonathan knew this because he awakened now and then from his drunken stupor and heard the ship's carpenter dragging heavy objects across the deck.

Toward dawn, Jonathan woke up. He dressed, picked up a bottle, went on deck and found Lawlor asleep there, his back against one of the forward hatches. Jonathan saluted the gray dawn by raising the bottle of rum and drinking copiously from it. Thus fortified, he shook Lawlor awake.

Together they hauled enough canvas aloft to sail the ship. It was tedious and difficult work, which left them exhausted, but they were very proud that they were able to handle it themselves. True, there were bare masts, but it wasn't necessary to provide speed, or even much durability, because Jonathan only intended to sail the ship just out of sight of land.

They hauled up the anchor, another muscle-straining job, but easier than setting the sails. Jonathan manned the wheel. The clipper moved slowly about, answering the helm well. There were no lines to throw off and soon they were sailing free and moving at about a tenth of the speed the vessel was capable of.

They sailed for the better part of an hour, with Jonathan enjoying every moment of it. There was no sadness in him because he was about to destroy this fine ship. He'd be glad to watch it slide beneath the water. His whole life seemed to depend on this. Besides, he was slowly getting drunker. Lawlor staggered about, laying to with a short piece of iron he'd found. He took a strange delight in smashing anything breakable, as if it were the culmination of a dream of destruction he'd had since a child.

Soon Jonathan judged they were far enough out. Together, clumsily and drunkenly, they lowered the sails, letting them fall where they might. They'd be good fodder for the flames. They cracked open the containers of oil. Jonathan raised one of the aft hatches, holding his nose against the stench, yet wanting to endure it just once more so he'd have a good memory of what he was destroying. He poured the entire contents of the cask down into the hatch.

Lawlor was showering the canvas with it. They opened more hatches, pulled and shoved oil-soaked canvas and threw it into the hold.

They uncovered a dimly remembered hoard of torches for emergency use and placed these at strategic spots. Finally, they were finished. The escape dory was tied to the ladder, all was in readiness for the execution of a fine ship and a bitter memory.

Jonathan uncorked a full bottle of rum. "Let's drink one more to the *Wyndward*," he shouted into the wind. He drank generously, handed the bottle to Lawlor and let go before Lawlor could grasp it. The bottle landed on deck, its contents spilling out. Jonathan roared with laughter and picked up another bottle. Opening this, he drank again and Lawlor made certain he got hold of it in time. He too drank.

Jonathan's wits were reeling by now. All that rum on a totally empty stomach—he'd eaten nothing and thrown up what little there'd been in his belly. The rays of the hot noonday sun added to his state of drunkenness.

"Light her up!" Jonathan roared. He got a torch going and hurled it into the nearest hatch. He repeated this until there was fire in each. Smoke began pouring out of the open hatches. Jonathan went below, lit another torch and hurled it at the bunk in his cabin. Another went into the crew's quarters. He struggled up the ladder to the deck. Lawlor was at the rail, ready to go overside. He was partially obscured by smoke.

"Time to get off," he yelled.

"Not yet," Jonathan called back. "The big hold ain't smokin' 'nuff yit."

He staggered over to the main hatch, the entry to the largest hold where the bucks had been chained. There was fire below, but all it did was make the stink worse. Jonathan swore lustily, lit another torch and threw that down into the yellowishly lighted maw.

Suddenly a sheet of flame burst from the hatch, driving Jonathan back. His hair was singed, so were his eyelashes and brows. His face felt as if it was on fire. He doused it with rum from the bottle he still held.

"Cap'n," Lawlor called desperately. "I'm goin' overside. Hurry—the fire's gettin' worse."

"Comin'," Jonathan called back. "I'm comin'."

He was now in the midst of hot, thick smoke that seared his lungs when he breathed. There seemed to be growing fire everywhere. It was coming through the deck now and curling its ugly crimson fingers up the companionways.

"Time to git the hell outen this," Jonathan mumbled.

He began to run. He couldn't see Lawlor any more. Likely he was waiting in the dory. He knew Lawlor would never abandon him so he felt perfectly safe as long as he didn't tarry.

A section of deck seemed to disintegrate to his left, and fell with a crash, its embers adding to the fires below. Jonathan felt the heat and broke into a run. Something seemed to tug at his right foot. He fell head first, stretching out on the deck. He seemed to be consumed by a wave of excruciating pain. He tried to get up. One arm worked, he could raise himself partly until the agony weakened him so that he fell flat again. He tried to use his legs. One moved, the other wouldn't budge. He couldn't figure this one. Here he was, on the deck of his blazing ship and he couldn't get up.

It took him a few more moments to realize that his left arm was broken, and so was his right leg. It was an impossible situation. Close by him, the bottle of rum rolled about casually. He reached for it, pulled the cork with his teeth and began to drink.

He could see what had made him fall. It was those goddamn rings with which he'd chained all those bucks to the deck months ago. They'd tripped him, stretched him out, rendered him unable to move, not even to crawl.

"Lawlor!" He screamed, but the noise of the flames and the breaking up of the tinder dry ship drowned out his call for help. All he could do was lie there and pray that Lawlor would come to see what had happened to him.

Lawlor had come. Three or four minutes after Jonathan tripped on the iron rings, Lawlor climbed the ship's ladder.

"Cap'n Turner," he screeched. "Cap'n . . . where are you?"

There was no reply because Jonathan lay stretched on the deck just after his fall his wits still befuddled. He didn't even hear the shouting. Lawlor tried to penetrate the smoke, but was unable to do so. A tongue of fire came flashing out of a porthole below him. If he was to get off this ship, it had to be now.

He guessed, hopefully, that Jonathan had been able to make it across the deck and jumped overside. If so, he would be in need of help. There was no way Lawlor could aid him if he was still aboard, so the best thing to do was get off, row the dory around and see if Jonathan was swimming.

Lawlor descended the ladder, barely missing a scorching from more flames spurting out of portholes.

He rowed away from the doomed ship as rapidly as possible and then began to circle it, looking for any sign of Jonathan.

Aboard the *Wyndward*, Jonathan winced as fire touched his flesh. He raised himself and drank. He kept on drinking until a deep breath carried with it an excessive heat and his lungs were seared.

He felt himself weaken. He tried to drink more. If he could pass out, it wouldn't be so bad. But the stench was gone. It would never foul the earth again. That much he had accomplished.

His head became a ball of fire. He dropped flat. He barely felt part of the deck give way. He didn't feel himself sliding slowly into the big hold where the slaves had been chained. He didn't feel anything. By the time his body slid off the shattered portion of the deck and hurtled below into the fiery hell, he was dead.

Twelve

"BE GODDAMNED," Fitz said, "we ain't even got anythin' lef' to bury."

"I loved him," Benay said. "I think he was one of the finest men I ever knew. I wonder what could have happened?"

"Well, you knows whut the ship's carpenter said.

Papa came aboard aimin' to sail the *Wyndward* out to sea, set her afire and watch her sink."

"All so he wouldn't smell the stench of the slave hold any more," Benay said quietly. "It was all in his mind, Fitz. I even think I know what brought it on."

"Missin' mama after she daid." Fitz offered his opinion.

"No, it was more than that. I think deep inside he hated what he did in those days. Bought slaves, carried them here an' sold them. I don't believe he wanted to do that, but there was a demand, he needed a great deal of money to buy this plantation, so he made the most of it. He never wanted to think back, but there had to be somethin' to make him, an' it was the smell from the ship's hold he remembered the most. So it came to be something that reminded him of those days he hated."

"Kinda figgered that myse'f some time back."

"But to . . . to set the ship on fire and not be able to get off in time . . ."

"He was drunk," Fitz said. "Reckon goin' back to whut he knew that stink was, he needed to be drunk. Don' know whut happened. Mayhap the ship burned faster'n he figgered and he got caught. The carpenter said he couldn't go back on board, 'count o' the fire, so it musta been mighty fast."

"We cain't dwell on this, Fitz. We got us a pow'ful lot of things to do now."

Fitz, who had been walking up and down the floor of his father's office while Benay sat in one of the black overstuffed leather chairs, now took his seat behind the desk.

"Reckon this mine now," he said. "Won't make much difference, Benay. Papa been porely so long I been doin' all the wuk 'roun' heah. We jes' goes on, 'ceptin' we don't have to go to papa and ask him 'bout things."

Benay patted her stomach. "I know I'm goin' to be some busy in a little while. Fitz, I'm glad your papa knew 'bout the baby 'fore he died."

"Knows it made him happy," Fitz agreed. "We runnin' this place now an' we makes it big as papa wanted it to be. Mayhap we lonely now, with papa gone an' Cousin Clarissa married to the Major's son. Been thinkin' mayhap you'd like your mama to come heah and live with us."

Benay shook her head. "It's nice of you to say that, Fitz, but I don't think mama would come. She's runnin' the horse farm my papa lef' an' doin' real good with it too, last I heered. Been thinkin' 'bout her. It's too long a journey here for her, but she kin make it to Richmond fine. Got regular stages runnin' now. Whut you think if I writes her and asks her to meet me in Richmond for a few days. Wants her to know 'bout the baby right from me."

"You do that. Days an' weeks comin' you ain't goin' to want to travel much. Bes' you take a vacation now 'fore you start swellin'. You goin' to meet her in, say two weeks from now, I'll meet you in Richmond a week later. Racin's startin' then and I'm bringin' a two-year-old that's showin' promise."

"I'll get a letter off right away," Benay said. "I'll send one of the houseboys to Lynchburg with it so it'll get to mama soon."

"That settled," Fitz said. "Whut we goin' to do with this heah gal the Major's buck raped an' near kilt?"

"If we send Viney back to the Major, he's likely to finish whut the big buck started. Reckon she suffered 'nuff, even for a nigger."

He grinned at her. "You'd said anythin' different don' know whut I'da done. Sent the Major a draft fo' fifteen hundrud dollahs and asked him to send me a bill of sale fo' the wench. We kin use her heah an' pair her off when she gits strong and healed up."

"Whut if the Major says he won't sell her?"

"He don't, I'll send word to ever'body in Richmond 'bout whut happened. One thing I scared of: whut if he sends Clarissa back?"

Benay laughed and felt a little better. She excused herself and went to her room to write the long letter to her mother proposing they meet in Richmond for a few days. She looked forward to it and wished she was leaving today, because Wyndward was a sad place since Jonathan died. Even the field slaves had slackened their work somewhat and nobody had the wish to drive them. There'd been much weeping and chanting amongst the blacks, because they'd truly loved and respected Jonathan. They'd considered him the finest and most generous master in Virginia.

From behind the desk, now his, Fitz went over the books and his father's papers. He'd known he was wealthy, but the figures were surprising. He leaned back to contemplate the future. In the parlor, Nina was busy dusting and tidying up. She didn't know he was watching her and she was a bit careless about the way she bent over. He knew that small, soft body so well. He began to visualize the rounded breasts, the flat belly and the slim, athletic thighs she used to wrap around him when they wrestled sexually in bed. Happily married, a prospective father, Fitz nevertheless felt the stirrings in his groin.

"Nina," he called.

She whirled about, startled. Then she approached the office door slowly, not quite certain what he was going to ask of her. She was hoping it would be a resumption of their once heated and gentle lovemaking.

"How that wench you takin' keer of?" he asked.

"Viney bettah, massa, suh, now I tells her she ain't goin' back to Richmond. Tell her you buys her."

"Soon's she gits about 'nuff, set her to wuk in the house. They's plenty to do, but not in the kitchen. Elegant drives too ha'd."

"Yassuh, massa, suh."

"Your mist'iss she goin' to Richmond come maybe a

week or two. She goin' to meet her mama there, so this time reckon you stay heah."

She began to realize what he was getting at. "Yassuh, I stays you says so, massa, suh."

"Don' want mist'iss to think I got anythin' to do with it. She say you go, you go, but she don't, you don't mention it."

"Yassuh, massa, suh, I don't say nothin'."

"Good. You seein' that big buck, Themba?"

Her face wore a frightened look for an instant. "No, suh. Don' see him, suh. Skeered o' him. Don' like him none."

"Good. Stay away from him. He one crazy nigger. Don' know why I say that, but he sure as hell is. That's all."

She left promptly. Favored or not, his wench for months or not, she obeyed because she was a slave. He expected it of her and she expected it of herself.

Later in the day, Fitz made his way to the stables where he examined the new, triple-strength stall created for the black stallion devil. It was isolated from the other stalls, and its walls were the thickness he had specified. There was ample room for the great horse. Fitz was, by no means, trying to penalize the animal for being so savage; in fact, he respected the horse for its sense of independence. The stall had a door that closed and opened in two parts; one half was rather high, so the stallion couldn't get his head over it. There were mares always ready and Fitz didn't want this stallion to break down the stall in an effort to reach a mare. The lower door gave entrance, but here too, when the lower door was opened, the stallion couldn't see out. Both doors were provided with large and very heavy bolts to resist any attempt on the part of the horse to kick the doors down.

Themba came out of one of the stalls, a pitchfork in his hand. He doffed his cap quickly and kept his eyes down, something unusual for Themba. All the other slaves did this because it was demanded of them, but Themba more often than not had a look of defiance about him.

"Heerd they got race tracks ready in Richmond in 'bout two or three weeks," Fitz said. "Thinkin' o' runnin' the two-year-old mare showed plenty promise when we times her last. She in good shape?"

"Yassuh, massa, suh. She in good shape awright. I gots two-three weeks mo' I gits her in bettah shape, suh. You takin' me to Richmond, massa, suh?"

"Maybe, maybe not," Fitz replied in the studied carelessness with which a slave's requests should be considered. "Give you a week an' we times her agin. How the jockey wukkin' out?"

"Kin I says somethin', massa, suh?"

"I asked you a question, didn't I?"

"That jockey got no time fo' wukkin' out with the hosses, suh. He foolin' 'roun' in the kitchen an' Elegant she makin' him so fat the hoss be carryin' too much weight."

"You wants me to send him heah an' you take charge o' him?"

"Yassuh, you wants him to ride an' win, massa, suh."

"Sends him tomorra. Wuk the goddamn fat offen him an' feed him on'y 'nuff to keep up his strength. He too fat come race time, I take it outen his hide an' I takes it outen yours too."

Fitz walked away from the man, not looking back. It was lucky for Themba that he did not, for Themba's face was a mask of rage, his eyes so wide the whites glittered with hatred.

The days until Benay's departure for Richmond flew by. Fitz had never quite realized just how much work his father had done, even during the last few months when he was moping about and more concerned with his imaginary smelling of the *Wyndward*'s slave hold than the plantation.

Benay's concern for Viney, the raped wench Fitz had bought from Major Apperson, had inspired her to take the girl to Richmond instead of Nina. Benay had expected tears and wailing from Nina, but there were none.

She used the stagecoach Jonathan had added to the vehicles owned by the plantation. Two bucks were given horses to ride and be in constant attendance on Benay. She was quite safe and very eager to see her mother again.

Fitz began to miss her before the last particles of dust fell back to earth and the stage vanished along the road to Richmond. He turned back to the house, but veered off before he got there and visited the tobacco fields, where the tender plants were beginning to shoot up nicely. In one warehouse were a hundred and seventy hogsheads of tobacco, tightly compressed for another year's curing when it would be as mellow and rich as the lot Fitz had sold in Richmond as the first money crop from the plantation. They'd set a reputation for the quality of the leaf then, and Fitz had no intentions of turning to cheap methods of production.

He ate alone in the big dining room, served by Nina as usual, and supplied with corn liquor and water by Calcutta who scooted about willingly. That would last a day or two until he got used to the idea that Benay was no longer here to sharply criticize his slothfulness.

For the first time, Fitz realized the utter isolation of the plantation. He'd been so busy ever since he got here that it had never occurred to him that it would take him practically all day to visit the nearest farm and get back to Wyndward.

After supper, his restlessness increased and he sat about, trying to think of something to do. He checked over the books again, impulsively wrote a long letter to Benay which he would send out for posting in the morning. By nine he had completed it. He called to Calcutta, bringing him on a dead run from the kitchen.

"Fetch me a whole bottle of cawn," he ordered. "An' a glass. I wants it now, not day after tomorrow."

Calcutta said, "Yassuh, massa, suh," already on his way to the kitchen. There he told Elegant what he wanted, for alcohol was kept locked up and away from the slaves. Nina, eating her meal of gravy-soaked hominy and fried pork, pushed her plate away, quietly arose and left the kitchen.

"Whar she goin'?" Calcutta asked. It was on his mind to one day try to get Nina on her back. He had need to look at her but a few seconds before he felt the urge for a woman. It was all he could do to keep the lust out of his eyes. He knew that if Massa Fitz so much as suspected he wanted Nina, there'd be a quick shift in Calcutta's duties and he'd find himself at the other end of the plantation weeding garden patches from sunrise to sunset.

Elegant didn't answer him and he repeated the question. Elegant seized the bottle of bourbon she'd handed him, slapped him so hard across the face that he staggered and almost fell. Then she thrust the bottle back into his hands.

"Yo' min's yo' own mizzable business, you no-count black bastahd. Yo' asts too many questions an' yo' gits yo' ass all hotten up with the whup. Now git . . . do as massa say an' keep yo' mouth shet."

Fitz, armed with the bottle, left the office and went to the stairs. Nina stood at the foot of them. Without a word, Fitz passed an arm around her waist and led her up the steps. She trembled with excitement and anticipation. It had been a long, long time and her feelings were overwhelming her.

In Fitz's bedroom, she quickly pulled down the bed and made it ready. She laid out his nightdress and then helped him undress. She'd hoped and prayed this would happen and during the late afternoon she'd gone to her room and prepared for it by bathing and generously applying cornstarch all over her body. She snuffed the candles between her fingers, peeled off her dress and slipped quietly into bed beside him.

For a long time she lay there, huddled against him, keeping her hands to herself, waiting for him to begin. Finally, he turned around to face her.

"Swore to myse'f I'd do no more wenchin' when I got married. Swore agin when I heerd my wife was knocked up, but it goddamn lonesome heah, and I ain't a man who likes to sleep by hisse'f. 'Sides that, you a goddamn good-lookin' nigger an' you ain't musky noway. Reckon you got so much white blood the nigger stink ain't pow'ful 'nuff to come through. I'm rapin' you tonight, Nina, 'cause I lonesome, but this be the las' time. Kin you git that through your haid, gal? No more, 'cause I goin' to be a papa, gots to behave myse'f. But I wants you 'round all the time."

"Yassuh," she said, impatient now, not caring about tomorrow or the next day or the next so long as her natural urgings were satisfied tonight.

He pulled her to him, turned her on her back, promptly entered her and she responded with an animal-like fury which startled and pleased him. Two more times that night they engaged in white-hot sex and then slept like the dead until well after dawn.

When Fitz awoke, Nina was gone. He washed, dressed, went down and found her ready to serve him breakfast. He patted her soft little behind and grinned up at her, remembering their night antics and still rejoicing in them.

"Goin' to Richmond to bring your mist'iss home, mayhap in two weeks. Goin' to see the judge theah and git the manumitts started for you, Hong Kong and Seawitch. Wants you to be free, Nina."

"Yassuh, massa, suh. Likes that, I do. But I stays heah, suh. You ain't sendin' me 'way?"

"You talk 'bout goin' 'way, I rips you manumitting papers an' makes you a slave agin. You stayin' heah to take care o' my son. I wants him brought up by you and your mist'iss. Knows you do a good job, treats him like he you own. That right, Nina?"

"Yassuh, massa, suh, like he my own."

Fitz didn't notice the tears in her eyes. What Nina really wanted was a child of her own, by Fitz. It was never going to be—unless, she thought, one had been conceived last night. The ferocity of their lovemaking might have made it possible, but she doubted it.

A week went by, busy for Fitz, empty for Nina, because he kept his word and when she stood at the foot of the stairs each evening, he merely granted her a smile and kept on going. Knowing he was up there, alone, made her restless and created in her a degree of passion she hadn't known she'd possessed. She sensed it was because she couldn't have him, and without him there was no one else.

Consumed by the restlessness, she took to walking about the plantation by night. She visited Hong Kong and Seawitch several times, partly to help tend Hong Kong's festered ear lobe which was improving slowly. She told them of Fitz's plans to have them all given manumission papers making them free, and they agreed that was a good idea, mainly because it would place them well above all other blacks and they could give orders far more effectively. They hadn't the slightest thought of leaving the plantation. Being manumitted meant only that they had a little more power, they'd be safe from whipping—as if any of them ever needed it—and they'd be given money for their work. It all seemed quite reasonable to them, but it only served to increase their devotion to Fitz and Benay.

In two more days, Fitz would journey to Richmond to join Benay and enter his horse in the racing at the new track. Nina, consigned to remaining behind this time, didn't mind that half as much as she minded knowing that in three more nights Fitz would be sleeping with Benay. Nina refused to consider the fact that she was jealous. She loved Benay too much for that and she knew her own place in the scheme of things. As long as Fitz slept alone upstairs in his own bed, she felt that she was still close to him. Going away to be with Benay meant a separation she felt unable to endure.

It happened the night before Fitz was to leave. Themba was busily engaged in seeing to the comfort of the mare they were going to race, and anticipating what he'd buy with the money Fitz would likely give him if the mare won. He knew what he wanted in Richmond, but it was going to be difficult deciding which books, which pens, and what kind of paper he'd buy.

It was a warm night and Themba was stripped to the waist. His magnificent chest glistened in the candlelight in the barn he used as his quarters. He had things ready, blankets, bags of feed, some tidbits in the form of carrots, apples, and a little dark brown sugar. Keeping the mare content during the long haul to Richmond was very important.

He was about ready to go up to the loft where he had a cornhusk-filled mattress and a couple of ragged blankets. There, in well-shielded candlelight, he could stay awake half the night if he chose. His companions would be the books, now dog-eared and musky with the sweat from his fingers and the sweat off his brow as he bent over them, trying to digest what the words meant.

He looked up, sensing rather than hearing the approach of the visitor. Nina stood there, in her thin dress, with candlelight behind her, shining through the material.

His desire for her rushed to the surface and made him angry. "Whut yo' wants heah?"

"Nothin'," she declared docilely.

"Whut yo' doin' heah then?"

"Comes to talk to yo', Themba."

"Talk 'bout whut?" he asked suspiciously. She was the master's wench and it was wise to be careful.

"Them books yo' done got las' time we in Richmond. Yo' says yo' learnin' how to read an' write. Wonderin' how yo' comin' 'long."

"I doin' fine. You aimin' to tell that to massa?"

"Ain't aimin' to tell him nothin'. Wish I was goin' to Richmond tomorrow."

"No call yo' goes. Massa got he mist'iss theah an' don' need no niggah wench servin' him like he do heah while mist'iss 'way."

"I tells massa whut you said an' you ain't evah goin' to see Richmond agin. Maybe you see nothin' agin . . . evah."

"Yo' ain't tellin' him," Themba derided. "Yo' wants to see whut I write?"

"Sho' I does. I kin tell yo' if yo' wrong. I kin read an' I kin write better'n yo' evah will."

"Massa knows that?"

"Nevah tells him."

"Mist'iss know it?"

"Nevah tells her neither. Ain't they business, way I sees it."

Themba grasped her wrist and half pulled her up the ladder to the loft. There he arranged the candle better for maximum light. He delved beneath the piled-up hay and brought up the brown paper-wrapped bundle of books, writing paper, pen and ink. One notebook was almost filled with his labored, stilted handwriting, but the words made sense. He'd copied things about the Abolitionist movement out of smuggled-in Philadelphia papers. He didn't know what much of it meant, but he understood enough to realize that there was a strong feeling in the North against the continuance of slavery.

"Yo' reads that an' tells me whur I wrong," Themba said.

She bent over the work, studying the words, noting

some of the misspellings and some of the awkward attempts to write the lesser-used letters of the alphabet. She was kneeling on the layer of soft straw and now she looked up to point out his mistakes. Themba was bending over her. His broad, black face was alight with desire. His mouth hung open and air whistled in and out of his throat.

She reached up to touch his cheek, then she held him firmly around the neck, pulled him down on top of her. She reached for his groin and the massiveness of him there. They spoke no word, they sought only to sate their desires. Themba's, long, long suppressed; Nina's, a need for a man, any man equipped sufficiently to satisfy her. He was painfully huge and she cried out in pain as he entered her, and then she forgot the pain and gave herself to the lasciviousness she was wont to practice.

They lay back, exhausted completely. There was a pounding in their ears, a numbness about their bodies. Neither heard Calcutta enter the barn and, totally innocent of what he'd find, scale the ladder. He held a bottle of corn liquor, about a third full, which he'd promised to bring to Themba.

Now, his head just above the loft floor, Calcutta stared at the two of them, naked, still flushed with their sexual excitement. His jaw hung open in plain astonishment. Then it opened wider as he gasped for air when Themba's gigantic hand clasped his neck in a throttling hold.

"Yo' goddamn no-'count niggah," Themba said tensely. "Sneakin' up, spyin' on us. Goin' to kill yo' daid, I am."

"Din' see nothin'," Calcutta screeched. "On'y yo' heah, Themba. Don' see nothin' else."

His eyes, bugged out at the sight of Nina so temptingly naked, were now bulging in terror.

"Yo' means that?" Themba demanded, relaxing the choking grip just enough to let some air whistle into Calcutta's lungs.

"Sweahs it, Themba. It dahk heah, cain't see nothin'.

Ain't goin' to tell. Likes yo', I do, an' I ain't goin' to tell massa whut you and Nina do . . ."

"Whar Nina? Yo' sees Nina heah, you no-good bastahd?"

"No, suh. Sees nobody. Dahk . . . cain't see nothin'."

Nina turned on her side. "Don' kill him lessen' he tells massa 'bout us, Themba. He do, then yo' kills him—or I do it. Makes no mind to me, 'ceptin' he daid."

"Ain't goin' to tell. Ain't goin' to tell," Calcutta whined. "Don' see nothin'. Brings you much cawn's I kin, Themba, yo' lets me go."

Themba released his hold and Calcutta promptly slid down the ladder, partly to get away from those powerful hands, but mainly because, in his terror, weakness of his leg muscles made it impossible for him to cling to the ladder and descend it in a normal manner. He hit the floor of the barn on his rump, with a thud that shook the place and made some of the horses in the nearby stalls whinny in nervousness at the unexplained racket.

Calcutta got to his feet and ran from the barn. He ran all the way back to the house where he scooted into the kitchen and dove headlong under the blankets in which he slept close by the stove. He shook for an hour with his fear.

In the loft, Themba laughed, seized Nina, pushed her flat, straddled her and entered her again. They made almost a full night of it, but wisely stopped in time for Nina to slip back into the house, reach her room and get cleaned up before it was time for her to help with Fitz's breakfast.

"Goin' to be lonesome heah," he told her. "Sent for Doc to keer for the place. He comin' later. Yo' stays away from him. He horny as hell all the time an' he like good-lookin', light-skin wenches. Yo' tells him yo' mine, an' he don' pester you none."

"Yassuh, massa, suh. I ain't skeered o' him."

"Bring you back somethin' real nice," Fitz promised.

She followed him down to the stables where the padded wagon into which the mare had been led waited, along with a wagon of supplies and a place for the bucks to sleep. Fitz was taking Themba and two others. They traveled light and fast.

As they drove away, Calcutta stood beside Nina watching them go. Nina began turning back toward the house. Calcutta trotted beside her.

"Sho' got me a likin' to pleasure yo', Nina. Let's me pester yo' some, I don' ever tell whut yo' an' Themba..."

She was small, but she was strong, and when she whacked him, he went back on his heels and landed on his rump. When he tried to get up, she kicked him in the face and then she bent over him.

"Yo' evah say that agin' to me, I have yo' whupped good. Ain't nobody goin' to believe yo'—'cause yo' a goddamn liah ever'thin' yo' say. 'Member now, yo' says yo' wants to pester me, means a whuppin'. Now git back to the kitchen whur yo' belong's 'fore I hide yo' myse'f."

She walked away from him, trembling within, but not letting him know it. What she'd done was wrong, and she was well aware of that, but Massa Fitz had stated clearly that he would no longer pleasure her. She was accustomed to being loved and could no longer do without it. Themba was too big for her, though she could accommodate to that and he was an unusual man. For a slave, he was extremely ambitious and he utilized his spare time trying to learn something. What he'd ever amount to was problematical. More likely than not, he'd swing from a tree branch before too long. But he was a man and he tried to be gentle for all his hugeness. Besides, he was someone she could talk to. Nina was not a girl who could go through life alone.

Thirteen

THE JOURNEY to Richmond was highly successful. Fitz knew now, without question, that he missed Benay too much not to be completely in love with her.

He enjoyed her mother, who turned down the suggestion she come to Wyndward to live.

"Like to," she admitted, "but got me a farm of my own to run. Sam spent his life gettin' it started an' all I kin do is keep it goin' out of memory and respect for him. 'Sides, it makin' money. When I gits old and cain't do for myse'f, then I comes, you still say so, Fitz."

"Any time," he told her. "But you kin visit, you comes by way of Richmond."

To this she agreed and Benay was grateful to him for his consideration of her mother's problems. On the second day, Fitz's mare won the race for two-year-olds and showed considerable promise. Major Apperson had no entry this year, even if the track was brand new and the race turned out most of the population. He had convenient business in Norfolk.

On his way back from the paddock, Fitz ran into Clarissa—by accident on his part, but hardly that on hers. She'd seen him and waited to get him alone. She came out from a group of racing fans and fell into step with him before he realized she was there.

"How yo' bin, Cousin Fitz?" she asked coyly.

"Fine," he said. "Jes' fine, Cousin Clarissa. You lookin' well."

"Oh, I got my troubles. Benay heah with you?"

As if she didn't know, Fitz thought. "Sure is. She be glad to see you."

"I'm stayin' in the same hotel, same room, where you pleasured me," she said. "My husband, he gone to Norfolk with his daddy. I kin sure stand some pesterin' you a mind to, Cousin Fitz."

"Ain't a mind to," he said tersely.

"You ain't goin' to give me the pleasure of yore comp'ny fo' one night, Cousin Fitz?"

"Not for one minute, Cousin Clarissa."

"Now 'sposin'," she looked up at him archly, "I tells Benay you raped me twice."

"I already tol' her," he said. "Ain't nothin' 'bout it she don' know. An' that means she knows how you tantalizin' that nigger boy and whuppin' him at the same time."

Clarissa waved her fan in front of her face and smiled blandly again. "You go to hell, Cousin Fitz."

"Yes'm, wouldn't be none s'prised I did. How you enjoyin' married life?"

This time she didn't smile and she closed her fan with a snap. "Nevah did think a cousin could be so unfriendly as to wish that no-good sonabitch on me. Oh, he got money—or his papa got it. I has ever'thin' I needs 'ceptin' whut I needs mos'. My husban' ruther trot down to the shed with his two personal body servants—an' they sure personal. They pleasures him so he ain't got nothin' lef' fo' me. Soon's I git 'nuff outen him and his pa I goin' to git a divorce, and they goin' to 'gree to it an' pay me well or I tells whut he is."

"Goodbye, Cousin Clarissa," Fitz said, turning abruptly and walking away so fast she was unable to keep up and finally dropped back. The rage she felt dissipated somewhat when she noticed a handsome young man eyeing her with considerable speculation. She opened her fan, brought it to a point just below her mouth.

Her mouth widened in a generous smile while her eyes promised much. As she lowered the fan, he came toward her.

Fitz told Benay about his meeting with her cousin. "Clarissa got 'nuff so she nevah be lonely," Benay said. "They always 'nother'n hidin' behind some rock to come out when she whistles."

"That's the kin' she deserves," Fitz said. "Reckon we start fo' home tomorrow, Benay. Cain't be much lef' in Richmond we din' buy."

"I want to go back," she said. "I'm part of Wyndward now, an' I hate bein' away from it. Mama's fine, got whut she wants an' she happy she kin be. 'Til now I nevah thought much how a man love a woman and a woman love a man. Your papa, he grieved for Sarah more'n I ever see a man grieve. Mama grieves for my papa, but if he alive, she nevah show she cares this much. Reckon we's growin' up, Fitz. Leastwise, I feel that way."

"With whut you packin' in there," he patted her belly, "you goin' to be grown up an' grown out pretty soon. Cain't wait."

"I kin," Benay assured him. "Wants a regular doctor when the time come, Fitz. Doc all right with animals an' niggers, but wants one from Richmond, you don't mind."

"Got one all picked out and he willin' to come. For a price, but he wuth it. No need to fret. Everythin's goin' to be fine."

They made love each night they were together in Richmond, but tonight they were both too tired and too excited over the prospect of beginning their journey back to Wyndward. Fitz had made all necessary legal arrangements to take over the estate. Bank accounts were now in his name. There was nothing more left of Jonathan Turner, except the memory of the man. That was burned into Fitz's mind so he'd never forget.

They pressed the trip back, making it half a day faster than usual. Doc greeted them, just as redfaced as ever, but a capable man for all his drinking. Nina was there too, shyly greeting Benay and accepting her gift and Fitz's with much excitement and then squeals of delight as she put on the long, jade-green earrings that went so well with her bronze skin. She raced to the house, forgetting all dignity expected of a slave, so she might find a mirror.

Later, Benay told her that Fitz had made the necessary arrangements for her manumission. It would take time, but there was no question that it would go through.

"While we waitin'," Benay said, "we aimin' to think of you as free. You're now in full charge of the house, Nina, and you gets yourse'f paid in money. You talks to Fitz 'bout that."

"Don't want no money, mist'iss. Don't need no money. Loves my earrings. Loves you fo' buyin' 'em."

"Another thing," Benay said, "now you free, you got to stop talkin' like a nigger. I'm goin' to teach you, Nina, 'til you talks as good as me. You learns how to write and figger too. 'Fore we get through, you goin' to make some light-skinned man a fine wife. You free now. You has to git married. Ain't no buck goin' to jes' cover you so massa git him 'nother sucker. Things be real different for you from now on."

Nina cried herself to sleep that night. Never before in her life had she felt she'd done wrong, but she felt guilty tonight. She'd given herself to Themba and that was wrong. She belonged to Fitz. His being married made no difference, nor did the fact that she was now all but a free woman. As soon as the legal papers arrived, she would be able to simply pack her things and walk away from this plantation and there would be none to stop her. The very idea made her shudder.

The days settled down to the thousand things that had to be done. Fitz took an almost abnormal pride in the little "hominy eaters," the black children so fat and shiny, squalling, romping, screeching. There were a hundred of them now, a hundred and more. He hadn't counted lately, though each birth was duly recorded in his book for such a purpose.

The bucks and wenches did their day's work without grumbling or slothing. They sang their songs in the evenings in the half-moaning, low pitch so peculiar to plantation Negroes. None looked forward to being sold, though they knew they would be. No plantation could support so many slaves unless the sale of some brought in added profits. They were a commodity, and they knew it. They also knew that when they went on the vendue table in Richmond or Norfolk, they'd step up there proudly, because they were Wyndward slaves and that was coming to mean a great deal.

It was almost two months before Nina's condition began to betray her. The first time she was carrying a tray of sizzling bacon to the breakfast table and she had to put it down hurriedly and rush off to vomit.

Neither Benay or Fitz thought much about it until it happened again, a week later. "You reckon Nina sick?" Fitz asked in a worried voice.

"Not in the way you think, Fitz. 'Member I been sick too, that same way . . ."

"She knocked up?" Fitz asked in total surprise.

"Likely it be that."

Fitz did some rapid calculating in his mind. It would be about this time that she'd show the first signs. He felt like grinning from ear to ear, but managed to control himself. He didn't think Benay would share his enthusiasm, but it seemed to Fitz that he was going to make it as a father twice, without much time difference between the babies. Of course, one wouldn't be white and he could never officially acknowledge him, but he was proud of himself nevertheless.

When Nina came back to finish waiting on table, Fitz

looked directly at her. "Nina, you knocked up?"

She nodded and gave him a wistful smile. "Reckon so, massa, suh. You ain't mad?"

Benay said, "Nina, of course we're not. I hope you have a big, healthy baby. He'll be born soon after mine. Reckon we'll have to put you on regular duty as a nurse, you got two of 'em to care for."

"Reckon I don't mind that none," Nina smiled.

It wasn't until a week later that Fitz was able to talk to Nina alone. Benay had taken a ride in the carriage, a habit she'd taken up, much to Fitz's concern, but she laughed at his fears she'd jolt the baby out of her. Nina came into Fitz's office and he told her to close the door.

"Wants you to know," he said, "that you an' your sucker be taken good care of. No veter'nary for you, Nina. Got me a big doctor comin' from Richmond 'bout the time your mist'iss in need o' him. Reckon be no trouble to git him to stay long 'nuff to take keer o' you too. Won't be too many days apart, I reckon."

"No white doctor keers fo' Nina," she said. "Nina a nigger."

"But a free nigger." He laughed at her discomfiture. "And whut I pays him, he thinks you white as fresh paper. That my son or daughter you carryin'. He's goin' to be a real mustee, mos' white he kin git, with on'y a little nigger blood. Wants him to grow up with my other son. Damn, they be girls, goin' to have to change my thinkin'. Anyways, wants them to grow up together. I treats 'em equal as I kin, 'thout forgettin' you baby got nigger blood. I'm real proud, Nina. Of me an' of you."

She could only nod as she backed out of the room and fled. Fitz chuckled. She was a strange girl all right. He looked forward to improving her lot until she was almost as good as a white girl. He wanted their child to be educated and clever, a splendid foil for his half-brother.

Of course Benay would know. One look and she'd not have to ask him who the father was. She undoubtedly knew now, but it was not her place to ask about such things. She knew perfectly well that so far as everyone was concerned, Fitz had but one offspring and that born to his wife, Benay.

And so the weeks brought forth another bumper tobacco crop of the finest possible leaf. Wenches were waddling about, heavy with child, and the sucker crop gave great promise. The horses were doing well, though Fitz had none quite ready for any more racing this year. Next, he planned to establish a stable right at the track in Richmond, with Themba in charge. It was his plan to enter every race where there was a chance for a win or place. Before long, the fame of the Wyndward horses would spread and become accepted as being as near perfect as a horse could be. Exactly as the slaves and the tobacco were accepted.

Jonathan had been right in his aim to raise only the best, to buy the best and improve them by proper breeding. Never stint, never create an unhappy, rebellious slave—or horse, for that matter. Though the black stallion was still trying to kick his stall to bits, and on the track he'd rear and kick and bite. But the few times they got him to run, he was like the wind itself. Longer than usual legs, a huge lung capacity for sustained speed, great strength for fast getaways—he had everything a perfect race horse should have except docility. With that he probably wouldn't be as good a horse, but there was still the problem of calming him down. Fitz figured it would take another year, but likely be worth it. If not, he'd be a fine stud.

The oncoming of winter created another clearing in the woods around the plantation, more fuel for the fireplaces and stoves—and more land on which to plant more tobacco.

Benay was swollen, moody, alternately cursing her

soon-to-be-born child, or praying it would come soon and be healthy and strong. Nina too was now grown all out of proportion to her delicate frame and small size.

"Sweahs she goin' to have two or three suckers," Benay said.

"That make you jealous?" Fitz asked her.

"All I wants is one. That'll do me fine, Fitz. Jes' one, that's all."

"Dr. Bruning, he comin' in 'bout 'nother week. He stayin' to take keer o' the baby after he borned and to see Nina comes through hers fine."

"You think Nina's goin' to be white?"

"Don' know," he confessed frankly.

"She bein' pestered by any of the bucks?"

"Not's I noticed. Reckon she tell me."

"Don't mind you tells me, Fitz. Knows you loves only me now, an' if you pestered Nina, it be long ago an' none o' my business. You think Nina's baby yours?"

"Said I don't know."

"But it could be?"

"Reckon," he confessed.

"When I in Richmond an' you stays here?"

"Got to be then. Wasn't 'fore that or after that."

"Nina most white. Her sucker goin' to be near white, reckon. We brings 'em up together, Fitz, but my son more impohtant than Nina's. Wants that understood."

"Reckon we all understands."

"Then I say no more. What's done is done. Ain't nothin' to git excited 'bout. My papa he got hisse'f six or seven suckers outen some of our slaves."

"Happen on mos' plantations," Fitz said. "Meaning to talk 'bout that. My papa he got suckers runnin' from Boston to Capetown, reckon. I nevah thinks much 'bout it. But now I'm growed up. Cain't see it no more. Nina the last wench I ever rapes. Promise you that."

"I'm glad to heah you say so, Fitz. I likes her and I

some worried 'bout Nina. She too big for such a tiny girl. Sometimes wenches like her have trouble."

"Knows that. Bringin' the doctor from Richmond. Mostly 'cause o' you, but to see Nina too. Tel' her and she real glad."

Fitz was secretly even more worried about Nina than Benay, for, as Benay said, Nina was swollen all out of proportion. She'd been relieved of all work and spent her time mostly with Benay while they industriously knitted baby clothes and talked about how they would bring up their children. Benay thought Nina was extremely worried about her condition too. That was not a favorable sign. Moreover, the way she'd developed, she would likely have her baby only a short time after Benay's was born. Some suckers born that soon were frail and sickly.

Fitz discovered another spark of danger. He came across Themba one evening as the big black sat in his loft reading one of the Philadelphia newspapers mostly concerned with the Abolitionist movement.

Fitz held out his hand for the newspaper, then studied it for a moment. "You kin read this, Themba. Don' lie. Knowed you could read ev' since I caught you with that other piece of newspaper. Whut else you got 'roun' heah?"

He began poking at the mound of straw by Themba's bed. The big slave moved to stop him. Fitz turned on him, daring him to make a move. The two huge men, who could be brutal when they chose to, eyed one another, but it was Themba's eyes that lowered first.

Fitz finally used a pitchfork on the hay, until he uncovered Themba's carefully-wrapped books, papers and pen and ink. Fitz examined them for a few minutes, paying particular attention to Themba's crude writings.

"Themba, you a slave. You 'members that?"

"Yassuh, I 'members."

"Niggers got no right to learn how to read an' write.

Niggers made to wuk an' to make mo' niggers. That's all they good fo'. Learnin' the wust thing a nigger kin do. Does you know I could hang you for this an' not be blamed?"

"Yassuh, I knows."

"Why you do it then? Think I'm soft? Think 'cause I treats my niggers good, I skeered of a big buck like you?"

"Naw, suh, don't think that, massa, suh."

"I'm goin' to tell you now whut you aimin' to do, you learn to read an' write. You goin' to run."

Themba braced himself. "Reckon, suh."

"That's a hangin' offense too. That all you wants? To git hung?"

"No, suh. Wants to learn. Thass all."

Fitz threw the books and papers onto the mound of hay. "Don't know whut I'm goin' to do with you, Themba. You the bes' man I kin git to handle the hosses. You he'ps me win two impohtant races. For that you got a double eagle. Mos' niggers spend that quick on wenchin', but you buys books. That agin the law, like I said. Now whut I got to do 'bout this, Themba?"

"Don' know, suh. Don' rightly know."

"I forgets this, you keep wukkin' with the hosses jes' like before?"

"Yassuh." Themba's face lost some of its grave concern.

"Mind now, you shows them books to anybody else, that be the end o' you, Themba. Don' mind you study 'cause it takes yeahs to learn, an' you ain't never goin' to learn much."

"Reckon I don', suh."

Fitz dropped his accent, the lazy, easy way of talking, and his words became the crisp, sharp style of Boston and the North.

"Themba, by the time you learn how to speak as I speak to you now, you'll be an old man incapable of doing much, with all of your learning. I don't blame you for wanting to know more, but slaves are not supposed to. I began learning to talk and think like this when I was two or three years old and I was eighteen before I was any good. Most of my friends of those days talk and write better than I do, and it took them years too. So if you want to study the primers . . . the schoolbooks—you may do so, provided you keep it a strict secret."

Themba stared at him wide-eyed. Fitz dropped back into his drawling way of speech. "Thinks you understan'd any of that, Themba? Whut I jes' said?"

Themba nodded. "Some, massa, suh. On'y some. Reckon you right 'bout me. I an old man I learns how to talk like you jes' done. Reckons wants to keep tryin', suh, yo' say so."

"Whut if I say no?"

Themba sighed. "Burns the books and the writin's and fo'gits it all, suh."

"I don't believe you. I still think you git yourse'f 'nuff learnin' to make you smarter'n other niggers, you goin' to run. If you do, Themba, I goin' to track you down and I goin' to hang you."

He descended the ladder and walked back to the house. He didn't know whether he'd made a mistake. Themba could become a highly dangerous man. It was impossible that he had studied enough to know what those articles in the Philadelphia newspapers really meant, but when he did, he'd be trouble. However, that would take a long time. Fitz planned to keep him so busy around the stables that he'd have little time to settle down with a book. That way he'd still have him, because he needed him. Very few blacks could do what he could around horses. White men hired for the same work would be lazy and incompetent. It was better to keep Themba and risk his turning into a rebel.

There was always a tree branch and a rope.

Fourteen

CHRISTMAS was not a time of great pleasure this year. Fitz and Benay remembered too well Jonathan's death. Besides, it was only a matter of days to the arrival of the doctor from Richmond and the expected birth of Benay's and Fitz's first child. So they celebrated moderately, although they sent for a black preacher from Lynchburg and turned one of the big curing sheds into a church for Christmas services.

According to the law, Fitz had to be present during the service in case it was turned into a mob of rebels, or speeches were made in favor of the abolition of slavery, as the northern newspapers so often advocated.

The Wyndward slaves were not rebellious and had no thought of running, except, perhaps, for Themba. Since Fitz had discovered he was trying to learn, Themba had been exceptionally polite and worked harder than ever. He'd never been shiftless, so the stables and the horses were really beginning to amount to something.

Next year, Fitz promised himself, things would be different. He'd sell some of the thoroughbreds, select a large coffle of slaves for the market in Richmond, and haul in his well-aged tobacco for auction.

He'd have his son then—his sons, likely, for Nina looked as if she'd soon burst if the child didn't birth itself. Next Christmas there'd be his son—his white son. Then they would celebrate. Nina's son would receive special attention, of course, and so would Nina for being faithful and obedient.

So the holiday season passed with only a large dinner on New Year's Day, which Fitz alone could enjoy because Benay was beginning to have pains and worried too much to care what she ate.

Dr. Bruning from Richmond arrived four days later. He was middle-aged, rotund, pompous and efficient. He examined Benay and sent her to bed promptly. In the morning he would give her a medicine to hasten the delivery. Fitz then led him to Nina's room. She was occupying Jonathan's room. It would make less steps for the doctor, and besides, Fitz wanted his son born upstairs.

Dr. Bruning frowned darkly. "She a nigger, suh. What she needs is a vet, not a doctor."

"She mos' white, suh," Fitz said. "She bein' manumitted now. She good's free this minute."

"That makes no difference," Dr. Bruning insisted. "She not white."

Fitz winked at him and grinned. "Child likely be white, suh."

Dr. Bruning pursed his lips. "I see."

"An' she bein' mos' white an' almos' manumitted, you entitled to charge as much as for my wife, suh. She not bein' treated like a nigger, you gits lots more'n a veter'nary would git. Thinks you understand, doctah?"

"Yes . . . it will be all right." He examined Nina carefully. Afterwards, he led Fitz into the hallway. "She's made very small. She's goin' to have a hard time. Your wife will have no trouble, but this wench . . . I can't swear she'll come through, Mistah Turner, suh. Seen too many of 'em like her die."

"Give you five thousand dollahs, she don' die, suh," Fitz said imploringly. "Don' keer whut you got to do, don' let her die. Please, doctah. She mean too much to me an' my wife."

"She must. Do the best I can. Want a woman to help tomorrow. You got somebody been around birthin'?"

"Yes, suh, got a fine woman. Fetches her in the mornin'. When do you think . . . ?"

"Don't rightly know to the day, suh. Your wife . . . maybe tomorrow. Time she gave birth now, but sometimes the first one a little slow."

"An' Nina?"

"Don' know. Baby wants to be born an' can't git out, we know 'bout it soon enough. Nothin' to be done tonight."

Fitz and the doctor sat and drank rum for part of the evening, corn later on. They kept Calcutta running—and drinking their dregs. It amused the doctor to see him begin to lurch and observe the tray tip dangerously.

"Understand you're one of the most successful and richest plantation owners in the state, suh," the doctor commented. "What I see of your plantation tells me why. Never did see so many fat and healthy suckers. I can see you treat them well and feed them well."

"Cain't sell an ornery nigger or a skinny one," Fitz said. "It be a matter o' good business, suh. We raises slaves to sell."

"I've seen some pretty poor specimens on the vendue table," Dr. Bruning commented. "Most folks don't care. A nigger is a nigger, but they take goddamn good care of their dogs and their horses. Hell of a lot more'n they give to the blacks. Some day there's goin' to be a big trouble. Can see it comin' sure. I go North often and the talk up there—well, it's not good. Don't know how long it'll be, Mistah Turner, but it's comin', rebellion or laws, don't matter which. By the time it comes, it'll be too late to stop it."

"I know," Fitz said. "I was born and educated in Boston, Doctor. I was never exposed to slavery until my father introduced me to it by way of serving on his clipper, which brought slaves to Norfolk."

Dr. Bruning chuckled. "You speak like a northerner too. Mind you, Fitz Turner, don't advertise that."

"Ain't aimin' to," Fitz grinned. "Papa he tol' me long ago, I livin' down heah, I talk an' I act an' I think like a southerner. Don't mind it. Fact, likes it better. But sometimes . . . a nigger needs a whuppin', I don't have the heart to do it lessen he awful bad. Then I gives it to him good. Oh, well, we got no trouble heah. Don't look for none."

They slept well that night, but Elegant summoned the doctor early next morning. Fitz saw Benay for only a moment or two before he was chased out. Seawitch, Hong Kong's capable wife, arrived at dawn ready to help, and she was experienced and capable, even drawing favorable comments from Dr. Bruning.

It was late afternoon that Dr. Bruning came slowly down the stairs, his face dark with a worry that made Fitz's blood pressure leap to heights.

"You're the father of a baby boy," Dr. Bruning told him.

"But Benay . . . whut's happened . . . ?"

"Your wife is fine. Give her a couple of hours to rest and then you can see her and the baby."

Fitz mopped the sweat off his face. "Way you looked comin' down the stairs. . . ."

"It's Nina. I hate to say this, but she's not goin' to make it. I can't get the baby out of her. It's fighting to be born, even now well ahead of her time, but the baby's very big and she's very small. Damn it, I see this so often and there's nothin' we can do."

"She goin' to die?"

"Yes . . . yes, she's goin' to die, but we might be able to save the baby. Hard to tell yet."

"I'm goin' up to see her. . . ."

The doctor shook his head. "Don't. She's in too much pain and she don't know what's going on. Might take another day or two, can't tell, but I'll be there to do what I can."

Fitz was beset simultaneously with happiness and fear. He'd never experienced this before. Benay was fine. Nina was going to die. He wanted both to live and he cursed the child that was responsible for this.

He saw Benay in the early evening, after she woke up. She kissed him and fretted over Nina. It was clear she hadn't been told the news and Fitz held it back as well.

Seawitch brought his first son, swaddled in his blanket, crying lustily and fighting the air with his little fists.

"Goin' to call him Jonathan," Fitz said. He glanced at Benay. "You don't mind none."

"I've already called him by that name," she said. "He's a wonderful baby, Fitz. You're goin' to be proud of him."

"Already am." Fitz poked a finger at the baby's cheek, causing Seawitch to yank the infant out of his reach while she scolded him indignantly.

"How's Nina?" Benay asked, after the storm died away.

"Reckon she awright," Fitz lied. "She don' say much."

"I know how she feels. Fitz, I'm very happy, do you know that? I've got everything I ever wanted in this world. A fine husband and a fine son."

"There be more," Fitz grinned at her.

Seawitch had returned the baby to its crib. Now she advanced on Fitz and stood before him, hands on her thin hips, scowling at him.

"You aimin' to git yo' wife so tahred she git sick, massa, suh? Yo' git. Comes back mayhap tonight, you kin see her agin. Go 'way now."

"All right. All right." Fitz gave in with a broad smile. "You a pretty good midwife, Seawitch. Mayhap we put you in business. . . ."

"You gits, massa, suh, or I calls the doctah. Ain't no time to be listenin' to yo' lyin' tongue. I ain't no better'n any othah nigger woman on this heah plantation an' yo' knows it."

"Yes, yo' is. You an' Hong Kong been manumitted. You know that makes you better."

Fitz kissed Benay rather awkwardly, but she patted his cheek and comforted him, though it had been his intention of comforting her. He went downstairs looking for the doctor, but he couldn't find him.

In the kitchen, Elegant worked among her pots and pans, yelling at the young slaves who helped her and at Calcutta who was seated on the floor near the stove, knees drawn up to his chin, eyes big in fear. Fitz noticed that but reasoned Elegant must have been batting him around the kitchen, as she often did when he betrayed his customary laziness.

"Doctah, he wid Nina," Elegant said, and her eyes were red from crying already. "Massa, suh, yo' reckon Nina she goin' to die?"

Fitz nodded. "Reckon so, Elegant. Ain't nothin' kin be done fo' her."

"She so li'l," Elegant wiped her eyes with the hem of her apron. "Been prayin' fo' her, but reckon it jes' ain't no use. Reckon she too good to live, massa, suh."

"I know. Grieves me too. Likes Nina, I do."

"Reckon," Elegant said, a trifle huffily, he thought. She was blaming him probably, and she had a right to. He wandered out back of the house and his steps took him to the small graveyard which Benay had had fenced in with iron grillwork brought from New Orleans. It had been painted white, with a low gate that screeched metallically. Fitz didn't open it. He straddled it and hauled himself over.

There were only two rounded graves, but there were three granite markers. One was for Jonathan. Fitz hoped none of them, his mother, his wife's father, would mind if a simple little light-skinned girl and her unborn baby lay close by. Fitz knew he was burying the living at this moment, but he felt as the doctor did, that Nina had no chance.

When he returned to the house, Calcutta was racing his way, his face alight in terror.

"Doctah say yo' comes right quick, massa, suh. Nina, she daid, reckons. Nina daid . . ."

Fitz's long legs streaked over the ground. He rushed up the stairs three at a time and burst into the room where the doctor sat beside the bed on which Nina lay. She was breathing, but that was about all. Even as he watched, her chest movements grew more and more shallow. After five minutes, the chest didn't move at all.

"Mistah Turner, suh," the doctor said, "Nina is now dead. But her baby may be alive. You gives me permission, I'll take the baby from her."

"You kin do that . . . ?"

"If it's all right. She's your slave. It's your child."

"Take it," Fitz gasped. "Don' know how you kin, but do it."

The doctor pulled down the bedsheet, exposing that poor, engorged figure which had once been so warm with life and so beautiful to behold and possess. The doctor had everything prepared. He used a large scalpel to make a deft incision straight down the center of that swollen belly. With a smaller knife, he enlarged the wound until he could reach inside the dead girl with his bare hands and gently lift the baby out.

He slashed the umbilical cord, tied it in a matter of five seconds, grasped the baby by the heels, swung it, whacked it smartly across the back. He did this half a dozen times before a lusty wail burst from the child.

Fitz was affected by the gore he had witnessed, by the strange way of birthing a baby from a dead mother, by the rough handling of the tiny infant before it squawked to life. But it was more than that which caused him to stand there breathless.

The baby was black! Not ordinarily black, but dark as any sucker Fitz had ever seen.

"How . . . that happen . . ." he managed at last.

"We got the baby out before it died, that's all . . ."

"Doctah, I knows that. Whut I means . . . the baby black as coal."

"Yes . . . that's very evident."

"If I the papa, the baby might be dark, or tan, or yella, but not that black."

The doctor laid the baby down on a blanket and wrapped it tenderly. "It's a boy, like your own son, Mistah Turner."

"That one . . . he's not my son, is he?"

"Obviously he couldn't be. I know in a baby only minutes old it's hard to say he looks like much of anything, but you can see for yourself that there isn't the slightest resemblance to you that there is in your wife's son. I can see you in him easily enough."

"Wasn't me," Fitz breathed. "All this time she knew it wasn't me, and she too skeered to tell me."

"Now don't do anything rash," Dr. Bruning advised. "We have a very healthy sucker here. Biggest baby I've seen in a long time."

"So goddamn big he kills her," Fitz said in a burst of anger.

"That's not his fault."

"Whose fault then? I asks you, whose fault?"

"Why—his parents."

"You lookin' at whut's lef' of his mama right now, Doctah, you reckon she big?"

"His father then."

Fitz nodded. "Reckon."

He turned away for the door. The doctor now focused his attention on the newborn baby. Halfway to the door, Fitz hesitated. Then he turned about, approached the bed and carefully covered Nina's body with the bedsheet and the blanket. He went downstairs to sit for the better part of an hour in his office.

"Elegant," he bawled in a loud voice.

She waddled in promptly. "Yassuh, massa, suh. Nina she daid, ain't she?"

"She daid, an' she birthed a boy. Big, awful big baby, an' he black as yo' ass. Yo' knows I always figgered he was mine, but he ain't. He somebody else's. Wants to know who."

"I don' know, suh," Elegant hastened to say. "Sweahs I don' know, massah, suh. I figgered he was yo' son. Nina she nevah say nothin' make me think anythin' but that, suh."

"You see her hangin' 'round' any buck?"

"No suh. Nina she stay by herse'f mos'."

"Whur Calcutta? He got his nose in eve'ybody's business. You sends him in heah and you tells him to bring two bottles o' rum. Two bottles, an' he sloth an' I bust his goddamn tail."

"Yassuh, massa, suh."

"You sends him heah, you goes to the fields an' tells Hong Kong, Nina daid. Tells him to git a coffin made. A nice one. Tell him to git a grave dug nex' to whar my papa would lie we had anythin' to bury."

"Yo' puttin' that pore chile to res' side yo' papa's grave an' yo' mama, an' yo' wife's papa?"

"Kin you think of a better place?"

"No, suh. Thinks Nina like that. Thanks you, massa, suh. Nina, she loves yo'. Says so agin an' agin. Don' blame her she git knocked up by some buck. She mighty lonesome yo' gone."

"Don' blame her none neither. Knows better. Do whut I says, and be quick 'bout it."

Elegant waddled out in a great hurry for her ample bulk. Presently Calcutta appeared, a bottle under each arm and somehow also holding onto a tray with a glass on it. He set the tray down, lined the bottles beside it.

"Took you long 'nuff," Fitz growled.

"Come fas' I kin, massa, suh."

"Nina daid, you knows that."

"Yassuh, I knows. Feels bad, I does."

"Feels that bad, you kin open one o' them bottles fo' yo'rse'f."

Calcutta didn't move except that his eyes grew bigger.

"Well . . . open it and have a drink. That's whut I goin' to do."

Fitz pulled the cork, poured an ample quantity of the golden fluid into the glass and drank copiously.

"Yo' tells me to drink, suh? Heah . . . wid yo', suh?"

"We both loves Nina and we drinks to her memory. Drink, goddamn your black hide."

Calcutta uncorked the bottle, tilted it and gagged. He wasn't accustomed to this undiluted, strong rum. Most of what he enjoyed had been mixed with spring water. Fitz drank more, poured more, indicated Calcutta was to keep on drinking.

The boy was drunk in fifteen minutes, clinging to the edge of the desk for support and grinning foolishly until Fitz mentioned Nina's name again and then Calcutta burst into drunken tears.

Fitz said, "Stop that, heah? Stop yo' crazy cryin'. Whut you cryin' for? That your baby up there. Heah me—that you baby? You pestered Nina?"

Calcutta sobered for a moment or two under the enormity of that accusation.

"Massa, suh, I don' pester Nina none. Wants to . . . wants to bad, but Nina say 'less I goes 'way frum her she goin' to whup me."

"Yo' lyin'. You covered her an' you knows it."

"Massa, I sweahs . . ."

"Goin' to have you whupped. Fifty lashes with the snake. When you half daid, goin' to string you up by the balls and cut 'em off 'fore I buries you 'live, like papa done to Marseilles. You knows 'bout that."

"I knows. Massa, suh, I don' rape Nina. I sweahs it. I nevah done nothin'. . . ."

"You didn't, who did?" Fitz asked casually, taking that drunken, terror-ridden mind so unexpectedly by surprise that he might get the truth out of the boy.

"Themba, he rape her, massa. He give Nina the suckah, suh. Wan't me. She tell me go 'way, but she lay with Themba."

"That's a goddamn lie. Nina hated Themba."

"Night fo' yo' lef' fo' Richmond, suh, I fetches Themba whut cawn lef' in a bottle. Sees him in the bahn, massa, suh. He on top Nina, he pleasurin' she mighty good an' she squealin' he so big. Massa, suh, not me. T'wasn't me, sweahs it Themba."

Fitz closed his eyes tightly for a moment, visualizing that wizened black face of Nina's baby. It was true, as Dr. Bruning pointed out, that it was difficult to distinguish features in a newborn, but that Fitz's features were plain in Benay's son. Themba's features were just as plain in the face of Nina's boy. Calcutta wasn't lying. He was too drunk to do anything other than tell the truth; even if he wasn't so scared of the snake, that alone would have forced him to tell.

That's when it must have happened, about the time of the last Richmond trip. He'd told Nina just before that, she would never again bed down with him. In sheer desperation, or in an attitude of rebellion, whatever the motive, she'd gone to see Themba and he'd raped her. Whether she'd been willing or not made no difference. He'd raped her—and, in so doing, he'd also killed her.

Fitz drank what was left in his glass. As he left his chair, Calcutta slowly sank to the floor in a drunken stupor. Fitz stepped over him and went out.

It was midafternoon. The word had reached the cabins and the fields that Nina was dead. There was nothing but a strange and intense silence over the plantation and no one could be seen. Fitz strode down to the stable area. On the way he picked up a long, dry branch fallen from an oak. He broke it near the end, leaving a sharp tip.

He walked up to the specially built stall where the black stallion was kept. He opened the upper part of the heavy door. The horse eyed him with angry eyes, as if challenging him to make him come out and perform. Fitz jabbed the stick into the horse's ribs. He jabbed him several more times while the animal screamed and kicked until it was frothing at the mouth. Fitz dropped the sharpened stick.

Themba was approaching him at a dead run, rubbing at his eyes. He'd apparently been asleep.

"Massa, suh, whut wrong?" he asked.

Fitz said, "Thinkin' 'bout shootin' that sonabitch hoss. Goes into the stall an' he like to kick me to pieces. Gits away, but drops my ridin' crop in theah and tryin' to git it out."

"Don' shoot him, massa, suh. He comin' long real fine, he do. He gittin' so he loves me, massa, suh, an' he do whut I say."

"I don't believe it."

"Massa, suh, I sweahs . . ."

"You ain't skeered of him no mo'?"

"No, suh. Like I say, he love me, he do."

"Go in there and fetch my ridin' crop you ain't skeered o' him. He lets you do it, I don' shoot him."

"Shows you, massa, suh. Yassuh, shows yo' . . ."

Apparently, Themba hadn't heard of Nina's death or the birth of his son. He was wholly unsuspicious of Fitz's motives. For his part, Fitz would have preferred to tell Themba what had happened, and then take care of his punishment, but Themba was a latent rebel and apt to fight. Fitz thought he could take him, but he was in no mood to dirty his hands on this nigger who'd killed Fitz's first love.

Themba opened the lower door, after he closed the upper one. He ducked under it and began looking for the riding crop while he talked soothingly to the nervous animal. Fitz slammed the lower door, shot the heavy bolt, opened the upper door and with the same stick he tantalized the already savage horse until it went berserk.

"Massa, suh," Themba screamed. "Massa, suh, yo' killin' me. Whut I do . . . ?"

"You raped Nina and she daid. She daid birthin' yo' son. Do you heah me, Themba? Yo' son! Goin' to raise him. Goin' to make him work hisse'f to death. Goin' to make him pay for your goddamn sins. Cain't make you pay, 'cause you dyin' right now. Dyin', Themba. For killin' Nina, I kills you."

The horse was bucking, kicking, biting, crushing at Themba's body with his powerful haunches. Themba's screams were muffled by the closed doors. His antics in trying to escape the horse only maddened the animal further and Fitz didn't find it necessary to tantalize the beast any more.

For fifteen minutes this went on until, finally, the horse subsided, because there was nothing moving in that stall to enrage him. Fitz cautiously opened the lower door. Themba's body, battered beyond recognition, was pushed up against it. There was no need to make any tests to determine if he lived. Half his brains had spilled out of a skull crushed under the power of the stallion's hoofs.

Fitz closed the door and walked back to the house. Hong Kong was waiting for him on the porch steps.

"You got the coffin for Nina started?" Fitz asked.

"Yassuh, massa, suh. Tells the cahpentah he makes it good as fo' white folks."

"You send the grave diggers?"

"Yassuh, massa, suh."

"You finds a place, down near the grove of poplars.

You has the grave diggers start a new cemetery. Themba, he killed by the crazy black stallion. Wants him buried soon's kin be done."

Hong Kong's face was impassive. "Yassuh, massa, I do whut you say."

"Got one more thing. You come with me."

Wonderingly, Hong Kong followed his young master into the house, up the stairs and into the room where the doctor had just finished with Nina's son. Without a word to the doctor, Fitz picked up the baby in its blanket and thrust it into Hong Kong's arms.

"That's Nina's baby. He Themba's baby too. You takes this heah sucker to your cabin. When Seawitch finish carin' fo' my wife, you hands her this baby and you tells her to bring him up. You tells her not to feed him too much, not to love him nohow. He cry, she hits him good. He grows up, he don't play with othah suckers. He locked up. He goin' to be the hardest wukkin' slave this plantation evah saw. He Themba's son and I hates him. Wants him to live, but whut Themba done to Nina, his son pays for. You understan' whut I sayin'?"

"Yassuh, massa, suh, I understan's."

"Git! Take that black sonabitch bastahd with you. Don't want to see him agin. I lays eyes on him 'til he full growed, I kills him. Take him 'way . . . git!"

Hong Kong cradled the child and left promptly. On his way down the stairs, he crooned softly to the baby.

Fitz sat down in the room which now contained only the doctor, silently gathering up his instruments, and the body of a dead girl, once beautiful, golden-skinned, loving and faithful. Fitz lowered his face into his hands and wept.

Epilogue

NINA'S SON lay in a quickly fashioned wooden crib in Hong Kong's cabin. Seawitch knelt beside the cradle and rocked it while she thrust her face against that of the baby and made it laugh in delight.

"Don' feed him much, don' let he play wid othah chillun. Raise him so he kin wuk he po' haid off, 'cause he pappy rapes the li'l gal massa loves. Massa crazy, Hong Kong."

"Reckon you does whut he say."

She got to her feet and faced him. "Yo' say yo'se'f massa say he don' wants to see this po' chile 'til he full growed. Reckon I sho' do whut he say far as not seein' the chile. But I feeds him good, I gives him the love I give yo' chile an' mine, Hong Kong. Wants a chile. Yo' cain't give me one so I takes this 'un like he sent to me from heaven. He goin' to be big an' strong—like massa's white son. They goin' to be alike, them two. They almos' brothers."

"Massa sho' kills us he finds out."

"Mayhap he do, but he don't kill this heah chile. He cain't he'p he hates him, but don' mean we hates him too. He mine, Hong Kong. He our'n. He our son. We raises him like we wants an' massa, he don' find out."

"Reckon," Hong Kong said. "Reckon that the bes' way. Loves yo', I does, fo' thinkin' like that. Yo' skeered whut massa say an' you raises this po' child like you say, I runs with him soon's he old 'nuff."

Seawitch was thinking deeply. "Mayhap, we gits 'nother man chile whut died an' we tells massa he Themba's chile, an' we buries him . . ."

"An' we raises yo' chile an' mine," Hong Kong derided. "How our chile git borned? I got no balls an' massa sho' knows that."

"We do somethin'," Seawitch said. "This heah chile Nina's. Loves her we did, an' we loves her chile. Po' thing cain't he'p it he got sonabitch fo' papa. Fo'gits that. He growin' up to be a good nigger. We goin' to be mighty proud o' him and some day, reckon massa be proud o' him too."

ROMANCE...ADVENTURE...DANGER...

THE BONDMASTER BREED
by Richard Tresillian   **(D81-890, $2.50)**
Carlton Todd, the Bondmaster, is a happy man. With his marriage to the young, copper-haired Milly Dobbs, he has a new chance to produce a legitimate, white, male heir to his estate. But from his liaisons of the past, others come to stake their claims. A novel of forbidden love in a hurricane of hate by the author of THE BONDMASTER.

BLOOD OF THE BONDMASTER
by Richard Tresillian   **(D82-385, $2.25)**
Following THE BONDMASTER the saga of Roxborough Plantation—the owners and the slaves who were their servants, lovers—and prime crop! In the struggle for power, there will be pain and passion, incest and intrigue, cruelty and death for these, too, flow from the BLOOD OF THE BONDMASTER.

THE KINGDOM
by Ronald S. Joseph   **(D33-074, $2.95)**
Out of the rugged brasada, a powerful family carved THE KINGDOM. Joel Trevor was willing to fight Mexicans, carpetbaggers, raiders, even Nature itself to secure his ranch. Then he won the beautiful Spanish Sofia who joined her heart and her lands to his. When control passed to Joel's daughter Anne, she took trouble and tragedy with the same conquering spirit as her father. These were the founders—and their story blazes from the pages of THE KINGDOM, the first book of a giant trilogy.

THE POWER
by Ronald S. Joseph   **(D36-161, $3.50)**
The children of Anne Trevor and Alex Cameron set out at the turn of the century to conquer the world in their own ways. Follow Dos, the reckless son, as he escalates youthful scrapes into crime. Travel with Maggie from boarding school to brothel to Congress. Meet Trev and the baby daughter to whom all the kingdom, power and glory will belong.

THE GLORY
by Ronald S. Joseph   **(D36-175, $3.50)**
Meet the inheritors: Allis Cameron, great-granddaughter of the pioneers who carved a kingdom in southern Texas. Go with her to Hollywood where her beauty conquers the screen and captures the heart of her leading man. Cammie: Allis's daughter, who comes of age and finds herself torn between a ruthless politician and a radical young Mexican. They were the Cameron women, heirs to a Texas fortune, rich, defiant, ripe for love.

If you like romance, you'll love Valerie Sherwood...

HER SHINING SPLENDOR
by Valerie Sherwood (D85-437, $2.75)
Lenore and Lorena: their names are so alike, yet their beauties so dissimilar. Yet each is bound to reap the rewards and the troubles of love. Here are the adventures of the exquisite Lenore and her beauteous daughter Lorena, each setting out upon her own odyssey of love, adventure, and fame.

THIS TOWERING PASSION
by Valerie Sherwood (D33-042, $2.95)
They called her "Angel" when she rode bareback into the midst of battle to find her lover. They called her "Mistress Daunt" when she lived with Geoffrey in Oxford, though she wore no ring on her finger. Wherever she traveled men called her Beauty. Her name was Lenore —and she answered only to "Love."

THESE GOLDEN PLEASURES
by Valerie Sherwood (D33-116, $2.95)
She was beautiful—and notorious and they called her "That Barrington Woman." But beneath the silks and the diamonds, within the supple body so many men had embraced, was the heart of a girl who yearned still for love. At fifteen she had learned her beauty was both a charm and a curse. It had sent her fleeing from Kansas, had been her downfall in Baltimore and Georgia, yet had kept her alive in the Klondike and the South Seas.

THIS LOVING TORMENT
by Valerie Sherwood (D33-117, $2.95)
Perhaps she was *too beautiful!* Perhaps the brawling colonies would have been safer for a plainer girl, one more demure and less accomplished in language and manner. But Charity Woodstock was gloriously beautiful with pale gold hair and topaz eyes—and she was headed for trouble. Beauty might have been her downfall, but Charity Woodstock had a reckless passion to live and would challenge this new world—and win.

BOLD BREATHLESS LOVE
by Valerie Sherwood (D93-651, $2.95)
The surging saga of Imogene, a goddess of grace with riotous golden curls—and Verholst Van Rappard, her elegant idolator. They marry and he carries her off to America—not knowing that Imogene pines for a copper-haired Englishman who made her his on a distant isle and promised to return to her on the wings of love.

ROMANCE...ADVENTURE...DANGER...
by Best-selling author, Aola Vandergriff

DAUGHTERS OF THE SOUTHWIND
by Aola Vandergriff (D93-909, $2.95)
The three McCleod sisters were beautiful, virtuous and bound to a dream—the dream of finding a new life in the untamed promise of the West. Their adventures in search of that dream provide the dimensions for this action-packed romantic bestseller.

DAUGHTERS OF THE WILD COUNTRY
by Aola Vandergriff (D93-908, $2.95)
High in the North Country, three beautiful women begin new lives in a world where nature is raw, men are rough...and love, when it comes, shines like a gold nugget. Tamsen, Arab and Em McCleod now find themselves in Russian Alaska, where power, money and human life are the playthings of a displaced, decadent aristocracy in this lusty novel ripe with love, passion, spirit and adventure.

DAUGHTERS OF THE FAR ISLANDS
by Aola Vandergriff (D93-910, $2.95)
Hawaii seems like Paradise to Tamsen and Arab—but it is not. Beneath the beauty, like the hot lava bubbling in the volcano's crater, trouble seethes in Paradise. The daughters are destined to be caught in the turmoil between Americans who want annexation of the islands and native Hawaiians who want to keep their country. And in their own family, danger looms...and threatens to erupt and engulf them all.

DAUGHTERS OF THE OPAL SKIES
by Aola Vandergriff (D93-911, $2.95)
Tamsen Tallant, most beautiful of the McCleod sisters, is alone in the Australian outback. Alone with a ranch to run, two rebellious teenage nieces to care for, and Opal Station's new head stockman to reckon with—a man whose very look holds a challenge. But Tamsen is prepared for danger—for she has seen the face of the Devil and he looks like a man.

DAUGHTERS OF THE MISTY ISLES
by Aola Vandergriff (D93-929, $2.95)
Settled in at Nell's Wotherspoon Manor, the McCleod sisters must carve new futures for their children and their men. Arab has her marriage and her courage put on the line. Tam learns to live without her lover. And even Nell will have to relinquish a dream. But the greatest challenge by far will be to secure the happiness of Luka whose romance threatens to tear the family apart.

INTRODUCING *THE RAKEHELL DYNASTY*

BOOK ONE: THE BOOK OF JONATHAN RAKEHELL
by Michael William Scott (D36-233, $3.50)

BOOK TWO: CHINA BRIDE
by Michael William Scott (D95-237, $2.75)

The bold, sweeping, passionate story of a great New England shipping family caught up in the winds of change—and of the one man who would dare to sail his dream ship to the frightening, beautiful land of China. He was Jonathan Rakehell, and his destiny would change the course of history.

THE RAKEHELL DYNASTY—
THE GRAND SAGA OF THE GREAT CLIPPER SHIPS
AND OF THE MEN WHO BUILT THEM
TO CONQUER THE SEAS AND
CHALLENGE THE WORLD!

Jonathan Rakehell—who staked his reputation and his place in the family on the clipper's amazing speed.

Lai-Tse Lu—the beautiful, independent daughter of a Chinese merchant. She could not know that Jonathan's proud clipper ship carried a cargo of love and pain, joy and tragedy for her.

Louise Graves—Jonathan's wife-to-be, who waits at home in New London keeping a secret of her own.

Bradford Walker—Jonathan's scheming brother-in-law, who scoffs at the clipper and plots to replace Jonathan as heir to the Rakehell shipping line.

If you liked Wyndward Peril, you'll want to read...

WYNDWARD PASSION
by Norman Daniels (D30-137, $2.95)
At Wnydward plantation, the Turners grew tobacco and raised horses, but slaves were their most profitable product. Jonathan Turner mated bucks to wenches and produced prime black stock for sale. Between white and black, passions turn to lust. Between Fitzjohn and Nina, lust ripened into love, and the very foundations of the Turner empire shook in the fury of the WYNDWARD PASSION.

WYNDWARD FURY
by Norman Daniels (D30-145, $2.95)
Of the land and the slaves they owned, the Turner men gave no one else an inch. For the women they loved, they battled all rivals. Against those they hated, they schemed, raged and fought. But such passions sow anger and jealousy in others, and it was inevitable that the Turners should reap the bitter harvest of revenge.

WYNDWARD GLORY
by Norman Daniels (D90-742, $2.95)
The Civil War is over, and in its wake lie the charred remnants of Wyndward. All that remain are Fitzjohn and his grandson Mark, determined to rebuild the family plantation and restore their name to glory. But as they struggle to recreate their world, reclaim their passionate women, and regain self-respect, the Turners face the greatest threat of all—a ghost returned from the past to destroy all he ever loved with hate.

To order, use the coupon below. If you prefer to use your own stationery, please include complete title as well as book number and price. Allow 4 weeks for delivery.

WARNER BOOKS
P.O. Box 690
New York, N.Y. 10019

Please send me the books I have checked. I enclose a check or money order (not cash), plus 50¢ per order and 20¢ per copy to cover postage and handling.*

_____ Please send me your free mail order catalog. (If ordering only the catalog, include a large self-addressed, stamped envelope.)

Name _____
Address _____
City _____
State _____ Zip _____

*N.Y. State and California residents add applicable sales tax.